DIAMONDS AND DIRT ROADS

BILLIONAIRES IN BLUE JEANS

ERIN NICHOLAS

DIAMONDS AND DIRT ROADS

Billionaires in Blue Jeans
Book One

PROLOGUE

From the desk of Rudy Carmichael...

1. **Move to Bliss.**
1 year. Live in house <u>together</u>

2. **Run pie shop.** → profit by year end. $$

3. **AVA– kitchen, baking, all products.**
<u>NO business!</u>
Date a guy from Bliss. Give it
6 mos. Have fun. No checklists!

4. **BRYNN – customers/waitress.**
Time with <u>people</u>, get to know them.
no kitchen, no business,
Date ~~a~~ guys from Bliss. ⁶

5. **CORI –books/accounting.** no baking.
leave customers to B.
make a commitment. but NO DATING ~~1 year!~~ 6 mos

1

Ava Carmichael was worth twelve and a half billion dollars. Billion. With a B.

She could afford a Rembrandt. Or a Van Gogh. But instead, she had a framed inspirational poster hanging on the wall behind the desk where her receptionist sat. Cori wasn't sure why that annoyed her. But it did.

Cori studied the poster and thought about her sister. Maybe the poster annoyed her because it read INSPIRATION and was a photo of a guy hang-gliding and she knew for a fact that Ava had never gone hang-gliding.

Or maybe it was because Cori was 99 percent sure that her sister had no idea what poster was hanging behind the front desk at Carmichael Enterprises. The stupid thing had probably been hanging there when Ava had taken over as CEO five years ago.

And yes, *that* was what irritated Cori about it. Ava had been so determined to follow in their father's footsteps that she hadn't even replaced the wall art in his office when he'd moved to Bumfuck, Kansas and put her in charge.

"Oh, Ms. Carmichael!"

Cori straightened from where she was leaning on the tall front desk as the receptionist, Sarah, came rushing around the corner with an armful of file folders. She dropped the stack in the middle of the desk, folders sliding precariously.

"I'm so sorry! I didn't know you were here! I didn't mean to keep you waiting."

"No worries. I just got here," Cori said with a smile. "Just didn't know which conference room we were meeting in." That was a bald-faced lie. Ava had texted her an hour ago that it was Conference Room A.

But there was no way Cori was showing up for that meeting on time. Being on time—or God forbid early—for this meeting would make it seem important. And she did not want it to seem, or to *be*, important. For her or for her sisters.

She was going to stroll into the enormous conference room with the table that could seat fourteen and the floor-to-ceiling windows that overlooked Manhattan, as if it was just one more thing she had to do in her day and was hardly worth a second thought. She'd even worn black jeans and her black T-shirt that said *Sorry I'm late, but I didn't want to come* under her red leather jacket. All of which would completely exasperate Ava.

But better Ava be exasperated with her than anxious about the documents the lawyer was going over with them today. Exasperated with Cori was a normal state for Ava. And Cori was determined to give her sisters—both of them—as much normalcy as she could as they listened to the lawyers go over the paperwork.

Yeah, the paperwork. Also known as their father's will.

"They're in Conference Room A," Sarah said. "Do you need some help getting everything down there?"

Cori grinned as she picked up the two cardboard trays of coffee cups, balancing one on top of the other, along with the whipped cream dispenser she'd set on the front counter. "Nope, I've got it."

"Okay, fourth door on the right," Sarah said.

"Thanks." Cori started down the long stretch of gray carpet. Gray. Of course it was gray. She hadn't visited the offices of her father's company in years, but she definitely had memories of lots of gray and white and black. Clean, professional, sterile colors for the décor that screamed money and intimidation and perfection.

She reached the conference room far too quickly, so she paused for a moment before stepping in front of the glass wall that separated the conference room from the hallway. She took a deep breath, dug for her this-is-no-big-deal-I-can-make-anything-fun side, and pasted on a huge smile. Then she tucked the stainless-steel canister full of whipped cream under her arm, balanced the trays in one hand, and reached for the door.

"Good morning!" she said brightly, as she stepped into the room.

Ava was standing near the windows looking every bit the CEO she was, in her black pencil skirt, white silk blouse, gold jewelry and Louis Vuitton sling-back pumps—the only part of her outfit Cori would have ever borrowed. Her other sister, Brynn, was at the table, a notebook and pen laid out in front of her. She wore blue capri pants that clashed with the salmon-colored cashmere sweater she wore. The white T-shirt under-neath was wrinkled, her hair was pulled back in a haphazard bun, and she had glasses perched on her nose. No doubt she'd been immersed in something in her lab when she'd remembered, at the last second, that she had to be across the city and in her sister's office by nine a.m.

Cori felt the tension from Ava and the worry from Brynn immediately, as if she was feeling it herself. She had no idea if all sisters felt each other's emotions that way or if it was because she, Ava, and Brynn were triplets, but she struggled to hold on to her smile as she set everything down on the gleaming mahogany tabletop and began pulling bottles from her pockets.

"You stopped for coffee?" Ava asked.

Dammit. It was only Brynn, Ava, and some guy sitting at the end of the table. A very good-looking guy. There was no way for Cori not to notice that. Despite her nerves jumping with the need to get this meeting over with, the urge to bolt coursing through her veins, and the determination it was taking to act nonchalant about it all.

He wore a white button-down shirt, sleeves rolled up to his elbows, no tie, no jacket. He had a folder in front of him and a notebook next to it, but there was nothing written on the page. Maybe because the damned meeting had clearly not started yet. He sat back in the leather chair, one forearm resting on the tabletop, one ankle propped on his opposite knee. And he wore blue jeans. Cori was shocked by that. Surely he wasn't an intern. No way would Ava let an intern wear jeans to the office. Maybe he worked for the legal team that was coming in. He could be a note-taker—what were those people called again?—or something, she supposed. He had dark hair, light eyes that could have been gray or blue behind dark-rimmed glasses, and a tanned, muscular forearm.

Cori tore her attention away from him. It was so typical that she'd be distracted by some cute guy while she was *trying* to help her sisters through this meeting. She always had good intentions, but her predisposition for frivolousness was often stronger.

Where were all the freaking lawyers? If they got the meeting started, she would be able to concentrate. She'd really thought being twenty minutes late would ensure everyone else would be present and that they would have covered at least some of the information by the time she got here. She didn't want to sit through the whole thing about Ava inheriting the business, and Brynn getting her research funding, and Cori not getting anything. This was all just some formality, and she hadn't been shocked to find out that she was required to be there, but she did resent it a little. She didn't really need to be told in a formal, legal document that her father had given up on her. That had been pretty clear for a long time.

"Of course I stopped for coffee," Cori said with a big smile.

She'd intentionally been late so she could make an entrance. She'd hoped the interruption would break up the tension that would have already built in the room. And she'd intentionally shown up with treats. Because that's what she did. She made things sweeter, sillier, and more fun for her sisters. That was her role in their triad and really the only thing she could offer here today.

She'd behaved every day since finding out their father had died. She'd bit her tongue when people talked about how great he was. She'd refrained from scoffing when people said how proud he'd been of her. She'd pretended that she knew his favorite church hymn when the funeral director had asked—hey, everyone liked "Amazing Grace", right?

But she'd be damned if she'd sit in this office and act sad listening to lawyers milk their hourly rates while doling out her father's possessions.

It was no coincidence that there was not a single *World's Best Dad* mug among those possessions.

So what if a few of the tears she'd shed had felt real? There was plenty to mourn when it came to her and her father. His death was not even number one on the list.

"The meeting was supposed to start at nine," Ava told her.

Cori nodded as she pulled one of the cups from the tray, grabbed the whipped cream gun and one of the plastic bottles, and rounded the table. "I got your texts."

"And it's now nine thirty-five," Ava said, accepting the cup with a frown.

Okay, she was thirty-five minutes late. She'd still beat the stupid lawyers. She took the lid off of the cup Ava held, tipped the silver can, and added a swirl of whipped cream to the top of Ava's chai latte, then shook a few tiny cinnamon cookie crumbs from the plastic bottle onto the top of the cream. "Well, I felt bad leaving the people in line behind me without whipped cream, so I let everyone else go first. And it was a long line." *Thankfully.*

"Then you stole the whipped cream gun?" Ava asked.

"Of course not. I bought it from the guy." She was aware that the man at the end of the table was watching her with a bemused expression, but he hadn't moved or said a word.

"Why?" Brynn asked.

"Because if I'd added the whipped cream to our drinks there, it would have melted by the time I got up here," Cori said. She removed the lid from the mocha latte she'd gotten Brynn and added a tall swirl of whipped cream. Then she chose another of the plastic bottles she'd brought and shook chocolate sprinkles over the top. She handed it to her sister. "I hate that."

Brynn took it, almost as if she was at a loss for words. She dipped her finger into the whipped cream, catching a few sprinkles with it, and stuck her fingertip in her mouth. And smiled. And that was all Cori needed to see. She took a deep, satisfied breath.

"You brought *a lot* of coffee," Ava commented.

She was already sipping her chai and Cori hid her smile. She might frustrate her sister, but Ava needed her. In the midst of a very not-fun meeting like this, Ava needed a latte with little cookie crumbs on top. She just didn't know it until Cori showed up.

"Sure. For the lawyers. It's all just black though," she said with a shrug. "Figured boring was probably the way to go with lawyers, right?"

"Actually, I love a good caramel macchiato."

Cori's gaze went to the only guy in the room again. "Do you?"

"Definitely."

"Cori, this is Evan Stone. He's the attorney from Kansas," Ava said. "Mr. Stone, our sister, Cori. And now that we're all here, let's continue. I'm sure we all have other places to be."

Well, that wasn't untrue. Cori didn't have anywhere else specific to be, but she could think of at least twenty places she'd *rather* be.

"Please call me Evan," the lawyer said.

The lawyer. Of course he was. But he liked caramel. And his eyes were definitely blue.

The only thing that matters is the lawyer part. Knock it off.

"It's nice to meet you, Cori," Evan said. "I'm sorry for your loss."

Yeah, she couldn't deal with that right now. Cori looked at Ava. "*The* attorney. As in, just one?"

"Just one," Evan confirmed. "But don't worry, I did have my assistant spell-check everything."

She'd pictured a room full of lawyers, some for her father, some for Ava, talking through multiple points regarding the transition of power of Carmichael Enterprises. Ad nauseum. She'd downloaded a new romance novel onto her phone just for the occasion. She wasn't going to get to start that today either.

Cori resisted sighing. Why was it when she prepared for something, actually spent time thinking it through and making a plan, it never turned out the way she'd imagined it anyway? Oh yeah, because plans sucked. She was much better at spontaneity and going with the flow.

Fine. There was one lawyer. Maybe that would mean the meeting would be shorter. And hey, he was wearing blue jeans. For some reason that made her like him a little bit. Sure, maybe in small-town Kansas that was typical dress code for lawyers, but she doubted very much that Ava had ever met with an attorney wearing denim before.

Feeling a little happier at the thought that even Ava couldn't have been fully prepared for this meeting, Cori took another of the cups from the tray and removed the lid. She swirled whipped cream on the top, picked up another bottle, squeezed a drizzle of caramel over the top, and took it to the end of the table.

"Caramel macchiato," she said, handing it to Evan.

He took it, one eyebrow arched. "You had a caramel macchiato?"

"My favorite," she said with a nod.

She headed back to her collection of cups that held only straight-up black coffee now. She took one and began doctoring it with sugar packets and creamer tubs that she also pulled from her jacket pockets. Then she squirted a copious amount of caramel syrup into the cup, stirred, added whipped cream, and drank.

It was only as that first swallow passed her tongue that she realized the room was quiet and that her sisters and Evan were all watching her.

She swallowed and asked, "What?"

"If you're finished?" Ava asked. "We can continue."

Cori dropped into the chair next to where she'd been standing. "Yes. Oh my God, please continue. Does that mean you've already started?"

"We did," Ava said.

Yes! Maybe not *every* one of her plans was going to crap.

"When you didn't answer my texts asking where you were," Ava added.

"My hands were full," Cori said. She'd felt her phone vibrating in her pocket, but she'd known it was Ava and exactly what Ava was asking. "But you can just fill me in on whatever pertains to me later."

She swiveled the chair, which was more comfortable and cost more than many beds she'd slept in over the past few years, so that she could prop her feet on the chair next to her. She cradled her cup in both hands and rested it on her stomach, settling in to pretend to listen, but to actually just enjoy watching Evan Stone. She could happily ogle his firm jawline and his broad shoulders and the long, thick fingers that wrapped around the coffee cup while he went over...whatever he was going to go over.

"Well, there are several things that pertain to you," Ava said.

There were? "Like what?" Maybe they just needed her to sign something that said she understood she didn't get anything. That was cool. She was all over that.

"Like going to Bliss," Ava said.

That little crease between Ava's eyebrows is getting deeper, Cori thought distractedly. Good thing for Botox. Then Ava's words sank in. That wasn't legalese. And it wasn't "sign here and move on with your life."

"What?"

Ava sighed. "You missed a lot, Cori. There are some...stipulations in the trust. Things we have to do to inherit."

Oh, well, that was no big deal. "I don't want to inherit," Cori said, waving that away with one hand. "None of that matters to me."

Ava crossed her arms, that forehead crease deepening again. "We *all* have to meet *all* of the conditions."

Cori frowned and shook her head.

"The company is being divided into three equal shares," Brynn said from across the table. "And we each have to follow the stipulations to inherit our third or *none* of us inherit anything."

The sip of coffee in her mouth turned bitter and Cori struggled to swallow it. "But I don't want a third of the company," she finally managed. She looked at Evan. "Can't I just give my part to Ava and Brynn?"

"You can do what you want with your third," he said. "*After* you inherit it. Which won't happen until the conditions of the trust are met."

Cori opened her mouth, but had no idea what to say. She was going to be *forced* to inherit part of her father's company? There was no way that was right. It was totally unfair to Ava and Brynn, for one thing. Ava had worked her ass off for the company since she'd been sixteen. Brynn had no interest in the business beyond the research and development branch where she worked as the lead scientist for their pharmaceutical companies, but she could at least fund her research with her third. But Cori…well, Cori not only had no interest in Carmichael Enterprises, but she had no talent, skill, or knowledge to bring to the company, and she didn't have any world-changing projects that she'd earmarked a few billion for.

Ava took a deep breath. "This is all or nothing, Cori. We all have to do it or it doesn't matter."

Cori focused on Evan instead, hoping he could make some sense out of this. Surely Ava was misunderstanding. Or overreacting. Or something. Because if that was true, then Cori was stuck. She'd do anything for her sisters. Which Rudy had, of course, known. And would have used if needed. She narrowed her eyes. "Can Dad actually make us do a bunch of stuff we don't want to do?"

Evan nodded and Cori felt her heart drop.

"It's perfectly legal for him to put any stipulations on the distribution of his assets that he wanted to." Evan paused and looked at each of them. "You don't have to do any of it, of course. But," he continued just as Cori tried to take a deep breath, "you then all give up all stake in the company and have nothing more to do with Carmichael Enterprises."

Which was exactly what Cori wanted. But that didn't matter. If she had to jump through a couple of hoops for Ava to inherit, she'd jump. And she'd freaking smile while she did it too. *So there, Dad.*

Cori practiced one of those I'm-totally-good-with-whatever smiles right then. "Okay, fine. I'm always up for anything. What are these stipulations?"

"Here." Brynn slid a piece of paper toward Cori.

For a second, Cori flashed back to calculus class in high school. Brynn was a master note taker. And Cori...wasn't. But it took only a quick glance to show that the handwriting on the paper was not Brynn's. It was their father's.

Instantly, Cori's throat got tight. That was stupid. It wasn't like he'd written her lots of—or really any—cards and letters over the years. But maybe that's why seeing his handwriting hurt now—because she hadn't seen a lot of it over the years. And now she wouldn't be seeing it again. She cleared her throat and shook that off. "What's this?"

"Dad's note," Brynn said. "The way this all got started. It's actually a pretty good summary."

It was a fairly small piece of paper, and Cori felt a little better. He couldn't have fit too many demands on something that size.

"There are a lot more details and, of course, it's written more...officially...in the trust," Evan said. "But yeah, that's the first note your dad made about all of this. And it does cover the basics."

Cori looked up, hearing a gruffness in Evan's voice. He seemed a little choked up. Okay, that was unexpected. She hadn't realized that the attorney had been close to Rudy personally, but it seemed clear that Evan was feeling sentimental about the note.

She swallowed hard and made herself focus on the paper.

It was definitely Rudy's handwriting. But there wasn't anything like "My dearest Ava" or "I'm sorry I didn't tell you I was sick" or "I wish we'd had more time." It was, more or less, a list. There were five main numbered points. Then there were some small notes written around each. Some words had been underlined or crossed out in red and other words were highlighted in yellow.

It took only a few seconds to read. And then a few seconds more for her to realize that she'd been wrong. He'd fit *a lot* onto that four-by-six-inch piece of paper.

1. *Move to Bliss. 1 year. Live in house together.*
2. *Run pie shop. Profit by year end.*
3. *AVA- kitchen, baking, all products. NO business! Date a guy from Bliss. Give it 6 mos. Have fun. No checklists!*
4. *BRYNN- customers/waitress. Time with people, get to know them. No kitchen, no business. Date 6 guys from Bliss.*
5. *CORI- books/accounting. No baking. Leave customers to B. Make a commitment. But NO DATING for 6 mos.!*

Cori read it three times. Finally, she looked up. She had no idea which thing to focus on first. It was all equally bizarre.

Except...it wasn't.

Not completely. Not the part about Ava having fun. And the part about Brynn spending time with people. And, yeah, even the part about Cori making a commitment. None of that was bizarre. It was all stuff that she and her sisters were not so great at.

The only thing that made it weird was that Rudy had realized it.

"You're telling me that *this* is what Dad said we had to do before we can inherit?" she asked the room.

"Yes. Basically," Evan confirmed. "Like I mentioned, there are a few more details in the trust itself, but...yeah."

Cori looked at her sisters. Ava looked pissed and Brynn looked worried. Dammit, she'd brought whipped cream and *sprinkles* to avoid those looks today. She glanced at Evan. He looked concerned and maybe just a little...curious. About her reaction? She wondered what he'd expected.

"You actually put all of this—" She pointed to the note. "—into a legal document?"

Evan glanced at Ava, then back at Cori. "Um. Yeah."

"And we *have* to do all of this or we lose the company."

"Yes."

Cori looked at the note again. Rudy wanted her to do

accounting and *not* date? She wasn't really the sit-at-a-desk-with-spreadsheets type. And she definitely wasn't the sit-at-home-with-Netflix-on-a-Saturday-night type. She had a tendency to, well, not stick. Not to jobs, not to places, not to relationships. She kind of understood why a typical, concerned father might feel the need to do something drastic to change all that. Like tie her sisters' happiness...and twelve and a half billion dollars...to her settling down for a year.

Then again, Rudy had never been a typical father.

Her gaze settled on the yellow highlighted part under her name. *Make a commitment.* Since that was followed immediately by BUT NO DATING! she had to assume that he didn't mean to a guy. Which left her sisters. Or a job. Or both.

Had Rudy known that when she saw her sisters, it was for forty-eight hours or less and involved doing something fun and ridiculous that neither Ava nor Brynn would ever do with anyone else? Cori blew into town, usually without much notice, dragged her sisters out for a fun, extravagant weekend, and then left before they got sick of her. And stayed away for at least a couple of months so they had a little time to miss her. But that wouldn't be possible in Bliss, Kansas. Living in the same house. Working in the same pie shop. That would require her to get serious. And stick around.

But *make a commitment* were not the only highlighted words on the page. *Have fun* was highlighted for Ava and *time with people* was in yellow after Brynn's name. Rudy wasn't wrong about those either. Ava did need to relax and have more fun, and Brynn needed to spend more time with people than with microbes and bacteria—or whatever she had in her lab. Her sisters were brilliant and successful and could do or have anything that they wanted. The fact that they chose to spend all of their time working was a concern of Cori's as well.

Dammit, Rudy, now we have something in common? Now that you're dead?

Cori felt tears pricking at her eyes again and she quickly blinked. Nope, there was not going to be any crying here today. She also couldn't be pissed off or worried. Ava and Brynn had those covered. Cori was the girl with the whipped cream gun. As always. Of course, usually that whipped cream gun was figurative.

"Okay, well, I guess it goes without saying that I can be ready to go first thing in the morning," Cori said.

"You...can?" Ava asked, clearly stunned *that* was Cori's answer.

She gave Ava a look. "I can always be ready to go first thing in the morning."

She didn't typically just pick up and go. She gave notice at work and let her landlords know when she was leaving town. Usually. But she *could* just decide to take off. She made sure she took jobs that were fun and different...and where it didn't matter if she screwed something up or decided to suddenly quit. At least, that it didn't matter in a cosmic, people-truly-depending-on-her way like her sisters' jobs did. She supposed there were some irritated restaurant and clothing boutique managers here and there, but overall, Cori's absence didn't change the course of history or leave any gaping holes. Exactly the way she wanted it. And yes, she realized that not being dependent on any of those jobs to pay her bills was definitely one advantage of having a trust fund that had kicked in when she'd turned eighteen.

Ava pulled a breath in through her nose and let it out slowly. "Well, don't worry about that. I'm going to do everything I can to find a way out of this. I will speak to my lawyers as soon as we're finished here."

Because of course you don't want to spend a year in Kansas with me and Brynn.

The thought flitted through Cori's mind unbidden. Whoa. Dammit. *She* didn't really want to live in Kansas for a year either.

It was good that Ava could snap her fingers and have some of the best lawyers in the country looking for ways out of this.

But for just an instant Cori wished she could see Ava Carmichael in small-town Kansas. Sure, she was stereotyping a bit, but there had to be some truth to the idea that there were towns where everyone knew your name within five minutes and all of your business within six. Where the idea of twenty-four-hour sushi was something they only saw in the movies. Where it would only take you a few minutes to get to a place where there were no other people, no noise, no lights. Yeah, she'd give some of her hefty-maybe-almost inheritance to see her sister in a place like that.

Cori glanced at Brynn. Hell, a place like that could be great for Brynn too. Where Ava managed hundreds of people, was on conference calls and in meetings all day, and even tied her social life to her work, Brynn could go days without speaking to another human being and be completely fine with it. She preferred her test tubes and microscopes to anything involving people and human interaction. It might be good for her to be in a place where she couldn't just blend into the crowd on the sidewalks or disappear into her lab for days.

Cori looked down at the note again. Yep. She was seeing a point to what Rudy had scribbled on this paper.

Okay, now she had to do her job here and make this not only no big deal, but maybe even fun. She had to figure out a way to add a few figurative sprinkles. But honestly, there were a few things in Rudy's note that could qualify as a good time.

For instance, the idea of Ava baking. Her sister was absolutely not domestic in any way. Seeing Ava outside of the boardroom and out of her pencil skirts, with some flour in her hair, and pie filling on her Gucci pumps would definitely be fun.

Also, the idea of Ava dating a small-town boy from the middle of America who, if there was a God, drove a pickup and would call her ma'am or darlin'. There had to be some hot guys in

Kansas besides Evan Stone. Guys that worked outside, with their hands, in blue jeans and boots. Guys that wouldn't be impressed by things like Ava's investment portfolio or that she could get last-minute reservations at any five-star restaurant in New York City. Yeah, a hot, country boy could be good for her buttoned-up, workaholic sister.

And for her brilliant, nerdy, microscopes-and-books-are-my-crack sister too. Cori reached over and snagged Brynn's notebook. She wrote *SIX GUYS!* and drew a heart and then some googly eyes. Brynn looked at the doodle and giggled slightly. Cori felt a surge of accomplishment at the sound. The idea of Brynn launching a social life was definitely fun now that Cori was thinking about it. Cori could help her with her hair and makeup. And hell, Brynn could borrow Cori's entire night-on-the-town wardrobe. She wasn't going to be needing it.

And there was a fourth fun thing on their father's list. Pies. It was really hard to not have good feelings about pie.

"I don't know, Ava," Cori said, summoning her come-on-you-can-trust-me smile and her I-dare-you tone of voice. That smile and tone of voice had gotten Ava Carmichael out of her one-piece swimsuit and into the Gulf of Mexico bare-assed naked two years ago. "This could be an adventure."

Ava gave her an I'm-allergic-to-adventure-remember? look. And Cori did remember. Adventures with Ava required a lot of spontaneity—i.e., not letting her think about it very long or hard —and a good amount of vodka. And proposing the plan while in a shoe store was even better. Preferably Gucci, but Louis Vuitton worked too. Shoe stores were about the only place on the planet where Ava Carmichael was at all frivolous and out of control. This alcohol-less meeting in a conference room that reminded Ava she was responsible and in charge was really working against this whole idea.

"What's this thing about a pie shop?" Cori asked Evan. "We have to open one?"

Evan had been watching her and Ava and Brynn quietly. Seemingly just studying their reactions and interactions. Now he leaned in again. "It's your dad's shop. He wants you to take over running it. As a team. You each have something particular to be in charge of."

"Our dad's shop?" Cori repeated. "You mean like a huge pie *company* that distributes to restaurants and grocery stores nationally or something, right?" The word "shop" brought to mind a quaint little place with a glass display case and chalkboard menu and air that smelled like cinnamon and sugar.

Evan shook his head. "No, it's just a little shop on Main Street. He made a few pies a week and mostly served them to his friends."

Cori stared at him as *Main Street* echoed in her head. There was a Main Street in Bliss. A slide show of Norman Rockwell paintings suddenly flashed through her mind. "Our dad, Rudolph A. Carmichael, CEO of Carmichael Enterprises, billionaire, owned a pie shop in Bliss, Kansas?" Cori asked. "Where *he* made the pies. And had friends." Cori wasn't sure that she knew of anyone she would have called her father's *friend*. He had a lot of acquaintances. Tons of business colleagues. Hundreds of employees. But friends? She couldn't think of one.

Evan nodded. "Yes."

And for the life of her, Cori could not picture Rudy in a kitchen even making a sandwich, not to mention making a pie. "*Why?*" That was maybe not the most important question at that moment but...it was really the one she was most fascinated with.

"Well, there was nowhere else to get pie in town," Evan said. "And it was his favorite dessert. So he decided to solve the problem by opening his own shop."

That made sense. She supposed. And pie was her father's favorite food. She hadn't known that. She had no idea what her father's favorite...anything...was. A stab of sorrow hit her in the chest again.

"And he must have really loved the town." She hadn't been expecting to say that but it seemed clear. If he'd found a place that made him happy, where he'd been content to run a pie shop versus a worldwide conglomerate, and where he'd had *friends*, that really was nice. Strange. But nice. And now he wanted his daughters to know this place. Hell, that was almost fatherly.

Evan didn't respond immediately, but after a second, he shifted and sat forward in his chair. "Bliss was very important to your father," he said. "He felt that living in the town changed him, for the better." Evan removed his glasses and took a deep breath. "Rudy had a lot of regrets at the end. The cancer progressed very quickly, and he realized that he had run out of time to say all of this to you himself. He believed that living in Bliss would help you see and learn the things he did and that this was the only way to get you there and for you to really give it a chance."

Cori couldn't respond right away. The words "cancer" and "a lot of regrets" and "at the end", and hearing them from Evan with that note of gruffness in his voice, made Cori's throat feel tight.

"That means his dying wish was for us to move to Bliss, for a year, and make pies," Brynn finally said. She looked at Cori and Ava. "Together."

"It was," Evan said.

Cori groaned internally. Brynn had to use the term "dying wish" didn't she? And yet the "together" made Cori's heart thump just as hard. She glanced down at the note again. Number one was *Move to Bliss. 1 year. Live in house together.*

Together was underlined in red.

And that part suddenly didn't seem crazy either. A little scary, for sure. Twelve months straight with her sisters was a *big* commitment for Cori. There were a lot of things she could screw up in that amount of time. But...Ava and Brynn would *have* to stay there with her anyway. Maybe that had been part of Rudy's thinking too.

"This is just all so over-the-top," Brynn said softly. "It's like you're talking about a stranger rather than our dad. He never did anything...dramatic."

Maybe once you knew you were dying, you started not caring as much that your actions might be perceived as a little over-the-top. Cori felt her heart thump again with the thought.

Over-the top was her specialty. It was how she did most things. So there was something else she and her father had in common. Now. Ironic, that. His demands of perfection and her tendency to overdo and not respect limits and rules had always been a wedge between them. And now he was the one doing something crazy. Well, she supposed it made sense that she was the one thinking they should go ahead with the whole thing.

Evan rubbed a hand over his face and for a flash, Cori thought *really hot* before he pushed his chair back and got to his feet. Evan stepped around the corner of the conference table, and Cori was again distracted for a moment. He was tall, probably six-two, his jeans fit very nicely, and she couldn't help but notice the way his arms and shoulder muscles flexed against the dress shirt as he tucked his hands into the front pockets of those jeans. And he was wearing tennis shoes. Had a pair of tennis shoes ever touched the carpet in this office before? But she quickly decided *no way.* And this guy clearly didn't give a crap. She might not normally be attracted to a guy in glasses who studied and practiced law, no doubt surrounded by leather-bound books and fountain pens, but she was definitely a sucker for guys who didn't give a crap.

"I didn't know Rudy prior to his car breaking down in Bliss five years ago," Evan said, his voice low and even. "All I knew was the eccentric, funny, incredibly generous man who came into my friend's diner looking for a mechanic and a cup of coffee. He got both. The cup of coffee from my best friend, Parker, and the best mechanic in four counties, my buddy Noah. All he got from me was some conversation, but it was enough to forge a friendship.

Over the three days it took Noah to fix Rudy's Cadillac, Rudy fell in love with my town. I had no idea that he was rich until he came to me asking for help with his trust. For four and a half years, he was just this goofy guy who made everyone smile and treated Bliss like it was his hometown." Evan's voice got a little gruff. "He was a friend of mine. Someone I watched die with regrets. Someone I miss every single day. Someone who, in the last couple of months, wished he could have done a lot of things differently, especially with his daughters. I tried to talk him out of some of this stuff. But in the end, when he asked me if I would be sure that you all knew the things he wished he'd said to you and shown you himself, I couldn't say anything but yes. Which means, I'm here to be sure that you all know exactly what he wanted and why."

Wow.

The man was nerdy hot, was from small-town Kansas, and had worn blue jeans to an important meeting on Madison Avenue. But in that moment, Cori realized that he was absolutely going to be sure that her father got his way. And that determination was very attractive. She also admired his defense of someone he considered a friend. Even if it was her father. Funny? Generous? *Goofy?* How could this be the same Rudy Carmichael who had said "Seriously, Cori?" more times than she'd ever heard him say anything else?

"Dad was paying more attention than we ever thought," Cori said.

Evan's expression softened slightly. "He loved you all very much. He realized he hadn't done a good job of being there for you, but he paid very close attention, especially over the past few years. He did a lot of soul searching, and talking with...local counselors."

"He saw a therapist?" Cori asked. That might have been the biggest shock of all.

"Well, he had coffee every morning with a group of guys who

were fathers and grandfathers and involved in their children's lives in ways he never was," Evan said.

Then his lips turned up in a half smile that was full of humor and affection, and Cori felt a little tingle. Dang.

"So a bunch of old guys in Kansas helped him see what a crappy father he was?" Cori asked.

"Pretty much," Evan agreed. His smile grew bigger. And her panties grew warmer.

"*Alright*," Ava interrupted, clearly out of patience. "Is that everything?"

Evan looked over at her, almost as if he'd forgotten she was there. He nodded. "It is. In a nutshell. You have the documents."

"I do." Ava turned on her heel and started for the door. "And I'm calling my lawyer. Dad was clearly out of his mind. Maybe it was the chemo or the cancer or whatever but I'm going to have Kevin look into his medical records and figure out a way—"

"Miss Carmichael."

Cori didn't know if Ava paused because she was surprised by Evan's tone of voice or because the low, firm, I'm-in-charge-here quality had sent goose bumps skittering over her body the way it had Cori's, but Ava stopped with her hand on the doorknob.

"Yes, Mr. Stone?" Ava asked, finally turning back stiffly.

"It would be in your best interest to understand a couple of things before you contact your attorney." Evan hadn't shifted his posture a bit, but his expression was now one of fierce determination.

Ava crossed her arms. "And what are those?"

"The first is that I took my job with your father very seriously and, while I may not have agreed with everything he wanted to do, my job was to make this trust what he wanted it to be. You are free, of course, to have your attorney look it over, but I can promise you that this document is well constructed and not something that you'll be able to have overturned."

Ava swallowed hard but didn't say anything.

"The next thing you need to know is that I am fully prepared to take the stand in a court of law and testify that he was of sound mind when he wrote it. As will a number of people in Bliss, including his physician, our Mayor, and a district judge. His mind was absolutely not impaired by his cancer or his treatment, and while I understand that you all had a complicated relationship with him, I won't allow you, or anyone else, to disparage him."

Cori shifted in her chair. Damn. That was hot too. She didn't often see people taking Ava down a peg, and typically she would have rushed to put herself between one of her sisters and anyone who dared challenge them. However, Evan was right. Ava was frustrated and Cori got that, but going after their father's mental capacity because she didn't like what he'd mandated in his trust was low.

"And finally," Evan said when Ava took a breath that might have been fueling a heated response, "I think I should point out that the time frame in your father's trust doesn't begin until you and your sisters move into the residence in Bliss. Which means that if you take several weeks, or even months, questioning this document or the stipulations within, and then realize that you are, indeed, bound to it, you are only prolonging the time it will take for you to resolve the terms and claim your inheritance. So it seems to me," he said, lifting a shoulder, "that your best move here is just to get your butt to Bliss and get this all over with."

No one said anything for several ticks.

Then Ava raised her chin slightly and said, "Thank you for making all of that so clear, Mr. Stone. But if you'll excuse me, I would like to consult with someone who is perhaps a bit more objective about the situation."

Cori watched Evan. It looked like he tensed his jaw, but finally he gave Ava a nod. "Fine."

"Fine," Ava agreed. Then she again turned on her three-inch, seven-hundred-dollar heel, jerked the door open, and then shut it quietly behind her.

Wow, that right there was a really good example of how Cori and her sisters were different. Ava would shut a door firmly, but quietly, always the picture of poise and professionalism. Brynn would never stomp out of a room in the first place. And Cori would absolutely have slammed that thing. Maybe after a good, loud, "Fuck you."

2

After a moment, Brynn sighed and got to her feet. "I'll go check on her," she said.

Cori nodded. She'd been expecting that. Brynn disappeared through the door and Cori turned her attention back to Evan Stone. He'd rounded the table and was gathering his papers.

"You're leaving?" she asked, pushing up from her chair.

He looked up. "I'm happy to answer any questions you have. I can review anything we covered before you got here."

Cori thought about that. Then glanced at Rudy's note again. "I think I'm clear on everything, actually."

"You sure?"

Rudy's three main objectives were crystal clear. "Yep, I'm good."

"Okay, then." Evan tucked a manila folder into the leather briefcase that looked like it had been taken out of the box that morning.

"They're not planning to buy furs coats or build a vacation house in Vienna or anything, you know," she said. For some reason, she felt compelled to make Evan Stone understand Ava's and Brynn's motivations. Provided Ava's attorneys couldn't undo the entire thing in the end. And the idea that they might actually get out of this sent a stupid twinge of disappointment pinging through her. She was definitely going to ignore *that*.

Evan gave her one of those half smiles. "Really? Rudy mentioned something about Brynn wanting a private jet."

"Only because it would make it easier to travel with her research and teaching," Cori said quickly. "And he probably also said that Ava has a limo, but that's so she can work while she's commuting. She never stops. Even on the way to the symphony or an art show, she's on the phone or her computer."

Evan's smile went from half to full, and Cori cursed herself for loving it.

"I know all of that. I'm just pushing your buttons."

Cori crossed her arms. She didn't have many buttons, but her sisters—and anyone's criticism of either of them—was definitely one of them. "Ava doesn't want the money for limos and shoes. She thinks that heading up this company is the only way to ensure security and safety for *us* long-term. She wants me to be able to travel and Brynn to be able to continue her research and our mother to continue her charity work."

"She thinks money can buy happiness?" Evan asked. He stood at the end of the conference table, his shiny had-to-be-new brief-case in one hand, the other tucked into the front pocket of the blue jeans that molded to his body in a way that said they definitely were not new.

Cori shook her head, pulling her thoughts away from the fact that she really liked a guy in blue jeans. "She knows that money can buy security and that the ability to pursue goals and dreams without limitation can lead to happiness."

"Ah."

Cori frowned. "This company's money allows my mother to fundraise for nonprofit organizations."

In fact, their father had provided their mother, Jennifer, with enough money to take care of Cori and her sisters and to continue her nonprofit work long before Ava had taken over at Carmichael Enterprises. Their mom and Rudy had never been married. They'd met at a fundraiser and he'd swept Jennifer, his junior by almost fifteen years, off her feet and into a love affair that had resulted in a pregnancy. With triplets. But he'd never been able to talk her into walking down the aisle. They'd always been friendly though, and Cori could admit that the way he'd respected and supported their mom had made it easier for Cori to like him. She'd often wondered if her mom was the one that got away for Rudy. He'd never had a serious relationship after her. At least that Cori knew of.

"It also lets Brynn to do life-saving research without politics and policies getting in the way of her funding," Cori went on. "They are literally working to make the world a better place with Ava's support."

"Ah."

What did *that* mean? "What they're doing is important. And it's important to Ava to know that we're all taken care of. She's very protective of all of us."

"I see."

Okay, this was getting annoying. Even with his sexy smiles and his well-fitted blue jeans, Evan Stone was beginning to irritate her.

"This company isn't just about making money to have money," Cori insisted. "It's about the things that money can help accomplish."

"And what about you?" Evan asked.

"What about me?" But she knew what he meant.

"What's your role in this make-the-world-better machine?"

Well, Cori did give money away. By the tens of thousands. And she had a lot of causes that could benefit from her share of twelve-and-a-half billion dollars. But no one knew that. Not even Ava. And Cori loved her even more because she supported Cori even thinking that all Cori was doing was partying her way around the world. That was part of why she kept those details to herself. Was it a way of testing the people who said they loved her because she'd had a father that she could never please? Well, that's what her shrink said.

But Ava passed with flying colors. Ava just wanted them to all be safe and secure and happy. And putting up with their father and working her ass off to be in position to lead his company was her way of making that happen.

Until now.

Until Rudy Carmichael once again decided he knew better than everyone else.

Cori lifted her chin and gave Evan one of her signature, mischievous smiles that she could, at this point in her life, conjure in a snap. "Oh, they don't need me to make things happen," she said. "I just show up once in a while to ensure they have some fun while they're kicking ass."

Evan looked at her for a long moment, and Cori's mind started to spin with what Rudy had possibly told Evan about her. But Rudy didn't know that she'd given almost her entire trust fund away already or that her travels had included volunteer work with a variety of organizations. It wasn't that she was embarrassed by any of that. But she liked being *unexpected*. It had given her a freedom that she appreciated greatly. No one in her family had ever valued enjoyment quite to the extent that she did, but she knew it was important to work *and* play. And if she sometimes had to force her sisters to have a good time, she didn't feel bad about it. Too much.

"You and I have a lot in common, Cori," Evan finally said.

"You're in charge of manicures and karaoke and chocolate Kahlua milkshakes when you and your sisters get together?" she asked.

He shrugged. "I prefer whiskey and both of my sisters are horrible singers, but yeah, something like that."

Cori felt a jolt of...something. Something that felt like...like.

For Evan Stone. "Are sex and dating the same thing?" she asked without thinking. Which was how she did most things.

Evan's eyes widened, but he didn't react otherwise. "I assume we're talking about the no-dating provision in the trust?"

"Right."

Evan took a breath and moved around the edge of the table. When he was on the same side of the mahogany monstrosity, he half sat, one ass cheek on the table, facing her.

"Your dad thought you were using partying and being the good-time girl as a way of being important to the people you care about without doing anything that's actually serious or responsible... because you don't want to mess up bigger things that really matter. You don't want to help them make career decisions that might not turn out well. You don't want to give them relationship advice in case you're wrong. You want to stick with Kahlua milkshakes. Because they always love Kahlua milkshakes. You can't screw that up."

Damn her father and his stupid, too-late insight. She swallowed hard. "Why would he think that?" she asked, acting as if she couldn't care less. Or trying to anyway.

"Because that's what I do."

Cori's gaze zeroed in on Evan's. "Oh."

"Yeah, your dad figured out that we're a lot alike early on. As he got to know me, he gained some insight into you."

"Great," she said dryly. "I really appreciate that."

"Sorry." He didn't look sorry. He looked a little stunned actually. Like maybe he hadn't been expecting to see all of this up close and personal.

"But that doesn't really answer my question," Cori said.

"Okay. Yes. I would say it's safe to assume that he wanted you to focus on something other than casual sexual relationships while you're in Bliss. Something bigger and more important. Like your sisters. The business. Yourself."

She cleared her throat. "Myself?"

"When the relationships are short and mostly about sex, it's easy to avoid really thinking about what you can—or can't—bring to a relationship and what it means to be a real partner, in good *and* bad times." He shrugged with another small smile, this one self-deprecating. "I've found that if all you're promising is a good time, then you don't have to feel bad about not delivering on what they need during the not-as-good times."

Whoa. Cori stared at Evan. So they *were* a lot alike. "Okay," she finally said with a nod. "Got it."

There was a stretch of silence where it felt like Evan wanted to say something more. And where Cori kind of wanted him to. She hated it, but she was curious about what other things her father had figured out and said about her and her sisters.

"I should go," Evan finally said, pushing to his feet.

"Yeah. Okay."

"Okay." He hesitated. Then said simply, "'Bye, Cori."

Cori watched him leave the room with his briefcase in one hand and his—or rather *her*—caramel macchiato in the other. After a moment, she started after him, paused, went back for her bag and whipped cream gun, and then followed him to the elevator. She stepped on with him just as the doors were beginning to slide shut.

"You're not staying to talk to your sisters?" Evan asked as he pushed the button for the lobby.

Hell no, she wasn't staying. The building was beginning to feel claustrophobic. Even if it was sixty-four floors. Cori shrugged. "They don't need me for what they're doing."

"What are they doing?"

"Ava is bossing people into figuring out how to fix this and Brynn is researching inheritances and trusts."

"And you're going to go home?"

"I'm going shopping." She waited for a beat—the length of time it took for people to think "of course" when an heiress to billions of dollars said something like that—then added, "For vodka, tiramisu, bacon and Nutella."

He looked mildly surprised. And interested. "Quite a combo."

"The vodka is for Ava—for chocolate martinis—and the tiramisu is for Brynn. Things they love, but never buy for themselves. That whole thing about being there for them but not getting too serious about it, you know?" And she knew that he did know. Somehow. So what if Rudy had kind-of nailed that right on the head?

Evan just nodded. "And is the Nutella or the bacon for you?"

"Both."

"Bacon *and* Nutella?"

"Bacon *in* Nutella," she said. "And don't think for a second my sisters will pass that up either."

He looked a little amazed and Cori liked that. She liked being amazing. If it was for something simple like junk food. And temporary. Being amazing temporarily was so much easier than sustaining it.

"You put the bacon in the Nutella?" he asked.

She nodded. "I dip it. I mean, you can make sandwiches or brownies with bacon and Nutella in them. Or coat the bacon with it. But that's all a lot more work than just dipping it."

"The bacon would have to be pretty crisp, right?" he asked, acting like he was taking mental notes about all of this.

"Definitely. And you have to melt the Nutella some. Of course."

"Of course."

Okay, she hadn't bonded with a guy over Nutella before. That was probably a good thing. She liked to keep things light and casual and that would be very difficult to do if there was Nutella involved.

The elevator arrived on the first floor and the doors swished open. Evan held a hand against one side and let her step off first. She walked to the middle of the marble floor of the lobby and turned to face him, not quite ready to say goodbye for some reason. It was probably the tennis shoes. She liked surprises, and somehow she sensed that this guy had a few more he could pull out.

"I better go," she said, stupidly wishing there was a good reason to stay.

This was the guy her father had hired to make sure she and her sisters behaved and did exactly what he wanted them to do even when he wasn't around to ensure it himself.

For a second, she felt like something had jabbed her right in the sternum. Again. Dammit. That sadness kept sneaking up on her. Yes, she'd lost her father. But she didn't think she'd ever really had him.

Maybe that was what was so damned sad about this whole thing.

"Oh, before you go..." She reached to take the lid off of Evan's cup and tipped the whipped cream canister over the half-full coffee drink, adding a new swirl. She replaced the lid and looked up at him with a smile. "Another reason to have my own whipped cream gun. I like to add more halfway through."

Evan nodded, watching her eyes. "Never too much sweetness with you, huh?"

Oh boy, that sounded like flirting. And she loved flirting. And she had never been good about *not* doing something she loved just because it was a bad idea. She grinned at him. "You got it."

Something flickered in his eyes. Something that made deep-down-feel-good muscles clench.

Evan gave her a long look. Then he said, "We have Nutella in Bliss."

Huh. That was good to know. "How about shoe stores? That's a biggie for Ava."

He chuckled softly. "No. No shoe stores." He reached out and flicked the diamond bracelet on her wrist. "No jewelry stores either."

It was the only expensive jewelry Cori wore on a regular basis, because her mother had given it to her, but she knew most people assumed she had an endless supply of precious gems. Cori tipped her head. "What *do* you have a lot of?"

"Wheat, corn, and hay fields," he said with a grin. "Pickup trucks. And dirt roads."

Something fluttered in her chest at his words. She looked down at her bracelet, then back up at Evan. "Do you know anything about diamond mining?" she asked. Because she did.

He shook his head. "Can't say that I do."

"Well," she said, giving him a big smile. "You can't get to diamonds without dirt roads."

He just stood looking at her for a long moment, a little bit of that amazement still there. Then he said, "When you end up in Bliss, you're going to have to introduce me to bacon and Nutella."

She laughed. "Don't you mean *if* I end up in Bliss?"

"No," he said slowly. "I think I mean *when*."

"Ava and her attorneys are really good. I wouldn't get too cocky, Mr. Stone."

"Yeah, well, you're about thirty years too late with that advice," he said.

Then he gave her another panty-warming grin and walked out of Carmichael Enterprises.

————

E van threw his leather bag—the one that he'd gotten for his graduation from law school and had used exactly one other time—onto the bed and shoved a hand through his hair. Noah had tried to convince him to run the bag over with his truck at least once, or rub some dirt on it at the very least. He said the shiny leather and the gold adornments were irritating.

But no, Evan had decided to carry the stupid thing into the meeting with the Carmichael triplets. Even as he was dressed in jeans and tennis shoes. At Rudy's request. Yes, that was what Evan typically wore to work. In Bliss. But even he knew that a meeting at Carmichael Enterprises headquarters required a tie. Still, Rudy had insisted Evan show up as Evan. And Evan would have done anything for Rudy, even before his friend was sick. Then, like an ass, had carried a nearly-new leather briefcase along with him.

He slumped back onto the mattress next to his are-you-fucking-kidding-me briefcase and sighed. The hard part was over. He'd told the girls about the stipulations on their inheritance. And they'd reacted exactly the way Rudy had predicted.

Except for Cori.

That thought floated through his mind and he found himself thinking about the three sisters and what he'd expected. Ava was every bit the cool, ballbuster that Rudy had described. He'd said that his oldest would be pissed off and would do whatever she could to get control of the situation. Brynn, the middle triplet, was quiet and thoughtful, if a little distracted. The three words Rudy had used when talking about his scientist daughter had been right on. Rudy had said Brynn would try to calm the situation and look at it more analytically.

But then there was Cori.

Rudy had made it sound like Cori was hell-bent on rejecting everything he tried to give her and rebelling against every bit of decorum. Evan had expected her to take one look at Rudy's note and say "no fucking way." But that wasn't what had happened. She'd said she could be ready to go in the morning. And she'd showed up with a whipped cream gun.

Evan ran a hand over his face. He had been prepared to feel a sort of kinship with the world-trotting party girl, but *damn*. There was a connection there, and he had the feeling he'd do anything to see that little mischievous smile of hers a few thousand more times.

Of course he was fascinated with Cori. Because he shouldn't be. But it was all the stuff Rudy had told him about how Evan had given Rudy insight into his youngest. The way she used partying and wild weekends to stay important to her sisters and make them happy without having to be too responsible. And she definitely had an air of trouble—and fun—about her. But she was also more self-deprecating that Rudy had let on. She had a sense of humor and was very quick to defend her sisters too.

And she had a thing for Nutella.

Evan ran his hand up into his hair. Okay, the Nutella didn't matter. The whipped cream and sprinkles didn't matter. Her red leather jacket and fitted black jeans and hot leather boots didn't matter. Nor did the fact that she'd written some little note to Brynn that had made her sister giggle at one point. Or the fact that the one thing that had made Ava's shoulders unwind even slightly was the latte Cori had handed her. And Cori's comment about diamonds and dirt roads didn't matter. He wasn't going to think about how that could be an analogy for what Rudy had found in Bliss—diamonds at the end of dirt roads. Figurative diamonds, of course. But literal dirt roads.

With an exasperated grunt, Evan sat up. He'd been in his head far too much lately. He supposed a friend's death would do that to a guy, but he wasn't going to sit around and think a bunch of deep, meaningful thoughts right now. He was going to get room service. And maybe a drink. And he was going to think thoughts about how to ensure the Carmichael triplets got their butts to Bliss. No, he didn't want to be in charge of making the girls bake pies. He definitely didn't want to oversee their love lives. But he would do anything for Rudy, and Rudy had been *adamant* about wanting his girls to live in Bliss.

Ava cannot end up with a man like me. She needs someone who can help her see beyond her office. And Brynn's never dated. God knows how men could take advantage of her. And Cori...Cori needs more. She needs to realize that she can be more than just a good time for someone.

He and Rudy had been over this. Multiple times. Evan was supposed to be like a big brother to the girls. Sort of. In a way. He was supposed to make sure Cori stayed home and that Brynn only dated nice guys who would treat her well and that Ava gave a regular guy a chance.

Evan's phone rang and he reached for it without looking at the number, grateful for the distraction.

"Stone."

"When will they be here?"

"Well, hey, Parker. Yes, my trip was great. Nice hotel. And I appreciated the pep talk text you sent me this morning before the meeting. You're a good friend."

"I didn't send you any texts this morning."

"I know."

Evan heard Parker sigh on the other end of the phone. "Just tell me the girls will be here in a couple of days and I will send you a dancing bear thingy or something."

Evan laughed. "Do you even know how to send a thingy, also known as a GIF, by the way?"

"I'll figure it out. Just tell me again how everything is going to be fine and they've already agreed to Rudy's crazy-assed plan," Parker said.

'They will agree to it," Evan said carefully.

"Which means they haven't yet," Parker said flatly.

"They're...looking things over."

"Dammit, Evan."

"We expected them to challenge it," Evan reminded him. "We knew they wouldn't just roll over."

"*Make* those Gucci girls get their pretty, spray-tanned asses to Bliss *now*," Parker said.

Evan rolled his eyes. Talk about a rock and a hard place. He had Ava Carmichael on one side and Parker Blake on the other. He wasn't sure which was a bigger hard-ass, frankly.

"There's no way out of the trust," Evan said.

"There's one way," Parker said. "And I promise you, if that's how this goes down, I will make your life a living hell."

Evan grimaced. Considering that Parker made about two-thirds of Evan's meals and that he, Parker, and Noah all intended to spend all of their lives in Bliss and die very old men, that wasn't a completely empty threat.

What Evan hadn't told Ava, Brynn, and Cori yet was that if they decided to not follow Rudy's mandates, then the town of Bliss would become the owner of Carmichael Enterprises. Rudy had already established the Bliss Foundation, given a ten million dollar trust to that foundation, and put Evan in charge of it. But if even one of Rudy's girls didn't follow through on her part of *this* trust, whether it be the provisions regarding the pie shop or their relationship statuses, then the company and all of its assets went to the town of Bliss with Parker as CEO, Evan as the CFO, and Noah as Vice President of something or other. It didn't matter what they called it. It meant the three men were in charge. And none of them had any desire to run a company based in New York City that did...hell, they weren't even entirely sure what Rudy's company did besides make tons and tons of money. It might sound crazy, but they didn't want to have billions of dollars under their control. They liked their lives in Bliss and part of that was the simplicity and straight-forwardness of it. Exactly the things Rudy had loved. So no, they did not want to take over Carmichael Enterprises. Which meant, they were even more invested in making sure Rudy's triplets did what they were supposed to do.

"It's going to be fine," Evan told his friend. "The trust is airtight and they want the money."

Evan really hoped Parker couldn't hear the note of hesitation in his voice. Parker had agreed to the provision of taking over as CEO to placate Rudy. But he'd pulled Evan aside and basically said he'd kill Evan if the triplets didn't come to Bliss.

Evan definitely needed to be sure the girls came to Bliss. There just wasn't another option. "I've got it under control," he finally told his friend. "I'm not leaving until tomorrow. I fully expect to talk to them again before then."

Even if he had to go hunt Ava down and convince her that Bliss was exactly where she needed to be for the next year.

"Do that," Parker said firmly.

"I'll see you tomorrow," Evan said.

"Don't make me pull the jalapeño burger off the menu," Parker warned.

"You wouldn't."

"You don't want to find out."

He definitely would. Evan scowled at the ceiling. "Cool your jets, Blake," he said. "No need to plan revenge for something that's not even going to happen."

"I'll believe it when I see those billionaires walking down Main Street in blue jeans."

"Goodbye, Parker." Evan disconnected before Parker could give him any more shit. Or give him anything more to worry about. He really liked that jalapeño burger.

But all he had to do was get the Carmichael triplets into blue jeans and to Bliss. How hard could that be? Hell, one-third of them had been wearing jeans today. And looking damned good in them.

Evan scowled at the ceiling. *Of course,* he was attracted to Cori. She was the fun one. The can't-be-tied-down one. There wasn't anything about her that he didn't like. Evan dug the heels of his hands into his eyes. But she was off-limits. And even if she wasn't, Cori wouldn't do a damned thing to make *him* more disciplined. The travel-the-world, party-in-every-country triplet would only feed Evan's own what-the-hell-you-only-live-once tendencies and he was trying to be a better man. Someone worthy of Rudy's trust in him. Someone who knew when and how to take things seriously and be responsible.

The girls weren't the only "kids" Rudy had worried about. He worried that Noah didn't trust himself to take care of the people he loved. Which he didn't. Rudy worried that Parker was a little *too* independent. And crotchety. Which he was. And Rudy worried that Evan didn't take things—or himself—seriously enough. Which he didn't. Most of Bliss trusted Evan to always show up with a cooler and a great idea about how to make any event even more fun.

Rudy, on the other hand, had trusted Evan to manage the Bliss Foundation, make decisions about how to spend ten million dollars, and his daughters' happiness.

Evan rolled his neck as the tension, that was becoming far too familiar, crept up the muscles on either side of his spine. He really wanted to do this. He really wanted to be deserving of Rudy's belief in him. But the last time someone had trusted him to do something *other* than throw a kick-ass Super Bowl party or hand out multiple orgasms, he'd spent four panic-stricken hours searching for a friend in Vegas and had to write a five thousand dollar bail check once he'd found him.

His phone dinged with a new text message and he grabbed it. He really didn't want any more of Parker's shit about how he had to get this thing done. He knew that. He just wasn't sure how.

But it wasn't Parker.

BBQ wienies or pigs in a blanket?

It was Jill Morris. A very good friend of Evan's. A Bliss girl, born and bred. And the woman he'd slept with three nights ago. And hadn't talked to since.

Evan winced and texted back. *Yes. Both. Always. Or pigs in a blanket and BBQ meatballs.*

Ah, meatballs. Good call.

Evan smiled. He and Jill had been friends since kindergarten. She was a great girl. *For your going away party?*

Jill had been offered her dream job in Omaha and was scheduled to leave in a couple of weeks. She deserved a big bash on her way out of Bliss.

Wedding reception.

Evan frowned. He couldn't think of any upcoming weddings. *Whose?*

Ours.

Evan looked at those four letters far longer than he should have needed to. But that answer made no sense.

You have the wrong number, he finally sent back. She was messing with him. He was sure. Ninety-eight percent.

Evan Michael Stone. Birthdate, August second. Great taste in action movies. Horrible taste in comedies. Will do just about anything for lasagna.

Well, that was him. Except that Will Farrell was always funny. But yeah, Jill's lasagna was exactly why they'd ended up naked together the other night in spite of a number of good reasons not to. Reasons that had kept them fully dressed when together for...forever.

It wasn't a lack of attraction or opportunity over the years. But their families were very close and even a *hint* of something beyond friendship between them would have stirred up a bunch of expectations for an ongoing relationship when all Evan and Jill would have wanted was a friends-with-benefits situation. Jill had always had her sights set on places far from Bliss and, frankly, they got along great, liked each other a lot, and yes, had some chemistry. But they didn't want to get married. A fact that their families, particularly their grandfathers, would never understand. Staying *out* of bed had been a solid plan.

Until the other night.

But there had been lasagna. And whiskey prior to the lasagna. And a funeral service for a very good friend prior to the whiskey.

And then after the lasagna, there's been a very sweet, beautiful, willing woman who had kissed him and then taken her clothes off and distracted him from how fucking miserable he'd been, and he'd gratefully taken her up on everything she'd offered. From pasta to...another P word he was very fond of.

Evan sighed. Yeah, he probably needed to work on the Being
A Better Guy thing.

What's going on? he finally asked. But he knew. Someone had
found out about their night together. Shit.

*I'm on my mother's couch, covered in Calamine lotion, and bridal
magazines. Oh, and two generations of hopes, dreams, and expectations
for me.*

Yeah, shit. Definitely. *Calamine?* He, unfortunately, understood all the rest of that.

Hives. From the strawberries.

Evan groaned and ran a hand over his face. Fuck. Fuck, fuck,
fuck. *You're ALLERGIC?*

Duh.

Good God. The way they'd used those strawberries...the
places they'd used those strawberries...she had to miserable. *You
didn't know?*

Of course I knew!

What?! *Kind of important information when someone is rubbing
something you're allergic to on your bare...skin.* There, he'd used a
more gentlemanly word than he could have.

I was blindfolded, remember? she replied, followed by an emoji
that looked like it was rolling its eyes. *Then it was too late. YOU
should have known!*

Evan frowned at the message. *How???*

*Strawberry patch. Fourth grade class trip. They called an ambu-
lance for me!*

Evan winced. Holy shit, how could he have forgotten that?
Oh, yeah, he wasn't really that good guy. But... *You didn't tell me
to stop.*

I got...distracted.

Evan couldn't help his grin. He'd distracted her from the fact
that she was going to be covered in head-to-toe hives. Or more
specifically, breasts-to-knees hives. That was something. And

then it occurred to him that thoughts like that probably didn't fall under the Good Guy column either.

I'm really sorry he told her sincerely.

I know.

But you're messing with me, right? No one knows?

My mother would notice hives. And me taking Benadryl like candy.

Right. Of course. Jill couldn't sneeze without her mom rushing to the pharmacy. Maybe because her daughter had been horribly allergic to strawberries and had ended up in an ER in fourth grade. *You told her about me?? You couldn't just say you'd eaten some?*

His thumbs were getting sore from all the back and forth, but he and Jill had always been pretty wordy texters, and now didn't seem the time to skimp on explanations.

Why would I eat something that I'm ALLERGIC TO? she asked. *And you shouldn't have used strawberries with MB! She told everyone! Mom knew I was bringing you lasagna that night and that I didn't come home...she's not stupid.*

Evan shook his head. Fuck. He and Marcie Brown had eaten strawberries together at the strawberry festival last June. And yeah, he'd taken some home. He'd also taken Marcie home. But it hadn't been nearly as...inventive...as it had been with Jill. Damn, small towns sometimes. And damn his inability to just say no to things that were a bad idea...

So... Mom knows. Jill sent. *So her sister knows. So my grandma knows. So my grandpa knows. So...*

So Evan's grandfather knew. Fabulous.

Ring size? He knew that Jill wouldn't take that seriously. She was as adamant about them being only friends as he was. And she was the one with the dream job out of state. She would never give that up for him. For one, she wasn't in love with him. For another, she knew him. Very well. She knew that he took fantasy football more seriously than he did anything else in his life, that he thought five-day work weeks were the worst invention ever, and that he was the state's best mediator—because he was a lawyer who didn't like paperwork or judges or going to court or, really, the law. And she knew that he was *not* good long-term boyfriend material. Because he'd been a short-term boyfriend, and an even shorter-term fling, to most of her friends at one time or another over the years.

Ha ha, she answered a few seconds later.

We just deal with it until you go to Omaha?

Well...

Evan felt his heart thud at that vague answer. No. She *had* to go to Omaha. Not to save him from a shotgun wedding, but because he could *not* be responsible for someone giving up a dream. It wouldn't take long for the regret to sink in and he couldn't live with that. He was the good-time guy. The guy everyone liked. The guy everyone invited everywhere. He wasn't a guy people gave up important things for, or trusted with huge life-altering decisions. And he couldn't be a guy someone regretted being involved with.

You are going, he told her. *It's an amazing opportunity. You can't pass it up.*

Of course not, she responded a moment later.

Evan breathed a sigh of relief.

But I don't want to deal with all of this, she added.

What's that mean?

We pretend to date. Them=happy, off our backs. Then big fight=I leave.

I can do that, he told her. He didn't love that plan, but he owed her. Putting Calamine lotion in some of the places she needed; it couldn't be pleasant.

OR, she sent a second later. *I explain I'm a grownup=sex with whoever I want. NOT wedding.*

Evan nodded, even though she couldn't see him. *Very adult.*

Yeah.

He started to respond with *I've got your back,* but he saw the three dots jumping, indicating she was typing.

But, that's a lot more energy and time than I really want to give.

He nodded again. He understood that.

She sent another message a moment later. *I don't really want to pretend. Or have you over for family dinners. Or have you along with me and my friends.*

Evan felt a prick of annoyance. He was a great guy. People loved having him around. He made sure of it. She didn't need to be quite so adamant about *not* wanting him around.

Yeah, yeah, he told her.

Sorry. She sent a big, grinning emoji. *I adore you. And...the other night...totally worth a few hives.* After the words, she added a flame, a heart, a firework, and a smiley face with its tongue hanging out.

He grinned. She had to say that. But Evan appreciated it anyway. He sent her an eggplant emoji to which she replied with a honeypot.

He snorted. Yeah, their friendship was fine.

Just need to pack and spend time with my friends—and even my crazy family—before I leave. Nothing personal.

Of course not. He knew she was a little nervous about the big move, and he didn't want to do anything to make the days leading up to it more stressful.

But I also don't want to have this big talk with them.

What do you want? What can I do? There, that was a good-guy thing to say. Evan was proud of himself as he pressed send.

Glad you asked.

Evan felt a niggle of trepidation, but he waited for her answer. The woman had hives because of him. He'd do whatever she wanted him to do.

You need to break my heart. She sent a broken heart emoji and a grinning devil.

Evan blinked at the words. What? He had typed the w and the

h when Jill's dots started dancing again. For a long time. This was going to be a long one.

Or they need to think you did anyway. Then I'm not disappointing anyone. And me getting out of town will make sense.

As soon as she sent that, he saw the dots again.

Plus, if I cry, my grandfather won't want *to talk about it at all. Can't deal with tears. He'll avoid the whole topic completely.*

Evan read Jill's explanation twice. And had to admit, it was pretty good.

I'll do it, he told her. *But this makes ME the bad guy.*

Right.

And I'm stuck here with them all hating me.

Good point. Will only have to put on the act for a few days! Whoo hoo! I could leave early. Since it'll be so painful to be around you.

Evan sighed. *But I WILL STILL HAVE TO BE HERE.*

Yeah. But you owe me. Lasagna. Hives.

Dammit. *Fine.* He sent her the broken-hearted emoji back. *How?*

There was a long stretch where there were no dancing dots. Then a message popped up that said simply, *Just be you, I guess.*

Evan frowned at that. *What?*

Don't be so sensitive. Do your usual. Don't call. Don't ask me out. Go fishing for the weekend instead. Take another girl home and do the strawberry thing with her. Without the risk of anaphylaxis of course.

Evan's frown turned into a scowl. *That makes me seem like an ass.*

There was no response to that for nearly a minute after that. Finally, Jill sent *Sorry. What part of that is NOT your usual?*

He scowled even harder as he typed. *You liked my USUAL. Twice.*

Yes, he had casual relationships. But they were mutually casual. None of the women in Bliss expected him to make any commitments beyond breakfast the next morning. And he'd given Jill coffee and English muffins. And orgasms. He'd held up his end of this bargain. But he didn't love the idea that people—okay, his mother and Jill's mom and their grandmothers—would think he'd treated Jill like all the other girls. Even if *she* was completely fine with it. They wouldn't know she was fine with it. They would think she was brokenhearted over it.

Yes. YES! she responded. *I did. Of course.* There was a pause and then she sent, *The coffee was delicious.*

Brat.

She sent a big grinning emoji again. Then, *These hives are REALLY itchy.*

At least he was a good enough guy to feel guilty about that. Exactly as she'd intended.

He was stuck. He had to do this Jill's way. It was his fault she was itching in very unpleasant places and that their families knew about it. And she was right, any attempt to rationally *explain* this to their families would take a lot of time and energy.

But Jill was Jill. He couldn't treat her like she was just some girl he'd spent the night with. Of course, he also didn't want to marry her. How could he break her heart without coming across as...his usual self?

He blew out a breath. Rudy had thought he was capable of being more than his usual self. And this seemed as good a time as any to start really trying. And a thought hit him.

He typed in *I have an idea.*

She sent a broken heart emoji with a question mark after it.

Yes. He typed as the idea formed fully. *I was really sad about you leaving. Figured I should take a shot...find out if there could be anything between us. And we had a great night. And we both thought that MAYBE it could get more serious. But then—*

He stopped typing as a message from her popped up. *They know it was after the funeral.*

Great. You being there for me then showed me I love having you in my life—true, btw—and I realized I should have taken a chance on you a long time ago.

Go on…

But then I had to come to New York for Rudy's trust. And I met someone.

So what if it was Cori Carmichael that popped into his head? She had definitely made him take notice. He'd always known that attraction between two people could be instantaneous, and now she'd proven that he could become fascinated within only a few minutes over caramel macchiatos and talk of Nutella.

There was a long pause before Jill's dot danced and then the dots bounced for several seconds.

Pretend girlfriend in NYC? Brilliant! They won't have to actually see you with anyone. Long distance=mostly texts and phone calls. Let it go for a while and then fake breakup. Nice!

Evan read her response and realized that would work. And would be a hell of a lot easier than what he was thinking about.

BUT then no dating anyone HERE for a while. No cheating on your long-distance girlfriend, Jill added.

Well, there was that. But something had been nagging at him ever since Rudy had showed him his "wish list" for his daughters. Cori wasn't supposed to date because she used dating and sex and partying as a way of keeping things light. Just like Evan did. As he'd told her, if all you promised was a good time, then no one had expectations of you during the bad times. But she was going to be taking time off from all of that. To work on commitment. To focus on more important things. To maybe figure out that she had more to offer her relationships.

And he couldn't shake the idea that maybe he should do that too.

He was really good at a few things—mediating conflicts, making people happy, and romancing women. Maybe he could use his talents for something actually…altruistic. Use what he was good at to help someone else. Like Jill. And Rudy. And the Carmichael triplets.

He'd admit that he wanted to date Cori Carmichael. Absolutely. But Cori didn't need what Evan had to offer. No one needed to show Cori a good time. She handled that all on her own.

It was Ava that needed a guy like Evan. He'd been thinking about setting her up with Brian Callahan. Brian was a great guy who owned a contracting business and played slow-pitch softball and poker with Evan and his friends. Brian was from Bliss and was genuinely a nice guy who knew how to kick back.

But now...

Ava was every bit the uptight, driven, cool business woman Rudy had told him about. Getting her to let her hair down might be a bigger job than Brian could handle. It would take someone who was *really* dedicated to the project. Someone who knew the whole situation. And someone who had something to gain from it as well.

Evan wasn't a complete fuckup, but he didn't take himself very seriously either. He didn't forget to pay his bills or anything, but he probably relied too heavily on verbal contracts versus written ones, considering he had a law degree and all. But if a guy couldn't make a promise over a beer with a handshake and then stick to it, then he wasn't someone who Evan wanted to do business with anyway. And maybe schedules were more like suggestions than hard and fast rules in Evan's life. And maybe he preferred conducting business meetings while sitting on the river bank with a fishing pole in hand. And maybe he didn't mind being paid in handyman services or with pot roast. That was all just fine with him.

And would make a woman like Ava crazy.

Evan frowned, irritated by those thoughts. He could be *good* for Ava. And helping others was part of being a better man after all. The girl was going to have an ulcer if she didn't already.

And she could be good for him too. She would make him toe the line and show up on time and tell him when he was failing. It wouldn't be all about partying and casual sex. It would be an actual relationship. Ish. There were bound to be some ups and downs with her relocating her life, taking on the pie shop, living with her sisters, and navigating the things Rudy wanted her to learn. Evan would have to be there for her through all of that. For six months. Exclusively. Monogamously.

That would be...new.

And maybe when that time was up, he would have changed too and would be ready to be more responsible and committed.

Or I could not pretend. Someone everyone would actually meet. And be wow-ed by.

Wait, Jill replied, *there's a real girl?*

There could be. He paused. How much did he want to share with Jill? Well, he was breaking up with her, kind-of. It stood to reason that he'd tell her about the new woman in his life. *Met her today. She's...something. Once she moves to Bliss it might be hard to stay away from her.*

Yes, he was thinking of Cori again. Dammit. But he *would* get his head on straight about the sisters. He was doing *Ava* a favor. And *Jill* a favor. And hell, himself a favor. It wasn't about Cori at all. It couldn't be.

Great!!!! A second message came almost immediately on the heels of that one. *Wait, is it one of Rudy's daughters?????*

Everyone knew that he'd come to New York to meet with the Carmichael triplets. *Yes. Ava.*

You ALREADY have a crush on one of Rudy's daughters???????

Evan read the question three times before replying with a completely truthful answer. *After hearing everything about her from Rudy for so long, I might have had a crush on her before I even got here.* And yeah, fuck, it was still Cori he was talking about.

But Bliss didn't know that. Jill didn't even need to know that.

I love this, Jill replied. *Then it's not lying when I tell everyone that you took one look at this woman you've been hearing about all these years and fell for her.*

Not really lying. Yeah, right. But Evan still responded with,

Spread that around, okay? While you're blubbering into your carton of ice cream over losing me, be sure you drop Ava's name.

Jill sent him an ice cream emoji, then, *Will do. Happy for you! Though now I do wish I was sticking around...seeing you finally fall in love would be entertaining.*

Evan felt a kick in his chest. He wasn't falling in love. With *any* of Rudy's daughters. Dammit. *Get your ass to Omaha!*

She sent him a heart emoji, a car emoji, and a penguin emoji.

Evan chuckled and tossed his phone onto the bed beside him.

Then he ran his hand over his face again. That was taken care of. Now he just had to convince Ava that this was a great plan. But he could do that. Probably. Ava wasn't the type of woman he'd be able to sweet-talk or charm, but she was a business woman. He'd just have to offer her something more appealing than sweet talk.

He'd make her a deal.

3

"I can't believe it. I seriously can't believe it."

Cori rolled her eyes and handed Ava another martini. It was her third, but she still hadn't shut up about how her attorney's advice had been to simply go to Bliss and do what Rudy wanted.

"All he said was that it was the *easiest* thing," Brynn commented, her words soft and a little slurry. She was definitely mellowed out from her one martini. But then Brynn was a lightweight.

It would take another couple of rounds for Ava to start to relax. The woman was so tightly wound that Cori was seriously concerned. Ava had always been driven and worked nearly nonstop, but this whole trust and Bliss, Kansas thing might just be the final straw.

Brynn waited until Ava had taken a huge drink, then said, "I think this could be a good thing."

Ava lifted one perfectly waxed brow, her glass poised before her shiny Coral Crush lips. She was in loose cotton pants and a tank top just as Cori and Brynn were, but where Brynn never wore makeup and Cori had already taken hers off—shoes, bra, makeup were the first things to come off when she got home, in that order—Ava still looked like she could pose for a magazine cover.

"You think us moving to Kansas for a year could be a good thing?" Ava asked.

Brynn lifted a shoulder. "Why not?"

Ava lowered her glass. "Why not? Why *not*?" she asked, her voice rising. Again. They'd already done this ranting and raving bit. "I have a company to run."

"Yes. A pie shop, I believe," Cori said dryly.

"Oh sure," Ava scoffed. "A pie shop. Because that makes tons of sense."

"You know." Cori shifted on her sister's custom-made sofa upholstered in the softest leather Cori had ever rubbed her body against. And she intended to do more of that before she left. "Maybe it does make sense."

Ava shook her head. "No. It doesn't."

"Listen, if Rudy wanted to give us each a new experience, something to expand our horizons, then coming up with something that is almost exactly opposite of what we're doing now makes sense," Cori said. She'd been thinking about everything a lot while she made dinner, and dessert of course, for her sisters. And she was on board.

She couldn't believe it, really. It irked her a little to be going along with Rudy's decree, honestly. But she couldn't deny that she was curious about Bliss. And her father's life there. She didn't know why she would take Evan Stone's word for it, but he said Rudy had changed, that he was a different guy than the one Cori knew. Cori wanted to see what that was about.

It was like every dare she'd ever taken—which would be any and all ever issued to her. Heading into a house they claimed was haunted? She had to see the apparitions for herself. Taking a bite of a pepper people claimed made grown men cry? She had to feel the fiery burn for herself. Visiting a town that claimed to have changed Rudy Carmichael into a decent human being? Yeah, she was going to have to live there herself.

And she was always up for an adventure. Living in a small town in the same house with her sisters for a year and running a pie shop might be the biggest one yet.

"So, I'm in," she said.

"For Bliss?" Ava asked, her eyes wide.

Cori nodded. "Yep." She looked at Brynn. "I think it could be good for us."

"You? World traveler, never-settle-down Cori? Seriously?" Ava asked.

Cori frowned at her. "Yes. Seriously."

"But you...you're...you."

"I don't know what you mean."

"Yes, you do." Ava seemed totally exasperated. "I'm not saying it's not a good idea in some ways. Lord knows of all of us you could use the most downtime."

"Whoa. Hang on there. Really, Ms. Workaholic? At least I know how to have fun and not let everything get so serious. I think *you* could use some downtime."

"Of course you know how to not let everything get so serious! Nothing is serious for you!"

"That is not true. I'm getting seriously pissed right now, if nothing else."

"I'm just saying that Brynn might be right," Ava said. "You could use some stability."

"And maybe it could pull that stick out of your butt."

"Hey!"

Suddenly they both stopped and turned to face Brynn. The sweet one.

Who was now frowning and looked almost on the verge of tears. "Knock it off."

Cori took a deep breath. "Sorry."

Ava looked sheepish as well. "Me too."

"*I'm* going," Brynn said. "I'll go alone if I have to."

She wouldn't go alone. But as Cori looked closer at her sister, she had to admit that Brynn looked as serious as she sounded.

"You can't go alone," Ava said.

"Oh, yes, I can. And I will. I will work in the pie shop and date the entire town of Bliss and...enjoy it."

But her hesitation over the "enjoy it" part was what finally made Cori say, "There's no way I'm letting you date an entire town without me there to help you."

Brynn looked relieved. "Okay. Good."

Cori grinned at her. "I have a feeling you're going to love Bliss." She gave her sister a wink and Brynn blushed.

Ava was watching them. "I don't want you to go without me."

"Why not?" Cori asked. "You can stay here and be miserable if you want."

Cori expected Ava to point out that they all three had to go to Bliss for it to count. But a little bit of Cori wanted to go anyway.

Instead Ava said, "But you'll have fun without me."

Surprised, Cori nodded. "Yep, we totally will."

"I can't believe you want to do this," Ava said to her.

"My therapist thinks it's a good idea. For all of us, incidentally. She said she thinks Dad knew us better than we realized." After picking up the groceries, Cori had taken a few minutes to call Karen. Even though she'd already known her shrink would love the idea of Cori making a commitment to her sisters that involved more than a wild weekend.

"You are seeing a therapist?" Ava asked.

"Uh, yeah."

"Why?"

"Well, shocker... I have issues."

"And you've talked to him about us?"

Cori laughed. "Her. And yes. You're my sisters. We're *triplets* for fuck's sake. You've come up. Especially with all of this."

"And she thinks we should all go?" Brynn asked.

"Yep."

"But you've...been talking to someone else?" Ava asked, still frowning.

Cori focused on her. "Yes. Why?"

"I just...shouldn't you be talking to us?"

Cori snorted at that. "To my kick-ass, no-one-tells-me-what-to-do corporate shark sister and my sweet, smarter-than-anyone-I-know sister about my feelings of inadequacy?" Cori asked. "How would that work? You can't tell me you're not all of those things and it would just make you feel bad."

"Like how I feel right now, you mean?" Ava asked.

Cori looked at her for a moment. She'd love for Ava to be someone she could go to with problems and questions. And vice versa. Like it used to be. "Come to Bliss. Be a little out of your element. Be *around* so I can talk to you."

Ava swallowed hard. Then she looked at Brynn. "And you're really going to date the town?"

Brynn nodded, but she looked less than confident. "Sure."

Ava sighed. "Well now I have to come."

She didn't look happy about it, but suddenly Cori felt a surge of anticipation go through her. "I know you love what you're doing and that you're good at it. But finding out you're good at other things, things you didn't even know about, is empowering. And finding out you're not good at some things is humbling. And being empowered but humble is awesome."

Ava narrowed her eyes. "You're *always* trying something new and going somewhere new."

"And I'm empowered and humble," Cori said. But she shifted on the sofa cushion. That all sounded a lot stronger than she felt.

"But now you're talking about going somewhere to live and do the same thing for a *year*," Ava said.

Cori swallowed. That was a good point. She was curious about Bliss. She felt like this was a dare from her father that she had to take. But doing it for a couple of months would be a lot better.

"Well, I—"

"You're right," Ava decided. "We should go."

Cori blinked at her. "Huh?"

"If I need to shake things up, then *you* need to...unshake things." She frowned as if that hadn't come out the way she'd intended. "You need to settle down some."

"Hey," Cori protested. "I'm fine. I guarantee that my blood pressure is lower than yours and when I take ibuprofen it's because of a muscle strain from climbing a mountain or a back ache from sleeping on the beach all night, not because of a tension headache or eyestrain from staring at a computer screen until two in the morning."

"You sure the backache isn't from having sex on the back of a motorcycle or a camel or something?" Ava asked.

"Having sex on the back of a moving motorcycle would be really dangerous," Cori told her.

"Well, obviously not while it's moving," Ava told her.

Cori didn't say anything. Because there had been this one time...

"Oh, my God, you've had sex on a motorcycle?" Ava asked.

"Hey, at least I'm getting laid. I'd highly recommend it for you, in fact," Cori shot back.

The sound of the doorbell interrupted whatever Ava was about to say. She gave a little *humph* sound, but set her glass down, tossed off the blanket she had over her lap, and pushed herself up. But the second her butt cleared the cushion, she wobbled and leaned to brace her hands on the glass-topped coffee table.

"Whoa there, princess," Cori said, coming up from the couch and guiding Ava back down. "I got it. You just sit."

"Okay." Ava sighed and leaned back into the thick cushion behind her.

Yeah, Cori really needed to get Ava drunk more often. She was a lot easier to get along with when she had some vodka coursing through her veins.

Cori went to the door and pulled it open.

"I have a plan. Just hear me out."

"Mr. Stone." Cori was completely surprised by the way her heart thunked in her chest, seeing Evan on the other side of Ava's door.

He was still wearing the jeans and white button-down shirt, but it was wrinkled now and his hair looked like he'd been running his hands through it.

"What are you doing here?" she asked him.

"I want to be your boyfriend for the next six months."

Cori felt surprise, then temptation shoot through her. And then comprehension.

But still, she had to hear this. She propped her shoulder against the doorframe. "Go on."

———

Ava Carmichael looked completely hot.

Maybe it was just getting her out of her office, or maybe it was his sudden desperation to make this work, or maybe it was that her long, blond hair was pulled back, her makeup was wiped clean, and she was wearing a tiny, fitted tank top that hugged her breasts...and no bra. Her nipples were prominent against the pink cotton top that also left a strip of skin bare between it and the top of the loose pants that sat low on her hips. Evan was surprised that the pants were covered in bright multicolored stripes. And that her feet were bare. But of course, she'd be barefoot at home. Just because she looked like she'd been born in heels didn't mean that she never took them off.

Yeah, he could definitely be *this* woman's boyfriend for six months. She might be cool and confident and give off a there's-no-way-I'm-ever-going-to-find-you-charming vibe that was, honestly, pretty foreign to him, but if he could keep her out of her pencil skirts and shoes, he might have a chance at not fucking this up. Because *this* woman? Yeah, there was a lot to like here.

"I fit all of the requirements," he said as she folded her arms —which plumped up those very nice braless breasts—and propped her shoulder against the doorframe and looked up at him with a mix of curiosity and humor.

Yeah, he could work with that too. If she'd go braless and smile, even every other day, he'd be okay.

"The requirements?" she asked.

"In the trust," he said. "Your dad said that you never go out with a guy until you know his grad school GPA, his political affiliation, and his cholesterol levels. And he said that you have to date a guy without knowing any of that about him."

She looked surprised at that, and Evan figured she'd had no idea that her father had been that observant. Evan wasn't sure how Rudy knew about Ava's checklist of characteristics for her dates, but he'd said that she made online dating sights look like child's play.

"I totally fit," Evan went on. "I'm from Bliss, I'm a nice guy, and there's no way I'm telling you my GPA, so you can't make judgments about that. I don't really have a political affiliation and even I don't know my cholesterol levels."

She seemed to take all of that information in. "GPA was that bad, huh?" she asked, a smile teasing the corner of her mouth.

He was surprised at that show of humor, but then he caught a whiff of liquor. Ah, so she'd had a drink to wind down after the long day. Not a bad idea. If she'd go braless and drink in Bliss, he'd definitely be good.

"I passed the bar, that's all that really matters, right?" he answered.

"Hmm," she said, noncommittally. "And how about the cholesterol thing? I mean, I don't need to know exact numbers, but I definitely need to know how you feel about onion rings and cheese."

Okay, there had to be at least an iota of honesty in their relationship, right? "I'm a huge fan of both. But I also run and take vitamins."

She laughed at that.

And Evan felt like he'd been punched in the stomach. Wow. Yeah, if Ava Carmichael was braless, drinking, and *laughing*, even some of the time, these six months would be a piece of cake.

"So what's the plan?" she asked.

The plan. The thing that was going to solve every problem for every person. Just that.

"Date *me* for six months."

"I didn't think we really...connected," she said.

Yeah, he hadn't either. But that didn't matter. "That's the thing," he said, "it doesn't have to be totally real."

One eyebrow lifted. "Oh?"

"I mean, it will be real enough," he amended. "We'll go out and stuff. I'll make sure you have some fun and don't work all the time. We won't talk business. We won't hang out with a single person who makes seven figures. We won't ever say the words *hedge fund*." Considering he had no idea what that even was, that would be easy. "That was what was important to Rudy. That you don't work all the time. That you see that there's more to life. That you have some fun. I can do all of that. But there won't be any expectations beyond the six months and really, there won't be any expectations *during* those six months. We only have to make it seem like we're in a relationship. And this way no poor unsuspecting Bliss guy will fall in love and be devastated when you leave." Evan gave her one of his best come-on-I'm-pretty-cute-right? grins.

"We don't need to talk and get to know each other? Spend time alone?" she asked.

He shook his head. "Only needs to be public."

She tipped her head. "What's in it for you?"

"It takes away one of the things that you're concerned and frustrated about," he told her. "Basically, it gets you to Bliss. That's important. It's what Rudy wanted." *And will keep Parker from poisoning me slowly and painfully.*

"And that's all you care about? That this would make Rudy happy?" she asked.

Well, and Parker and Noah. And... He took a deep breath. "Okay, there's also this girl."

"Ah." She nodded. "Okay, there *is* something direct in it for you. You need her to think you're taken."

He supposed it was good that Ava know this. So that if his grandmother—or Jill's—ever walked by and he suddenly grabbed and kissed her, she'd know why. "I need the town to know I'm taken by someone other than her."

"The town wants you to be taken by her?"

At least part of the town did, Evan thought. Then he realized that no, pretty much the whole town probably did. "Yes."

"And why can't you just tell them you're not interested?"

"Because I've known Jill all my life and she's awesome and any guy would be lucky to have her. *Not* being interested...now... would make me seem like a commitment-phobic ass. I need a really good *reason* to not be interested. Like you." He gave her a wink that worked to soften up the woman he was talking to nine times out of ten. "Because, on paper, Jill and I seem like the perfect couple."

Ava gave him a look that said *I know that you think that wink works for you nine times out of ten.* "But you actually *are* a commitment-phobic ass?"

"It isn't actually a phobia. Per se," he protested. "It's being responsible."

"Sleeping with women you have no intention of committing to is responsible?"

He stared at her. "How did you know we slept together?"

"Because you're trying to talk a woman you just met into pretending to be your girlfriend so that your hometown doesn't think you and this girl, who you've known your whole life, should be together *now*." She tipped her head. "Something must have changed between the two of you and everyone must know about it."

Evan blew out a breath. She was good. "Okay, we slept together. But it was mutually a friends-with-benefits thing. She doesn't want anything more either. But it's up to me to come up with a really great reason for us to not be together." Something Ava had said a minute ago occurred to him. "And by the way, never promising to give them anything more than I can deliver is responsible."

"What can you deliver?" She looked curious. And slightly amused.

He could work with that. "A few laughs and a few orgasms."

She lifted her shoulder. "Well, that's not nothing."

Evan grinned. It felt like he was talking to Cori again. Of course it made sense that Ava and Cori would have things in common. He supposed as triplets even their sense of humor could be crazily similar. That was good. He was attracted to Cori. Which meant, he could be attracted to Ava too.

"You're just not into serious relationships?" Ava asked.

"Well..." He wanted to be. Or he wanted to want to be. "Mostly, I can't be responsible for penguins being cared for by a sub-standard vet."

Ava's eyes widened. "Penguins?"

"Jill's a wildlife vet. Specializing in penguins."

"And there aren't a lot of penguins in Bliss?"

"Not a one."

"But there are in..."

"Omaha. At the zoo. It's her dream job."

"Ah." Ava took a breath. "You're worried that she'll give it up and you won't live up to the hype."

Well, no. Not exactly. Okay, maybe. A little. He lifted a shoulder.

"Was this the first time you'd slept with Jill?" she asked.

"Yes."

"And why now?"

"It was an unusual situation," he said carefully. "Normally I wouldn't have let it happen."

"What was the situation?"

Evan rolled his neck, but he said, "It was just after your dad's memorial service. I'd had a few drinks and she brought me lasagna and—"

"Well, that explains it."

"It does?"

"It's *lasagna*."

Evan would not have pegged Ava Carmichael as a comfort-food girl. But he also wouldn't have imagined how relaxed and normal she'd look at home. There were some layers here. That could make the next six months much more interesting.

"Exactly," he said. "I was sad and drunk and there was a lasagna and she said that she was there for me, anything I needed and..." He trailed off, assuming she could fill in the rest.

Ava groaned. "You Harry-ed her?"

He paused. But no, that didn't make any sense even when he repeated it in his head. "What?"

"You Harry-ed her," she said again. When he shook his head, she sighed. "*When Harry Met Sally*? The movie? Billy Crystal and Meg Ryan? They're friends forever and she's really sad one night and he comes over to comfort her and they end up sleeping together and afterward she thinks their relationship has changed, but he doesn't."

Evan stared at her.

"You Harry-ed her," she said again, as if to drive the point home.

"But I was the one that was sad and needed comforting."

"Well, maybe you Sally-ed her." Ava scrunched her nose up, thinking.

And he found that adorable.

He sighed. "And neither of us thought the relationship would change. But okay, *we* screwed up. So, I propose this—you come to Bliss, and we act madly in love, and Jill will act broken-hearted and like she can't wait to get away from having our happiness rubbed in her face, and everyone will give up on the idea of her and me. Then she'll escape to Omaha, you'll fulfill the dating provision in the trust, and I'll prove that I'm a changed guy who is capable of being with a woman for more than sex."

"Except that you won't be a changed man. You'll be a man trying to get out of a sticky situation."

He leaned in, propping his elbow on the doorjamb just above her head. "But maybe you *can* change me." That tone of voice always worked. And this was a good idea. For both of them.

She didn't look amused. Or particularly turned on. But she didn't move away from him either. She simply asked, "Do you want to change?"

Fine, she should probably know this too. "I need to take things a little more seriously. I'm kind of...the life of the party now. A lot like Cori. I love to have a good time, try new things, make sure everyone around me is having fun. But people want to hang out with me if there's beer and wings involved, not as much if there are big decisions to be made."

She tipped her head. "You're a *lawyer,* right?"

He grinned. "Yeah, well, I'm very content mediating disagreements between people I've known my whole life, helping people draw up land purchase agreements, trademark their homemade soy candles, and adopt babies. Nothing big or fancy or serious."

"Babies aren't serious?"

He shook his head, still smiling. "Come on. You know what I mean. I'm a good guy. But I could stand to settle down a little."

She finally nodded. "Okay, I get it." She took a deep breath. "But you're not like Cori."

Just her name made his heart thump. That could be a problem. "No?"

"Sounds like people love to have you around."

Evan felt his eyes widen. "What's that mean?"

She lifted a shoulder. "A little bit of Cori goes a long way."

He felt his brows pull together. "Rudy always said that Cori was the fun one." Surely that wouldn't offend Ava. Surely, she knew.

"Oh, she is. She's great in small doses."

A strange surge of protectiveness went through him. That could also be a problem. But it didn't keep him from saying, "That's weird. I got a small dose today. And definitely wanted more."

Her eyes went wide. He probably shouldn't have said that. But if Ava was going to criticize Cori, they were going to have issues.

Yeah, that was definitely going to be a problem.

"You wanted more from Cori?" Ava asked. Her voice sounded strange.

Absolutely. But that wasn't going to work. Obviously. If he was dating Ava, he couldn't even flirt with Cori. Though he wasn't sure he'd be able to help it. "I found your sister...delightful."

He wasn't sure he'd ever used the word *delightful* ever before. And certainly not in reference to a woman he wanted to sleep with.

"You did?" Ava asked. Her eyes were even wider now.

"I did."

"It was probably the whipped cream."

Again, he felt himself frowning and wanting to defend Cori. "It wasn't the whipped cream."

She arched a brow.

"It wasn't *just* the whipped cream," he amended.

"Evan—"

"I like your sister," he said. "But this is part of how I'm going to start changing. *We* both need *this*." Ava was the one to shape him up. Cori was the one to...yeah, that didn't matter.

She just looked at him for several seconds. Finally, she asked, "Do you cry a lot?"

"Excuse me?"

"Do you get all sad and despondent and in need of lasagna often?" she asked.

"I'm generally a pretty happy person," he said dryly. "Though I will admit that I'm in need of pasta every once in a while even when I'm in a good mood."

She nodded. "Noted."

And he could have sworn she was suddenly fighting a smile.

"No risk of accidental sex, then?" she asked.

"I can honestly say that 99 percent of the sex I have is very on purpose."

Yeah, she was definitely fighting a smile. And he really liked that. And it made him think about sex. With this woman. It was interesting, and surprising, that he hadn't really thought about sex with Ava before this. He'd noted that she was gorgeous and that she looked damned good in her heels and that if they'd met in a bar, he probably would have hit on her. But that was as far as that had gone. Because she'd opened her mouth and the frosty-CEO thing didn't do it for him. He'd actually thought briefly about how a six-month public relationship with her would keep him essentially celibate, but then he'd quickly *stopped* thinking about that when he'd started to hyperventilate.

He'd told himself he could make it for six months. He was a grown man, for God's sake. He could sacrifice for a greater good. People went off to war, after all. And into space. And...other places where they couldn't have sex for long periods of time even if he couldn't think of one at the moment. But he could be a fucking soldier here. So to speak.

"I assume if we're putting on this relationship show in your little town, we're going to have to make it believable," Ava said.

He nodded. "Definitely. There's no way anyone will believe that I'm serious about someone I'm not attracted to."

Evan could have sworn she moved closer. That was...interesting.

"But I'm not sure we have any chemistry," she said, her voice a little husky now.

He wasn't sure they did either. But he knew that he liked her in this tank top. And he really loved her smile and her laugh and the way she seemed to know that he was full of shit.

"Well, there's only one way to know for sure," he said, to them both. Then he stepped in, wrapped an arm around her waist and drew her up onto her tiptoes and against him.

She took a quick, soft breath, but didn't seem shocked. And didn't move to put more space between them.

"So far so good," he said gruffly as his body responded to having her up against him.

"Yeah," she said, staring at his mouth.

He had no choice but to cup the back of her head...and kiss her.

Because, seriously, they needed to know how much acting this whole chemistry thing was going to take.

And the answer was clear almost immediately. *Not one fucking bit.*

Regardless of the hoity-toity attitude, the shoes that cost more than his truck had—and that admittedly made her legs look amazing—and the fact that he really wanted to eat bacon dipped in Nutella with her sister, kissing Ava Carmichael was going to be absolutely no hardship whatsoever.

In fact, the kiss had him thinking about other things to do with Nutella.

And if Cori's face was the one that flashed through his mind when Ava first dragged her tongue over his bottom lip, then it wasn't *totally* his fault. They were identical after all.

Evan curled his fingers into her hair as her hands gripped the front of his shirt. She made a little needy sound at the back of her throat and Evan took the step that put her up against the door and his body more firmly against hers.

Without her heels, she was a little short of the perfect height for making out against a door, so Evan scooped under her ass and lifted her slightly so he could press his suddenly aching cock into the soft apex of her thighs.

She groaned and wrapped her legs around him, her arms slipping around his neck.

He groaned in return.

Yeah, the next six months was going to be just fine.

As their tongues tasted and danced, he memorized the perfect curve of her ass, the feel of her breasts against his chest— also perfect—the smell of her skin, and the way she squeezed him with her thighs, almost as if she was trying to hold him in place.

He had no intention of going anywhere any time soon.

"Hey! Who was at the door?"

Unless of course one of her sisters interrupted.

Evan pulled back and stared down into the big blue eyes that were filled with heat and surprise, if he wasn't mistaken.

She took a long breath, then called back, "Evan Stone."

"Oh, is there a problem?" the other voice asked.

Her mouth curled up and her gaze went to his lips. "Well, maybe just a slight one."

He lifted an eyebrow, but also loosened his hold on her, letting her feet swing to the ground. He stepped back, still able to feel her butt in his palms.

"That didn't feel like a problem," he said. "This plan will work."

She took a deep breath, ran a hand over the front of her tank, where her nipples were even more prominent now, and said, "There's just one little thing."

"What's that?"

"You're really going to have to learn to tell us apart."

Evan felt trepidation skitter down his spine as another beautiful blond appeared at the end of the hallway inside the door.

"Mr. Stone? What can we do for you?"

"He'd like to talk to you about your requirements in the trust," the woman he'd just been kissing said.

And Evan felt that trepidation sneak around to his gut and form a hard knot.

"Oh?" the other blonde said. The one in a similar tank top and pants. But this top was green. And she was wearing a sports bra. "What about them?"

Evan met the first Carmichael sister's gaze. He lifted a thumb and ran it over his bottom lip, where she'd nipped him slightly.

"He has an idea," she said to her sister, even while she returned his stare.

"Well, great," the one in the green tank said. "What is it?"

"I'll just leave you and *Ava* alone," the sister who was now clearly Cori, said.

Apparently she wasn't going to mention his mistake. Or the kiss. That was great. He supposed.

Evan watched her as she walked down the hallway and disappeared around the corner. And all he could feel for a few seconds was regret.

Then Ava asked, "What's your idea?"

And Evan focused on the woman who was going to be his girlfriend for the next six months.

———

"What's going on?" Brynn asked as Cori walked to the couch and dropped onto the end cushion.

What was going on? She was knee-deep in a crush on a guy who was, at that very moment, convincing her sister to be his girlfriend.

Her very beautiful, put-together, successful, intelligent, driven sister. Who practically *had* to date him. While Cori wasn't supposed to date *anyone*. She grabbed a throw pillow and hugged it to her stomach.

"Evan Stone has a solution to Ava's part of the new dating rules around here," Cori told Brynn.

"Really?" Brynn asked. "He can get us out of that part?"

Cori couldn't help but smile. Brynn actually looked concerned. "No, you hussy, you still get to try on a bunch of different guys, no worries."

Brynn tucked her hair behind her ear as her cheeks got pink. "I wasn't worried."

"You know, you could still start dating a bunch. Even if it wasn't mandated in some stupid trust," Cori said. "There are lots of ways to meet nice guys."

Okay, there were lots of ways to meet guys. There were a few ways to meet *nice* guys. But doing it in Bliss, Kansas seemed like one of those ways. Evan Stone sounded like he was a bit of a player and even he was *nice*.

"But the trust thing is such a great excuse, right?" Brynn asked with a grin.

Cori laughed. "Well, I guess if you need an excuse, then yeah."

"Honestly, I've never needed an excuse, because I've never really wanted to date," Brynn said.

"No?" Cori had always assumed that Brynn was just shy and a workaholic. Not in the same way Ava was, of course. Ava did it because she was proving herself. Brynn did it because she honestly loved what she did.

Brynn shrugged. "I guess I've always assumed when I met the right guy, I would just know. And he'd be it."

"The first guy you date will be the last guy you date?" Cori asked. That was...a completely absurd idea.

But Brynn nodded. "I guess going out to dinner and the movies with someone I'm not sure of seems like a waste of time."

Cori got more comfortable on the couch. This was fascinating. "But how do you know you're sure, or not sure, until you spend some time together?"

"I'm just not the type to meet a guy in a bar or something and spend time getting to know him. I think I'm more likely to end up with someone I already know from work or a research team or through one of the forums I'm a part of or something. I think I'll really know the guy *before* we go on a date. And then that will be it."

Cori thought about that. Wow. That would be really nice actually.

"How's Evan going to help Ava?" Brynn asked.

"He's going to play my boyfriend for the next six months," Ava said, coming into the room. Alone.

Well, that hadn't taken very long. Why had it taken him more time to tell Cori about the plan? Oh, yeah, because there had been flirting. And making out.

"What are you talking about?" Brynn asked.

Ava reclaimed her seat, put her head back, and her feet up. "Yep. This is perfect actually." She yawned.

"Perfect?" Cori echoed. "Really?"

Was Ava feeling an attraction to Evan too? And why did that idea make Cori's stomach feel weird? Just because Ava wasn't as fun or spontaneous or flirtatious as Cori and Cori really wanted *that* to be Evan's type? That wasn't fair. Ava was awesome. And there were extenuating circumstances here, for both of them. And Cori wasn't supposed to date anyway.

But, seriously, how was she supposed to embrace the not-dating thing after a kiss like that? Sure, the idea of spending a few Saturday nights on the couch with the Hallmark Channel on was really appealing. But she was really going to miss kissing. Maybe Hallmark wouldn't be the best choice. Too much romance. She might have to rent some thrillers. Scary stuff. Like the idea of never having Evan Stone's mouth on hers again.

Fuck. She was in trouble.

Ava rolled her head to look at Cori. She was clearly still a little tipsy. "It's perfect because it's easy. And fastest. The six-month clock starts right away. This way it will be over sooner. Meeting a guy, establishing a relationship that could last six months, but not longer, would all be complicated. But Evan knows what's going on so we can just do the minimum to meet the requirements—go out a few times, maybe have fun, do... something...date-ish."

Ava frowned and Cori laughed, in spite of the fact that Ava was talking about doing something date-ish with Evan. "You do know how to date, right?" she asked. "I mean, you do go out with guys."

Ava sighed. "Yeah, but I guess maybe Dad was right. I don't date just for fun. And I pick guys based on things like their job and their future prospects. And I like to multitask. Which means that I like to go to dinner at restaurants where other CEOs, or senators, or foundation presidents will also be having dinner. And I like to talk about PR plans and investments while we run. And I love when we have mid-week drinks and he can introduce me to new contacts. And I like gallery openings, because they're great opportunities for business conversations that don't feel like business conversations. And I love weekend getaways skiing or at the lake where I have access to influential people for an entire forty-eight hours while they're 'relaxed' and happy and a little drunk."

Ava used air quotes around "relaxed" and Cori shook her head. "Do you ever actually spend time alone with any of these guys?"

"I said we run," Ava replied.

"And talk business the whole time," Cori said.

Ava shrugged.

"Do you talk about the stock market while you're having sex too?" Cori asked.

Ava didn't respond right away. Cori felt her eyes widen. "Don't tell me that the words 'market shares' and 'depreciation' get you going."

"Of course not," Ava said. She paused. "But 'cash flow' and 'acquisition'? Definitely."

Cori threw the pillow at her. "Stop. That makes me sad. Foreplay should include words like 'tonight I'll be the professor and you be the grad student' and 'all fours *then* cowgirl' and 'naked waffles'."

There was no response and Cori looked from Brynn to Ava. They were staring at her, their cheeks pink.

"What?" she asked. "I like to role-play." She really did.

"Naked waffles?" Ava finally asked.

"Yeah. That's not really role-playing but it's fun. One of you is the waffle. Then there's butter and syrup and—"

"Yep, got it," Ava said. She looked at Brynn. "I don't..."

"What?" Cori asked.

Ava shook her head. "I don't have sex like that."

I'll bet Evan Stone does. Okay, that was a completely inappropriate thought. Cori shook it out of her head and focused on her sister. "Do you have sex at all?" she asked Ava.

Ava shrugged. "Of course."

Cori was pretty sure how that went. "Let me guess. You like to be on top and you get up afterward and check your email."

Ava rolled her eyes. "I don't get up afterward to check email." She paused. "I can check it on my phone from bed."

Cori laughed. But for some reason it was really important to Cori that her sisters, both of them, have good sex more than sometimes. She swallowed hard and ignored the twist in her stomach and said, "Maybe you won't want to check email when you're with Evan."

Ava sat up quickly, then groaned slightly. But she shook her head. "I'm not going to sleep with Evan Stone."

"Why not?" Cori asked, legitimately confused. "He's hot and funny and I think he'd go for naked waffles." Or Nutella and bacon.

"You and your food," Ava muttered.

Yeah, well. "I'm just saying that sex should be fun," Cori said. "And satisfying. And something that makes you forget about your email. At least for the night."

"Nothing can make me forget about my email." Ava slumped back into the couch.

Evan Stone totally could. But she'd already done the bigger-person thing by saying he was hot and funny and even mentioning the idea of Ava and Evan and naked waffles in the same sentence. Now she was shutting up.

"I guess that means Dad was right," Ava said.

Hearing about Ava's dating life, Cori couldn't disagree. "So, we're going?"

Ava sighed. "It's still crazy."

"Maybe that's what we need," Brynn said. "I have to admit that there's been a severe lack of crazy...and naked waffles...in my life."

Cori almost laughed. But then a thought hit her. "And maybe I've had too many naked waffles." Maybe the fact that her mind went from the idea of dating, straight to naked waffles and role-playing, meant that she wasn't doing so great at basic dating and getting to know people either. Or even really dating at all. She didn't make business deals during fancy-schmancy wine tastings and art shows, but she didn't go to the movies or on picnics in the park either. Maybe a step back from incorporating butter and syrup into her sex life wasn't a horrible idea.

And wow, she'd come up with that without having to pay Karen three hundred dollars an hour.

"Okay, then," Brynn said. "We're going."

"Yep, we're going," Cori agreed.

Ava nodded too. "Look out Bliss, Kansas. The Carmichael sisters are moving in."

4

"Wow."

"No kidding."

"Not at all what I expected."

"Oh yeah, that's totally what *I* expected."

"Bullshit."

"Seriously."

"I mean *wow*."

"What the hell did you put in their hash browns this morning?" Evan asked Parker as his friend topped off his coffee.

"Their hash browns?" Parker asked, leaning onto the counter across from where Evan sat in the diner.

Evan tipped his head toward the booth behind him where four of Bliss's favorite residents sat having breakfast. Ben, Hank, Roger, and Walter had been diner regulars until Rudy had moved to town and opened the pie shop, where they could sit and gab for hours without anyone making not-so-subtle comments about how they should either keep eating—and buying—or move on. But now that the pie shop was closed, the men had been forced to relocate back to the diner if they wanted someone to make and serve them coffee. And no, their own kitchens were not an option. Apparently.

"Oh, they're not talking about my hash browns," Parker said.

"No?" Evan looked up to find Parker's attention focused over Evan's shoulder.

"Nope." Parked pointed out the window.

Evan took a bite of toast and turned to look. And almost choked.

There was a long black limo parked across the street from the pie shop. And leaning against the side of it were three long-legged, gorgeous blonds. Who were identical other than what they were wearing.

Evan swallowed hard.

"Let me guess. Left to right—Brynn, Cori, and Ava," Parker said.

He'd nailed it. Brynn was wearing a blue sundress and a pink sweater. She had her hair back in a ponytail, her black-rimmed glasses on her nose and she was clutching a book to her chest.

Cori was in the middle in a red-and-white striped dress, short black boots, and her red leather jacket. Her hair was loose and curly. And she was holding a champagne glass. Evan felt his body stir even from this far away. He wasn't sure if it was the jacket or the boots, but he didn't think he'd have her take either off in bed.

And because he was *not* supposed to be thinking about Cori and beds in the same thought, he tore his eyes away and looked at her sister. Ava's hair was stick straight and she wore a black skirt, white blouse, and, sure enough, heels. And she was holding a briefcase.

Evan cleared his throat. "Good guess," Evan said to Parker. He knew Rudy had told Parker as much about his daughters as he'd told Evan.

Parker chuckled. "We're in trouble, huh?"

"What makes you think that?" Evan asked, knowing his eyes

should be on his "girlfriend" but finding they were back on Cori. Crap. He was definitely in trouble.

"Those girls don't know a damned thing about living in a town like Bliss."

That was an understatement. "Could be fun."

"Could be a pain in the ass."

Well, he couldn't argue with that.

"And I told you that you needed to get them into blue jeans," Parker added.

"Yeah, well, I got them into the state of Kansas. One thing at a time," Evan said. He stood from the stool, fished a ten out of his pocket and tossed it on the counter.

Parker swiped it up as he reached to return the coffeepot in his hand to the warmer. There was no such thing as a best friend discount in Parker's diner and he fully expected Evan to tip.

"The scenery in town just improved. Times three," Noah said as he slid onto the stool next to Evan's and picked up the cup on the counter and held it up for Parker.

Parker sighed and grabbed the pot again. He was always annoyed filling coffee cups. He made crappy coffee on purpose and overcharged for it, and yet people still insisted on coming in to drink it. He filled the cup. "Don't get all gaga over those girls," he warned Noah. "They're here with very specific instructions. And if they don't do what they're supposed to, we're all screwed."

Noah took a sip. "I'm just saying that this front row seat might not be all bad."

Parker rolled his eyes.

Evan took a deep breath. "I'm going to go introduce the girls to their new business," he said. "And get them out of sight."

"Yeah, like that's gonna matter," Parker said.

Half the town had already seen them, and they'd be talking to the other half of the town—Evan glanced around and noticed a number of people on their phones—if they weren't already.

"Damn." This was going to be...interesting. Good thing Evan loved the unexpected.

As his hand hit the door, he heard "Hey, Evan, is that your new girl?"

He'd started the rumor about him and Ava immediately upon returning to Bliss two days ago. It had been easy enough. He'd simply told Parker while sitting on the very stool he'd just vacated. During the lunch rush. With Shelly Perkins sitting right next to him. Shelly owned the hair salon. It had only taken two hours for the news to spread. In fact, in that time the story had grown from Evan and Ava having a love-at-first-sight reaction when they'd met in New York to them having an online relationship for the past few months before actually meeting. For possibly the first time in his life, Evan appreciated the Bliss rumor mill and its absolute inability to keep any fact straight.

"Yep, that's her," he said.

"She's out of your league," Hank told him.

"No shit," he muttered, pushing his way through the door.

But he couldn't help but grin as he headed for the three newest residents of Bliss. They looked completely out of place, and Evan felt a stirring of anticipation. He loved his hometown, but he had to admit that things were pretty routine around here. Evan loved a good shake-up, and there was no question the Carmichael triplets would be providing that. Ava, Brynn, and Cori might not be ready for Bliss, but Bliss wasn't ready for them either. At worst, this was going to be something new. At best, it was going to be a hell of a good time.

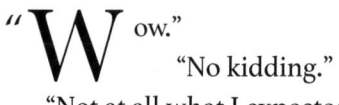
"Wow."
"No kidding."
"Not at all what I expected."

Cori stood between her sisters, staring at the front of the pie shop that they now owned and were to operate over the next year.

Besides the fact that it was a *pie shop* and none of them knew a thing about running a pie shop, there were a few more details demanding their attention. Like the fact that the storefront was, well, green and pink. A not-quite-neon green. A not-exactly-lime green. It was more...

"Avocado," Cori decided. "That color is the color of the inside of an avocado."

Ava and Brynn nodded.

"And the pink is kind of..."

"Bubble gum," Brynn said.

"Or Pepto Bismol," Ava said.

Cori nodded. "Yep. Definitely."

The siding was painted in the inside-an-avocado green, while the front door and the shutters on the windows were pink, with a green-and-pink-striped awning over the door.

Even more surprising, the colors didn't stand out on the main street of Bliss, Kansas. All of the buildings were painted in bright colors. There was pink and yellow and a light blue and even lavender. They didn't all have awnings, but most had huge picture windows, and a couple had benches or chairs in front. The sidewalk that ran in front of the stores was so white it almost required sunglasses to look at it directly. There were lampposts with old-fashioned-looking lanterns at the top, a median in the middle of the street that held grass and flowers that were just as bright as the siding on the shops, and right in the center was a tall post that hoisted an enormous clock high above the street. Directly across the street from the storefronts was a huge park with lots of trees, beautifully kept grass, and flowers everywhere.

"And that name?" Ava asked. "Seriously?"

Cori focused on the sign above the awning in front of them. The loopy green script read Blissfully Baked.

"It sounds like a pot shop," Ava said.

It did. "Maybe it was a marketing strategy," Cori said. "Nothing like pie when you've got the munchies, right?"

Ava sighed. "I wouldn't know."

Yeah, well, she could take Cori's word for it.

"Do we go in?" Brynn asked.

Considering they didn't know where anything else was, like the house they were going to be living in, that made the most sense. The GPS had gotten them to the pie shop, but they didn't have an address for the house. "Did you call Evan?" Cori asked Ava.

"No, why?"

"Well, someone should probably tell *someone* that we're here. And we don't know anyone else. And it should probably be you since you're his girlfriend." Cori grimaced slightly as she said it. That was going to take some getting used to.

Ava sighed. "Fine."

She pulled her phone out, but just then Brynn said, "No need."

Cori looked over to see Evan coming toward them. And she was shocked by how happy she suddenly felt.

He's your sister's boyfriend. Keep it in your pants, girl. But she couldn't help her smile when she saw that his gaze was on *her*. *Pretend boyfriend. He's Ava's* pretend *boyfriend*, she couldn't help but think.

"Don't you just hate when the car rental company is out of practical cars and puts you in a limo instead?" he asked, coming to a stop in front of them.

"Actually, no," Ava said.

"Let me guess," Cori said. "The last limo to roll through Bliss was on prom night?"

He grinned. "Jaci and Seth Marshall's wedding last September, actually."

And of course, he knew the people's names and the exact date. Because Jaci and Seth were two of only fourteen hundred and sixty-three people living in this town, according to the sign they'd passed on their way in. A lot of things about this situation were going to take some getting used to.

"A limo can be practical, actually," Ava told him.

"Because it color coordinates with your outfit?" he asked, moving closer to her.

"Because I was able to plug in my laptop and Cori had champagne," Ava said.

Cori held up her glass. "The champagne on the plane was better, but I'm not complaining."

The champagne was definitely taking the edge off of traveling all day with Ava, who literally had a spreadsheet to keep her other spreadsheets organized. She had one for work, one for packing, one for items she'd need in the new house, one for things to check on with the pie shop, and God knew what else. Cori had tuned her out after hearing that she'd been in contact with some chef she knew in New York who knew some other chef who did something with pies.

Cori would love to give the pies a shot, honestly. She loved being the kitchen. There was something about creating recipes that would give someone else pleasure. But, after a brief session with Karen yesterday, she'd realized that maybe finding some of that same satisfaction would be good for Ava too.

Evan looked like he wanted to comment on the champagne thing, and Cori waited for it, knowing that it would be flirtatious. But Evan swallowed and looked at Brynn instead. "And was the limo practical for you too?" he asked.

Cori felt a stupid sense of disappointment.

Brynn nodded. "Plenty of space. To keep those two apart," she said, pointing at her sisters.

Evan laughed at that and Cori sighed. She liked when he laughed. This was going to be the longest year of her life. *He only has to date Ava for six months*, she reminded herself. There were six more months in the year after that. Then he leaned in and kissed Ava's cheek, and Cori felt her eyes widen. Yeah, all she had to do was leave him alone for six months. And not hate her sister for getting even the pretend Evan kisses.

Ava looked similarly stunned when he leaned back.

"We're being watched," he said quietly. "Look over my right shoulder."

Ava did and Cori almost did.

"But not all of you at once," Evan said, just as Cori was turning.

Instead, Cori watched Ava's eyes go round. "There are about thirty people looking out the window of the—" She squinted and finished, "—the diner."

"Probably more like fifty," Evan said. Then he looped an arm around Ava's waist and started toward the pie shop. "How about we get inside where we can talk more freely?"

Cori scowled at the sight of him touching Ava. And then told herself to chill out and consciously relaxed her expression. She couldn't go around glowering at Evan for the next six months. And a big part of this trip was about Cori reconnecting with her sisters. Karen had talked her through that too. So she couldn't hate Ava for going along with this plan that was for all of their goods. This *pretend* plan.

"They can hear us from here?" Brynn asked, following Evan and Ava across the street.

"I swear to God, even the trees here have ears," Evan said.

Cori was the last to start for the pie shop and she made a point of not looking in the direction of the diner. Or watching Evan's hand on Ava's lower back as he reached to pull the door open for her. He also held the door for Brynn and Cori, and as Cori passed him, he said softly, "Needed something stronger than Nutella today?"

She paused in the doorway and smiled up at him, unable to help it. "Nutella is for when we're hanging out for a few hours and Ava has vodka and I have pajamas on. When I'm stuck in airborne tin cans with her and I'm wearing a push-up bra and she's organizing everything from what time we get to the airport to what carry-on bag I can use, it's definitely champagne. Or whiskey."

She didn't miss how his eyes dropped to her breasts at the mention of her push-up bra, and she felt a twist of heat in her stomach. But almost immediately, his eyes were back on hers. He gave a soft chuckle and Cori actually sucked in a quick breath at the deep, rumbly sound that seemed to vibrate through her chest. And they weren't even touching. They were just standing a lot closer than a guy and his girlfriend's sister should be.

"Well, I included Nutella and bacon on the list of things they stocked the house with," Evan told her.

Evan's hand was still on the door and there wasn't much space between them, and for that moment, she let herself just enjoy the close proximity, turning to face him fully. "Someone stocked the house for us?"

"And cleaned it, made the beds, all of that," he said. "I'm sure there are a few casseroles in the fridge too so you don't have to cook for a while."

"Are you serious?"

"I am."

"Why would they do that?"

"They loved Rudy and you're his daughters. And they're glad the pie shop is opening again. Well—" he grinned, "—Parker is, anyway, and his mom was one of the women getting the house ready. And—" He broke off and looked past her.

But Cori understood. "And they love *you* and think your girlfriend is living in that house," she said.

He didn't say anything, but he didn't have to. Everyone in Bliss already knew that he and Ava were supposedly a couple. Awesome. Which meant Cori should really move *away* from him.

Don't you dare ruin Nutella for me, she thought as she stepped through the doorway. *Don't be sweet and flirtatious and make me think dirty thoughts about my favorite snack when you're out of reach.*

But she already liked him, so him being out of reach was a *good* thing, she reminded herself. She wasn't supposed to be dating. Which was also good, because she was not in a position to leave or avoid him after she called it quits. Karen had also brought that up when she'd pointed out that Cori was committed to being in this one place for a year now. Her shrink loved that there would be no moving on after a few weeks or months when Cori started to feel like she'd used up her welcome. She had to stay now, and she knew Karen was hoping that she'd see she was able to contribute to a relationship long-term. But Cori was going to concentrate on that relationship being with her *sisters*. Because they had to keep loving her anyway.

Shaking all of that off, Cori concentrated on looking around the little shop that now belonged to her, Ava, and Brynn.

The lights weren't on, but two of the four walls were made up of windows and the sunlight poured in onto the white linoleum, the six tables with mismatched chairs, and the long Formica counter that stretched along the top of an empty glass case. There was an opening that gave access to the area behind the counter where, presumably, the pie shop staff would be positioned, ready to help the customers. And behind that was a white swinging door that had to lead to the kitchen.

The place was dusty and drab and, frankly, a little sad. Especially after seeing the bright and cheery outside.

"This is..." Ava started.

"Dull," Cori supplied.

Ava sighed. "Not what I expected." She turned to Evan. "I thought you said that he'd had it renovated."

"It used to be a soda fountain," Evan said. "But the building had been empty for a long time. Rudy hired a guy from Kansas City who specializes in rehabilitating old buildings in small towns. He came in and helped with things like removing the soda fountain and fortifying the interior walls and updating the plumbing and electricity. But Rudy liked that it was...rustic."

Cori snorted. "I don't think that word means what he thought it meant."

Evan smiled. "He wanted it to be basic. He wanted the bare minimum. Said he wanted people to come for the pies and the company. He thought that doing a lot of fancy upgrading might change that."

"Yeah, heaven forbid people come in because the place looks nice," Ava said. She turned a full circle. "Well, we're going to have to do...something."

"We can easily paint, get some new furniture, put in a photo booth," Cori said, also turning a circle and taking it all in. When she'd turned all the way around she stopped. And realized that they were all looking at her. "What?"

"A photo booth?" Ava asked.

"Sure. That would be fun," Cori said. She looked at Evan. "Is there already a photo booth in town?"

He shook his head slowly. "No."

"Then it would be something unique," she told them. She frowned as they continued to just stare at her, looking confused. "A photo booth," she repeated. "One of those things where you get in with a bunch of friends or a date and it snaps a strip of photos and you pose differently for each of them."

"Yeah, we know what a photo booth is," Ava said. "What does it have to do with the pie shop?"

"It would be something that could pull kids in," Cori said. "And people on dates. We could call it something about Sweetie Pie. Oh!" she said as another idea occurred. "We could do pies shaped like hearts and serve one with two forks. This could become the new *it spot* for date night. And we could have a photo wall. If people want to hang their photos up here, it would show all the fun people have when they come in." She turned to Evan again. "Is there a jukebox anywhere in town. At the diner or anything?"

He shook his head. "No. Definitely not at the diner. But no."

"A jukebox would be fun too," she said, scanning the room and mentally putting the photo booth into the corner by the glass case. "We might have to take part of the case out though. But that thing is huge. We don't need that much display space."

"We could..." Ava trailed off. "I don't even know where to start with all of that."

"Well, and obviously we wouldn't just focus on sweetie pie stuff," Cori said. "There's a lot of other types of customers too, but that just came to mind."

While her sisters were looking at her like they had no idea what language she was speaking, Evan was looking at her with a mix of amusement and wonder. She kind of liked that mixture.

"You walk into this shop and immediately things like photo booths and sweetie pie specials come to mind?" he asked.

She shrugged. "I guess so."

"It's a basic, boring shop," Ava said. "Of course, she immediately starts thinking up ways to make it more fun and...unique." Ava gave her a smile. "It's how she's wired. She can't help it."

Cori decided to take that as a compliment. "It's okay if you use the word crazy instead of unique," she told her sister.

Ava laughed. "Well, I think we have a ways to go before we can start adding photo booths and things, but yes, we need to do *something* here."

"But shaped pies would be cool," Cori said. "And that's gotta be easy. I mean, all the pie stuff stays the same, we just need different pans."

"Do they make different shaped pie pans?" Ava asked.

"If they don't, they should," Cori said. "We'll commission something. It could be a side business."

"Oh, I could talk to Brent Gerwin. He's into restaurant supplies, I think," Ava said.

"Great. Email him tonight."

"Wow."

They both stopped talking and looked over at Evan. He was standing next to Brynn and they were watching Ava and Cori with wide eyes.

"You haven't even seen the pie pans that you already have," Evan said.

Cori crossed her arms. "Are there heart-shaped ones?"

"Definitely not."

"Well, then."

Brynn looked at Ava. "You've never even made a *round* pie. You sure you're ready to get into different shapes?"

Ava looked pained. "I'm not ready to even go into the kitchen."

"Right. Maybe one step at a time," Brynn said.

Okay, she had a point. But Ava was right. Cori couldn't help that her mind started spinning with new ideas that seemed like fun. It was a problem, actually. Her ideas were often a little wild, and she loved to just jump in. Doing this with Ava and Brynn was a good thing. They could keep her craziness reined in and tell her when her ideas were too much. Which was probably about eighty percent of the time.

"Okay," Cori agreed. "We'll just start with paint and some new tables and chairs." She looked the current furniture over. Honestly, it looked like Rudy had picked up the various pieces from different yard sales or something. But that made her wonder... "Evan, do you know where Rudy got this stuff?" she asked.

He looked the room over. "Around town. Yard sales and stuff," he said.

So she'd nailed that.

"Like I said, he didn't want this to be fancy," Evan said. "Just the basics. Just a place where people could come and sit and chat. Like a friend's house."

The tables and chairs were mismatched and clearly not new, but there was something nice about them being from people in town. "Maybe we could just give them a makeover," she said to Brynn. "Paint them or refinish them, add some cushions to the chairs, some tablecloths, little centerpieces." She pulled her phone out and quickly did a search. Then she held her phone up to Brynn. "We could do something with little tartlet pans like these for centerpieces so it's sort of pie themed."

Evan stepped forward and wrapped a big hand around her wrist, lowering her hand and phone. "The front of the shop is Brynn's. The pies, of all shapes, are Ava's. Come here." He started behind the counter, pulling her along with him.

Cori wasn't sure she'd ever felt tingles from a guy holding onto her *wrist*, but she did with Evan Stone. That was how complicated this was, of course, going to be.

He took her through the swinging door into the kitchen at the back of the shop. It was...a kitchen. Which she'd guessed. But this looked like the kitchen in a house, not a restaurant. There was a stove and oven—one, basic, white stove and oven— a refrigerator, which was yellow, a sink, and countertop that was a gray granite, and some oak-colored cupboards. Nothing matched in here either. And there was no stainless steel, no restaurant quality appliances, no enormous center island, no racks hanging overhead displaying copper pots and pans. Yes, she'd imagined copper pots and pans. She wasn't sure why. But she realized as Ava came through the door behind her that she'd actually envisioned the kitchen in the pie shop. And it was nothing like this.

"Let me guess, the appliances and stuff came from yard sales too?" she asked.

"He bought the stove from a woman who was remodeling and was getting new stuff. He bought the fridge from a guy whose mother had passed away and was cleaning out her house. He got the countertop from a guy who does remodels and had extra.

And he took the cabinets and cupboards out of a house they were tearing down."

"Wow," was all Ava said to that.

Evan chuckled. "The pie shop was more like a clubhouse for him and his friends and he set it up with odds and ends. He made pie and coffee and hoped people would come by and sit for a while and talk. It wasn't about looks, but about function," he said. "This is why no one had any idea how much money he had. Everything was really basic with him. He didn't mind second-hand and he lived pretty simply." Evan shrugged. "I can't explain it better than that. This pie shop totally fit your dad."

Cori felt that getting-familiar stab of sadness. She shook her head. "Not the guy we knew."

Evan's expression softened and the fingers around her wrist tightened briefly. Those tingles zipped up her arm, effectively distracting her from thoughts of how she would have really liked to get to know the Rudy Carmichael who collected stray furniture and rescued unwanted appliances so that he could make pie for his friends in his version of a clubhouse. She supposed if little boys had the ability to put ovens into their tree houses, they'd do it. For the frozen pizzas, if nothing else. And she supposed that her father hadn't had a clubhouse or a tree house growing up. And maybe he hadn't had that many friends either. Cori hadn't known her grandparents on her father's side, but Rudy had been raised with money and had grown up in a Manhattan penthouse and had gone to private schools.

Just like Cori, Ava, and Brynn had.

Hell, they hadn't had clubhouses or tree houses either. And suddenly she felt like she'd missed out. And like maybe this pie shop could be something similar for them too.

"You okay?"

She focused on Evan, finding him watching her with a look of concern. He was also stroking his thumb across her wrist, over her pulse point. And it had a strange combination effect of increasing the tingles, but also making her feel calmer. She nodded. "Yeah. Probably." *Especially if you keep touching me.*

He looked like he wanted to say more, but Ava pushed past them and further into the kitchen.

"This is not what I expected," she said. Then she sighed. "I wonder when I'm going to quit saying that in regards to this whole thing." She started opening cupboards and drawers. Then she turned toward Evan. "There's nothing here."

"Well, there are measuring cups and stuff," he said.

Ava held up some plastic measuring spoons. "There are these." She held up a wooden spoon. "Two spoons." And she stepped out of the way of the cupboard she'd opened. "And one set of bowls. I don't even see measuring cups."

Evan shrugged. "Simple. Basic."

Ava tossed the spoons back into the drawer and rubbed her forehead. "Not what I expected."

Evan started across the kitchen, tugging Cori along with him again. He stopped in front of a door. "Ava's in charge of the kitchen, Brynn has the front, and this—" He turned the knob and pushed it open, "—is *your* domain."

He dropped his hold on her now, and Cori felt the instant loss of comforting tingles. If there was such a thing. Though it really seemed that there was.

Evan flipped on a light switch just inside the door and Cori peered around him, with admitted trepidation. Trepidation that was absolutely warranted as she took in the room. Or rather the closet. That had a card table, a folding chair, and a file cabinet in it.

"This is the office," Evan said. His voice held a hint of humor.

"Wow. The *whole* room and everything in it is mine?" she asked.

"Yep." Evan grinned at her. "But don't get your hopes up for that file cabinet. The top drawer has about every fifth receipt and invoice in it that it should and maybe some pens, and the bottom drawer has a broken phone in it and a stapler."

Cori lifted her hand to rub her forehead, but stopped just short of exactly mimicking Ava. "I probably need to make a trip to the bank."

Evan nodded. "I have all of his account information and the paperwork you need to access it."

"Great." She glanced back at the closet. She stepped to the file cabinet and opened the top drawer. "Well, the stapler is in here." She pulled it out, along with a box of paperclips and two folders. Yes, just two folders. She bent to open the bottom drawer. "You're right about the phone. And—" She reached in and pulled out the only other thing in the drawer. "Measuring cups. No pens in here though."

"I'll check the oven for them," Ava said dryly.

"I assume I can take this stuff home?" Cori asked Evan. "I can't work in here."

"Sure. As long as *you're* the one taking care of it," Evan said agreeably.

"Uh, guys?" Brynn came into the kitchen, holding a piece of paper. A plain white sheet of paper with words printed on it in black marker. In Rudy's handwriting. Cori recognized that immediately.

"Is this the menu?" Brynn held it up to Evan.

He nodded without even looking at it. "Yep."

Brynn lifted an eyebrow. "There are four things on it. And one is coffee."

"Simple. Basic," Evan said.

Cori gritted her teeth. He was hot and funny, but that was getting damned annoying.

Brynn turned the page to look at it and read, "Cherry pie. Apple pie. Peach pie, parentheses sometimes. Coffee." She looked up again. "Seriously? This was all he served?"

Ava grabbed the page from Brynn. "Three kinds of pie?"

"Sometimes only two," Evan said.

Ava looked at him. "How is this a *pie shop*?"

"He served pie," Evan said with a shrug. "Look, I get it. It was—"

"I swear to God, if you say 'simple' or 'basic' again, I will smack you," Cori told him.

He cleared his throat. "Rudy wasn't in the pie business to make a lot of money. He liked pie and he felt that there were things about business that he wanted to learn up close and personal. He wanted to do things with his own two hands. He wanted a place that was all his own." Evan looked at all three of them. "All of the things he wants you all to learn and experience now. So, he kept it..." Evan trailed off and glanced at Cori. "Easy," he finally said. "Straightforward."

She rolled her eyes at him to let him know that the synonyms weren't much better. But then she focused on her sisters. "Well, I guess there's less for you to learn to make this way," she told Ava.

"It's *ridiculous* to build a business on *three* products, one of which is only available *sometimes*," Ava said. "I suppose that could create some kind of demand for the peach since it's not available all the time. But having only two other kinds of pie? I don't even like pie, and I can name off at least five others that are so commonly known that it should be assumed that a *pie shop* would have them."

Cori almost laughed. Almost. But seeing Ava riled up about pies was funny. Her sister was officially in CEO mode one hundred percent of the time. Which meant that Cori was going to have to split her time between the books for Blissfully Baked and making sure Ava remembered how to not think in terms of profit margins and investment strategies twenty-four-seven. Which meant keeping Ava *away* from those books and in this kitchen.

Maybe Rudy had gotten this right. The thought occurred to her and it didn't make her flinch. Maybe giving his girls a *simple* and *basic* business to work on together would teach them all something. Maybe it wasn't about the business at all. Maybe it was about letting go of their ideas about how they wanted their world to work. Ava was used to running everything and making money. Now she would be making pies. And that's all she'd be doing. Brynn was used to being able to hole herself up and not interact with anyone for days at a time. Now she had to make sure that the shop was inviting to the public. And Cori didn't like to be tied down, not by a job or a relationship or even a lease. Now she co-owned a business and had to stay in this town for a year. Yeah, this had to be about more than the actual business of pies. Besides, the trust said simply that the business had to be profitable after the year. That meant, as long as they had one dollar in the bank after expenses, they'd made it.

Piece of cake. Or pie, as the case may be.

"Are there recipes in here somewhere?" Brynn asked, looking around the kitchen.

"There's hardly anything in here," Ava groused. "I need to get on the computer and start ordering supplies."

"How do you know what to order without a recipe?" Brynn wanted to know.

Ava frowned at her, as if bringing up that point was irritating. "Well, I'm guessing I need flour. And sugar. And..."

Now Cori did laugh. "Good guesses," she said, as Ava trailed off. "I can help you come up with a list. And we can look around the house too. Maybe some of the stuff, like recipes, is there."

"I don't think he had recipes," Evan said. "He was trying to make pies that tasted like the pie his grandmother made when he was a kid. He was never able to track down a recipe and he tried over and over to replicate it. I think he threw all recipes out after they disappointed him."

"There has to be a starting point at least," Ava said. "And how am I going to know if they taste like his grandmother's pies?"

"You won't," Evan agreed. "You'll have to make them your own. Customize your recipes for Blissfully Baked."

Ava tipped her head back and groaned. "I have no idea how to do that." She looked at Evan again. "And can we change the shop name? Does it say in the trust that it has to stay the same?"

"It doesn't," Evan said. "But I wouldn't do that."

"No?"

"At least not right away," he said. "Everyone in town is happy to have you here, but also...hesitant."

"Hesitant?" Ava repeated.

"You're new. You're from New York. In the five years your father lived here, you never came to visit. People are just not sure how you'll fit in and how this will all go. I wouldn't come in and start changing a lot of things up, if I were you," Evan said with a shrug. "It is your shop now, but you'll be dependent on these people to support you and come spend money here."

Ava nodded. "Okay, fair enough."

"And you shouldn't order the groceries. Go to the store here and spend your money in town."

Ava sighed, but she didn't argue that. She did tip her head to the side, regarding Evan. "Though I am dating one of the town's favorite sons. That has to help me some."

He flashed her a grin, and Cori felt her gut clench at the sight.

"You are, at that," he said. "And it will help them give you the benefit of the doubt, bring them in the door at first. But if they don't like the pie, you might be in trouble. And *I'll* hear all about it. So, you probably need to learn more about pie than the fact that it requires flour."

Ugh. That wasn't even flirtatious and yet, hearing Evan and Ava talk about dating—even pretend dating—and seeing them grinning at each other was officially Cori's least favorite part of this day. She should have brought the bottle of champagne in with her.

And then it got worse because Ava laughed lightly and said, "Well, I know there's sugar involved too."

That actually was a little flirtatious. For Ava, anyway.

"I can help," Cori interjected, wanting to say *anything* that would keep Evan from making any kind of comment about sugar and Ava. "I can name all of the ingredients that go into a cherry *and* an apple pie."

That succeeded in getting Ava's eyes off of Evan. "I was hoping you'd say that," she told Cori.

"But the baking is supposed to be your thing," Evan said. "The trust is very specific. Don't forget that."

"Of course," Ava said. "But it also doesn't say anything about me not getting help."

"It doesn't?" Cori asked.

"No. As long as I'm *in charge* of the pie, that doesn't mean that someone else can't help," Ava said. "Isn't that right, Mr. Stone?"

Cori had no doubt Ava had scoured the trust for every detail...and loophole. And she was back to calling him Mr. Stone. The kind-of flirting was over. Thank God.

"That is correct," Evan said carefully. "You can get help. As long as you're still the primary baker. But we, you, need to be careful not to interpret things too loosely. It does say that Cori isn't supposed to be baking. Your father had a very specific intent behind his provisions. In your case, it was for you to be hands-on with your product."

"Of course," Ava said, soothingly. "I'm perfectly fine staying inside the legal boundaries of the trust."

Evan frowned and Cori had to admit that it didn't sound like Ava was overly concerned with their father's *intentions*. But as long as she abided by the trust, everything would be fine. Supposedly.

"You're not going to be here with us every day, are you, Mr. Stone?" Ava asked. "I assume that you have other clients and obligations?"

Evan's eyes narrowed but he nodded. "I do have other obligations. And no, I didn't intend to be here every day. Though," he added, as an afterthought, "since we *are* dating, you should probably plan to see a lot of me."

Ava gave him a smile that seemed less than sincere. "Wonderful."

"And if you're thinking about having Cori baking the pies because no one is going to know anyway, you need to be careful," he said. "I am dedicated to fulfilling all the terms of the trust as your father *intended* them to be fulfilled. And I'm not the only one aware of the provisions."

Cori really did like when he got firm like that. She had the impression that Evan was easygoing and fun-loving a lot of the time. But when it came to her father, his friend, and this stupid trust, he was resolute.

"I can promise you that I will touch every single pie that this pie shop makes," Ava said.

Evan shook his head. "I understand that your reputation as a tough negotiator is well-earned, Miss Carmichael."

Yeah, Cori liked when he called Ava Miss Carmichael *way* more than when he talked about her being his girlfriend.

"But," Evan went on, "this isn't something to negotiate. This is your father's trust. And your future. Your sisters' future."

"I'm aware," Ava said coolly. "And I also assure you that if anyone *but* me bakes these pies..." She lifted a brow. "...you will never know it."

"But I will."

They all swung to look at the owner of the new male voice.

There was a tall guy with dark hair and a deep scowl standing by the back door of the shop. In spite of the scowl and the way he had his arms folded, which made his biceps look big and firm, he was definitely good-looking.

"And that's not happening," he said.

"And who are you?" Ava asked, her chin going up and her chilly CEO voice firmly in place.

"Parker Blake."

Ava just lifted a brow. "I'm sorry, Mr. Blake, but I'm not sure how this is any of your concern."

"Oh, it's my concern all right, sweetheart. You are *not* fucking this up. Read a cookbook, look at a few online videos, take a cooking class. But you're making those pies and if I have to come over here every day to babysit you while you do it, I will."

Whoa. Cori turned wide eyes to Brynn. Nobody talked to Ava like that. Or if they did, they had their balls in her pocket when they left her office.

"Wha—you must be—there is no way—" Ava spluttered.

"Okay, Parker," Evan said, holding a hand up. "Take it easy."

"I'm just saying," Parker told Evan.

"I know."

"Who the *hell* do you think you are?" Ava demanded.

"I'm the guy who's taking this place over after you go back to New York," he said. "I'm also the guy who owns the diner right next door, so I can pop over and check on you any time I want. And I am the guy who does *not* want to have anything to do with Carmichael Enterprises. So, you *will* figure this pie thing out, sweetheart, and you're going to have me watching every move you make while you do it."

Ava seemed to have finally regained her composure, at least slightly, because she said, "What the hell would you have to do with Carmichael Enterprises?"

Huh, that was a good question. Whereas Cori was thinking that there were worse things in the world than having Parker Blake watching every move she made.

Parker glanced at Evan. Evan shook his head. Parker rolled his eyes. And suddenly Cori really wanted to know what *that* was all about.

"If you girls don't fulfill the provisions of the trust, or if you fuck it up," Parker said, "*we* take over Carmichael Enterprises."

Ava's eyebrows were nearly to her hairline. "Excuse me? Who is 'we'?"

"Me, Evan, and Noah."

"Hey." Another guy stepped into the room from behind Parker. "Am I late?"

"Noah Bradley," Evan said, "Meet Ava, Brynn, and Cori Carmichael. Ladies, Noah Bradley. And you now know the jackass, Parker Blake."

Noah lifted a hand in greeting, though he looked chagrined. His gaze lingered on Brynn, and Cori caught her sister's shy smile before she averted her eyes. Okay, Noah was going on the list of guys Brynn needed to date.

"*You* all take over the business if we don't fulfill the trust?" Ava asked.

"That's right. I'm going to be on your ass the whole time you're here," Parker said.

Ava gave him a very unimpressed look and Cori was *impressed* by that. How did she not have a few stray dirty thoughts going through her head when a guy that looked like Parker and had that firm, dominant air about him, said something about being on her ass?

"You are going to get your hands dirty," Parker told Ava. "So, you might want to cut your nails and take off the polish."

"I will handle my nails, my hands, *and* my pie business all on my own, thank you very much, Mr. Blake," Ava said.

Parker shook his head. "No. You won't. Because your sisters are supposed to help."

Ava blew out a frustrated breath. "Yes, of course. I meant without *you*. And if you ever set foot in my kitchen again, I'll have you...arrested for trespassing."

Cori choked on a laugh. That was so over-the-top that it was clear that Parker was rattling Ava.

Parker got a sly smile on his face and unfolded his arms, tucking his hands into his front pockets. "You want to tell her or should I?" he asked, his eyes on Ava.

Who was he talking to?

But then Evan sighed. "Actually," Evan said, looking almost like he already regretted what he was about to say. "Parker is the official manager for Blissfully Baked. It's allowed him to continue paying the bills and for the business to go to him when the year is over. He actually has the right to be here. Whenever he wants to, really."

It didn't take long for Ava to process that. And what it meant. "You're my employee then," Ava said to Parker.

His smug smile faded slightly. "I wouldn't really call it that."

Ava glanced at Evan. "Would *you* call it that?"

"He works for you and Cori and Brynn," Evan confirmed, looking amused suddenly as he glanced at his friend.

"So I can fire him," Ava said.

"Actually, no," Evan answered. "It's also in the trust that Parker stay in his position. He can't be fired. The only way for him to be removed would be if he was in prison. Or died."

"I see." Ava's eyes narrowed. "I'll keep those options in mind."

And to Cori's shock, Parker gave Ava a slow grin. "How about you just use all the brilliant brain power and determination that your dad never shut up about and learn the pretty basic skill of making a pie?"

And it seemed that Parker Blake had already figured Ava out. He'd just issued a challenge to her intelligence and drive. There was no way she was backing down from that.

"How about you get out of my kitchen and I won't make you do all the dishes that I'm going to be getting dirty."

Parker gave a small smile at that. "Sure thing, Boss."

The word boss had never sounded more sarcastic.

Parker turned for the door. "But if you need any help figuring out how to actually *do* dishes, I'll be right next door." Then he was gone.

"I, uh, just wanted to say hi," Noah said. "Guess I'll be going too." He grabbed the knob, but then turned back. "Oh, and Elvira's right out front." He tossed a set of keys in Cori's direction and she caught them without thought.

"Elvira?" she asked.

"Your dad's Caddy." Noah's smile was full of affection. "She's clean and filled up and should run for at least a couple of months, but if you have any trouble, just bring her down."

Her dad's Caddy. That was named Elvira. That Noah had kept for them. "Just a couple of months?" Cori asked.

"She's an old lady," Noah said. "But she's tough. Just needs a little loving nudge once in a while to keep going."

Cori nodded and smiled at him. "Well, thanks."

Then he disappeared through the door too.

"We have a Cadillac," she said to her sisters.

"And an employee," Brynn added.

Ava ignored the subject of Parker entirely. "Guess we can send the limo home then." She seemed disappointed.

Cori laughed. "I'm guessing our commute from the house to here isn't long enough for a conference call anyway."

"Conference calls you're not supposed to be having," Brynn added.

"I can still have calls," Ava said. She frowned at Evan. "I'm not CEO and I have to make pies, but the trust didn't say anything about not working for Carmichael Enterprises at all."

He nodded. "But don't get too many things scheduled on your calendar," he said.

"Why not?"

"Because your *boyfriend* is going to be taking you out and making sure you have some fun, remember?"

Ugh. Cori remembered. And hated it more every time she heard it.

"Right." Ava, on the other hand, seemed exasperated. "Fine. But we need to put together a schedule for things so that I know when I can work and when I can't."

Evan shook his head. "That's part of the deal. A little less planning, a little more spontaneity in your life."

"Argh!" Ava ran a hand through her hair and looked around the kitchen again. "Let's get out of here for now. I can't start making anything without supplies."

"There should be enough here to get started," Evan said. "After all, Rudy was baking up until a couple of days before he..." Evan trailed off, cleared his throat, and finished, "...up until just a couple of weeks ago."

For a moment Evan looked overcome. But Cori made herself stay put. It would not be a good idea to grab her sister's boyfriend and hug him tightly. But damn, it was difficult. She wasn't very good at squelching her urges.

"I'm just going to pretend that there's a really good reason for me not to dive right in to baking today," Ava said. "You know, other than the fact that I have no idea what I'm doing and will likely suck at it."

And then Evan, being the nice, sweet guy that he was, stepped toward his girlfriend, put an arm around her shoulders, and said, "I'm guessing you're not used to not knowing what you're doing and sucking at things."

Ugh. Yuck.

Ava smiled up at him. "No, not really."

Gross.

Evan squeezed her and started for the door with his arm around her. "You're going to be fine. It's just pies. You can do this. And we're all here for you."

Ick.

Cori hung back, took a couple of deep breaths, gave herself a pep talk about only wanting Evan because Ava had him, and then started after them.

But when Evan kissed Ava goodbye on the lips, beside the limo, in full view of the diner, Cori actually said the *ugh* out loud. And then had to tell Brynn that it was nothing.

The limo had to go to the house since all of their bags were in it, but Cori volunteered to drive Elvira home. Evan gave the limo driver the address and directions—which were, "go a couple of blocks, take a left, it's the fourth house on the right", and then stepped back as they pulled away.

Cori was scrambling to get into Elvira before he came over and said something sweet and flirtatious to *her*. She wasn't even sure he was aware of the fact that he was flirting with two sisters. Because *ugh*. Even if one was pretend. Though it didn't seem entirely pretend with Ava. It seemed like Evan Stone just couldn't shut it off.

"Need help?" he asked as she failed, again, to get the key to unlock the door.

She fumbled with the keys. "Nope, I'm good." Then they dropped to the ground. Well, who the hell had old-fashioned car keys anymore? What happened to keyless entry and fobs and stuff?

She bent to retrieve them, but Evan got there first. He rose with the keys in hand. "You sure?"

"Absolutely sure," she said, focusing on the car door instead of him as he inserted the key, turned it, and opened the lock.

He pulled the door open and stepped back to let her in. But before she slid into the seat, he moved in close. "Cori."

Don't look up. Seriously.

But she did. "You shouldn't stand like that," she told him.

"Why?"

"Because it looks like you're going to kiss me. And you can't."

His gaze flickered to her mouth. Then he sighed. And didn't deny that's what he'd been thinking about. And stepped back.

Cori managed to shake her head and shut down the *say to hell with it and kiss me anyway* thought. "I'd better go or Brynn will claim the best bedroom without drawing a single straw."

"You girls draw straws to make decisions?"

"Yeah, but we always make sure she wins anyway," Cori said, sliding into the seat.

"You let Brynn win?" Evan asked. "Why?"

"Because she never asks for anything or makes any demands," Cori said. "And she's going to be stuck living with me and Ava in the same house for the next three hundred and sixty-five days. She deserves the best bedroom." She started the car as Evan laughed.

"Well, look at it this way, today's more than half over. It's more like three hundred and sixty-four days."

Right. But who was counting? Oh, just the girl who had to resist this guy for at least one hundred eighty-two days.

5

It wasn't right for a guy to think "oh, shit" when he saw his mother. But that was exactly what went through Evan's mind when he saw his mother approaching the pie shop from the opposite direction three days later.

In part, because she was with Jill's mother, Holly, and Jill's best friend, Liz.

And in part, because he was lying to her about his relationship with the woman who she was no doubt heading to the shop to meet.

Evan lengthened his strides and managed to reach the women on the sidewalk before they got to the pie shop door. "Hi, Mom," he said with a huge smile. "Ladies." He gave them all a quick smile as he leaned in and kissed his mother's cheek. "What are you doing here?"

Diane Stone looked a little sheepish having been caught trying to meet her son's girlfriend without him present. "We decided we were in the mood for pie," she said, glancing at her longtime friend, Holly.

Holly nodded. "We were so happy to hear that the pie shop was open again."

"They're not open again just yet," he said focusing on his mother and trying to sound regretful that he was going to thwart this particular attempt to ambush Ava. "Soon. The girls are working hard to get it cleaned up and ready for business again."

"Are you *sure* they're not open?" Holly asked, looking past Evan's shoulder to the front of the shop. "There sure are a lot of people in there."

Evan glanced toward the huge window as well. Then paused. There definitely were a lot of people in there. And one of them was Cori Carmichael. And she was, finally, in blue jeans. Kind of. She wore what looked like they'd once been jeans but had been cut off for shorts. The white fringes hung from the bottoms, brushing long, smooth, tanned thighs. Thighs that were streaked with green and pink paint that matched the façade of the pie shop. She was also wearing a fitted baby-blue tank top with a long sleeved white button-down shirt—also streaked with green and pink—open over it. Her hair was piled on top of her head in a messy bun, but a long strand escaped as she tipped her head back and laughed.

Holy. Shit. For a second Evan couldn't think of anything other than that. But the next second it hit him that he'd been coming to see her. That shouldn't have been a revelation, of course. He should know why he was going somewhere. He'd left his office and turned in this direction with the purpose of coming to the pie shop. But he'd ignored the fact that he'd wanted to see Cori. Not Ava. The woman he was supposed to be dating. The woman he was now going to have to act boyfriend-ish with in front of his mother and two women who would really like for him to *not* be serious about Ava. *Dammit.*

"Weren't you on your way in?" Holly asked.

He had been. Because Parker had called to tell him that the back door of the pie shop and the back door of the diner were both open and he'd heard glass breaking and swearing coming from the pie shop's kitchen. When Evan had asked why Parker didn't go check on things, he'd laughed and said that was above his pay grade. Since Evan didn't know, without looking it up, what Parker was getting paid as the manager of Blissfully Baked, he couldn't argue.

And it had been the perfect excuse to come down and see his girlfriend's sister.

Evan rolled his eyes. "I am," he finally answered. "Had a break and wanted to see how the cleanup is going."

"Well, even if there's no pie, coffee sounds good," Holly said. "And it looks like they're serving that."

Evan was able to look back in the window and not just see Cori this time. Now he took a quick attendance and realized that all of the guys who used to hang out with Rudy were inside. Parker had to be happy about that at least. They weren't taking up booth space and wanting constant refills at the diner.

"I guess it does," Evan had to admit.

"Oh, and while we have you, we'd love to have you over for dinner tomorrow night. Your mom and dad are coming too," Holly said.

Diane nodded.

"I'll have to see if Ava has plans for us," Evan said. She would. He'd make sure of it. "But maybe."

"Oh. Ava," Holly said. "I guess I was thinking it would be nice to have *you* over to catch up. It's been a while."

Evan lifted an eyebrow. "Just you and Larry and mom and dad and me?" he asked, knowing that was not what she'd meant.

"And Jill, of course," Holly said.

Yep, *that* was what she'd meant.

"She might be leaving in a few days, you know," Holly added.

He definitely caught the *might*. And the unspoken words *unless something changes her mind.*

Evan gave her a smile. "I don't know how Ava would feel

about me having dinner with a beautiful woman I have a history with."

"Oh, you and Ava are really that serious already?" Holly asked. "She got you on a short leash quickly."

"Well, maybe she knows how much *wandering* he does," Liz said. "Even as recently as a couple of weeks ago."

Technically, Jill had "wandered" over to his place, but he didn't think pointing that out was a great idea. Both Holly and Liz were looking at him with barely disguised disdain. Evan sighed. He couldn't even blame them. He'd slept with Jill and, according to the rumor already going around town, broken her heart. The whole story about him, Jill, and Ava had been startlingly easy to spread. And it seemed the town in general had no trouble believing that Evan had done Jill wrong. But it was, apparently, harder for them to believe that it was because he was madly in love with someone else.

He definitely needed to sell the idea that he'd already been interested in Ava because of the things Rudy had told him and that it had become much more once they'd met. For one, because while Jill was the leaving town, on to bigger and better things, Holly and Liz weren't. Ever. And they could make his life very unpleasant if they held a grudge. For another, the more skeptical everyone seemed over his ability to actually have real feelings for a woman, the more determined he became to prove to them that he was, in fact, capable of a committed, adult relationship.

And then he remembered that he and Ava were faking the whole thing. And then he became even more determined to actually *be* a boyfriend to Ava. Maybe not in the usual sense of the word—at least in *his* usual sense of the word—but he could be there for her as she went through this transition in her life, help her adjust to living in a small town and running a new business, and make sure she relaxed and had fun too.

In fact, he had to. That was part of their deal.

"This thing with Ava...was unexpected..." Well, that was true.

"...for me too." He glanced at the window and saw Cori, a hand propped on her hip, talking to the men at the table, all of whom seemed to be hanging on her every word. "It's amazing how quickly a bond can be formed, though," he said, *not* talking about Ava.

Cori was going to be a definite wrench in his Ava plan. Of course. Because he was naturally drawn to fun. Especially when he was *supposed* to be doing something responsible.

"You're not just filling in as the guy she needs to date to get her millions of dollars?" Liz asked.

He turned his attention back to the women on the sidewalk. "It's billions, actually," he corrected dryly. Then added, "And once you meet Ava Carmichael, I think you'll agree that she doesn't need to ask anyone to 'fill in' for that. Or for any other occasion. Ever."

That was true enough. Ava had agreed to this plan because it was a simpler means to the end. Not because she wouldn't have had any other eager, temporary-boyfriend candidates. The guys in Bliss would have been lining up to spend six months with her.

"I went to New York to help her and her sisters understand the will, and I was prepared to be their liaison for anything they needed here, and their friend. But once we met, it became much more." That was true too. They'd met and formed this plan. Which was more than just showing her around town or keeping track of the trust from a legal perspective.

It was him spending time with and committing to a woman for more than sex. Or, more accurately, for something *other than* sex. It was her settling him down and teaching him to be a boyfriend and not just a hookup, dammit.

Which was not something Cori could help him with.

Evan frowned. Where had that come from? That thought was completely unwelcome and probably unfair. He only knew what Rudy had told him about Cori, and he got the impression that neither Rudy nor Cori had really known the other that well. And just because Rudy had mentioned that Evan and Cori had a lot in common didn't mean they had *everything* in common. Evan only went for short-term flings and fun, but that didn't mean she did. And hell, there was nothing wrong with that anyway. She was a gorgeous, adventurous woman who liked to have a good time. So what if she didn't know how to make a commitment or have a long-term relationship? He was hardly one to judge.

And none of it mattered at all. *Ava* was the one he was involved with. With Ava, it was a win-win situation. Cori and her feelings about relationships and settling down had nothing to do with him. Even if it felt like it all really mattered anyway.

"Anyway, I definitely shouldn't be having dinner with another woman," he told Holly. That was also true. He was serious *enough* about this relationship with Ava and what it meant for both of them to not fuck it up. He hoped.

"Well, then I'm even more interested to meet her. Since we also haven't seen you out together. At all," Holly said.

Right. The public appearance thing. The being in love in front of people. They were going to have to do that. Convincingly. Evan nodded. "She's been very busy, relocating her life here, getting the shop up and running, dealing with her grief."

He'd laid that on a little thick, but Holly did have the decency to look slightly abashed with that reminder of all that Ava was going through.

"Of course," Holly said, her tone gentler now.

"Maybe we should come back another time," Diane said.

Evan gave her a grateful smile. "That might be best. Maybe next week sometime." After he'd had a chance to talk to Ava about how they were going to act in public. It might be best for them to not be overly touchy-feely. That would require less acting and would mean less chance of screwing something up. Ava was beautiful, but they didn't have much chemistry. Every bit of *this won't be so bad* that he'd felt in the hallway outside of her apartment had been because it was really Cori that he was feeling it with.

And there he was with Cori on his mind again. Or still.

"If you're this serious, then there's no reason for her not to say hello to your mother," Holly said, pushing past him. "We won't stay long."

Evan sighed. Ava was a bright woman. She knew what was going on. Surely she'd be able to act happy to see him. "Fine. A quick hello." He put a hand on his mother's back and steered her around Holly to the door. When he pulled it open, he was surprised by the merry tinkle of a bell overhead. He looked up. Rudy had never had a bell. Then he was hit by the smell of fresh paint.

He hadn't been able to see the entire shop through the window...okay, that wasn't true. He hadn't looked past Cori to see anything else about the shop.

Now the scene inside made him think of a preschool. There were bright pastel colors everywhere, it was a huge mess, several voices were talking at once, and someone was saying, "Okay, hold up your cups if you want more" in an upbeat, yet firm voice.

He zeroed in on that voice. Cori. She was refilling the coffee cups that had been hoisted into the air over one of the tables. That table had been pushed to the side, off of the huge plastic drop cloths that covered everything else. There were buckets of paint, brushes, two ladders, a long-handled roller, several rags, and paint trays scattered throughout the room. The wall behind the counter had been painted a robin egg blue, the wall to his left was the same green as the front of the shop, the wall behind him —he noted as he turned to take it all in—was a sunshine yellow, and Brynn was up on a step stool painting the last wall bubblegum pink.

"Hi."

He focused on Cori again. She was coming toward him with a

bright smile and a coffeepot. Two of his favorite things. Smiles and coffee. Not *Cori* and coffee. No, of course not.

"Hi."

"What do you think?"

"I think it looks like a rainbow tornado hit the place," he said with a grin.

She nodded and laughed. "Right? But hey, if the town likes bright colors, we thought, why not? The trim and the floor will be white. So will the chairs and tables, but we're going to do different colored cushions on the chairs. Mix it up. Like a giant crayon box got dumped out."

Her grin was contagious. "I didn't know you were open for business," Evan said, looking pointedly at the men sitting at the table.

She shrugged. "The door was unlocked, these guys came in and asked if I had coffee, which of course I did, and so they pulled out chairs and sat down."

"She asked me if I wanted caramel and cream in mine," Walter said. "I said I'd never tried it and she said that she couldn't let me leave here without at least one cup."

Evan grinned. "And?"

"Maybe the best thing I've ever tasted," Walter said. "Then again, I'm pretty sure Cori could make anything taste good."

Great. Cori had a fan club. As if he was surprised. It hit him that Cori had the same openly accepting and warm air that Rudy had always had. He knew that she wasn't aware of that commonality with her father. And he really wanted her to know that. He wondered if that was part of why these men were so drawn to her. It was clear that they were. Sure, the short shorts didn't hurt, but Cori's wide smile and willingness to drop her work for a cup of coffee and some conversation were definitely a lot of it.

Cori laughed. "I think the paint fumes are getting to them," she said. Then she whispered, still loud enough for them all to hear, "I figured the fumes would get rid of them actually, but they've been here for over an hour."

Evan gave her a once-over, which he made sure she noticed, then turned to where Brynn was stretching up to paint a high spot on the wall. She also wore shorts and her T-shirt pulled away from the waistband as she reached.

"Hot girls and hot coffee?" he asked. "They're never going to leave."

"Well, maybe we have our new marketing plan," Cori said. "Like Hooters only with pie and coffee."

"I'm in," Walter told her.

"You'll be rich," Hank agreed.

Evan couldn't help but laugh at the irony of that statement.

"Now you need to invest in a cappuccino machine or one of those fancy espresso things?" he asked.

"Can't afford it," Cori said. She tipped her head to the side. "Did you know that we're broke, by the way?"

Ah. She'd been doing her job with the books and had made a visit to the bank. Yes, he did know that the pie shop account was dry. But Rudy had told him that the girls were supposed to figure everything out themselves. "Rudy and I—"

"Ahem."

His mother elbowed him in the side and Evan realized he'd forgotten about the women who had accompanied him inside. Damn. But they were a great reason to not delve into the pie shop business right now. And the fact that he hadn't warned the triplets about the financial situation. "Oh, hey, Cori, I'd like you to meet my mom, Diane. Mom, this is Cori, one of Ava's sisters."

"Hello, dear," Diane said. "It's very nice to meet you."

"Evan's mom?" Cori repeated. "Wow! It's really nice to meet you too!"

"And this is her friend, Holly," Evan said. "Her daughter Jill is a classmate and good friend of mine."

Would Cori remember the conversation in the hallway

outside of Ava's apartment in New York? Would she realize who Jill was?

"Oh, Evan told me about Jill." She grabbed Holly's hand and pumped it up and down. "It's amazing that she's a wildlife vet. She must be so smart. He is really proud of her and the new job she's going to be starting. I totally got sucked into that giraffe cam thing they had at that animal park in New York," she said. "Does Jill work with giraffes?"

"Penguins, actually," Holly said, looking a bit flummoxed.

Evan was impressed. Cori had managed to warmly welcome Holly, compliment her daughter, make Evan look like a great friend, and strike Holly practically speechless all at once.

"Oh, penguins are so cool," Cori said. Then she flashed Evan a grin and a wink. "Get it? So cool?"

Holly actually laughed too and Evan felt a wave of affection for Cori that he couldn't quite understand. She was...something.

"Jill and Evan have been friends their entire lives," Liz interjected. "They've always been close. It will be hard for her to be away from him."

Evan sighed. "Cori, this is Liz. One of Jill's best friends."

Cori nodded at her. "Hey, he must have that effect," Cori said. "Ava was a *bitch* to live with for those few days when Evan came back to Bliss and we were still in New York."

Evan bit back a smile. And the urge to kiss Cori. He had no doubt Ava had been hard to live with as they packed up their lives for a trip to Kansas they hadn't expected and didn't want, but missing him had nothing to do with it.

"But I've got to ask you something," Cori said, moving closer to Liz and dropping her voice, even though everyone in the place could still hear every word.

The men drinking coffee at the table had gone silent. Evan rolled his eyes.

"What?" Liz asked.

"Well, in a town this size, since there aren't that many people your age, do you all just eventually hook up at some point or another? I mean, I figure that must be the way it is."

Clearly Cori had figured out that Jill wasn't the only classmate and longtime friend that Evan had messed around with. Suddenly Evan had the urge to pinch her. The brat. Maybe right on the ass. Or spank her. On that ass that looked like it was made to wear cut-off denim...

Liz's cheeks got pink, but she said, "Yeah, kind of."

Cori nodded. "I knew it. I mean, Evan and Noah—"

She waved her hand in Noah's direction, and Evan realized for the first time that his friend was even in the room. He had to have been out of the room when Evan had first walked in. But he was now rolling pink paint onto the wall right next to Brynn. How had Evan not noticed him coming into the room? Noah wasn't exactly small. The ex-marine stood six-one and was wide and muscled. He was generally pretty quiet, and he supposed Noah's training had taught him to be stealthy and stuff—Evan wouldn't really know since Noah never, ever talked about his time in the Marines —but damn.

Of course, Cori Carmichael did have a way of pulling all the attention to her. At least *his* attention.

"—and Parker," Cori went on. "I mean, you have some very hot guys here. No way would I be able to keep my hands to myself if I'd grown up here."

Yep, she was definitely why he hadn't even noticed his friend painting a wall pink.

Liz's cheeks were even redder now, but she was smiling. "We do have some really great guys here." She'd married one of those great guys she'd gone to school with, in fact.

Cori sighed dramatically. "Too bad I'm taking a dating hiatus," she said.

"Your dad said that you really like dating," Hank said as he took a drink of his coffee.

Cori turned to him with an arched eyebrow. "Did he now? I'm not sure it's very gentlemanly of you to repeat gossip about me."

Hank chuckled. "Nobody's ever accused me of bein' a gentleman, darlin'."

Cori's face broke into a huge grin. "Then you're just my type, Hank. Too bad I'm taking a break."

Damn, no wonder they were all in love with her. Not only was she gorgeous but she had this...light. Something that seemed to glow from inside her that made a person want to get closer.

Or maybe that was just him.

All of the men at the table laughed at that, and Roger said, "I think you'd kill him on date one, Cori."

Hank nodded. "But what a way to go."

Okay, not just him.

Cori laughed, without so much as a faint blush, Evan noted, and said, "Well, I kind of like you, Hank. How about we keep our relationship about dark roast and caramel syrup and keep you alive?"

Hank held up his cup. "As long as we've got whipped cream too, darlin'."

Hearing Hank, who was seventy-one and widowed, call Cori *darlin'* annoyed Evan. Strangely. And stupidly.

But Cori winked at Hank and said, "There's not much that I do that doesn't involve whipped cream."

And suddenly it hit Evan that he was incredibly happy about her dating hiatus. He couldn't handle Cori dating the town of Bliss. With—or without—whipped cream.

Cori focused on Evan and the ladies with him, who were all watching her with avid fascination. "But thankfully, Ava's *not* taking a hiatus and she grabbed this guy right up," Cori said, gesturing at Evan with her thumb. "I'm guessing he's got a waiting list of girls."

Okay, now that was a little close to the situation with Jill possibly. She really was a brat. Evan's gaze dropped to her ass again.

"He does," Liz said with a nod. "Except that Evan isn't the settling-down type."

"Oh?"

"He enjoys dating, but he doesn't take anything too seriously," Holly said as if Evan wasn't standing right there. "In fact, there have been many times over the years that his grandfather has said that the only thing Evan takes seriously is not taking anything seriously."

His grandfather had definitely said that. Still, it was not okay that his mother's best friend was warning his girlfriend's sister that he wasn't a good risk. "Holly," Evan started, "I don't think—"

"Well, then, everyone knows where he stands and no female hearts are getting their hopes up for a diamond ring, right?" Cori interrupted.

Whoa. Evan looked at her. But she was staring Holly down. Still, that was...the most defense anyone had given him in a long time.

"I mean, if Evan's always been the fun-loving guy who doesn't get serious, then the girls who...go out with him..." she said, clearly indicating that she didn't mean *only* going out with him, "...shouldn't be surprised when he's that same guy the next morning, right?"

Yep, she knew exactly what Holly was getting at. And it was definitely getting harder to fight the urge to kiss her. Evan could feel the surprise radiating from Holly and he had to bite back a grin. He turned, grabbed a chair from the next table, and pulled it up between Hank and Walter. This was getting good.

The guys scooted a little to make more room and, almost as if she did it on autopilot, Cori grabbed a cup from behind her, filled it with coffee, squirted caramel syrup into it, and then added a swirl of whipped cream from the dispenser she'd obviously brought from New York. He grinned and lifted the cup for a sip.

Then sat back in the chair, crossed one ankle over the other knee, and waited for the show to go on.

"Then your sister is aware of who he's going to be...in the morning?" Holly asked.

Holly gave him an irritated look, but he'd perfected *not* reacting to jabs about his personality and habits years ago. If he could withstand digs from his own grandfather, Holly had nothing in her arsenal that could get to him.

"Oh, no doubt about it," Cori said. "Evan's been very up-front about what he wants from Ava."

Well, that was true enough. Evan sipped again. And the girl made delicious coffee.

"Your sister doesn't take things seriously either?" Holly asked. "She has a penchant for...sprinkles...too?" Her tone and the way her eyes dropped to the coffee cups on the table in front of her, made it clear that *sprinkles* meant all kinds of unflattering and unserious things.

Cori leaned over and shook some sprinkles on top of Evan's cup. "Oh, Evan doesn't want sprinkles from Ava." She mimicked Holly's tone perfectly on "sprinkles", making it just as clear that she knew that Holly had meant it as an insult. And that Cori didn't care.

And it was true that he didn't want, or intend to get, sprinkles of any kind from Ava. Sure, he'd entertained the thought of a fling when he'd had her pushed up against the front door of her apartment and had been kissing the hell out of her. But then again, that had actually been *Cori*. And her sprinkles were a whole other thing.

Holly sniffed. "Well, Evan definitely needs fewer *sprinkles* in his life. He needs..."

"Plain coffee?" Cori supplied when Holly trailed off, unable to complete the analogy.

Evan had to cough to hide his chuckle. The men around the table were all watching, obviously taking mental notes to share with everyone they ran into later. Even Noah and Brynn had stopped painting to turn and watch. Liz looked a little uncomfortable, but she was watching Cori with a hint of admiration. And Diane had inched closer to the door.

A flash of irritation went through him. Just once, he'd love for his mother to stand up to someone. Even if it was *him*. She had never told him not to do something or that she was displeased with him. She'd left the stern lectures to his grandfather. She'd never once grounded Evan or even withheld his allowance. He hadn't been a bad kid, but he'd, as Holly pointed out, never taken things very seriously—including school and chores and schedules and rules.

"I was going to say, he needs a nice girl to settle him down," Holly said.

Cori shrugged. "I get it. But the thing is, when you combine coffee and sprinkles, the coffee doesn't make the sprinkles less fun. The coffee becomes sweeter and more enjoyable because of the sprinkles."

"What are you getting at?" Liz asked, her eyes narrowing.

"Evan is the sprinkles," Cori said, as if it was obvious.

Evan swallowed his coffee down the wrong pipe and coughed hard. Hank reached over and thunked him on the back, without ever taking his eyes off of Cori and Holly.

He was the sprinkles? But as he coughed again and finally cleared some of the coffee from his windpipe, he realized that yeah, he was.

"Well, 'sprinkles' can make a big mess," Holly pointed out with a frown.

Evan's eyes, and everyone else's, dropped to the table where there were sticky spots of whipped cream and caramel, and sure enough, several stray sprinkles all over the surface. Evan had to admit that he was impressed that she'd been able to make *that* analogy.

"No doubt about it," Cori agreed. "And if you can't deal with the potential mess, you shouldn't choose sprinkles for your coffee in the first place. Or whipped cream. Or caramel syrup. You should stick with black coffee. In a cup with a lid. And one of those ring thingies that keep it from being too hot to hold."

There was a beat of silence after that comment. And the insinuations.

God, he really liked her. The thought seemed to jump out of nowhere and smack Evan in the face. But yeah, he *really* liked Cori Carmichael.

"But *you* go for...sprinkles?" Holly asked.

Cori laughed. "Oh, I *always* want sprinkles on my whipped cream."

Heat shot through him at that seemingly simple, but oh-so complicated—and hot—comment. And Evan realized that he had a not-at-all-small crush on his fake girlfriend's sister.

"But there's so much more under all the toppings, right honey?" Hank asked with a wink.

Cori smiled, but shook her head. "No, not always. Sometimes it's just the fluffy, fun stuff."

As her words sank in, Evan felt his hand squeezing his mug so hard, he was shocked it didn't crack. There was so much meaning in what Cori had just said. He had no idea if everyone else in the room heard it, understood it, *felt* it. But he did.

And holy shit, he wanted to grab her and hug her and tell her that when the whipped cream and sprinkles were as good as hers, they became their own underneath.

"Maybe you and Evan both need to think about taking things more seriously," Holly finally said.

Okay, enough was enough. Evan shoved his chair back and stood.

But Cori was already talking, "I think Evan and I have a lot in common, but, I wouldn't say I don't take *anything* seriously. I mean, there's food. I *really* love food. And there's Robert Downey, Jr. I don't joke around about him. And," she said, her smile fading as she met Holly's eyes directly, "there are my sisters. I take them and their happiness very seriously. I'd feel sorry for anyone who screwed with that."

Holly's eyes widened, Liz coughed, and Diane glanced toward the door as if wondering if she could escape. Evan opened his mouth to interject—though he had no idea with what. Especially considering that he really liked the whipped-cream-loving Cori, but he felt a definite jolt of *damn* when she got serious and came to her sisters' defense.

Suddenly, fortunately, there was a loud crash from the kitchen, followed by a fervent, "*Fuck, fuck, fuck!*"

Evan saw Cori wince slightly, and the men around the table all picked up their cups, while Brynn and Noah returned to painting. All as if this wasn't the first time they'd heard those things from the kitchen.

Oh, yeah. The reason Parker had called Evan down here in the first place.

"And that would be my lovely girlfriend now," Evan said, breaking into the tense moment and hoping like hell they could now move on. Because that urge to hug Cori wasn't getting any weaker.

"Good Lord," Holly said.

"Yeah. She's a firecracker," Evan said with a tight smile.

There was a loud crash that sounded like metal hitting tile. Then another few expletives. Then it was quiet. The whole shop seemed to be holding its breath for a moment. Then Cori said, "Okay, who needs more coffee?" and three hands at the table shot up.

There was another loud crash from the back and Evan had to admit that, whatever she was doing in there, Ava had great timing.

"Should someone go check on her?" Diane asked, her eyes wide.

Cori and Brynn exchanged a look, then Cori set the coffeepot on the table, Brynn turned on her stool, and they quickly did *rock, paper, scissors.*

"Dammit," Cori breathed when she did scissors to Brynn's rock.

Brynn just grinned and went back to painting.

"Sure," Cori said with mock brightness. "I'll go check on her."

"Tell her we'd love to meet her," Holly said, moving to another table and pulling out a chair. "And I don't care for *whipped cream* or *sprinkles,* but I would love some plain black coffee."

"Shocker," Evan heard Cori mutter.

Then she opened her mouth to say something louder, but Evan took her elbow and turned her toward the kitchen. "They probably don't have enough cups, Holly. They weren't expecting to have customers today."

"Oh, they've got a bunch behind the counter," Ben said, pointing. "Cori had to bring her collection down here because Ava told her she didn't want them taking up all the space in the cupboards at Rudy's place."

"You have a cup collection?" Evan asked Cori.

"Just one from everywhere I've traveled."

He didn't let go of her elbow, enjoying touching her way too much. "How many?"

"Forty-seven."

He let out a quick laugh. "And you brought them all here with you?"

"I'm going to be living here for a *year.* Of course I did." She smiled. "The bright side is that we don't have to buy cups for the pie shop. And considering we have no money, that's awesome."

"Son of a bitch!"

He and Cori both sighed.

"You sure *you* don't just want to go in and talk to her?" Cori asked, hopefully.

Hell no, he wasn't going in there alone. He gave her a look

that his mother and friends couldn't see. "Maybe you could take over for her back there while she comes out and chats for a bit," he said. That wasn't ideal either. He wasn't sure Ava was in a mood to make a good impression. And this would be their first real public appearance. In front of his mother. And two women who really wanted him and Ava to not work out. This was going to be great.

"But the kitchen is Ava's domain," Cori protested.

"Nice try," he said, for her ears only. "But no dice." Evan started for the kitchen with her elbow still in hand. "I'm sure Ava will appreciate your help," he said for the room.

He was definitely not facing Ava alone.

Cori sighed, but let him steer her into the kitchen. "Help yourself to coffee," she called out behind her.

"She has chocolate syrup too," Walter said.

"Of course she does," Evan thought he heard Holly mutter.

They stepped through the swinging door to the kitchen just as the back door to the kitchen slammed shut. The swinging door bumped Evan from behind as he and Cori stared at the back door.

Ava had just left.

And the kitchen was a disaster. There were bowls and spoons and measuring cups scattered over the countertops. There were four open egg cartons, all empty. There was a pile of apples next to the sink and the cupboard door under the sink was hanging open and water was slowly dripping from one of the pipes. The top of the oven was covered in pies. Or what should have been pies. Three were clearly burnt. One looked fine but had a hole dug out of the middle, as if someone had tasted it, and immediately abandoned it. And there was a fine dusting of flour over...everything.

"Wow," Evan said simply.

Cori blew out a breath. "Yeah, she really sucks at this."

"And you're not helping her?" Damn, the skin on the inner

side of her elbow was really soft and warm. And she smelled amazing.

Cori grinned at him. "Are you kidding? Did you hear the crashing and swearing?"

"Yeah, you could be helping her not swear and throw things, couldn't you?" he asked. If he had to guess he'd say Ava had thrown the metal mixing bowl that now lay on its side against the far wall.

"No way," Cori said. "She *needs* to yell and swear and break things."

"You *want* her doing that?"

"That girl has so much emotion wound up tight inside of her she's about to burst," Cori said. "This is therapeutic."

Evan looked around the room. "She's really this bad at cooking?"

"She had to Google 'whisking'," Cori said with a grin.

He turned to face her. This woman who had defended him to Holly, who seemed to just *get* him, who thought she only had fluff to offer. "*You* know how to whisk, though."

"Ava likes to figure things out for herself," Cori said with a shrug.

"Did you even offer?" he asked, somehow knowing she hadn't.

"She'd still look it up to be sure I was right."

Evan shook his head. "Then you *tell her* that you're right and insist she start trusting you."

Cori swallowed and stared up at him. "There might be a better way," she said with a shrug.

"A better way to whisk?" he asked. "Better than your way?"

She nodded. And he knew that she knew that this wasn't about whisking. And that she wasn't talking about Ava doubting Cori's knowledge or skill. He suddenly hated that Rudy was taking this woman out of the kitchen, where she could show off her talents and get enthusiastic. Instead, she was adding and subtracting columns of numbers.

What a waste.

Evan's phone dinged in his pocket and he reluctantly let go of Cori to reach for it. It was a text from Parker.

Come remove this woman from my kitchen.

Oh, boy.

"Ava's over at the diner. In Parker's kitchen," he told Cori.

Cori looked around the room. "Okay, tell him to send her home. She's had enough of this for the day."

Evan typed that in and sent it, then paused. "If she goes home, she can't meet Holly and my mom."

Cori lifted a brow. "Do you really want her to in this mood?"

Of course he didn't.

Parker responded *She wants eggs. She came and took butter earlier. I'm not supporting the grocery bill for that pie shop.*

Evan sighed. *Send her home or keep her busy. She can't come back over here. My mom's here.*

What am I supposed to do with her?

Teach her to whisk something. Evan grinned in spite of himself as he sent that and tucked his phone into his pocket.

"If they don't meet her now, they'll find her somewhere else, another time, when I'm not around," Evan said to Cori. "I'd feel better if I was there to mediate the situation."

Cori pulled her bottom lip between her teeth. Her eyes roamed over his torso from shoulders to waist.

Evan felt his body stirring, even with just her eyes on him. "Cori?"

She stepped forward and ran her hand over his chest. "Take your shirt off."

Uh. Okay. Who was he to argue with...

Cori shrugged out of the shirt she was wearing over her tank top.

"Um, what are we doing?" Not that he was protesting.

"Take your shirt off," she repeated. Then she stripped her tank off.

And Evan's only thought was *should have grabbed the whipped cream gun.*

When he still hadn't moved, Cori stepped forward and started unbuttoning his shirt. His gaze dropped to the amazing breasts that were now cupped in peach silk. He'd subconsciously memorized the shape and feel of them when he'd seen them under the tank top and then had them pressed against his chest in New York.

Yeah, he wasn't going to be able to do something as complicated as unbuttoning.

"Cori?"

She looked up at him as she freed his last button and ran her hands up over his ribs to his shoulders where she pushed the shirt off. "Yeah?"

"I really like your *sprinkles*, but is this the best time for this?" *And when will be the best time, because I can be available whenever.*

Her mouth curled into a half smile. "I like your sprinkles too, Counselor. But right now we need to convince Holly, and everyone else, that you're crazy about *Ava's* sprinkles."

Ava. Right. The reason that there wasn't going to be a best time for him and Cori. Fuck.

She reached behind her and grabbed a plastic measuring cup. She threw it on the floor, where it bounced and then slid up again the oven. "Dammit." She looked around, grabbed a glass bowl and chucked it, sending it arching and then crashing into the floor. She smiled at that. "Better."

"What the hell are you—"

But all thoughts of, well, everything else in the world, were obliterated by the feel of Cori's hands untucking the T-shirt he wore under his dress shirt and sliding up underneath to touch his bare skin.

"I really need you to take this off," she said, her voice huskier than it had been before.

And he officially didn't care who walked in or who thought

what or even what was going on. Because Cori was going to reach behind her and unhook her bra next. Evan reached behind his head, grabbed the back of his T-shirt and yanked it off.

Cori's gaze tracked over him and she started to lift a hand, but seemed to think better of it at the last minute. Instead, she held her hand out. "Can I have it?"

"My T-shirt?"

She nodded and he handed it over. Her eyes stayed on his chest as she put her hands through the armholes of his shirt and then pulled it over her head. So no naked breasts. Great.

"What are you doing?" he asked as the white cotton draped over the body that he officially wanted to never have covered again, ever.

She tugged the neck hole until the shirt hung off one shoulder and then tied a knot in the bottom, making it hug her waist. "Changing my clothes as much as I can," she said. She stepped past him and took an apron from the hook beside the door. She put it over her head and tied it behind her. "They need to think I'm Ava."

"Oh." He looked at the swinging door.

"She's not here and we don't really want her back in this mood. But I can stand in for her."

"Oh," he said again. He supposed that would work. He shrugged back into his dress shirt.

Then Cori reached up and pulled on something, causing her hair to tumble down. The wild waves cascaded past her shoulders, and Evan felt his cock stir again.

Without thinking, he reached up and threaded his fingers into her hair at the base of her head. Cori seemed to freeze. He drew his fingers through the warm, silky tresses, untangling them. "No one's ever going to believe you're Ava," he said, his voice strangely rough.

"They will," she said softly, with a nod.

"You're...too...different." That wasn't really what he'd meant to say, but how did he go on and on about how much freer and warmer and happier Cori was without seeming like an obsessed idiot? Which he feared he was becoming where this woman was concerned.

Cori's eyes softened for a moment, but she shook her head. "You just don't know her."

Of course Cori would defend Ava.

"I'm way more attracted to you than I am to her," Evan confessed. "They'll be able to tell the difference when I'm with her."

The heat in her eyes flared, but she shook her head. "People see what they want to see. If we make this first impression, then that's what they'll see in the future even if there's less..."

She trailed off and Evan smiled slightly. He didn't think Cori was at a loss for words very often. He knew she was right about people seeing what they expected to see. At least at times. Yet, he suddenly hated that in her experience people didn't look deeper. But they didn't have time to go into all of that at the moment.

"Less heat?" he supplied. "Less chemistry? Less chance that someone is going to end up with flour all over her bare ass?"

She lifted an eyebrow, and he looked at the flour-covered countertop and then back to her.

She swallowed and nodded. "Yeah, less of...*that*."

"We're going to go out there and you pretend to be Ava long enough to satisfy them and get rid of them," he said. He looked at the door again.

"Do you think that you can act like you're crazy about me?" she asked. "Act like *we're* the ones who fell head over heels so quickly?"

Evan looked down at her and felt a jolt that went from his chest through his gut. He cleared his throat and said, "Yeah, I think I can pull that off."

Cori broke the eye contact, reached for some flour and

dashed it onto her cheek and chin. "Okay, then. Let's go introduce your mom to your new girlfriend."

———

W hat the hell was she doing?

Oh, yeah, playing a very dangerous came of pretend. Pretend to Be Crazy About the Guy You're Crazy About While Pretending To Be Your Sister.

Yeah, nothing could go wrong here.

But Cori pasted on a bright smile, then dialed it back about three notches so it was more like an Ava smile, and pushed her way through the swinging doors with Evan's hand in hers.

"Hi, everybody," she greeted, sounding exactly like Ava. It wasn't like this was the first time they'd pretended to be one another. Switching Places was Chapter One in the How to Be An Identical Twin or Triplet handbook.

"Everyone, this is Ava," Evan said, wrapping his big, warm arm around her waist and resting his hand possessively on her hip.

And Cori had to bite back a moan. Stripping off their shirts together had been spontaneous and she hadn't thought of the consequences—like raging lust after seeing his chest and abs—before she'd done it. Which was typical. Thinking through consequences was *not* a strength of hers.

She caught Brynn's eye. Her sister arched an eyebrow, but Cori knew she wouldn't blow her cover.

"Ava, it's very nice to meet you," Diane said. "I know you're busy. Thanks for coming to say hi."

"Well, of course." Cori thought for a second about hugging Diane. She was Evan's *mom* for God's sake. But Ava would never do that, so Cori held back. She turned her attention on Liz and stuck out her hand. Ava was definitely a hand shaker. "Hi."

Liz took it with a polite, "Hello. I'm Liz. I'm an old friend of Evan's."

Uh-huh. This woman had slept with Evan. Somehow Cori knew that Evan had messed around with a lot of girls in Bliss. And Jill's bestie was on that list. Liz had seen him naked. She'd had his hands on her... Cori tamped those thoughts down quickly. Clearly, it hadn't meant anything. And Cori wasn't the jealous type anyway.

And if she *was* going to be jealous of someone, it would be her sister, who, pretend or not, could be out here right now with Evan's hand on *her* hip and his big, hard body pressed up against her side, and his soft cotton shirt caressing *her* skin and surrounding her with his scent in a horribly wonderfully distracting way.

"Nice to meet you," Cori said, coolly and politely as Ava would.

"And this is Holly, Jill's mom," Evan said. Then he added, "The one I told you about."

Ah. Evan wanted an Ava response to Holly and her earlier bitchiness. Cori had been surprised by how blatant the woman had been about her disapproval of Evan and her suspicion about his relationship with Ava.

Okay, truthfully, she was probably right to be suspicious if Evan really was the laid-back playboy that it seemed he was. And okay, there wasn't really a relationship, so she was kind of right in that case. But the way she'd been all judgmental? And the way Evan's own mom hadn't stepped in? What the hell?

"Oh, yes, Mrs. Morris. I'm glad I have the opportunity to assure you that you don't need to worry about Evan getting his *sprinkles* on anyone else around here. I intend to keep them all to myself from here on out."

Yes, that was really more something that Cori would say. But they didn't know that. And the snooty voice she'd used was all Ava.

Holly was clearly taken aback. "I just hope that Evan can take this seriously enough for you."

"Well, I find it interesting that you're so sure he *can't*, yet you want him to be with your daughter," Cori said. Because that really was weird in her opinion.

"Jill and Evan would be great together," Holly said.

"Well, I think Evan, and Jill, both deserve better than great." Cori knew, even as she said it, that she was issuing a challenge. That her sister was going to have to meet. But she couldn't help it.

Holly lifted her chin. "I guess we'll see. I'd hate for you to have moved to a new town, started a new business, and a new relationship, just to see it all fall apart."

Cori felt Evan's fingers curl into her hip. "Holly," he said, his voice low and full of warning. But Cori had this. Or Ava did anyway.

"There's something about Ava Carmichael that you should probably know," she said, with complete honesty. "She's never *not* gotten something that she wanted and worked for." Talking about 'herself' in the third person was obnoxious, but it was all true. And that truth was what was keeping Cori optimistic about the pie shop that had no money in the bank, a loan to pay off, and— for now anyway—no baker.

"Then I hope it all works out," Holly said, her tone chilly.

Yeah, Cori did too. And if she was doing this on her own, she'd have her doubts. But she had Ava and Brynn. And Evan. He was definitely on their side. And that made her feel strangely better.

Holly stood up from her seat and stepped toward the door. "I've changed my mind about the coffee."

"Sorry to hear that," Cori said.

Holly clearly knew that she didn't mean it. "Liz, are you coming?"

"Sure." Liz smiled tightly at Evan and then Cori. "It was nice to meet you, Ava. Take care of him."

Cori hugged Evan against her, even as she felt like a piece of lead had settled in her chest. *She* wanted to take care of him. But not only did he not really want that, but she wasn't good at that.

Holly and Liz headed out the door and waited on the sidewalk for Diane to join them.

"I would love to get to know you better, Ava," Diane said. "Maybe lunch sometime."

This time when Cori felt Evan's fingers dig into her hip, she knew it was a warning. She smiled brightly and said, "I'd love that."

Evan's hand slid to her butt and he gave her a little pinch. She jumped, then smiled bigger to cover it.

"We'll set up a time then," Diane said. She looked at her son. "Can I walk with you back to your office?"

"Sure, Mom. I'll be right out."

Diane joined her friend on the sidewalk, and Evan turned to Cori.

"You're trouble," he said.

"You have no idea."

"Oh, I think I just might." Then he slid his hand into her hair, tipped her head back, and kissed her.

The kiss was definitely not a goodbye kiss. This was a see-you-later-and-you-better-meet-me-at-the-door-naked kiss. She took a fistful of Evan's shirt and arched closer. She ran her tongue along his lower lip and his resultant groan rocketed through her, settling low and deep and hot in her pelvis. He stroked along her tongue with his own and she could practically feel the just-wait-until-I-get-you-alone.

Finally, he broke the kiss, lifted his head, and stared into her eyes. "Well, I'm convinced," he said gruffly.

She ran her tongue over her tingling lips and asked, "Convinced of what?"

"That we're crazy about each other."

Oh. Yeah. Damn.

He let go of her, gave Noah and Brynn—who Cori had completely forgotten about—a brief wave and then sauntered out of the pie shop, joined his mother in front of the shop, turned back and gave her a wink, and then sauntered on down the sidewalk.

Cori lifted her hand to her lips as she watched him go.

Sprinkles, indeed.

6

I n possibly the strangest moment of their relationship, Cori sighed and told Ava, "I'm sorry, but no. I can't authorize this purchase."

Ava set her cup down with a *thunk*. "I need stuff."

"I can't sign off on buying a new oven right now," Cori said, wondering who she was becoming. She never said things like *no* and *can't afford*. "For three reasons."

She put a plate down in front of each of her sisters.

"What's this?" Brynn asked.

"S'mores pie," Cori told her with a smile. She'd never made it before, but it had been easy and had turned out perfectly.

"Are you trying to rub this baking thing I can't do in my face?" Ava asked, even as she picked up her fork and drug it through the toasted marshmallows on top of the chocolatey pie and lifted it to her lips.

"I'm really not," Cori said, "But I have some ideas for our menu. Adding easy, new pies. If we're talking about different promotions, like the sweetie pies, we could do kids' pies too. This and a peanut butter and jelly pie, for instance."

Okay, they hadn't been talking about different promotions,

and no one had mentioned the sweetie pies since Cori had the first day in the shop. Ava was completely consumed with learning to bake—when she wasn't on her computer and/or phone conducting Carmichael Enterprises business—and Brynn was working on making colorful cushions for the chairs in the shop. Making them because they couldn't afford to buy them or pay someone else to do it. Her genius-IQ sister had picked up sewing faster than her CEO sister was picking up whisking, but needles and thread were more than a little outside of Brynn's area of expertise, so it was slow going.

"When kids like eating somewhere, they talk their parents into going. Look at the burger chains with the toys in the kids' meals and the pizza places that have the games and stuff. Kids can get their parents in the door. And they're a cute way to expand the idea of a pie shop."

Cori stopped rambling as she watched Ava set her fork down and sigh. "I can't even do cherry."

"You'll get better," Cori assured her. She was seventy percent sure that was true. There were very few things that Ava couldn't do if she set her mind to it, but she was turning out to be completely terrible at pies. She didn't have the patience and she wasn't focused. She was always trying to do three other things at once, and Cori very much doubted if Ava's mind was on pies even when she was in the kitchen. And the more she messed up, the more frustrated she got and the less patience she had. Clearly, cooking and baking weren't going to be the fun, stress reliever for Ava that they were for Cori.

"I didn't even know you can toast marshmallows in the oven," Ava said, taking another bite of the marshmallows on her pie.

"Well, it's even easier if you have a blowtorch," Cori said with a grin.

Ava's eyes went wide. "A *blowtorch*?"

Cori nodded. "Yep."

"Where did you find a blowtorch in Bliss?" Brynn asked.

"I brought it with me," Cori said with a shrug. At her sister's amazed looks, she added, "You never know when you might need to make crème brulee." But it was kind of true. The top of the brulee was the hardest. She could use the broiler, but it wasn't as good as with a blowtorch.

Plus, blowtorches were more fun.

"See, I need *tools*," Ava said.

"Do you even know how to use a blowtorch?" Brynn asked around a bite of chocolate and graham cracker.

"Well, no. But I can't get better without proper...stuff," Ava said, with an uncharacteristic inability to find a more eloquent word.

"Ava, I mean with this all the love in my heart," Cori said. "But the problem with the pies is not the oven or the lack of tools and stuff."

Ava frowned and opened her mouth. Then she shut it and nodded. "I know."

Cori smiled at her good-at-everything sister. Well, her good-at-almost-everything sister. She hadn't liked the fact that Evan had shown that insight into Ava's personality. But that was more because she was stupidly jealous and that had seemed like a connection between them. She didn't want them to have a connection. There. She'd admitted it. But truthfully, that part of Ava's personality was obvious. To everyone.

"What are the other reasons not to buy a new oven?" Brynn asked. "I assume number one is because it won't make a difference in quality." Brynn just grinned as Ava stuck her tongue out at her.

Cori knew there were several CEOs around the country, maybe even the world, who would be shocked that classy, cool Ava Carmichael had *ever* stuck her tongue out at someone. Especially while wearing cut-off sweatpants and licking chocolate pie off of her index finger.

"Reason number two is that we don't have enough business to

justify the need for an industrial oven. Which goes with reason number three—we have no money," Cori said.

"Sometimes you have to invest in the business to increase revenue, right?" Brynn asked.

Ava nodded. "Sure. With a solid business plan, we should be able to justify some purchases."

Cori nodded and leaned back. "Sure. But we don't have a business plan." And neither sister had said, "that's brilliant!" to Cori's idea for kid-friendly pies. She hadn't even told them she thought they should make them smaller, kid-sized, and called them "kiddie pies" to go along with the "sweetie pies."

"We'll write one," Ava said.

Cori swallowed her sip of coffee and shook her head, trying not to show that even the mention of Evan's name, made her heart flutter. She wasn't the type to just sit around and want something. When she had an urge, of any kind really, she just went for it. So this thinking longingly about something, or someone, was very strange. She supposed there was a good lesson in there somewhere. Maybe wanting something she couldn't have would be character building or something.

"Not 'we'," she said to Ava. "You're not supposed to help with the business side of things. Dad put it in his note. But I don't need help anyway," Cori said. "It doesn't take long to add zero to zero. I have time to learn all about business plans." Which was, apparently, part of this whole crazy plan—for them to all *learn* things.

"Zero?" Brynn asked.

"Almost literally," Cori said. She leaned her elbows on the table. "We have six hundred dollars in the bank account and we owe on a loan and we haven't brought in any new money."

"A *loan?*" Ava had just run her finger through a bit of chocolate and paused with it partway to her mouth. "Dad took out a *loan?*"

Cori shrugged. "Yep. Went to the bank yesterday to go over everything."

Ava put her finger down without licking it, a sure sign of shock.

"Rudy Carmichael, one of the richest men in the country, took out a loan from a bank in Bliss, Kansas for a pie shop that's basically a hole in the wall?"

Cori nodded. She had to admit she was just as surprised, but for some reason...she liked it. It made things more complicated. They had to make the business profitable by the end of the year, and they weren't just starting from zero—they were in the negatives. But she liked that Rudy hadn't blown into town and started throwing money around. There was no Rudy Carmichael Memorial Sports Complex or a wing on a building or a street named after him. And yeah, even his own business was a hole in the wall. She liked that no one had known he was rich.

It surprised her, but she liked that too. It had been eighteen years since Rudy had surprised her in a good way. She'd been eleven and he'd given her a pair of purple boots she'd mentioned liking when they'd walked past them in a store window on Fifth Avenue. He'd turned her into the store and bought them then and there. She'd worn them nonstop for almost three weeks.

She'd given up hoping for another pair of purple boots— literal or figurative ones—but she had to admit that the pie shop was beginning to feel that way.

"We need to come up with about 10K," Cori said. "We owe five on the loan, then to pay for supplies and advertising and stuff. And of course electric...and all the eggs and sugar we keep going through."

Ava rolled her eyes.

"I've got a woman making valances for the front windows, but we need to pay for the material and her time," Cori went on.

"You've got a woman making us valances?" Ava asked.

Cori shrugged. "Walter's wife's sister. She's pretty inexpensive but not free."

Ava almost looked impressed. "How did you pay for the paint and stuff? I assumed you'd used the account."

"I applied for a business credit card online," Cori said. "I fudged and used my own bank account on the application even though we're not supposed to be spending our own money on the business. I figure we're not *spending* it. We're charging it and will pay it off with pie shop profit."

Ava's look of admiration grew.

"Fudging? Like when you kissed Evan?" Brynn asked. "Since kissing isn't really dating."

If it wasn't for the glint of mischief in Brynn's eyes, Cori would have been more irritated, but she really did like the little bits of spunk in her sister. Cori looked at Ava. She'd told Ava about pretending to be her for Evan's mom and Holly, but she hadn't shared the kissing part.

"You *kissed* Evan?" Ava asked. "When? Where?" Her voice grew panicked as she sat up straighter. "Cori! You can't do that! If I don't have a steady boyfriend for six months we're screwed. And I don't know if you cheating with my boyfriend will be great for business."

"Calm down," Cori said. "Everyone thought it was *you*. It was at the shop with his mom."

"Oh." Ava deflated slightly. She frowned. "What kind of kiss?"

Cori swallowed as the memory of the kiss played in her mind. She felt like she'd just rubbed hot sauce on her lips—tingly and hot.

And maybe dropped it on her nipples. And a little lower.

"It was hot," Brynn supplied when Cori didn't answer right away.

Ava groaned. "It was?"

"Very," Brynn confirmed. "His hand in her hair, her clutching his shirt, tiptoes, tongues—the whole thing. And everyone thought so. Noah did this 'damn' thing under his breath."

"Hey, yeah, you and Noah are hanging out a lot," Cori commented. "Is he date-boy number one?"

"No," Brynn said quickly. "Those aren't dates."

Cori lifted an eyebrow.

"*And*," Brynn added, "don't try to distract me from you and Evan."

"So, Noah distracts you," Cori said.

But Brynn shook her head. "Nice try. Let's talk about how you practically climbed Evan in the middle of the pie shop."

"I did not." But her protest was weak.

"Well, *crap*," Ava interjected.

"What? They all thought it was *you*," Cori insisted. "I promise Brynn and Evan were the only two who knew it was me."

"And Noah," Brynn added.

"Yes, Noah. Brynn's new best friend who she is *not* dating even though she sees him almost every day and he's doing stuff like painting and finishing chairs and tables, and even stitched the edges of some cushions the other day."

Brynn frowned. "How did you know that? No one was there."

"I noticed the Band-Aids on the tips of his fingers. He's a mechanic, good with his hands, I'm sure." She waggled her eyebrows, loving Brynn's slight blush. "The only reason he'd need Band-Aids is if he's using little tiny needles that he's not used to."

Brynn rolled her eyes. "He's a *mechanic*. He scrapes his knuckles and pinches his fingers all the time."

"No way does ex-Marine, mechanic extraordinaire Noah, use Teenage Mutant Ninja Turtles Band-Aids. Like the ones *you* bought the other day." Cori grinned as Brynn shifted on her chair.

"They were the only ones they had at the grocery store the other day," Brynn said.

"Did you kiss his fingers better when you put the Band-Aids on?" Cori asked.

Ava laughed. "I haven't minded having Noah around," she

said, adding to the teasing. "That guys looks very nice without a shirt while sanding and sawing and *pounding*."

The same CEOs who would have been shocked by her sticking out her tongue, would have probably fallen over, hearing Ava say *pounding* in a tone that clearly didn't mean nails.

Brynn's face was bright red—she was the only one of the triplets who blushed—and she said through gritted teeth, "Cori kissed the *hell* out of *your* boyfriend in front of his *mom*."

Ava's frowned. "Oh yeah. Dammit, Cori."

"What? I totally pulled it off," Cori said. "Everyone thinks you're crazy about each other. You're *welcome*."

"But now *I* have to kiss him like that," Ava exclaimed.

And Cori's stomach tightened. Well...crap.

"If you kiss like that in public, obviously you're all over each other in private. We have to keep up the hot and horny thing now," Ava said.

"I don't know if I'd say *horny*," Cori protested.

"I would," Brynn said cheerfully, obviously happy to have the conversation off of Noah and his half-naked pounding.

Ava shoved her pie away, hardly touched but for the marshmallows and two tastes of chocolate. "Dammit."

"It's not like I set you up to have to eat broccoli every day or something," Cori said, annoyed. Though she wasn't sure if it was because Ava would be kissing Evan, at least in public—which meant Cori might have to see it—or if it was because Ava didn't want to.

Which was *stupid*.

"But I *like* broccoli," Ava said.

"You don't like Evan?" Cori asked, actually feeling offended. She did not want Ava to kiss Evan. She did not want Ava to want to kiss Evan. But regardless of the kissing, Evan Stone was very likeable.

Ava blew out a breath. "Sure. I like Evan. Evan's fine. He's certainly easier to get along with than Parker." She scowled briefly.

"You don't like Parker?" Brynn asked. "He's growly but seems...nice." Though she said the last word as if that wasn't quite the right word.

Ava snorted. "Nice? Um, no. I saw someone ask for sugar the other day. When he found out they were going to put it in their tea, he took it away."

"The sugar?" Brynn asked.

"The tea. The whole glass."

Brynn's eyes were wide, but Cori grinned. "Hey, that can only be good for *our* business, right? The only other food place in town."

Ava suddenly slumped back. "I wouldn't call us that."

"You'll get the hang of the pie," Cori said. "I promise."

"We're not really known for food though," Ava said.

"Um, *pie* shop. Baked is in our title." Though it still didn't sound so much as the eating kind of baked as the smoking kind of baked.

"Dad's pies sucked," Ava said. "No one came for the food. Parker told me. The pies were bad, he undercharged, it was all just...like he ran away from home and found the most opposite thing he could do."

"Like make bad business decisions?" Cori asked.

But Ava didn't smile. "Yeah. It was like he left New York and his success and hard work and just...stopped. Stopped working, stopped planning and strategizing and...*trying.*"

"Evan makes it sound like he was happy though," Cori said. It was puzzling. But things just didn't always make sense and go according to plan. She'd learned that away from New York. Maybe that was part of what Ava needed to learn.

"Yeah," Ava nodded, clearly thinking. "I guess Parker does too."

"Noah too," Brynn added softly.

"But we don't have the luxury of not working or strategizing," Cori said, fully aware that those were not words she typically used.

Her sisters were aware too. And seemed slightly amused by it. And maybe a little worried. Well, they weren't the only ones. But Ava wanted to buy an oven and Brynn wanted to just spend all day 'painting', i.e., watching Noah's naked, tattooed arms and shoulders, and Cori wanted...well, a photo booth and heart-shaped pie pans. But first she needed to get them out of debt and a positive bank balance.

She rubbed her middle finger on the center of her forehead and then caught Ava doing the same thing.

"Okay, business plan. New menu items—"

Ava's phone rang and Cori sighed. Ava never didn't take a call. She glanced at the screen. "I can't handle more or new," she said, getting to her feet. "Hell, I can't handle what I have. Let me work on that."

"But we have to start bringing in—"

"I have to take this," Ava said. "It's my eight o'clock call."

She picked the phone up as Brynn said, "Crap, it's already eight? I need to check in with Jeffrey." Jeffrey was one of the scientists in Brynn's lab who was keeping her updated on what they were doing.

Ava was already up from the table and headed toward the room off the main living room that she'd designated as her office.

"Go ahead," Cori told Brynn. "We'll talk later."

Brynn leaned over as she came around the table and gave Cori a quick hug. "We'll make it work."

"Well, at least Noah's working for a currency we can afford," Cori teased, squeezing her.

"What's that?" Brynn asked, straightening.

"Time with you. And the view of you in shorts on a ladder."

Brynn blushed again, but didn't deny it.

"You're sure you're not dating him?" Cori asked.

The tattooed ex-Marine mechanic wasn't the nerdy scientist type Cori would have thought of for Brynn, but he was hot and could definitely take care of the head-in-the-clouds, or rather head-in-the-microscope, Brynn. And he seemed a little enamored. Brynn deserved enamored. And hot.

"I'm *not* dating him," Brynn said firmly. She paused, then confessed, "Because then I'd have to stop. Right? Six different guys in six months."

Ah. Suddenly it made sense. "If you don't *date* him, you can keep seeing him."

Brynn blushed. "I don't know if he feels the same, but that's how I'm looking at it."

Cori grinned. "Good for you. Just enjoy it."

With a smile that was definitely a little dreamy, Brynn headed upstairs to the fourth bedroom that she'd taken over for *her* office.

There were five bedrooms in the huge, old two-story house, along with three bathrooms, a living room, formal dining room, enormous kitchen, den, full basement, and attic.

But none of those were serving as Cori's office. Cori didn't need an office. Cori didn't do work that required an office. Well, she'd been a personal assistant to a publisher for a while. And she'd run the front desk at an eye doctor's office for about six months. But like everything she did, she hadn't stuck with either of those jobs long enough to count them as any kind of career.

Cori sighed and got up from the table, gathering the dishes. Her sisters hadn't gushed over her s'mores pie either, dammit. Baking and cooking were two things she was good at, and she'd really love to have someone gush over something she did. And, not that she was shocked, she thought of Evan. She'd love to feed Evan. She'd love to do a lot of things to and for and with Evan.

Now she was the owner of a pie shop where she couldn't bake, doing books that were barely books, and lusting after a guy who was going to have to now kiss her sister like he wanted to do her up against the nearest firm surface. Because yeah, that's exactly how *she* and Evan kissed.

She threw the dirty spoons into the dishwasher with a satisfying clang. If Rudy's intention had been to give her a lesson in deprivation and self-control, this was well played.

She was nearly done cleaning up when the doorbell rang. The doorbell—a grand chime with three tones—fit the old house with the high ceilings, original woodwork, built-in china hutch, and wall sconces perfectly and made Cori smile as she headed for the foyer.

She pulled the heavy old door open, not even bothering to look through the window first. And her smile immediately widened.

Evan Stone stood on her front step. Well, *their* front step.

"Hi." He gave her a big grin.

Did he know which sister she was? Was he grinning at *her* or just whoever opened the door? Evan grinned at people all the time. She just knew it. He looked really good wearing that grin too. And she really wanted him to know who she was. "Hi."

She did not want him kissing Ava. The thought was hardly shocking, but the intensity with which she felt opposed to the idea was a little.

Movement behind him caught her eye, and she glanced over his shoulder to see their neighbor across the street, Jason, taking a box from the back of his truck. He lifted a hand in a wave.

And it seemed clear what she needed to do. She stepped forward, wrapped her arms around Evan's neck and pressed her body against his, kissing him like, well, like she wanted to put him up against the nearest firm surface.

Evan didn't hesitate for an instant. He cupped her ass, pulled her up against him, and opened his mouth.

Tongues and tiptoes. That was what Brynn had said of their kiss at the shop. The tiptoes made her taller and the tongues, well, those made her think of hot, wet thrusting of another kind.

Evan's hands were in her hair again and she was glad she had it down tonight. It allowed him to slide his fingers against her head and then drag them through the long strands in a deliciously decadent way that made her want those hands and fingers all over her body.

No. He could *not* kiss Ava like this. Dammit. Cori couldn't handle that.

She finally pulled back, but Evan didn't let her head go as he looked into her eyes, breathing a little harder.

"Hey, Cori," he said gruffly.

Relief swept over her. She hadn't admitted it, even to herself, but that first night in New York had been bugging her. That he'd poured all of that heat into a kiss with another woman. And that had been before she'd gotten to know him better. That was why the kiss at the shop two days ago had felt even more satisfying. He'd known it was her. And had kissed her like he'd never get enough.

"Hey," she said, just to confirm that he was completely correct. Then she went back in for more.

Their lips met and the kiss turned hungry almost immediately. He backed her up against the door and slid his tongue along hers. One of his big hands ran from her butt to her thigh, lifting it so that he could press against the hot, aching spot where she needed pressure. And friction. And a lot less clothing.

His other hand slid into her hair, gripping gently. He angled her head to the side and moved his lips over her jaw to her neck. "Damn girl," he said huskily. "You smell like chocolate, and you feel like the place I want to be for the next several weeks, straight, and you kiss me like you've had every dirty thought about me that I've had about you."

A little chorus of *yes, yes, yes!* sang in her head. He knew it was her. And hell yes, she'd stay right here for the next several weeks—although with the less clothes thing—and she'd love to share a few of those dirty thoughts.

She gave a soft laugh, then a moan as he sucked gently on the skin just behind her ear. "Man, I hope so. I don't want to be kissing someone who doesn't have the kinds of thoughts I've had."

"Those thoughts are keeping me up at night," he confessed, his hand sliding down her back and then under the edge of her shirt.

Her skin erupted in goose bumps as he trailed his finger over the bare skin just above her shorts.

"I could tell you about a few of them," he said, running his hand higher, spanning her rib cage and getting *so close* to her breast.

"One of mine includes us breaking one of those little round tables in the pie shop," she told him, arching closer, hinting that she wanted his hand higher.

He pulled back a little, his eyes burning. "Oh, really? One of mine has to do with the very big, very sturdy table in the conference room in New York."

She laughed. "Probably safer."

"I think sturdy will be important."

She caught her breath. He'd said *will*. As in it *will* happen. "Good."

He lowered his head and kissed her again, *finally* moving his hand to cup her breast. Her shirt pulled up on her stomach and cool night air hit her suddenly feverish skin. Evan ran the pad of his thumb over her nipple and Cori felt it in every inch of her body. Some more than others, of course. Then he rolled it between his thumb and finger and all of the tingles all over her body seemed to laser focus into a pulsing need between her legs.

"Evan," she moaned into his mouth.

"Cor—"

But he was interrupted by a car driving past the house. And the little *beep beep* the driver gave that said they'd seen it all.

Cori sucked in a breath and looked down. She was still mostly covered, only her stomach exposed, but it was very clear where Evan's hand was.

The hand that he slid out from under her shirt as he leaned back.

"I've had a few dirty thoughts about you against doors and walls too," he said, his voice rough. "But we should maybe not do front doors. Or at least, not the outside of front doors."

Cori ran a hand through her hair and Evan's gaze dropped to the breast he'd just had in his hand. She dropped her arm, very aware that her nipples were pressing insistently against her shirt, begging him for more attention. She coughed. "Yeah, that's maybe a good plan."

"Wouldn't want to scandalize our little town," he said with a grin.

Our little town. Was Bliss her town? Strangely, that didn't seem completely...strange.

And then the word *scandalize* sunk in. Yeah, doing her sister's boyfriend against the front door—or any door for that matter— would be scandalous.

Even if no one knew about it?

From the street, they wouldn't know that she wasn't Ava, but seriously? Did the fact that no one knew that she and Evan were messing around make it better? And did it help that he wasn't *actually* cheating on Ava? And did it make it okay that this was definitely not a usual relationship for Cori? She'd met Evan Stone two weeks ago. She'd never wanted a guy like this, flirted with a guy like this, *kissed* a guy like this, and *not* already slept with him. Hell, some of her relationships would be over by now. In the overall cosmic view of right and wrong and good and bad intentions and all of that, did any of these things really make it all right?

"You knew it was me? Even before I kissed you?" she asked.

"Yeah. Though I don't mind you confirming it that way."

Cori looked up at him, hating that she loved that he'd known her. He wasn't hers. Couldn't be. At least for a few more months. And maybe not even then, really. Because going from one sister to the next would probably be scandalous too.

On impulse, Cori gathered her hair in one hand, lifting it away from her neck. "Here," she said, tipping her head and pointing behind her right ear.

He leaned in to look, his warm breath caressing her neck and shoulder.

She felt her body react, tingles skittering down her arm and her nipples tightening. She cleared her throat. "We each have our first initial tattooed behind our right ear. "

He lifted a finger and traced the small C. Her tingles got tingles.

"That's really cute," he said, his voice husky again.

God, he smelled good. She resisted the urge to put her face against his chest and inhale deeply. And she gave herself more points for again resisting a very strong impulse.

She let her hair drop. "Now you'll always have a way of knowing. For sure. Just...in case."

He didn't ask in case of what. For which she was grateful. Because she couldn't say exactly. She just had this feeling that she really wanted to *always* know he knew her.

"Our mom used to use a marker to put our initials there. It helped babysitters and our grandparents and teachers. We did the tattoos on our eighteenth birthday as a kind of tribute to her getting us to adulthood mostly on her own. We don't tell many people."

"Thanks for telling me."

"Sure."

They stood looking at each other for a long moment. They were no longer touching but he was very definitely in her personal space. And she'd never wanted to have her body against someone else as much as she wanted to be up against Evan Stone in that moment.

"And *you* knew who I was when you kissed me," he said.

"Of course. But *they* didn't know who I was."

"They?"

"The neighbors," she said, waving her hand in the direction of Jason's house.

"Ah. And it wouldn't be okay for them to think that you were Cori greeting me at the door?"

She cleared her throat. "Just thought it was a good opportunity to further cement this thing between you and Ava."

"Ah. Well...thanks."

Finally she sighed. "Actually, that wasn't it. I just...had to."

His smile faded and he nodded. "Yeah."

"Yeah?"

He blew out a breath. "Yeah."

"Oh." So he was feeling the longing too.

He nodded again. "And it makes it even more awkward to now ask if your sister is home."

That made Cori straighten. Right. The neighbors could think she was Ava. From a distance. But there would be a point where Evan had to actually be with the real Ava. "Yes. Right. Of course. She's on a conference call. Is everything okay?"

"Yeah. Well, no." He shifted his weight, suddenly seeming uncomfortable. He cleared his throat. "We, um, need to go out. Me and Ava. We have to be seen together. In public."

"Oh. You're here to ask my sister on a date." *Ugh.*

"Yeah." He took a small step back.

Double ugh.

"Well, that *is* awkward." *Especially considering I want to strip down and introduce you to my pastry bags and decorating tips.* Cori coughed. "I don't know when she'll be done with her call but—" Suddenly Cori wanted more time with him. It was like there was a timer ticking now that would signal the end of...whatever this was. "Do you want to have dessert and coffee with me while you wait?"

Slowly he nodded. "I do. I really do."

"Are you okay?" He seemed pained.

"Just kind of wishing dessert and coffee was a euphemism," he said. "For which my answer would still be *I really do*, incidentally."

Cori felt heat curl through her belly and then dive into her panties.

"And then I was feeling bad that I wished that," he went on, cooling her down a little. "And then I was remembering that this thing with Ava isn't really real. And then I realized that this— going for the feel-good stuff instead of the responsible stuff I promised—is exactly what I always do."

Wow, that was all...pretty much exactly how she felt. No matter how warm and tempted he made her feel, couldn't she, just once, *not* give into her urges? Could she resist saying *what the hell* just one time? Apparently not, because Cori heard herself say, "But you just have to be sure Ava has some fun and doesn't work all the time." *You don't have to sleep with her. Or fall in love with her. Or even feel guilty about wanting to kiss someone else.*

"That's true," Evan said, his gaze on her mouth now as if he'd read her thoughts about the kissing.

"And I'm not saying my s'mores pie won't make you feel good, but giving me your honest opinion about a potential addition to the pie shop menu would be helpful. And helping someone out is responsible, right?"

"I guess you've got a point."

"So we're fine." If Brynn painting with Noah wasn't dating, then... Yep, there were loopholes everywhere. And she was honing in on every one of them. Typical.

"I mean dessert with a guy who's here to ask my sister out doesn't count as a date for *me*, right?" Having a conversation with a guy in her kitchen over pie and coffee was definitely not a classic date scenario in Cori's life. There would be a distinct lack of hard liquor, for one thing. And a lack of sexy panties—she had on plain white cotton tonight. And a lack of dirty dancing, NASCAR racing, and Tae Kwan Do instruction...which were the ways she'd met her last three boyfriends. Oh, and there would be a hell of a lot more *talking*. Even if her pastry bags and decorating tips were right there in the drawer by the oven.

Evan shook his head. "Probably not."

"*Probably* not?"

He paused, then his voice went a little lower. "Still kind of feels like a date."

Yeah it did. A pretty plain, sweet, she-still-wanted-it date. Cori shook her head and decided to lighten things up. Because light was definitely more her style. "Oh, that's just because of the kissing. Kissing always makes things seem more serious than they are," she said with a wave of her hand.

But Evan didn't take the lighten-up hint. Or smile. He just said, "Funny. Kissing is usually my go-to for keeping it casual."

She swallowed. Crap. Her too. Kissing was way easier than talking. "Well, I guess we could kiss in the kitchen instead of making conversation. If you insist." She gave him a smile that she was sure looked as wobbly as it felt.

"Strangely, I don't think that will make this more causal."

Oh, boy. "Okay. What will?"

"I'm not sure anything will."

How about dating my sister? Will that make things seem more casual between us? Talk about being out of her element. Cori never got too serious. If anything, she didn't get serious enough in her relationships. Now this one...she couldn't seem to pull back on the reins.

She took a deep breath. "Pie is the only answer. It will make you feel like you're giving in to all kinds of temptation, but you won't have to make a phone call in the morning."

"Why do I feel like you're not a phone-call-in-the-morning girl?" Evan asked. Still not letting her lighten the moment up.

"Oh, hell no, I'm not." She laughed. She really wasn't. She

always wanted some space the morning, and day, and sometimes week, after.

"And why do I also feel like you're a girl I'd really want to call?" Evan asked.

She swallowed. "Because you're a contrary personality. Like me."

He took a few seconds, but finally he nodded. "Probably. Okay, let's try the pie.

7

The girl had to start wearing a bra. That was the only solution.

Evan watched as Cori stretched to reach into the cupboard for a plate, her short T-shirt pulling away from the black cotton pants that hugged her hips and ass, and found himself leaning slightly to the side on the stool. No way was that shirt going up above her breasts—the shape of which he now had permanently imprinted on his palm—no matter how high she reached, but damn, the idea of it almost put him on his ass on the floor beside the breakfast bar. That would have been hard to explain.

"It smells amazing in here," he said, trying to distract himself from the hard, little points that were poking against the bright pink words *That's a horrible idea. What time?* on the front of her shirt.

But if a girl wore something that bright, she had to expect people to look, right?

She glanced over her shoulder with a smile. "Thanks."

"You cooked?"

"Chicken piccata," she said as she turned to scoop a piece of chocolate pie onto the plate. "And s'mores pie."

She set it in front of him, but before he could reach for it, she picked up a blowtorch. It was a kitchen-sized blowtorch, but a torch all the same. She lit the end and touched it to the marshmallows on top, toasting them quickly. Then she set a fork on the edge and pushed the plate toward him.

Evan couldn't help it. He laughed and shook his head. "Even dessert has a little something extra with you," he said.

Cori shrugged. "I love toppings."

He picked up his fork, trying to ignore the way his body stirred. After their mini-make-out session on the porch, he wasn't sure there was anything she could do that *wouldn't* stir his body. And maybe even his emotions.

"Toppings?" he asked.

"Oh, yeah," she said.

Then she tried, again, to kill him by leaning onto her elbows just across the bar from where he was sitting. The neckline of her shirt gaped, and the smooth, tanned skin drew his eyes. The breast and nipple he'd only gotten the briefest feel of were *right there*. And he noticed the shimmer. Holy shit, she was wearing shimmery body powder. That had to be it. Her skin glowed and yes, actually, sparkled in the warm light of the kitchen.

"Toppings can make or break a dish," she said. "I mean, without those marshmallows, that's pretty much just chocolate pie. I could have drizzled caramel over it instead and it would have totally changed it. And toppings and sauce can change a chicken breast from piccata to teriyaki like that." She snapped her fingers. "I'm all about the embellishments."

For some reason, that seemed like one of the most honest things he'd ever heard. Cori Carmichael *was* an embellishment. She seemed to make everything bigger and better. And yes, changed things. He couldn't put a finger directly on what it was, but since the triplets had come to town, Bliss had seemed more fun. Nothing major had changed. The outside of the pie shop looked exactly the same, and they hadn't opened to business again, so the interior changes weren't obvious. The girls weren't really out and about in town—much to the chagrin of all of the busybodies and gossips. Of course, the old men who stopped in for coffee every morning at the pie shop delighted in being some of the few people to actually have any amount of time with the Carmichael girls. And yet, there was something in the air, Evan could swear it. Something had changed slightly...and had gotten better when they'd come to town.

"Try it," Cori urged, gesturing at his plate.

Right. Pie. He was sitting here eating pie with Cori while he waited for Ava. So he could ask her out on a date. That wasn't weird at all. He took a bite of the pie.

And holy shit. If he hadn't been a little crazy about her already, that would have done it. He swallowed and looked up at her. "Damn, Cori, this is amazing."

Her face lit up, and for a second, Evan stopped chewing and just looked at her. The shimmery body powder had nothing on that sparkle in her eyes.

"You think so?"

He swallowed the bite. "Of course. How would anyone not think so?"

She shrugged and straightened, wiping at something on the counter with her finger and not meeting his eyes. "Brynn and Ava didn't seem impressed."

"Well, they're probably used to you coming up with amazing things." He took another big bite.

"Yeah, something like that."

That sounded completely sarcastic and he watched her as he chewed and swallowed again. "This is going on the menu?" he asked.

She looked up. "I want it to." Again, she lit up a little. "I have a bunch of ideas for new items."

It was one thing to be wound up after the kiss at the front door. And having the feel of her breast in his hand. The smell of chocolate and sugar that filled the air around him, the braless breasts with the look-at-me tips teasing him, the fact that even her T-shirt was sassy all made his I-want-that reaction make some kind of sense. But that excited, eager look on her face? Why did *that* turn him on? But he heard himself asking, "Like what?"

She leaned in again, the skin on her throat and chest again shimmering in the light and drawing his eyes. Yeah, it was the sparkles. It had nothing to do with the cleavage. Or the memory of how she felt in his arms. Or the way her mouth touching his made everything in his body tight and hard.

"Along with the Classics menu that would be the cherry, apple, and peach, we could do a whole kids themed menu too. Peanut butter and jelly pie, mac and cheese pie, corndog pie," she said. "And we could do a soda fountain theme. Root beer float pie and orange creamsicle pie and I think I could even figure out a way to do a cherry cola pie."

Evan knew he was staring. But... "Root beer float pie?" Evan asked. "Peanut butter and jelly? Seriously?"

For a second he saw a flicker of uncertainty cross her face and that made something else in him go tight. His chest. Or his heart.

"Well, it's just an idea," she said, carefully. "I just like the idea of some unique promotions. Like the sweetie pie idea." She looked down at the counter again. "But it's a little much, probably."

He cleared his throat. It was a little much. But it was also creative and unique and clearly something she was excited about and totally and completely Cori. Which meant, he loved it. Fuck. "Can Ava pull all of that off?" he asked.

Her gaze came up. And she looked disappointed. "Um... maybe. None of them are super hard. But—"

"But?"

"She doesn't want to tackle anything new right now."

"Ah." He could tell she was waiting for him to tell her that she could go ahead with those things. But Rudy had been very specific about why he'd chosen the job for each girl. And Evan was dedicated to making sure everything went the way Rudy had wanted them to. No matter how tempted he was to say fuck it. Actually, he should be *more* dedicated *because* he was tempted to say fuck it.

"I guess the new stuff will have to wait." Dammit, he hated that he had to pull Cori back here. But Ava had a lot to learn about products and customers, up close and personal. And Evan was beginning to suspect that Rudy had known how much Ava would struggle. And that it would be good for her. But what about Cori? What about staying out of the baking was good for her? Clearly, she had a passion, and talent, in the kitchen. This might all be good for Ava, but suddenly Evan was having a hard time caring about the woman who was supposed to be his girlfriend.

And wasn't that just typical? Something bright and shiny and fun came along and he forgot what he *should* be doing.

"Yeah. But I'm hoping she'll at least be open to adding blueberry to the classics," Cori said, her enthusiasm definitely muted.

Evan gritted his teeth against the urge to say *you're amazing, do whatever you want, fuck anyone who tries to hold you back.*

"Maybe that's what your dad was going for," he said. "To see if you could stick with it even if it's not fun and new and exciting. Accounting definitely isn't. But maybe that was his point—for you to care enough to do this thing anyway. Even the boring parts."

And if he thought a lot of that applied to him as well, he wasn't going to go there.

Cori took a breath, then nodded. "Maybe. I guess that makes sense."

He focused on the pie. The thing they were *supposed to be* talking about. Blueberry pie. Now *there* was the way to a man's heart.

"Tell me you're adding pecan pie to the menu too and I'll

probably do anything you want me to do," he said, shoveling in the last bite of s'mores pie.

She didn't say anything to that and he looked up. She was watching him. Well, she was watching his mouth. He pressed his lips together and swallowed.

"You like pecan?" she asked.

"Love it."

"Have you ever had chocolate toffee pecan?"

He stared at her. "No. Is that real?"

"It can be."

"Marry me."

There was a beat of silence after his teasing comment. Yeah, teasing. That's what that was.

Then she smiled. "That might be complicated since you're dating my sister."

He nodded and forced a smile too. "True. Then I guess I need to hang on to that relationship 'til Thanksgiving so I'm invited over for family dinner."

It was supposed to be light and joking, but it didn't sound like it. And there was a quick flash of *something* across Cori's face. Something like jealousy?

"I can make that pie in September too," she said.

September. When the six-month pretend relationship with Ava would be up. Cori knew it exactly without thinking. Had she added up when that would be over prior to this?

"Yeah?"

She looked at his mouth again and nodded. "Yeah."

Okay, this was suddenly very...not joking. There was a tension in the air that he didn't understand completely. But he didn't hate it. It felt like anticipation. And temptation. And like September was very far away.

Finally, Cori cleared her throat and straightened, propping her hip against the counter. "Can I try to teach this stuff to Ava? Or is that against the terms of the trust?"

Yeah, it was better to stop talking about tempting things he couldn't, or shouldn't, have. Like chocolate toffee pecan pie. And his fake girlfriend's sister. Or chocolate toffee pecan pie *on* his fake girlfriend's sister.

He nodded. "I think you can. If you're just instructing. As long as Ava's there and actually doing it."

He couldn't see how that was an exact violation. Just like Cori kissing him at the front door wasn't a *direct* violation of anything. He was still going to make sure Ava got away from work and had a good time and Cori wasn't *dating* him. She was just making him want to date her more than he'd ever wanted to date anyone.

Hell, he'd never really wanted to *date* anyone at all. It was just kind of what happened when you lived in a small town and had known the women you slept with since birth. Fucking around in Bliss turned into shooting pool at the bar, going to movies, and the occasional backyard barbecue with their families—who he'd also known since birth—for the few weeks that the fucking around was occurring. Even when everyone, even their families, knew that it was nothing serious, there was still an underlying expectation of making it *seem* like it was more than casual sex. And hell, he liked movies and barbecues. No harm, no foul.

But he couldn't help but wonder how going to the movies with Cori would be. It would be...different. Somehow. It would be *more*. Of something. It would be better.

He was so fucked.

"But I should definitely start with blueberry. And maybe pecan. Those are traditional pies. Things people would expect when they came into a pie shop, right?"

Evan felt his brows pull together. "Yes. But that doesn't mean you can't do some of the other ideas."

"Really?"

"Definitely."

She tipped her head, chewing her bottom lip for a moment. "Are you a good judge of when things are over-the-top?"

He almost laughed. Because that was a really good question. "Maybe not," he said honestly.

She sighed and nodded. "Yeah. Me either." She paused a moment, then said, "When I was fifteen, my dad invited me and my sisters to his birthday party for the first time."

Evan didn't know where this was going, but he felt a sudden need to hear this story. They'd already established the fact that the Rudy he'd known was not the father Cori had known. And he wanted to know more. About both Rudy and Cori in the past. He pushed his plate back and folded his arms on top of the breakfast bar, giving her his full attention.

"My dad threw these really big, fancy parties for his birthday and invited all of his big rich friends. It was always in some posh place with tons of food and drink and music—a huge gala."

Evan just nodded.

"But we were never invited. We were just little girls and he didn't want to have us underfoot. Which was fine. I didn't even know about them until I was about thirteen or so. Well, by the time we were fifteen, Ava was working part-time for the company on the weekends, and she'd impressed Dad and he wanted to show her off. Well, he couldn't take just her. Everyone knew we were triplets and Mom never let him get away with spending time with one of us more than the others. So he invited us all."

Evan simply couldn't picture Rudy at a big fancy New York party. The man he knew wore blue jeans and T-shirts with a flannel shirt over the top in the cold months, and work boots. He loved cheeseburgers and onion rings and drove an old Cadillac that ran about three-fourths of the time.

"Well, I didn't want to go in the first place," Cori said. "And then he gave Mom a dress code and all of these 'be sure the girls know' things and I was just done. He wanted us there to make him look good and didn't trust us to do that being ourselves." She was frowning now and had her arms crossed. "I went along because Ava really wanted to go and Brynn, of course, was just going with the flow. I sucked it up and put on the stupid dress and showed up. Dad introduced us to everyone and then forgot about us. That's when I decided to be sure that he never *wanted* me at one of his parties again."

Evan felt his brows rise. "Oh, boy. What did you do?"

"That year? I got into the liquor. Got puking drunk and sang karaoke."

"Your dad had karaoke at his big New York party?"

She actually smiled at that. "Nope."

"Ah." Evan grinned too. "So no more invites?"

"Oh, no, that would have been too easy. The next year I had to step up my game. I got caught making out in his office with one of his biggest client's sons." She frowned. "I had no idea that he was thirty and engaged. And he had no idea I was only sixteen."

Evan actually choked. "Holy shit, Cori."

"I know. But we really were just kissing and he got about halfway to second base. And I'd hit on him. And I'd dragged him into the office, so consent wasn't an issue. And no way was Dad going to make a big deal about it. Nothing really came of it. Well, except for a broken engagement."

Evan couldn't stop staring at her.

She shook her head. "I *know*. But they got back together. And that one worked, because the next year, Ava asked me not to go to the party."

There was a flash of emotion in her eyes, and Evan could have sworn it looked like regret. "That's what you wanted right?"

She shrugged. "Yeah. I thought so. But, stupidly, hearing that they didn't think I should go hurt a little." She gave a light, humorless laugh. "Maybe it was hearing it from Ava that stung. I wouldn't have cared if Dad had said it. That's what I wanted, I guess. His attention. An emotion from *him*, even if it was disappointment. That's what Karen says anyway. That I wanted attention from him that was about *me*, not about him. I wanted approval, but I wanted approval based on something I did, not on something he wanted me to do. And it seemed that whenever I didn't do things his way, he just ignored me. Any emotion would have been better than that."

Evan took a breath. He couldn't hug her. That wouldn't be appropriate. Would it? It seemed like a bad idea, but he couldn't pinpoint why. He wasn't *actually* dating her sister.

But in the next second, he knew the reason. Because if he hugged her, it would start a domino effect of feelings and actions and reactions that could definitely screw with their plans. Plans like dating Ava. And Cori not getting involved with anyone.

Yep, he was totally fucked.

"Who's Karen?" he finally asked.

She gave him a small smile. "My shrink."

"Ah." Yep, that all sounded like shrink talk. As if he would know. He didn't know any shrinks. Not that people in Bliss didn't need psychological help. They just had to drive about thirty minutes to get it. "No more birthday parties then?"

"I didn't go that year," she said. "But then, surprisingly, the next year, when we were eighteen, he invited us again and he personally asked me to come."

"That was...nice." Evan hoped it was nice. He had no idea at this point. This man sounded nothing like the one he knew. The one who had, without question, loved his daughters. And regretted a lot of his decisions regarding those daughters.

"It was. I was actually, stupidly, touched by it. Decided that if he was going to trust me again, I'd do better. No shenanigans." A sheepish look crossed her face.

"What happened?" Somehow he knew something had happened.

She sighed. "Okay, once, when I was ten, Dad and I were together for the afternoon. It was rare that any of us had one-on-one time with him. I mean, I guess that's normal when you have three kids and especially when those kids are triplets. Plus, I don't think he really ever knew what to do with us, so it was easier when we were all together because we kept each other company and entertained one another."

Evan nodded. He was completely enthralled here.

"Anyway, it was just the two of us because Ava and Brynn had been selected for this Quiz Bowl thing at school and were doing that. I, of course, wasn't so I was free." She flashed a smile that was part amused and part chagrined. "We were walking along and almost got knocked over by this huge St. Bernard. And my dad actually laughed, squatted down by this dog, let it lick his face, petted it, got hair all over his suit and...I about died. I had *never* seen him like that."

And *that* was the Rudy Evan knew. For some reason, it felt good to know that there had at least been hints of that man even back then. That she'd seen at least a tiny bit of it. He smiled. "He liked dogs."

"He did. But I never knew that. He said that he'd always wanted a dog. He'd grown up in a penthouse in Manhattan, so obviously he couldn't have a dog, but that had always been something he'd wished for." Cori had a look of faint amazement on her face even now, remembering.

Evan felt himself smiling. And being grateful that Rudy and Cori had had that moment together.

"Anyway," she went on, "when he invited me back to his birthday party, I remembered that. And had the sudden desire to do something special for him and to show him I remembered that afternoon."

Evan shook his head. "What did you do?"

"I got him a puppy."

Evan let that sink in. Then laughed. "Oh my God."

She nodded, a mischievous smile teasing her lips. "And I brought it to the party."

Evan groaned. "Don't tell me it was a St. Bernard."

Her smile grew. She nodded. "Of course it was."

"You got your dad a St. Bernard puppy and brought it to his fancy birthday party?"

"I did. But it was with every good intention," she said quickly. "I wasn't trying to cause trouble. I really wanted to give him a meaningful gift that he'd never expect and that he'd never get for himself."

"Did he even have room for a huge dog in his home?" Evan asked.

"Oh sure. He had the entire upper floor of his building. More square footage than most homes. And he could have afforded to hire someone to take care of it, walk it and stuff."

Evan nodded. "I guess. Was he touched by it?" He almost hated asking, somehow knowing the answer.

"Well, he was *surprised* by it. But he didn't really have a chance to let the...gesture...sink in," she said. She winced slightly, but she was also clearly fighting a smile.

"What happened?"

"The dog was *very* excited about the party," she said, her lips twitching. "He went barreling in, knocked over some lady on really high heels, stopped and peed in the middle of the dance floor, and then headed straight for the buffet table." She paused, clearly remembering the scene. "There was this horrendous crash, the total silence, then the sound of my father bellowing 'Corrine Michelle Carmichael!' louder than I'd ever heard him yell."

Evan grimaced. He couldn't imagine Rudy yelling. He really couldn't. He could, however, imagine Rudy loving a St. Bernard puppy. "And then?"

"He grabbed the dog by the collar, me by the arm, marched us both to the elevator, took us down to the car, shoved us inside, and told his driver to take us straight to the Humane Society and then home."

"Oh. Wow." Shit.

"Well, we didn't go to the Humane Society," she said. "I took the dog back to where I got it and then went home. And didn't speak to my father for six months. Which was fine, because he wasn't talking to me either."

"Damn, Cori."

"I know." She sighed. "But you see what I mean? I have this way of making things...too much. I go overboard. I get an idea and then it just keeps growing. I could have gotten him a watch. Or a tie. But no, I had to get him a puppy."

Evan paused, not sure he should say what he was about to. Then he went ahead. Because he wasn't huge on thinking through consequences either. "I don't think you could have."

Her head came up. "What?"

"I don't think you could have just gotten him a watch. That didn't even occur to you, did it?"

She didn't react right away. But finally she shook her head slowly. "Not until afterward."

He nodded. "Exactly. You can't just make pecan pie. I mean, you can, of course. But why, when you can make choco-late toffee pecan pie? When you can make it more and better?"

She stared at him for a long moment. "Damn," she said softly. "I really want to make you that pie."

And he really wanted her to. And "that pie" was suddenly symbolic of a lot more.

"I guarantee that he never forgot that birthday party. Because of you. Was he embarrassed at the moment? Maybe. Irritated? Maybe. But I promise you that the other parties he had all blurred together, but he always remembered the parties you were at."

She laughed. "Well, there's that."

"And I'll bet the parties after the ones you went to seemed boring and quiet."

Her grin softened into a smile and she gave him a look that stirred him. Physically. For sure. But it was more than the braless thing going on, and he felt the stirring somewhere else. Somewhere deeper.

"Thanks, Evan." Her voice was soft and husky and that stirring intensified. Everywhere.

"My pleasure."

"Oh, hi, Evan."

He jerked his attention away from Cori and focused on the woman who had just come into the room. The woman who was supposed to be his girlfriend. "Hi, Ava."

It was stupid to feel guilty, like he'd been caught doing something he shouldn't have been doing. Maybe he shouldn't have been imagining Cori spread out on the kitchen countertop with chocolate pie spread all over those teasing nipples. But he hadn't really been doing anything wrong. He wasn't cheating on Ava. And he hadn't actually licked one inch of Cori Carmichael.

Yet.

He made himself concentrate on Ava instead. "How was the conference call?"

"Fine." She opened the fridge and pulled out a bottle of water. She opened it and took a drink. "Just so you know, Jack Mitchell is making everything twice as hard as it needs to be."

Jack Mitchell was the acting CEO of Carmichael Enterprises while Ava was in Bliss. Evan shrugged. "Sorry."

"You're not."

"There's nothing I can do, Ava. The trust is clear. I'm just the messenger."

She sighed. "Yeah. I know. It's ridiculous, but I know."

"Which reminds me," Evan said, determined to fulfill *his* part of this deal. Even if it killed him. "We need to go out to dinner tomorrow night."

Ava took another drink, just watching him. "You and me?"

"Yep."

"Something romantic, I assume?"

"Probably. Mostly just something public, but yeah, probably

more than a beer and a game of pool." Though seeing Ava shooting pool might be interesting.

"What do you have in mind?"

"There's a nice place over in Morris," he said, naming the little town about fifteen minutes from Bliss. "They do steak and pasta and some seafood."

Ava sighed, but nodded. "Okay."

He couldn't help but grin. "Your enthusiasm is overwhelming."

Ava gave him a little smile. "Sorry. I really am. It's nothing personal."

Evan nodded and couldn't resist glancing at Cori. Yeah, it was nothing personal. Because there was nothing between him and Ava. But *personal* felt like it described him and Cori well. Too well. "I get it," he told Ava. "But we need to be seen in public together. And," he added, thinking about the other reason they were "dating", the *main* reason, "you need to get away from work. We'll go to dinner and then maybe do something fun after."

"Something like what?"

He regarded the straight-laced triplet. He didn't have to know her well to know a few things about her. "Just leave it to me."

Predictably, her eyebrow arched. "Oh?"

Yeah, Ava Carmichael didn't let other people take the reins very often. Or ever. And he was pretty sure she didn't like surprises. Again, he couldn't help but glance at Cori. Cori loved surprises. Somehow he just knew.

He looked at Ava again and nodded. "Yep. I'll surprise you with something fun."

She didn't look any more enthusiastic now. "Fine."

Yeah, a reluctant "fine" with a touch of skepticism was exactly what a guy wanted when asking a woman out. But he still smiled. "Fine."

"Okay, I'm going to head to bed," Ava said. "Text me to let me know the time and details for tomorrow?" she asked.

Evan lifted a shoulder. "I'll pick you up here at six. Wear a dress. But nothing too fancy. And I wouldn't go too high on the heels."

Ava again looked less than thrilled, but she nodded. "Dress. No heels. Six o'clock. Got it."

And just because he knew it would be funny he said, "Be sure to put some vanilla on."

She frowned. "Vanilla? *On*?"

"Vanilla extract. It's a great bug repellent without the chemicals."

That was true.

"I'm going to need *bug repellent*?" Ava asked.

He'd been right, that was funny. "Don't worry. I'll be happy to check you for ticks after."

He heard a little choking sound from Cori. But Ava just stared at him. "I don't know what that means."

Checking someone for ticks meant looking them over very carefully, head to toe, for any of the little buggers that liked to hide where it was hard to find them. In personal places. But even though ticks were a possibility when you spent time outside in the grass in the country, getting checked for ticks was actually code for getting a girl naked.

"I'll explain everything. Tomorrow," he said with a little wink.

"Um, okay."

Yeah, he wasn't going to check Ava Carmichael for ticks. But it was fun to tease her. And he just needed to get her smiling. And away from work.

He glanced at Cori and found her frowning at her sister. She must have felt him watching her because she looked over. Her frown didn't ease.

And something in Evan's chest warmed. He grinned. Her frown deepened. Cori was jealous of the idea of him and Ava together. He liked that. And that was a really bad idea.

"Okay, then. I'm going to head back upstairs," Ava said. She looked back and forth between Cori and Evan. "Everything okay in here?"

"Completely," Evan assured her. It was much more than okay. And so much worse.

"Yep," Cori agreed. Though she was still frowning.

Ava nodded. "Okay. 'Night." She turned on her heel, heading for the staircase.

When she'd disappeared up the steps, Evan slid off the stool. He needed to get going. He'd done what he'd come over to do. And if he didn't leave now, Cori might end up on the kitchen counter after all.

"I'm going to head home," he said.

Cori chewed on her bottom lip. Then she pushed away from the countertop. "I'll walk you out."

He'd been hoping she'd say something like that. Or *stay*. Or *my bedroom's the one on the right at the top of the stairs*. Yeah, he needed to go.

He waited for her to round the breakfast bar and they walked to the front door together. She pulled the door open and he stepped onto the porch, but he turned back.

She propped her shoulder against the door, reminding him of the way they'd stood the first night in New York.

"Thanks for the pie," he said, instead of all of the other things he wanted to say.

"I'm glad you stopped by."

There was something in her voice, and her eyes, that made him step closer.

"You realize I could have called Ava and asked her out," Evan said. Because he suddenly had to.

"I didn't really think about that," Cori said. "But yeah, I suppose you could have."

"And she basically has to say yes to that kind of stuff, right?"

"Yeah, I guess so."

"But I wanted to come over in person."

Cori didn't say anything for a moment. Then *she* took a step closer. "Why?"

"Do you think I should say it out loud? That makes it more official," he said.

"I know."

They were definitely on the same page. Something was happening between them and acknowledging it was going to make it harder to ignore.

Then she nodded. "But yeah, I think you should say it out loud."

Okay then. Not going to ignore it. "I wanted to see you."

She nodded. "And I really don't want you to check my sister for ticks."

"And I really don't want to check your sister for ticks."

Cori blew out a breath. "Thank God."

"You didn't really think I did, did you?"

"I keep thinking there's no chemistry but then I think that maybe it's because I don't want there to be."

He finally lifted his hand to her face. "There's no chemistry between me and Ava."

She covered his hand with hers. "You're not attracted to her?"

"No."

"She looks just like me."

That was true. And yet...she didn't. "Doesn't matter." He leaned in as Cori went on her tiptoes.

"You're not attracted to me?" she asked.

Evan knew she already knew the answer to that question. "No," he said sincerely.

"No?" But she didn't move back.

"I don't think attracted is the right word for it. Too tame."

Her lips were nearly against his but they weren't kissing. Yet. "What's the right word for it then?" she asked softly.

Just her warm breath against his mouth made his lower body harden and heat. Several words tripped through his mind at her question. Words like *lust* and *need* and *obsessed* and *desire*. But none of that was accurate either. Because there was more. He liked her.

He loved just talking to her. He wanted to check her for ticks. With his tongue. But he also wanted to make her laugh and hear all of her stories and take her to a town picnic and to a movie and to a million other seemingly boring, usual things—because he knew that she would make them fun and new—and he wanted to watch her make a pie.

"Captivated," he finally said. He slid his hand up her arm to the back of her neck and pulled her against his lips. "Completely fucking captivated."

She sighed—a sweet, happy sound—and he felt her smile against his lips. "No one has ever used that word for me before," she said softly.

"Good." He wanted her to feel appreciated and liked and cared for, but he, by God, wanted to be the one doing it. He wanted to be something new and different for her too. But, instead of saying anything else that might complicate things even further, he kissed her.

It was a slow, leisurely kiss. Where the others had been hot and passionate and surprising, this was fully intentional and all about tasting and exploring. And with every long stroke of his tongue, he wanted more. With every sigh from her, he wanted more. With every flex of her fingers against his chest, he wanted more. She tasted like sugar and chocolate and something he could only call *every craving he'd ever had.*

It took minutes, long delicious minutes, before Evan even thought about lifting his head. When he did, he let her go slowly and rested his forehead against hers. He breathed in deeply, sucking her scent into his lungs.

"Boy I hope some of the neighbors were watching that," she said huskily. "*That* was very convincing."

He gave a soft laugh. "I should probably go before we convince them of anything more."

She took a deep breath, then let him go, seemingly reluctantly. "I guess I'll...see you."

Yeah, she would see him. He was dating her sister. "It's a small town." There was that too. And the fact that there was no way he was going to be able to stay away from her.

"Right."

Cori took a step back. "Um...thanks for sampling my pie."

A wave of pleasure shot through him as she almost looked embarrassed for a moment. "It was my pleasure."

She gave a little laugh, then stepped back and looked up at him. They stared at one another for a long moment.

"Cori!" One of her sisters—maybe Ava (and he should probably figure that out for sure once and for all)—called from inside the house. "Can I borrow your boots tomorrow night?"

Yeah, it was Ava. And she was asking about Cori's boots. For her date with him. And he was hoping they were the short black ones Cori had worn her first day in Bliss. Because those were hot. On Cori.

Fuck. He ran a hand through his hair and Cori took a deep breath, then blew it out.

"Don't let her borrow those boots."

"Why?"

"Those boots make me...they're *your* boots and I really want to kiss you, a lot, but I need to be her boyfriend, and...I'm just kind of messed up about what I should be doing and feeling here."

Cori pressed her lips together as she studied his face. Finally, she nodded. "Okay."

"And, because of all of that I should probably stop kissing you." God, he didn't want to say that. Or do that.

She simply nodded again.

He was rejecting her. That seemed like a harsh word for it, and she really seemed more resigned than devastated, but he felt like an asshole. This was all his fault. "I'm sorry, Cori. I shouldn't have kissed you in the first place." Fuck, he hated every word he was saying.

She gave a sigh. "You only kissed me in the first place because you thought I was Ava."

She was right. They both knew that. But it felt like kissing Cori was exactly what should have happened.

"And I was the one that kissed you first tonight," she added.

"Because of the neighbors."

She hesitated, then shook her head. "Not really because of the neighbors."

Yeah, he knew that. This was really complicated. Fuck. He dug deep. At least that's what it felt like he was doing. It wasn't like digging deep for the fortitude to be a better man was something he was all that familiar with. He used his gut, or his heart, more than he used his head. He went with what felt good, what seemed fun at the moment. He simply didn't think much beyond *this will be great* very often. And being with Cori Carmichael, in every way, would be great.

"I just...I promised to do this thing with Ava. It's what's best for her and Jill and really both you and Brynn too. And I'm supposed to be making sure you don't have casual flings and that you focus on your sisters and the shop. Kissing you and wanting to do a hell of a lot more than that, isn't helping with any of those things. I need to think about that. What I *should* do, instead of what I *want* to do."

Cori wet her lips—an action that shot straight to his cock—and nodded.

"You're right. Being jealous of my sister because she gets to go out with you is not the way to get closer to her. Hoping that you have no fun and no chemistry with her is not the way to be supportive of what Ava needs to do for the trust and everything."

Damn. He grasped the back of her neck and pulled her close.

He rested his forehead against hers and said, "With the taste of you still in my mouth, it's going to be very difficult to be... convincing...with Ava."

She took a deep, shaky breath. And then she said, "Yeah. We need to be good. For everyone."

He squeezed her neck gently, then let her go. "Yeah. Good. I'm working on that."

She swallowed. "Goodnight, Evan."

"'Night, Cori."

She gave him one last lingering look and then turned and headed into the house.

As he watched her go, only one thing went through his mind. *Please, God, help her remember not to loan Ava those boots.*

8

"Is it just me or is this the most awkward date in the history of dating?" Cori asked.

"She definitely looks tense," Brynn agreed.

"And he looks annoyed," Cori said.

"He's smiling," Brynn pointed out.

Yeah, he was. But it wasn't real. Maybe no one else in the restaurant could tell, but Cori knew that Evan was forcing it. He'd given Ava a few genuine ones too throughout their dinner. But this one was definitely fake.

"Well, you can't really blame the guy, can you?"

Cori looked up as Noah pulled out one of the empty chairs at their table and dropped into it.

"Hey," Brynn said, with a big grin, "what are you doing here?"

Cori wondered if Noah realized how unusual that grin was for Brynn.

"I'm here for the show, same as everyone else," he said, reaching for a roll from the basket in the middle of their table. He pulled off a chunk and put it in his mouth.

"The show?" Cori asked.

"Evan's first date with Ava, of course."

Cori frowned and glanced around. "*Everyone* is here for that?"

He nodded as he chewed. He gestured around the room with the rest of the roll. "Ninety percent of these people are from Bliss," he said. "And the other ten percent know Evan and all about Ava."

"And she's super interesting?" Cori asked.

"Well, she and Evan are super interesting," Noah said, reaching for a cherry tomato from Brynn's salad. Did he know that Brynn didn't like tomatoes? "Ava is very different from Evan's usual."

Ugh. Evan's usual. For some reason that made her stomach hurt. Because he had a lot of usual and because his usual women who were probably a lot like Cori. Him being with someone *not* like Cori was interesting to everyone. Great. Ironic that the woman so interestingly unlike Cori looked exactly like her.

"Well, he doesn't look like he's having a good time," she couldn't help but point out.

"There are two things going on over there," Noah said, dipping the remainder of his roll in the house Italian dressing on Brynn's salad.

Cori would be amused by how comfortable the two of them were together—if she wasn't so unamused by her other sister and the man she was clearly uncomfortable with.

"What two things?" Brynn asked.

"One," Noah said, "Evan has never been out with a woman he couldn't charm before."

"You don't think he can charm Ava?" Cori asked.

"Can anyone truly charm Ava?" Noah asked.

Okay, that wasn't a bad point. "What's the other reason?" Cori suddenly wanted to know.

"He's never dated someone while the woman he's actually crazy about is sitting right across the restaurant."

Cori swallowed as Noah focused on her. "I assume that's

because he always gets the woman he's crazy about to go out with him rather than sit across the restaurant."

But Noah shook his head and gave her a small grin. "That's because he's never really been crazy about anyone before."

Cori felt her heart bang against her rib cage as *yes* went through her mind. But right on the heels of that burst of pleasure was a cold wave of *dammit*. She loved that Evan was crazy about her. She was feeling the same way. But he couldn't be. She couldn't be. She wasn't supposed to date and, more, he was supposed to be dating. Ava. For Ava. For him.

"I should go." She pushed back from the table, preparing to stand.

"What? No," Brynn said.

"Yeah, it's fine," she said. "I'm distracting them. Making them uncomfortable. And it's not like watching them on their date is making *me* feel good either. I'll just go. Noah will stay here with you."

"No," Noah and Brynn both said together.

Cori frowned at them. "Come on. This is *the* date place." Or so the guys had told her when they'd come in for their morning coffee. "You guys stay and—"

"*No*," they both said again.

Cori shook her head. "Still no dating, huh?"

Brynn blushed, but she shook her head. "We're just friends. Noah just stopped over to say hi."

"I need to spend time with Brynn so I can figure out which guys would be the best ones to take her out."

Cori lifted a brow. "I thought Evan was kind of in charge of that?"

"Evan seems to have his hands a little full," Noah said drily.

"Okay. Whatever." There was something going on there, but Cori wasn't in the mood to get into someone else's love life. She had her own problems. Not that this had to do with her *love* life.

Because that would be ridiculous. She pulled her phone out. She'd text Ava and tell her to relax.

"Maybe they need to drink more," Noah commented.

Cori looked up from her typing and followed his gaze. Evan was leaning in and Ava actually pulled back slightly, before clearly stopping herself, and giving him a stiff smile. Cori glanced around. Why was he leaning so close— but she saw the reason a moment later. Jill's mother, Holly, had just entered the restaurant on the arm of the man Cori assumed was Jill's father.

And Holly had already noticed Evan and Ava.

"Well, shit." Yeah, they needed more than liquor. Or texts.

Evan reached for Ava's hand, but rather than linking his fingers with his girlfriend, he bumped the bottle of salad dressing sitting next to Ava's plate. The bottle tipped, hit the edge of her plate, rolled, and lost its stopper.

Ava shot back from the table but not before oily Italian dressing dripped onto her skirt.

"Shit!" Evan also shoved his chair back, standing, and reaching toward Ava with his napkin. In his hurry, his hand hit her water goblet as well, sending ice water splashing into her lap before she sprung to her feet.

"Oh, boy," Cori muttered.

"This is a disaster," Brynn said, sounding a little more amused than she should.

"Okay, I've got this," Cori said, pushing her chair back.

"You've 'got this'?" Noah asked. "What's that mean?" he asked Brynn when Cori stood up.

"Just...be cool," Cori said. She caught Ava's eye, then looked toward the hallway at the back of the restaurant.

Two minutes later, Ava pushed open the door to the ladies' room. Cori pulled her inside, then shut the door and locked it. There were three stalls in the room, so the main door didn't typically need locking, but Cori couldn't risk someone joining them at the moment.

"You and Evan are screwing this up," she told her sister. She pulled her shirt off. "And you *can't* screw this up."

Ava just crossed her arms. "What are you doing?"

Cori popped the snap on her jeans and pulled the zipper down. "I'm saving the day."

That—or Cori continuing to undress—clearly surprised her sister. Ava frowned. "What?"

"I know, I know. Fixing things isn't really my forte. But I can help."

"How are we screwing this up? What's *this*?" Ava asked.

"You and Evan are supposed to be falling for each other. But you have no chemistry. No one in that restaurant thinks you're crazy about each other. And you have to pull this off, Ava. For the trust and the shop and for Evan."

"For Evan?"

Cori took a deep breath. "He wants to do this because he promised you. And Dad, I guess. He promised to help make sure we fulfilled the trust and this is one way he's doing that. If it doesn't work out, then he's let you and Dad down." She frowned, remembering their moments on the porch from last night. "He said something about doing what he's supposed to do rather than what he wants to do. I just get the impression he's trying to prove to *himself* that he can follow through on this."

"And that matters to you?" Ava asked. "That *he* feels good about this?"

Cori focused on her again. "He's a good guy."

"He is."

"And I'm not totally sure he thinks he is all the time." Okay, that was weird. That hadn't really occurred to her, at least not as a full, complete thought, before just now. But yeah, she definitely got that impression. He was fighting against the urge to be irresponsible as hard as she was. Or maybe harder. Because she was completely ready to go out into that restaurant and have a *ton* of chemistry with him.

"And how are you going to fix all of this?"

Cori pushed her jeans to the floor and stepped out of them. "Take off your clothes."

"Excuse me?"

"I'm going to be you."

"But...this isn't like the shop. I've already been out there. Everyone's already seen me."

"I know. But no one but Brynn will know which of us is which if we change clothes and I go out there as you, I promise. People see what they want to see."

"You really think this will work?"

Cori sighed. "It's our best shot. Look—" She faced her sister squarely and took a deep breath. "I know I should have just left him alone. But I didn't. Of course. And now he's all distracted and I'm loving that you have no chemistry and kind of *encouraging* it even. Like by flirting with him and kissing him and stuff I shouldn't be doing. I should be trying to help. Like telling you how great he is and what an amazing kisser he is and how funny he is and that you should give him a chance. And telling him how smart you are and how to get you to relax. And I really should want you to go out with him. For all the reasons Dad wanted this to happen. You work too much, you take everything too seriously, and you could really use some fun...some hot, sexy fun. But I don't want to tell you or him that stuff. Because... that would be the mature and sensible thing to do and God knows, I'm allergic to both of those things. Let me try to help this way."

Ava was regarding her with a bemused expression. "When things get messy you usually just leave."

Cori gave a short, humorless laugh. "Yeah. I get out of the way. But this time I can't. I'm stuck here in Bliss. Sorry."

Ava shook her head. "God, Cori, don't be sorry for being here. I couldn't be handling any of this without you."

Cori stared at her sister. "Really?"

"Really. This is all *crazy*. And crazy is your specialty. As long as *you're* smiling, I know we're not totally off the rails."

That was...unexpected. She knew Ava had fun when Cori was around, but she wasn't sure she'd ever *reassured* Ava before.

"Well, don't go by me," Cori said. "I'm usually the one pushing you all off the rails."

"Yeah, but...okay, if I'm going off the rails, I want someone with me who has experience. Who's survived that before."

Cori laughed. "You need someone who's climbed the mountain before?"

"I was thinking more like I need someone who's been in the scary, haunted forest and been chased by a creepy clown with a machete but who's made it out alive."

Cori snorted. "That makes Bliss the haunted forest and Evan the creepy clown?"

Ava grinned. "Okay, maybe it's not quite that bad." She paused. "Actually, I know why the haunted forest came to mind. Do you remember the haunted house we went to when we were thirteen?"

"You were supposed to be sixteen to go in, but I sweet-talked the guy at the door into letting us go," Cori said.

"I was scared to *death*," Ava said. "Even before we got inside. But you were...giddy about it. I just knew that if you could get that excited and think it was fun, then there wasn't anything to be *really* scared of."

"You hated that haunted house. We all had to sleep in the same bed for like two weeks, with you in the middle."

Ava nodded. "But you did that for me too. And honestly, that haunted house has always stuck with me. You were diving in because of the adrenaline rush. Brynn wasn't scared because she was able to look at everything and immediately figure out how they'd pulled off the illusions. It was just me...too uptight and not smart enough to avoid being scared."

"Hey—" Cori started.

But Ava shook her head. "But in the end, I got the best deal. You two, sleeping on either side of me, laughing and giggling until way past our bedtimes, for two whole weeks." She gave Cori a soft smile. "Totally worth it."

Cori blew out a breath. "You think Bliss can turn out the same way?"

"With you making it all fun and exciting and Brynn making it all practical and breaking things down step-by-step? Yeah, I think it can be the same way."

Cori reached out and squeezed Ava's hand. "I've got you, sis."

"I'm counting on it."

"Okay. Now take off your clothes for fuck's sake."

"I hate to ask you to sacrifice like this," Ava teased, but she began unbuttoning. "I mean, *making* you go out there and act all goofy over Evan."

"Yeah, yeah, more unbuttoning, less talking," Cori said, but she was smiling as they exchanged clothes.

Within minutes Cori was in a silk blouse and pencil skirt that was slightly tight through the hips. She needed to lay off the carbs. Or she needed to get her sisters eating more of them. Triple the wardrobe was one of the most obvious benefits of being triplets.

"Okay, let's do this fixing everything and making it all totally fine again," she said, as she slipped Ava's heels on. These were Gucci rather than Louis Vuitton but seriously, Ava had great taste in shoes.

"Hang on." Ava stepped forward, pulling the clip out of her hair. "Let's do it right."

Cori turned and she felt Ava gather her hair back and then twist it and secure it with the clip.

"Okay, *now* let's go. I can't wait to watch this," Ava said, actually looking like she was looking forward to it.

A minute later, Cori approached the table where Evan sat. She tried to keep her heart from pounding and her breathing from increasing. She wished she could blame it on nerves, but it was pure and simple lust. She wasn't nervous at all about sitting across the table from him. Or acting like she was falling for him.

That was, unfortunately, something that was as real as the diamond bracelet she'd also taken from Ava.

"Everything okay?" he asked as he stood and held her chair for her.

She gave him a smile and a nod. "Sure."

Be Ava. Be Ava. Let him scoot your chair in. She knew how that was done, of course, but she didn't hang out with guys who did it much. Of course, no one really held a barstool for a woman.

She gave him a smile as he returned to his seat in the chair perpendicular to hers. "Okay then, what were we talking about?" She definitely should have asked Ava that question. Instead she'd been busy apologizing...and being shocked to find out that Ava really liked having her here.

Evan hesitated, then he leaned back in his chair. "Cori," he said simply.

For a second, she thought he'd recognized her and was saying her name to confirm. Then she realized that he meant he and Ava had been talking about her.

Surprised skittered through her. She wet her lips. She should tell him who she was. He could be in on the ruse, of course. And she would. In a minute.

"Cori. Right. What about her again?"

"Her crazy idea about the party in the park."

The surprised rippled through her again, stronger this time. "Did...I...tell you *all* about it?" Cori asked, remembering partway through the sentence that she was supposed to be Ava.

"Is there more to it?" he asked. "She wants to call it Parking and Pie and have everyone come to the park for pie and a movie. Like a drive-in. She wants to make a bunch of kids' pies, like that s'mores pie she made the other night, and really appeal to the kids, who will then bring their parents. She wants to show that animated movie, *Jelly Jam*. That one is about a bunch of kitchen appliances and tools that cook and bake at night to save their owner's restaurant, right?"

Cori nodded and reached for her water glass. She was biting her tongue. She had to let *him* talk, see what he already knew, and act like *Ava* about the whole thing. And Ava was not practically jumping up and down in her seat over the idea. That much Cori did know. She'd told her sisters the idea that morning and had been met with not a lot of enthusiasm. Ava was worried about the pies and the general logistics of pulling something like that off when they hadn't been in town long. Which was, of course, why Cori thought it was a great idea. What better way to meet the town and show them that the girls wanted to be a part of the community? Brynn, the more practical one, talked about things like licenses and permits. Which was where Evan could, obviously, come in. He knew the laws and he knew everyone in town. Or maybe even the county. But Cori had figured *she* would be the one to bring it up to him, and she was surprised Ava had done it. Maybe they hadn't had anything else to talk about.

"And I told you about the charity part of it, right?" Cori asked. "Where we're going to give half of the profits to the before-school breakfast program and the snack program for the daycares?"

She'd asked the coffee club that met in the pie shop every morning if there were any food-related charities in the area—a shelter or food bank or something—that they could donate to. The guys had suggested the food bank in Great Bend, but she'd wanted something right in Bliss if possible. Thankfully, the guys had grandkids in the school system and one of them had a daughter who did daycare, so they'd known about both the breakfast program at the school and the program that provided nutritious snacks and nutritional education to daycare providers in the county. Which tied in perfectly with the kids' theme for the event, as well.

"You did," Evan said. "And I agree that knowing it's partly for charity will make everyone even more likely to come and participate."

"Oh, good. I didn't remember if I'd mentioned that."

Cori felt a little warm that Ava had brought all of this up. Cori had wanted to tell Evan about it. As more than the local attorney and guy-in-the-know. She'd wanted to tell him because...okay, because she'd wanted to impress him. The entire Parking and Pie event idea wasn't for Evan's benefit. The idea had come to her in the shower actually. But, she'd wanted to let him in on her idea and see his reaction. It was stupid, but she'd liked the look on his face when he'd accepted that first cup of caramel macchiato, and heard about Nutella-dipped bacon, and when he'd heard her talk about putting a photo booth in the pie shop, and when he'd watched her toast the marshmallows on the s'mores pie and taken that first bite. She liked the look of amusement combined with a touch of admiration on his face. It had seemed as if he'd liked all of those ideas, but even more, he'd been kind of intrigued by her out-of-the-box thinking.

Captivated.

The word whispered through her head and she had to fight a smile. That was the word he'd used last night to describe how he felt about her. She freaking *loved* that. And yeah, she wanted more. She wasn't throwing a pie party in the park—and she also really loved that alliteration—but she did want to tell Evan all about that party. And yes, she also had the feeling that he'd jump right in on that good time and help her make it even better.

"But I do agree that it's probably taking on too much too soon," he said, picking up his wineglass and taking a sip.

Cori let that sink in. "You don't think we should do it?"

"Not yet. Not if you're not ready."

Pop. Cori swore she could hear and feel her little bubble of excitement break.

"You need to get things at the shop going smoothly before you take on a big publicity stunt."

"But it's not a *stunt*. It's a way to get people trying our pies, first and foremost. And we need *something* to do that. And in addition, this would associate our business with fun and show we want to participate in the community."

Evan's eyebrows rose. "I thought you *didn't* like this idea?"

Oh yeah, shit. *Ava* didn't like this idea. "Well, I'm just surprised that *you* are dismissing it so quickly," she said honestly. "This seems like something you'd enjoy. I know you organize the 5K every year that raises money for the medical clinic here." It was a satellite clinic to the big medical group in Great Bend, but it provided all of the basic care the people here needed as well as bringing specialists in on a monthly basis for consultations. She'd heard all about that from her coffee group as well. Walter was followed by a cardiologist once a month and Ben had just been in to get his prostate checked. She'd heard way more about that than she's wanted to.

"I do," Evan said.

"And I know that it's more than just a 5K. You give it a theme every year and the runners and spectators dress up accordingly and the after party follows the theme as well."

He nodded. "Running kind of sucks. Even if it's for charity. I wanted to make it more fun."

Yeah, she'd loved hearing about that. The guys that sat in the front of her pie shop and raved about her coffee and kept her constantly buying more whipped cream, had given her more insight into the town—and Evan—than she could have ever hoped for. She'd gladly buy sprinkles and caramel syrup out of her own account in exchange for the steady flow of information. And laughter. The guys were great, and she couldn't help but think that if these guys had been her father's friends, then there was definitely more to Rudy than she'd thought.

"And I know that you do a lot of your business meetings while hunting or fishing. And that you throw amazing tailgate parties...

and have everyone throw in money toward the youth football program while they stand around and talk sports."

Her heart thumped again as she repeated the story that Roger had told her a few mornings ago. Everyone knew about Evan's fondness for a good party and having fun. But those extra things, like the fact that he preferred talking business while floating on the local fishing pond, or the fact that he found ways to make the fun into something more, were not as widely known. Or at least, they weren't as widely talked about. Not every party or get-together turned into a client meeting or charity event, of course, but the idea that some of them did made her stomach flip. Evan was a good guy. Just as she'd told Ava. A really good guy. Who didn't really see it about himself. This all seemed like something he just did without thinking about it. And she was incredibly grateful, again, that her sister was not attracted to him.

"It's easier to get generous donations when people are full of beer and brats," he said, again casually lifting his wineglass for a drink.

She nodded. "I'm sure. But my point is, you're all about having a good time and you're all about supporting this community. *And,*" she said, leaning in slightly, "you're all about supporting me and my sisters. What's with your hesitation on this park party?"

That bugged her. Sure, he thought she was Ava, and Ava had probably spelled out all of her concerns earlier. But still, this really seemed like something Evan would get into. She hated hearing he didn't like it. She had bad ideas sometimes. She had crazy ideas a lot of the time. And she'd accepted the fact that sometimes people were not going to buy in. But she hadn't expected it from Evan and it stung more from him. Whatever that meant.

And she didn't really want to know what that meant.

Evan shifted on his chair, leaning in and resting an elbow on the table. He met her gaze directly. "It's just a lot," he said. "The stuff I do has evolved over time. The 5K was always for charity, but someone else did it for three years before I took it over."

"They didn't have themes or a big after party though, I'm guessing," she said, knowing that those had to be Evan touches.

If he was surprised that "Ava" would have that kind of insight, he didn't show it. He just smiled. "That started out because the prior Halloween, Noah told me there was no way I could ever get Parker to dress up. Doing it for charity was my only chance. And I won fifty bucks off of Noah for that."

She laughed at that. She couldn't help it. Surely Ava would too. If nothing else, the idea of Parker Blake in a costume of any kind was just too funny.

"But the tailgates were just an excuse to get drunk and be loud at the game at first," he said. "And the fishing...I like fishing. One day a guy and I went out on the pond. We weren't going as client and attorney, just as buddies. But while we fished, we got to talking. And I found that he was a lot more amenable to the other side of the case while the fish were biting."

"You mediate a lot more than you actually sue or take people to court or whatever," Cori commented, unable to help it. Walter had told her that little tidbit and it had fascinated her. Of course, Ava wouldn't have said "whatever". She would have known the right terms for all the legal *stuff* Evan did. But Cori could hope he didn't know that.

"I do," Evan confirmed. "This is a small town full of people I've known and cared about my whole life. I don't like when they fight."

He gave a little smile, and Cori felt that flip in her stomach again.

"And don't you want these people you care about to have an amazing pie party in the park?" she asked.

Evan's smile dropped and he took a deep breath, his gaze going to his wineglass instead of holding hers. "I just think you girls might get in over your heads with it. Maybe next year."

Yeah, well, they weren't supposed to still be here, running the shop next year. And Cori couldn't deny that she felt a stab of sadness at that idea. Sure, things were anything but smooth and easy, but she couldn't say she'd hated her time in Bliss so far. Hanging out with her sisters at the shop all day, painting and stitching with Brynn, coaching Ava and resisting the urge to just push her sister out of the way and take over, listening to the coffee club, watching Noah and Brynn pretend not to flirt, watching Ava and Parker face off, anticipating seeing Evan...it had all been fun.

She shook all of that off. There was a long way to go before this year was over. She might feel differently by this time next year.

Okay, this party thing *was* a lot. And her sisters didn't love it. And Evan wasn't sold on it. But it was a good idea, dammit.

Cori took a drink of water, then said, "Well, Cori isn't very good at very many things, but she definitely knows how to throw a party. Maybe we should let her develop the idea a little bit."

Evan nodded. "Yeah, a huge, blowout good time seems right up her alley. But—"

"But?" Cori asked.

"I wouldn't say Cori isn't good at very many things."

"Oh?" Cori set her glass down, her palm suddenly feeling a little tingly. "What do you mean?" She was very good at kissing this guy, that was for sure.

"She's very good at making the coffee guys feel welcome even when they're completely underfoot. She's very good at making you and Brynn smile. She's very good at being absolutely exactly who she is, even when we're all telling her to pull back. And she's very good at winding me up tighter than any woman ever has, simply by laughing, or wetting her lips, or taking a drink of water."

His gaze was focused on her mouth now, and Cori wet her lips without thinking as her heart pounded in her chest. His eyes darkened and he reached out for her hand, then tugged her close as he leaned in as if to whisper in her ear.

"In my dreams, your nipples taste like whipped cream," he said softly, huskily, against her neck.

Shock—and lust—shot through her. Followed immediately by confusion. Before she could speak, however, he lifted a hand and traced his finger over the C tattooed behind her ear.

Oh.

She turned her head and put her lips against his. "Funny, your cock tastes like whipped cream in *my* dreams."

He gave a soft groan and kissed her. Not deep and hot the way she wanted, but more like a promise of the deep and hot to come.

"When did you know it was me?" she asked, when he lifted his head.

"When you walked across the restaurant toward me."

"Really?"

"You and Ava move differently. And…"

She pulled back to look in his eyes. "And?" she asked, arching a brow.

"The skirt is a little more snug on you than her," he said, almost hesitantly.

"Dammit, I knew it," Cori said. "I gotta lay off the pie."

"Cori," Evan said seriously, looking into her eyes. "You're perfect. I love every fucking curve. And I'd like to love them even more. Up close and personal. With my hands and lips."

She blew out a breath. "Well, I'd say all of this is much more convincing than what you and Ava were trying to pull off."

"And I think I should take you home," he said.

"Okay."

"And fire up the gossips about how long we sat in the truck in your driveway before you got out with your hair messed up, your blouse buttoned wrong, and a very big smile on your face."

She swallowed hard and nodded. "I can probably pull that off."

"I can definitely help."

They stood simultaneously and linked hands as they started for the door.

"Fuck." Evan pulled up short all of a sudden.

"What?" Cori felt almost breathless and it wasn't from the quick walk to the door.

"I should probably pay." He gave her a sheepish grin. "Kind of got distracted there."

She laughed and watched as he pulled his wallet out and headed for the waitress to settle the bill. She caught her sisters' gazes. They looked amused. And happy. For her. And Cori felt a warmth in her chest. The shared looks, the knowing what they were thinking from across the room, the joke that the rest of the town wasn't in on, the fact that they wanted her to be happy...it was all just really good. And it was thanks to being forced to be together. By their father.

"You ready?" Evan was back at her side.

She gave him a huge smile and linked her fingers with his again. "So ready."

9

Evan worked very hard to drive carefully to the Carmichael house. But he cussed every single stop sign and other driver between the restaurant and their driveway.

By the time he pulled into the drive and parked just past the sidewalk, he was wound tight and had only three things in his mind: how Cori smelled, how Cori's breast felt in his hand, and how she sounded when she moaned.

He turned off the truck and started to turn toward her, but before he'd even shifted an inch, she was already crawling toward him.

"Let's steam up these windows already," she said playfully as she started to lift her leg to swing it over his thighs. But she got stopped mid-swing. "Dammit," she muttered, putting her knee back on the seat.

He reached for her, mostly because he had to touch her *now*, than because he thought he could be a lot of help with...whatever the problem was. His hand skimmed her side to her hip as she braced herself on all fours over his front seats. "You okay?"

"This skirt is too tight," she said with a sigh.

He gave a soft chuckle. "Lose the skirt, Cori."

She looked up at him. "Yeah?"

"Unless you don't want me to put my hands where I intend to put them as soon as humanly possible."

She wet her lips and, as always, the action sent aching heat straight to his cock. "I want your hands *everywhere*."

"Then we are definitely on the same page."

"Well, we *have* to do this," she said. "for the sake of the neighbors."

Holding her gaze, he reached for the zipper on the side of the skirt. Yeah, he'd made a note of where the skirt zipped up. A guy had to be prepared. The rasp of the zipper going down filled the cab as Cori's breathing got faster.

She pushed back to kneel on the seat and slid the skirt down over her hips. Then shifting side to side, she moved out of it and tossed it on the floor. She started toward him, but then paused. She looked at the skirt, sighed, picked it up and then folded it over the back of the seat.

She caught him watching her with a smile and shrugged. "It's Ava's."

"Right."

Evan was grateful to the city of Bliss for positioning the streetlights where they had. And for whichever sister had turned on the porch light before leaving tonight. Along with the moonlight, they provided just enough light for him to see Cori's face as she knelt on the seat in only her panties, heels, and the white silk blouse. She looked turned on, if not slightly hesitant.

He held out his hand. "What are you waiting for?"

"I was just thinking," she said. "I'm not sure the last time I made out in a truck."

He smiled. "That's a semi-regular thing around here."

"And I'm not sure the last time I did this with a guy I like as much as I like you."

His smile died. There was suddenly an ache behind his breastbone and he wasn't sure if it was because his lungs had stopped working or because his heart had just taken the hardest beat of his life. Evan cleared his throat. "I like you too."

She nodded. "I know. That makes this different too."

The happiness he felt knowing that she knew he liked her was strange. "I find it impossible to believe that the other guys haven't liked you."

"They liked what they knew," she said. "But they didn't know much."

She was going to kill him. Just when he thought he might be at risk of dying of pent-up lust because of this woman, she made him realize that he might just die of wanting. And not wanting physically. At least not wanting *just* physically. But wanting everything. To be everything and give her everything and do everything she needed.

"Cori," he finally said, aware that his voice was rough and that he probably looked like a man in pain, "I really need you to come over here."

With a deep breath, she took his hand. As corny as it sounded, the moment their hands touched, Evan felt a shaft of need and *this is perfect* knife through him. He tugged her forward and she knee-walked across the leather.

This time when she swung her knee up, she had plenty of range of motion and she quickly straddled his thighs. Evan reached for the lever that would move the seat back, giving them extra room. Then his hands settled on her hips, the heat from her skin seeping into him from his lap and palms.

"Kiss me." His voice was still rough, but he knew she could hear the raw desire.

She put her hands on either side of his face, looked him directly in the eyes, and said, "I really need to do more than kiss you."

"Yeah?" He was definitely on board with that. Whether or not he should be. At the moment, with Cori Carmichael on his lap and in his hands, he simply couldn't care about anything else.

"I've also never kissed a guy as much as I have you without doing a hell of a lot more," she said with a smile.

That smile made things knot up in places Evan didn't even know he could feel knotted up. "You shouldn't say stuff like that if you want to get lucky tonight," he said, trying desperately for teasing rather than going completely serious and deep. Because he sucked at serious and deep, and he was going to die if Cori climbed off of his lap before he'd seen and touched and kissed a whole lot more than her lips.

"No?" she asked, tipping her head.

Evan reached up and squeezed the clip that was holding her hair up. He tossed it on the dashboard as the long blonde tresses fell to her shoulders and he pulled his fingers through them. "It kind of makes me want to just keep kissing you," he said. "I like being different for you." On one hand, he wanted to consume her, to brand her, to make sure there wasn't an inch of her that hadn't been touched by every inch of him. But on the other hand, being the guy that she wasn't immediately seducing sounded damn good too.

Though he definitely felt seduced. By things other than her amazing body and her playful daring in the bedroom. And he didn't need to ask to confirm that Cori was playfully daring when it came to sex. That was as much a part of her as her laugh and her sassiness and her love for sweets.

"Evan," she said, her voice soft and serious.

He felt his frown. Cori wasn't soft or serious. "Yeah?"

"You are different. No matter if everything from here on out is stuff we've both done a million times. You're different."

His heart gave one of those almost painful *whumps* and he had to swallow before saying, "Thank God. Because I'm sitting here feeling like a regular, dumb-ass guy who just happened to rub a lamp and ended up with a goddess genie in his lap and I was hoping to get a really good taste of you before you figured out how much better you could do."

The look on her face was a combination of amazement and disbelief and happiness and humor that seemed to reach in and wrap a fist around his heart.

"I thought this was going to be a wild and fast chance for us to both get rid of some of this crazy sexual tension," she finally said.

"And it's not?"

"Well, it might be that too," she said with a smile. "But it's also turning into...more."

Fuck yeah it was. Then Evan frowned. Fuck. Yeah, it was.

Then she wiggled on his lap and all Evan could think was the *yeah*.

"Kiss me, Cori."

This time she did. No more talking. No more making him wonder if his heart would continue to function adequately. Or if it had *ever* really functioned before this. Just her mouth on his, her hands on his face, his hands on her hips.

For about ten seconds. Then their hands began moving. She slid hers to the back of his head and into his hair. He ran his down her thighs—her bare thighs—to her knees and back up. She shifted in his lap and pressed closer to his cock. He gripped her hips and brought her down against his hard length. The feel of her against him was relief and torture at the same time. He slipped his fingertips under the edge of the scrap of silk that was all that covered her sweet ass and the wet heat that he was now grinding against his fly.

"Evan," she gasped as his fingers stroked the bare skin of her butt.

"Unbutton," he said hoarsely.

She sat back slightly, which brought her against his cock more firmly. They both groaned and she quickly went to work on the buttons of the blouse.

"Hurry up, Cori," he said, his tone more commanding than he'd intended. Not that it seemed to bother her at all. "I don't want to rip Ava's blouse. But I fucking will."

Her eyes flew to his, the heat there obvious. "Damn, Counselor, I do love that firm tone of voice you pull out once in a while."

"Do you now?" he asked, sliding one hand higher on her ass and squeezing. "I can get a lot more demanding than that." Several demands went through his mind in a heartbeat, in fact.

She parted the front of the shirt and then slipped it off, leaving her in panties and bra and heels only. She reached to drape it over the seat on top of the skirt. The motion pressed her breasts against his chest. He wanted to dip his head and take one of those tips into his mouth, but he held back. For now.

"I don't know," she said, sitting back, settling her butt against his thighs. "You're such a nice guy. Born and raised in Bliss, Kansas. The guy everyone wants around for a good time, but nothing too serious. Right?"

He watched her eyes, miraculous with those tempting-him-since-day-one breasts right there. He *was* a nice guy. And he was a hell of a good time. But he knew that she didn't buy the whole nothing-too-serious thing. And that made him want her even more. She saw beneath his everything's-a-party façade. Because she was the same person. She was more over-the-top, bold and beautiful and bright than he was, but yeah, she got him.

Which was why this absolutely felt serious. And he knew she wanted him right here, serious as hell, about everything that was about to happen. "Well, I can be demanding *and* polite," he said.

"Oh, yeah?" A teasing smile lifting one corner of her mouth.

"Oh, sure. You don't think I can say things like "Miss Carmichael, wrap those gorgeous, sassy lips around my cock"?" he asked.

He watched her swallow hard, but she said, "You didn't even say please."

He lifted a hand to the back of her hair, threaded his fingers through it, and tugged gently, bringing her mouth against his, "*You're* going to be the one saying please."

When he kissed her, it was hungry, but he held her still, so that he was the one taking it all from her. Then he released her lips, and said gruffly, "I want to see your nipples."

She licked her lips and reached behind her.

"The one time you're actually wearing a bra," he muttered as her back arched so she could undo the tiny hooks.

She laughed, quickly tossing the bra away.

And he was finally eyes-on with the breasts that had been haunting him since New York.

Then Cori tried to kill him again by lifting her hands and cupping the gorgeous mounds, teasing the tips with her thumbs. "I hate bras."

"You should never, ever, wear a bra again," he said, unable, in spite of being a nice guy, to tear his eyes away from her playing with her nipples.

She laughed, the sound shooting to his cock as surely as the sight of her naked from the waist up.

"On second thought," he said, without much thought, really, "you should always wear a bra. Unless you're with me."

She paused. "That sounds a little...possessive."

"Yeah," he looked up. Should he tell her he was never possessive of women? Never jealous? Or should he lie and say that this was totally normal for him?

"I don't usually tolerate that," she said, almost thoughtfully.

"But?" he asked, knowing there was more there.

"With you, it feels..."

"Tolerable?" he asked with a slight smile.

"Good," she finally finished.

He took that in. Then slowly nodded.

She started to drop her hands, but he said firmly, "Keep going."

Cori squirmed on his lap as she rolled her nipples between her thumb and fingers. "I want you to touch me, Evan."

"Where?"

"Anywhere. Everywhere."

"Does that make you wet?" he asked, finally lifting his eyes. "Does playing with your nipples make your clit ache?"

She blew out a breath. "Yes," she said softly.

"Would having me suck on them make your pussy clench?"

"Holy crap," she breathed. "You Kansas boys are dirty talkers, huh?"

"Well, you do think dirty talk is *nice*, don't you?" he asked with a grin he was sure looked a little wicked. She did. He could tell in everything from the way her breathing quickened to how her nipples tightened to how she was looking at him.

"I love dirty talk," she admitted.

"Then tell me how to make you come, Cori," he said, his voice like sandpaper, his tone firm even without him consciously trying.

He was a dirty talker. It came naturally to him. And with Cori, hell, he had all kinds of things he could say about the things he wanted to do to her and how she made him feel, how he wanted to make her feel. But as he opened his mouth to say something about his tongue and her clit and the bed of his truck, he suddenly couldn't say those words. It occurred to him that the things he wanted to say were more along the lines of worshipping her and that he needed a lot more room for the things he wanted to do and that she was going to need to let her sisters know she was going to be late to work in the morning. And none of that really felt dirty. He wanted her more than he'd ever wanted another woman, but it felt like...more. Damn, that was becoming the theme between them.

"Tell me how to touch you," he said, focusing on her nipples. "Tell me exactly what you want." There, maybe she could do the talking part.

"Your fingers," she said after a second. "Ever since you took that caramel macchiato from me in New York, I've been thinking about your fingers curling around and holding that cup."

Yep, he could do that. His fingers were practically itching.

"And I'm afraid I'm going to have to taste those sweet nipples. See if I was right about the flavor," he told her.

She lifted herself slightly off of his lap, kneeling on the seat while straddling him. He leaned in and finally took the tip of one breast between his lips, licking, then sucking. She moaned and shifted impatiently, and Evan really had no choice but to run his hand up the back of her thigh, slip a finger under the edge of her panties, and slide over the hot, slick folds underneath.

She gripped his shoulders as he sucked harder and slid higher, dipping into the sweet wetness between her legs.

"*Evan,*" she panted. "More."

I want to bury my face right here, he thought as he slid into her tightness. *I want to spread you out and lick every inch of you. I want to hold your hair back so I can see your hot mouth around my cock. I want to feel your hair spread out over my chest and stomach. I want to smell my soap on you in the morning. I want to make you late for work and know it's because we were lying in bed laughing and talking even though everyone will think it was because I was fucking you on the kitchen counter.*

Shock and trepidation and confusion rocked through Evan as his thoughts spun. He had the most delicious nipple in his mouth, his fingers deep inside the hottest, sweetest pussy he'd ever touched, and he was thinking about laughing and talking with her.

He should just *say* the stuff about having her spread out with his face between her legs. Cori would like that, he knew it. Hell, it was the kind of stuff he said often enough. He'd actually love to hear some of the things she said in response. But his tongue seemed frozen. Well, not frozen exactly. He was doing something right to her nipple, judging by the moaning and way she was gripping his shoulder, and the wriggling against his hand. But he suddenly couldn't talk dirty. To the woman who'd maybe had more of that than any of the other women he'd been with. To the woman who had admitted to loving it and who could, no doubt, give as good as she got.

What. The. Hell?

"Evan, please, more," she said, lowering her mouth to his and giving him a hot, deep kiss.

That wasn't dirty either. She wasn't saying "fuck me" or "spank me" or even "harder" and yet her plea fired his blood. Well, he could at least do *more*. He moved his thumb over her clit and slid a second finger deep. He circled his thumb as he pumped in and out and took her other nipple into his mouth, sucking, then nipping slightly.

She moaned and moved against his hand, and it was only a couple of minutes before she was gasping his name and coming around his fingers.

She paused for a few seconds, breathing hard, and Evan moved his hand and mouth. She slumped against him then, wrapping her arms around his neck, and putting her face against his throat.

And they just sat like that. No dirty talk, no clothes being ripped off, no one fumbling for a condom.

They were in the front seat of his truck, she was mostly naked in his lap, and all he wanted to do was rub his hand up and down her back and enjoy the feel of her hair against his hand and arm, the smell of her body spray and shampoo surrounding him, the feel of her hot and spent in his arms.

If he'd been able to take his hands off of her, he'd run one over his face. And probably say something like *fuuuuuck*.

Finally, she lifted her head and took a deep breath. She leaned back to look at him. "Um, sorry about that."

He lifted a brow. "Excuse me? Sorry for what?"

"It doesn't usually go that fast. At least not without some toys or the chance of being caught or at least some liquor." She frowned as if thinking about that. "We didn't even really do the dirty talk, did we?"

"First of all, *never* be sorry for *that*," he told her as he worked to tamp down thoughts of her doing all the toys-getting-caught-liquor stuff with another guy. "That was hot and sweet and... pretty much the best part of my year so far." He gave her a grin. "And hey, I did say clit, pussy, and cock."

"Yeah. And that was hot. But I guess..."

"What?"

"I guess I kind of thought when you and I did this, we'd go at it really fast and hard and dirty."

Yeah, he would have thought that too. He nodded. "Yeah."

"So..." She chewed on her bottom lip. "Should we try that?"

He wanted to. He wanted to reach between them, unzip his pants, and thrust deep. He honestly did. But he also...didn't.

"You're going to think I'm crazy," he said. Hell, *he* thought he was crazy. "But I think maybe I should head home."

Her eyebrows rose. "Seriously?"

"Yeah." At least he could be remembered as the only guy on the planet to *not* go for fast and hard and dirty with Cori Carmichael when invited to. Because there wasn't another guy in the world who would say no to that.

"Um. Okay, then." She clearly didn't know what to say. She reached for the blouse draped over the seat and shrugged into it.

Evan clenched his fists to keep from reaching for her and clamped his jaw shut to keep from asking—begging—her to stay.

Then she ran a hand through her hair and slid off of his lap. She gathered the skirt and bra to her chest, opened the door and got out. She ducked down to look at him. "See ya, Evan."

Yeah, there'd be no avoiding that. What with him dating her sister and all.

"'Bye, Cori."

And with the length of time they'd been out here, her hair a mess, and her heading up the front in her panties only...the neighbors were definitely going to be talking.

"**Y**ou're in love with her, you dumb-ass." Parker set a cup of coffee in front of Evan without being asked.

A sure sign he was concerned about his friend. At least as concerned as Parker got. Frankly, Parker felt like the people in Bliss, particularly his friends, had pretty great lives and he didn't get too worked up over the minor dramas that cropped up here and there. Even when other people thought they were major.

"I'm sorry, *what*?" Evan asked.

"That's why you couldn't fuck her in the front seat of your truck like you do all the other girls," Parker said, his tone making it clear that he thought this was obvious. "She's different for you. The same old stuff—the dirty talk and the front seat and all of that—doesn't feel right with her."

As much as he hated to admit it, that made sense. The idea that he was in love with Cori wasn't nearly as shocking as he would have thought it would be. It actually made sense. The girl was loveable. Plain and simple. And he was a highly intelligent guy. Okay, he was moderately intelligent. Anyway, he was smart enough to realize that she was special and to fall for that.

Evan was glad that Parker had to get to the restaurant at five to start serving breakfast at six. And he was glad that his friend had opened the front door for Evan in spite of the fact that Parker really hated when people messed with his schedule.

He was also glad that Noah had answered his text and joined them for the impromptu meeting. He didn't often ask his friends, or anyone for that matter, for advice. Because, he agreed with Parker—they all had it pretty easy and great here. He just rolled with the punches and didn't let the little things bug him much.

"You can't talk dirty to the girl you're in love with?" Noah asked. "That sounds like bullshit to me."

"Of course you can," Parker said. "But you have to understand that in the middle of telling her that you want her bent over the couch so you can fuck her with a dildo, you might also think about how you want to take her to the fair so she can ride the carousel and that you want to get her a necklace with her birthstone in it for her birthday."

Evan and Noah didn't say a word. Evan looked over at Noah to find the mechanic staring at Parker like he'd never met him before. Okay, so it wasn't just him.

Evan turned back to Parker. "*What?*"

Parker sighed.

"Seriously? This isn't hard to understand. When you're in love, all of that stuff gets mixed up together."

Parker straightened, and Noah and Evan swiveled on their stools to face the man who'd just walked in.

"You didn't lock the damned door behind you?" Parker asked Noah.

"Sorry."

"Hank, you know we don't open until six," Parker said.

Hank slid into the first booth. "Lights were on, door was unlocked, and coffee was being poured."

"Private meeting, Hank," Evan said. "I've got some...issues."

"Yeah, you're in love. I heard," Hank said. "But you should be glad I'm here. At least I've actually been in love. Unlike these two yahoos you're getting 'advice' from." Hank even made the air quotes with his fingers.

"Maybe you should get a bell above the door like the pie shop has," Evan said to Parker. "I didn't even hear him come in."

Parker was already filling a cup and handing it to Noah to hand to Hank. "I'm not putting a little tinkly bell above my door," he said flatly.

Hank gave a long, happy sigh after he took his first drink. "This coffee sucks, Parker," he said.

"I know, Hank," Parker returned.

"But at five twenty in the morning, who the fuck cares," Hank said.

"What are you doing up so early anyway?" Noah asked. "You guys usually come in for breakfast at seven thirty."

"I started getting up to work the farm with my dad at five a.m. when I was ten years old," Hank said. "You can't break habits like that. I was just taking my morning walk and saw the lights."

"You don't need to finish your walk?" Parker asked.

"Coffee trumps walking. Any time of day," Hank told him.

Evan grinned. It wasn't the coffee—because Parker's coffee really did suck—it was the company. Hank had lived in Bliss his whole life and had a number of friends. But that didn't mean in the wee hours of the morning, or night, he wasn't lonely. His wife had died about six years ago and he lived alone now.

"Okay, well, you've got a point. You've been in love before. It's normal to have all of that—" He broke off with a cough. Could he discuss his sex life with Hank? "—everything you feel and think," he finally went with, "get all mixed up?"

"Of course." Hank shook his head. "That's how you know it's love. When you want to do more than fuck."

Evan's eyes widened at Hank's blunt statement. But he realized the man had a point.

"Well, Evan's messed around with some girls he's friends with," Parker decided to interject.

Evan gave him a frown.

"I mean, he didn't just want sex from them," Parker went on, ignoring Evan.

Hank nodded. "But when you were messing around, what were you thinking about? Tits and ass, right?"

Noah almost spit out the drink of coffee he'd just taken.

Evan thumped him on the back and said to Hank, "Yep, pretty much."

"Well, when you're in love, things like hearing her laugh at the jokes on the Late Show make you just as hot as how she looks when she bends over," he said, rolling his eyes at Noah when he again choked slightly on his coffee. "And the way she cheats, badly, at Scrabble makes you want her just as much as the way she looks in lingerie. And even when she's bare-assed naked, you make a note to get a bag of gumdrops the next time you're at the store because they're her favorites. It all gets mixed up together."

Evan looked at the older man for a long moment. That all made perfect sense. And was all something he'd never experienced before Cori Carmichael blew into his life.

But he turned to Parker. "Okay, how the *hell* did you know all of that?" Parker had never, to Evan's knowledge, been in love.

"You think Hank's the only one that talks like that?" Parker asked, passing Noah the coffeepot so he could refill Hank's cup. "They all do. They give advice like that—and on lots of other topics—to anyone who will listen."

Evan shook his head. "Too bad we don't have a bar in this town. That seems more like bar talk."

Parker sighed. "You're telling me."

But Evan knew that his friend actually loved being the hub for all the gossip, political debates, sports talk and yes, even relationship advice, in Bliss.

"Hank, your coffee's on me," Evan told him as Evan slid off the stool. He needed to wrap his head around all of this. That he was in love with Cori. That it meant he *could* get dirty with her, even while he wanted to buy her a St. Bernard puppy, and that he could want to cover her naked body in pie filling and then lick it off, slowly, even while wanting to take her to the nearest photo booth and take strip after strip of photos with her.

"Well, I would hope so," Hank said, saluting Evan with his cup. "Glad I could help you realize how you felt. I hope you and Ava are happy for as many years as I got with Maryann."

Evan froze with a ten dollar bill suspended over the countertop.

Ava.

Right.

He was supposed to be in love with Ava. For four and a half more months.

Parker plucked the money from his fingers and said softly, "Breathe, buddy."

Breathe. Yeah, okay, that was a good first step.

After which he really had no idea what to do.

10

"Evan and I have decided that we're probably best off if we keep our dates a little less public," Ava announced as she came into the front of the pie shop, a pie in hand.

Or more interestingly, an unburnt, seemingly fully baked, pie. Which would make it a rarity in the pie shop.

"You talked to Evan?" Cori asked, pretending that her heart wasn't suddenly racing.

"He just called," Ava said. "He's coming over for a movie night tonight."

It had been three nights since Cori and Ava had switched places at the restaurant. And Evan had given Cori an orgasm in the cab of his truck. And then kicked her out of the cab of that truck.

"Movie night sounds like a good idea," Brynn said from where she was hanging a set of the new curtains in the front window. "That's a totally normal thing for a dating couple to do, his truck will be in the driveway, but it's not out in front of everyone."

"Exactly." Ava set the pie on the counter.

"But you have to actually watch the movie with him," Cori said. "That's the deal. *You* doing fun, normal dating-type stuff."

"I know. I intend to. He's going to bring dinner and the movie over."

"What time?" Cori asked, knowing she was going to either need to hide in her room or avoid the house. She didn't know exactly what had happened the other night, but things had been intense. And no matter what emotions and thoughts had been swirling around in that truck, the bottom line was that her sister's supposed boyfriend had had his hands on *her* bottom line.

She and Evan needed to behave, and apparently the only way to really do that, was to avoid one another.

And yeah, her ego was a little stung. Or very stung. She'd been half-naked on his lap. A lap that had purportedly had a lot of half-naked in it. And he'd said goodnight.

That bit of humiliation was making avoiding him a lot easier.

"Around seven," Ava said.

"Okay." It sucked that Bliss didn't have a bar. And she couldn't really go over to the next town that did have a bar, drink, and then drive home. Dammit. She was going to have to find something to do that didn't involve liquor.

She was pretty sure she could do that. Probably.

"Come taste this," Ava said. "I think I've got it."

"You've got it?" Brynn asked. "As in, you made a good pie?"

"I think so." Ava looked pleased, and both Cori and Brynn set down what they were doing to join her at the counter.

She handed them each a fork. Cori and Brynn looked at each other and quickly did *rock-paper-scissors*. Cori lost.

"Seriously?" Ava asked, as Cori stepped up to be the first to try the pie.

Cori just shrugged. "No sense in both of us having to wash our mouths out."

Ava rolled her eyes. Cori dug her fork into the pie at one edge. It was cherry, which was generally her favorite. She took out a tiny forkful and gingerly lifted it to her lips.

"Oh, for God's sake," Ava muttered. She picked up another fork and dug a huge bite out, putting it in her mouth.

Cori took the bite and chewed. Then she frowned, and scooped up another bite. The second was as good as the first. "Holy crap, Ava. You *did* do it."

"Really?" Brynn grabbed a fork. She was nodding within seconds. "Wow, you did. This is really good."

Ava smiled, nodded, then grimaced.

"What's going on?" Cori asked, taking one more bite, then thought about how Ava's skirt had been too tight on her and set her fork down. Then she thought about how she'd taken that skirt off and everything that happened after it, and she smiled and got a little flushed and then frowned and picked her fork back up. Because all she had now was pie. Because she was crazy about Evan, and Evan was really, really good with his mouth and just as good with his fingers...and she hadn't gotten to know how good he was with other parts. But she sure as hell had imagined it all night long.

Yeah, she was going to eat pie. Because the guy she was falling for had tossed her out of his truck after giving her one of the fastest orgasms of her life, and he was now coming over to watch movies with her sister.

"Okay, I *made* that pie," Ava said.

Brynn and Cori nodded, both still chewing.

"But," Ava went on. "I didn't make the parts of the pie."

Cori narrowed her eyes. "What do you mean?"

"I paid a woman for *her* pie crusts. And I bought the pie filling."

Cori set her fork down. "Ava."

"I know, I know. But listen," Ava said quickly. "I am making the pies. I'm getting my hands messy. I'm learning my way around the kitchen. That's the point, right? That's what I'm supposed to be doing." She sighed. "I can't make a pie crust to save my life. I don't get it and it's making me crazy, but I can't. And we can't keep going like this. We have to get the shop open and since it's a pie shop, we need to have pie."

"So you found a loophole," Cori said. She glanced at Brynn. "You are both finding all these loopholes in this plan." She had to laugh. "I'm impressed. I thought I was the only loophole girl in this little trio."

"Well," Ava said. "How am I doing?"

Cori looked down at the pie, then at her sisters. "It's homemade crust?"

"Yep. And," Ava added, "I paid her to adapt the recipe to make it something that would be exclusive to us. She won't make it any other time, even on her own."

"How did she adapt it?"

"I have no idea."

Cori couldn't help but grin. "Okay, we have an exclusive, homemade crust that *you* have to bake."

"And fill," Ava said.

Cori and Brynn laughed. "That's gotta count. At least partially," Cori agreed.

Ava smiled, but she looked earnest as she said, "It's just that if Dad wanted me to learn about creating the product from scratch, I'm doing that. I know *about* making pie crusts now...I just suck at it. And I *am* making the pies—at least I'm putting them together. But I've also realized the weakness in my process, and I've fixed it. It's resourceful."

Cori shook her head. "No wonder you always get your way in the board room."

Ava gave her a smile. "Well, maybe not *always*."

Yeah, well, ninety-eight percent of the time was pretty much always.

"We have pie now," Brynn said. "When can we open?"

"How many crusts to do you have?" Cori asked.

"A dozen," Ava said. "I figure that's optimistic for our first week."

Cori would love to debate that, but she thought Ava might have a point.

"Okay, but you're going to have to hide the pie filling cans," Brynn said, pointing at Ava. "You know Parker will be all over that."

"Ugh," Ava said, with an eye roll. "Don't worry, I'll figure that out. But you—" she said, pointing a finger at Cori's nose, "—have to keep your trap shut around Evan."

Cori dug another scoop out of the pie and said, "No worries." She chewed as her sisters shared a look.

"What's that mean?" Ava asked.

"Evan is avoiding me. And vice versa."

They shared another look.

"Why?" Brynn asked.

Cori took another bite and shrugged. "Because I was myself," she said around the mouthful of deliciously flaky crust and sweet-and-tart filling.

"And what's *that* mean?" Ava asked.

Cori swallowed. "A nice guy steps up to help me and my sisters take care of the crazy-assed crap our crazy-assed father put in his crazy-assed trust and what did I do? I flirted, I kissed him, I fell for him, and then when he gave me a ride home, while I'm pretending to be my sister don't forget, I climbed into his lap and had an orgasm."

Brynn started choking and Ava's mouth, literally, fell open.

Cori took the final bite of her pie and seriously considered taking another piece. She chewed as she watched her sisters process everything.

"You had an orgasm just sitting on his lap?" Brynn asked.

Cori swallowed and pushed her plate away. But not too far. "Well, Evan helped."

Brynn nodded. "Okay, that makes more sense."

Cori snorted, in spite of the fact that she was feeling stupid and sheepish.

"So he helped. That's good. What's the problem?" Ava asked.
"Why is he avoiding you now?"

"Because—" She blew out a breath. "I brought a St. Bernard
to the party," Cori said.

There was a pause, then it was Ava that snorted. "Oh, honey,
that's not what you did."

"It is," Cori said. "He wanted me there. I'm not saying that he
didn't. But he didn't realize that I *always* get carried away."

"You made out—and very well from the sounds of it—with a
guy you like, who really likes you. I sincerely doubt he regrets
anything about it," Ava said.

"Then why didn't he keep going?" Cori asked. The question
had been nagging her ever since. Evan Stone didn't seem like the
type of guy to pull back from a very clear offer from a half-naked
woman. Hell, he'd slept with Jill and he said that he'd known,
even at the time to some extent, that he shouldn't have. "After the
dog debacle, Dad escorted me out of the building immediately
before I could cause any more damage," Cori said. "The other
night Evan got me out of the truck as quickly as he could. He
didn't even unbutton his shirt."

Brynn was biting her bottom lip and looking unsure.

"Maybe it was just that it was our driveway and we weren't too
far behind and..." Ava trailed off.

"It wasn't the right time or place," Cori filled in.

"Yeah," Ava agreed.

"Yeah." That was the story of her life. It seemed she had a lot
of trouble finding the *right* time and place to be herself.

———

I nstead of hanging out at the house or trying to kill time at the
diner or heading to the bar in the next town, Cori spent
"movie night" in the kitchen at the pie shop. She wasn't supposed
to be the one creating the pies for the customers, but that didn't

mean she couldn't be in the place at all. And it definitely beat hiding in her room or, worse, joining Evan and Ava on the couch for their date night. In their living room, there would be no reason for Cori to stand in for Ava, and even though she knew nothing was really going to happen between Evan and Ava, seeing Evan after the whole...*thing*...the other night did not sound fun.

But having the pie shop kitchen all to herself was perfect. She could experiment with some new pie ideas and, for the first time, feel like she was working while Ava was relaxing.

And she was being supportive. She'd made Ava and Evan two kinds of popcorn and had put extra pillows on the couch, because you couldn't have a good movie night without pillows and popcorn. Everyone knew that.

It wasn't until she had the pie ready for the oven that she realized that Evan was here with her anyway. She'd made Nutella bacon pie.

With a sigh, she slid it into the oven. Well, it wasn't like Nutella and bacon was a bad idea. Ever. But it was annoying that even when she was trying to be good and stay out of the way, all of the things she really wanted wouldn't leave *her* alone. She couldn't leave Bliss the way she used to leave places when she started to feel restless or in the way. She could hang out at the house *with* them, but she'd never been very good at resisting temptation. Which Evan Stone most definitely was. And, evidently, she wasn't very good at distracting herself.

She did the dishes, and then looked around. The quiet was nice. Time alone was nice. Living and working with her sisters meant they spent a lot of time together. Having a break was great.

Really great.

Super great.

Oh, who was she kidding? Cori sighed. *She* was the social one. She'd lived alone here and there, but she did prefer roommates. It often worked out to sublease from someone since she tended to not stay in one place for the entire length of a typical rental agreement. Hell, she could use some *more* noise and conversation that wasn't about pie and paint. At the house, her sisters were busy and kept to themselves unless she made them come out of their rooms/offices and socialize.

Cori wandered to the front of the shop, taking in the new paint and cushions and curtains. It was looking really nice and there was no way this wouldn't be a huge surprise to the people of Bliss when they came in. If they came in. She blew out a breath as she turned in a circle. People had to come in. Because she and Brynn and Ava needed the money. That wasn't a position any of them had been in before, and it felt strange having to worry about paying bills. How did they bring in more money? How much could they bring in? If they only brought in so much, what should they spend it on? They needed to take care of the essentials, of course. Thankfully, the cost of living in Bliss was very low, and the few hundred dollars in the bank account were keeping the lights and water on at the shop. But the bills would keep coming, and then she really would like to buy some less-than-essentials. New pie pans. A bigger mixer. Of course, Rudy had gotten by with a hand mixer for years...

Cori shook her head. If it wasn't Evan on her mind, it was Rudy. Or both.

She sat down at one of the tables and checked out the shop from that perspective. They needed something on the walls behind the front counter. Maybe a framed inspirational poster. She laughed. Okay, maybe not. But framed artwork would be nice. And she really wanted to put a chalkboard menu up. And then she'd need colored chalk. Lots of colored chalk. She loved colored chalk. Well, colored everything.

But chalk—colored or otherwise—was way down the list of priorities.

They had to make the shop profitable, and the adjustment from not-a-financial-care-in-the-world to where's-the-grocery-money-going-to-come-from was taking a while. They all had personal accounts and credit cards. They weren't supposed to use those for the shop—they were using the business account and the new card Cori had gotten for that—but their own checking accounts were keeping the fridge stocked and the utilities on at the house. They were secure, not homeless or starving, but they definitely had to figure the shop stuff out. They had some time, but they were going to need it.

And she knew that had been her father's plan.

They needed time to realize that it was *not* a game. That it was real. And important.

And the thing was, it was becoming both of those things. Far faster than she would have ever expected.

Cori pivoted to look out the front window from the table. The curtains had turned out great. They were white with cherries, strawberries, lemons, grapes and blueberries. They weren't making strawberry or lemon pie. Yet. And probably wouldn't be making grape pie. Though she did intend to use grape jelly on some of the peanut butter and jelly pies. Still, the curtains were great and appropriate. And what she liked the best about them was that she and Brynn—and Noah—had made them together.

Okay, Dad, you might have known what you were doing.

Rudy Carmichael had been a brilliant businessman. But now Cori was starting to think that maybe he was just brilliant.

Cori rested her chin on her hand and studied the view outside her window. Her window. That didn't sound as strange as it should. The shop was at the east end of Main and she could see the edge of the park from here. The park was huge. It ran through the middle of town with Main Street bordering it for five blocks and then continued seven more blocks to the man-made lake at the edge of town. There was a walking/running/bike trail, a playground area, three picnic and barbecue spots, and an impressive enclosure at the center that could be used for birthday parties and reunions and such.

Maybe she should start doing the books here. She'd been doing them at home when Ava and Brynn went to work. But the adding and subtracting didn't take long. Here, at least she'd have something nice to look at while she pretended the work took longer than it did. The view outside the window was pretty and inside it smelled like sugar and coffee and...pie. Crap! Cori shot out of her chair and ran to the kitchen where her pie was hopefully not too done.

She pulled it from the oven just in time. She set it on the cooling rack and tossed the hot pads on the counter. Then she turned and surveyed the kitchen. The kitchen that still perplexed her.

It really did look like a kitchen in a home. A big kitchen, but still very...homey. Which was the root of the confusion. This was Rudy's kitchen. Ava had been working so hard to figure the pies out, that she hadn't changed a thing. This was what their father had surrounded himself with purposefully for almost five years. It was where he'd spent his last days.

And the best way to describe how that made her feel was perplexed.

She'd looked through the house, but there was mostly just normal house stuff—dishes and furniture and a few books. But no papers or photos. Parker had told Ava that the guys had cleaned out Rudy's clothes and shoes. But there was no indication that they'd taken any personal items out of the house.

And that *didn't* perplex her. Prior to moving to Bliss, Rudy had lived in a professionally decorated penthouse with expensive furniture and artwork and no personal touches. In Bliss, he lived in a...house. A comfortable, homey house that had no professional touches. But also didn't have many personal touches.

Prior to Bliss, he'd worked in a professionally decorated office with expensive furniture and artwork and no personal touches. But now, looking around the pie shop, Cori saw personal touches. Sure, the furniture and appliances were someone else's, but he'd clearly preferred these over buying restaurant-grade stuff, and he didn't have any connection to the appliances that had cooled and cooked his food before moving here. He'd had cooks to do all of the prep. She doubted that he'd set foot in the kitchen in his penthouse more than a handful of times, if that. Yet, in Bliss he'd not only gone into a kitchen on a regular basis, but he'd actually had *two* kitchens. And had spent most of his time in one of them. This one. With the regular bowls, the beat-up wooden spoons, the pot holders with cows on them that he could have easily bought at Target—and the idea of Rudy Carmichael in a Target made her almost giggle—the shop was more like a home than his home in New York had ever been. Was it possible that this place had turned into the home he'd never had? One that he'd always, on some level, wanted?

The pie was still too warm to eat, so Cori was stuck with a situation that rarely turned out well for her—she had time on her hands and nothing to do.

On impulse, she headed for the "office". The closet with the folding table in it was as far from Rudy's office in New York as he could have gotten. She pulled the door open. No way had he worked in here. Of course, from the looks of his books, he hadn't done much office work at all.

But still...she couldn't help but wonder what else might be different here. She regarded the middle drawer in the file cabinet with her arms crossed. They hadn't opened that one. They'd—she'd—assumed that it only had an empty tape dispenser or a broken pencil in it. Or nothing in it.

But now, if she opened that drawer and there was nothing there, she'd be disappointed. She couldn't lie. She wanted this place to have been different for Rudy on every level. When she was a little girl and had gone to his office and had opened his drawers, they'd been full. They'd had fancy pens in them and engraved stationary and everything had smelled like leather. If this drawer had nothing in it, that would be different, she supposed. The broken phone and stapler were different. But she wanted...more different.

And if that drawer smelled like leather, she was going to be upset.

She glanced over at the pie pans, rolling pin, and canisters that held flour and sugar. Okay, there were lots of differences. There wasn't a gold gilded clock or a gold gilded lamp or anything that was gold gilded anywhere in the building. Maybe the town.

Rudy had made pie. For his friends. True friends, not business acquaintances. Men who knew nothing about, well, anything Rudy did in New York. He'd had coffee every day with men who made their livings running the hardware store on Main, teaching science at the high school, farming, and building houses and barns. Rudy Carmichael had nothing in common with these men. But they mourned his passing more than people who'd known him for over forty years.

She blew out a breath and reached for the drawer of the cabinet.

It was empty. Except for three photos, all obviously printed off from the internet. Her hand shook slightly as she reached for them. The top one was of Ava from an article about her winning a women in business award. The next was Brynn's photo from the lab's website. And the last was of Cori.

Her heart flipped.

This one was from her Facebook page. Which meant that not had he gone looking for it, but it was completely candid. She was standing on a mountain with a huge grin with lots of white, sparkly snow behind her. She remembered that day. But she barely remembered the two girls with their arms around her. She'd spent a winter at that resort working in the shop where they rented out skis and snowboards. It had been one of many jobs and places she'd lived temporarily, and she'd never made a point to keep Rudy updated on where she was, but it looked like he'd found her. At least once.

She wondered if Ava and Brynn remembered the day they'd had their photos taken. Probably not. What they were wearing and where they were posed were the same as a hundred other days in their lives.

She looked at her photo and then at her sisters' photos. They were so different.

But her smile was bigger.

She wondered if her dad had noticed that.

Cori sniffed. Okay, this place was not what she'd expected. But she'd always liked surprises and she thought she was ready for a few more.

She pulled her phone from her back pocket and dialed. A minute later the man she wanted to talk to most at the moment answered.

"Hey, Hank. It's Cori. I was wondering if you and the guys were available for some pie and coffee and conversation."

———

She somehow managed not to go straight to Evan's house after her two hours of pie and conversation with Hank and the guys.

Well, she did go straight to Evan's house. She'd heard so many stories about her dad that her head was reeling, and for some reason, she'd thought that Evan would love to know.

But she'd kept herself from actually knocking on his door. His house was at the end of a short dirt road—she didn't miss the symbolism of that, at least the symbolism in *her* mind—and she'd stood at the end of the road in front of his house for a good ten minutes. But she hadn't gone any closer. Or knocked on his door. Or thrown pebbles at his windows. Or called him.

She'd been proud of herself.

But the whole stuck-here-for-a-year thing was rubbed in her face three nights later. Because Ava had decided to have a game night. And apparently game night included Cori. And Brynn and Parker and Noah. And, of course, Evan. In fact, she was seated straight across from him at the dining room table, trying to avoid looking at him while Brynn considered her poker hand.

Not looking at him was incredibly hard. Harder than not knocking on his door. Because she really liked looking at him. And because she really liked how he looked at *her*.

Finally, Brynn laid down her straight flush.

"It took you that long to put those down?" Cori demanded, then laughed. "You were just making us sweat."

"The sweet ones are the ones you have to look out for," Noah said, smiling as he watched Brynn scrape her winnings toward the already huge pile of chips in front of her.

"There's more to me than you might guess," Brynn said cheekily. The cheekiness was aided by the beer she was drinking, but it was absolutely as cute as it would have been without the drink. She narrowed her eyes then. "You didn't let me win, did you?"

Ava laughed. "I should let you think that."

"You *let* her win sometimes?" Noah asked.

"They let me win so it feels better than me just beating them all the time," Brynn said.

Ava laughed. "You've *never* drawn the long straw without help."

"But every spelling bee you've ever won was because I let you," Brynn told her.

Cori gave a low whistle. Ava knew that but they'd never said it out loud.

Ava sighed. "Yeah, okay. But I really was a better public speaker."

"Still are," Brynn agreed. "And I beat you at every science fair."

"What did you win at?" Evan asked Cori.

Dammit, now she was going to have to look at him. She gave him a tight smile. "Against my sisters? Nothing. Ever."

"You guys never let Cori win at anything?" Evan asked Brynn and Ava with a frown.

Oh, boy, that little bit of protectiveness was way too nice. "It wasn't like that," Cori said.

Ava laughed. "Cori would never have *let* us help her win anything."

"Yeah, we were all in that spelling bee," Brynn said, slurring *spelling* with *bee* slightly. "We all got up there and since they went alphabetical by last name, we went in a row. Ava spelled hers right, I spelled my first one right, and then Cori got up there and got the word *macaroni*. She spelled it wrong on purpose. The very first word."

"You added an extra C or something?" Parker asked.

"Oh no," Brynn jumped in enthusiastically before Cori could reply. "She spelled it *i-h-a-t-e-t-h-i-s* and then took a bow and walked off the stage. Right up the center aisle."

Parker snorted. "Not into spelling bees, Cori?"

"Not into performing for our dad," Cori said, before she really thought better of it.

"What's that mean?" Evan asked, with another frown.

Cori sighed. These guys all thought Rudy was amazing and she was starting to understand that maybe he had been. Here. With them. But he hadn't always been, and if these guys were going to be their friends, then they needed to know where the girls were coming from. "That was our fourth-grade spelling bee. It was the first time that our dad came to any of our school stuff. And it was when the three of us were up against each other. He was really into us being better than everyone else. And he was into which of us was smarter and tougher and better under pressure. I wasn't going to stand up there and compete for his entertainment."

Everyone was quiet for a few seconds until Ava lifted her glass of beer and said, "From then on, I was good at all the big public stuff and Brynn was good at all the behind the scenes stuff."

"And Cori was good at..." Evan asked, clearly wanting her sisters to fill in the blank.

"Making sure we never missed a scary movie and knew every move to every popular dance and that we each colored our hair at least once."

Cori felt a little catch her chest at the way her sister was looking at her. It was an expression full of affection, and for a second she felt stinging in her eyes.

"Only because she was *letting* you both be all kick-ass and—"

"Evan," Ava interrupted. "It was awesome. We loved all of that."

Cori pressed her lips together to keep from saying anything, or grinning, at the look on Evan's face.

"What color?" Noah asked into the awkward moment.

"What color what?" Brynn asked.

"What color did you color your hair?"

Brynn grinned. "I had black stripes for a while."

Noah lifted a brow.

"And I was a redhead for a while."

He nodded slowly. "Nice."

"She rocked that red hair," Cori said.

"I'll bet." The look on his face was thoughtful. "But I like the blonde."

Brynn blushed at that. And Ava laughed. "I was just going to say that your poker face is scary, Nerd Girl," Ava told her. "But maybe it's not as rock solid as I thought."

"Shut up," Brynn muttered, still blushing.

"Seriously though, I might need you at the negotiating table," Ava said.

"Well, maybe I can just come to a meeting some time and pretend to be you," Brynn said. "Like Cori's been doing."

Cori felt her cheeks flush. Everyone thought Brynn was the sweet one, but she'd just thrown Cori under the bus to get the attention off of her and her reactions to Noah. Wow. Cori turned to Parker, desperate for another topic. "Well, I guess if game night is supposed to be a date, then it's you and me, huh?"

Parker opened his mouth to reply, but Noah and Brynn said, simultaneously, "This isn't a date."

"Well, hey, you can be my date then, Brynn," Parker said, and Cori wanted to kiss him.

But Noah scowled at him. "What's that mean?"

"Nothing," Parker said with a shrug. "Evan and Ava are a pair and Cori isn't my type. So if you're not gonna date Brynn, then maybe I should."

"Hey," Cori protested, not really caring but unable to let it go by without comment. "Why am I not your type?"

"You're too much fun," Parker said.

"And that's bad?"

"I don't like to have fun."

Cori snorted. "Oh, then you *need* someone like me."

"He's fine." The two firm words came from Evan.

Cori couldn't help but glance at him again. It would be really nice if he'd stop talking. And getting offended on her behalf. And acting possessive. Like he was now. He was watching her intently. And he didn't look happy. Yeah, well, she wasn't happy either. Though, she had to admit that she didn't feel *unhappy*. Just kind of...unsatisfied. Tense. Itchy. Yeah, itchy fit. Itchy like her clothes were too tight and scratchy and in the way. Like she wanted to take them all off. And have someone...scratch her itch. Someone with big, strong hands and long fingers.

She cleared her throat. Parker had long fingers. Hell, Noah did too. And he did manual work with his hands. If Brynn wasn't going to date him, maybe Cori should.

Of course, she didn't want to.

"And you're not supposed to be dating anyone," Evan said.

And then there was that. "Well, then it's a good thing this isn't a date for anyone but you and Ava," she said.

He looked like he was about to reply, but Noah said, "Yeah, you don't need to date Brynn," to Parker. "This is date night for Ava and Evan. Only."

Okay, this was sufficiently distracting. And entertaining. Cori leaned in. "But Brynn is supposed to be dating," she pointed out. "And she hasn't even started."

"She's got plenty of time," Noah said, still scowling.

Brynn's cheeks were bright red. "We just got here."

"Well, and you've been busy," Cori said. She paused, then added, "With painting, and sewing, and stuff."

All things that Noah had been around for.

"Right. Exactly." Brynn sat up straighter. "Should we play again?" She started shuffling.

"Sure."

"You bet."

"Ava and I are just getting our signals down," Evan said.

"Signals?" Brynn asked.

"Sure, the ones we're using to cheat," Evan said, giving that teasing grin that made Cori want to take her clothes off and climb right back into his lap, regardless of the fact that the last time had been kind of a bust.

"You're cheating?" Brynn asked.

"We're trying," Evan said.

Brynn laughed. "Neither of you have won a single hand."

"Well, we're still figuring it out." He gave Ava a wink and Cori shot to her feet.

"Who else needs a refill?" Cori honestly wasn't sure how much more friendly, not-a-date-but-kind-of-a-date poker she could take. At least without more vodka and pomegranate juice. Or beer. Since that was what was being served tonight.

She took orders and headed for the kitchen with empty glasses and bottles. She rounded the corner into the kitchen and put a wall between her and Evan and all that fucking charm he just couldn't shut off. It didn't matter that Ava seemed unaffected by it all.

"Do you need help?"

She squeaked as Evan pushed through the door right next to where she was leaning. She straightened quickly and managed to not drop anything. "Nope, I'm good," she said, moving toward the sink.

"You can't carry all of that by yourself."

"I'm very strong." She set the glasses down. "And have wonderful balance." She turned to face him, leaning against the edge of the sink. "And I'm incredibly flexible."

Yeah, okay, she maybe shouldn't have said that. That was taunting him. Or poking him. Or something. But honestly, she was lucky that was all she'd said.

"I'm sorry," he said.

She lifted a brow. He was going to apologize for tossing her out of the truck?

"I thought tonight would be a good idea. Something fun for Ava that I'm guessing she doesn't do often, or ever. But not public. But not just the two of us."

Oh, that. Cori shrugged. "Hey, I'm all for game night."

He watched her for a long moment. Then said, "But you didn't have anything to do with this game night."

"What do you mean?"

"I mean, we're playing poker and eating chips and dip and drinking beer," Evan said.

"So?"

"So, you made strawberry popcorn for us the other night."

Cori swallowed hard and crossed her arms. "You didn't like it?"

He laughed and took a step closer to her. Then seemed to realize that he shouldn't do that and stopped and tucked his hands into his pockets. "I loved it, Cori. It was great. So was the chili lime popcorn."

She relaxed a little, but tried not to show it. "Well, I didn't know if you'd prefer sweet or savory."

Again there was a long moment of quiet. Then he said, "Sweet." His voice sounded a little gruff. "If I had to pick, it would always be sweet."

She cleared her throat. "What's your point?"

"You made popcorn, and not just any popcorn, for *other people*. There's no way that if you were in charge of game night that we'd be having chips and dip from a container."

"You don't like the dip?"

He blew out a breath and gave her a look. "Of course, I do. It's fine. It's stuff I've eaten a million times. I like it. I'll eat it again, another million times."

"Then what's the problem?"

He didn't answer. Instead he asked, "What would you have done with game night?"

"I don't know what you mean." But she shifted against the counter. No, none of tonight was her idea. Ava had set it up. And it *was* fine. Chips and beer went perfectly with poker, and poker was a great game. Lots of fun.

"Yes you do. Come on," he said. "What would you have done with game night?"

"I didn't think about it." She hadn't. She'd very specifically *not* thought about it.

"So think about it now."

"I need time to plan something. I can't just pull an idea out."

"Yes you can."

"Why is this so important?"

"Because...I just want to know," he finally said. "And I want you to see it."

"See what?"

"That even things that are completely fine, good even, are better with your touch."

Oh man. She wasn't good at resisting things she wanted on the best day. But when that thing said things like *that*? *Character building. This is character building.* She squeezed her arms, reminding herself she needed to be hands-off with Evan. "Yeah, well, sometimes I *touch* things too much."

He shook his head slowly. "Not for me."

Geez.

Finally, he sighed and turned. "Okay, back to poker."

He pushed the door open and Cori felt her mouth open without conscious command. "Adult Candy Land."

He turned back. "How do you play?"

"Each color means you have to do something different. Sing, act out a scene, do the hokey pokey, give someone a compliment, take a shot."

"With all different kinds of candy for snacks?"

"Candy themed shots," she said. "And spiked gummy bears."

He gave her a big, satisfied smile. "That's my girl."

Then he went back to the dining room. And Cori went back to pretending that she wasn't falling in love for the first time in her life and complicating everything when she wasn't even supposed to be dating and when her life had half a chance at being pretty simple for a change. Because that would be just a little too typical.

11

"This is your main office?"

Evan's heart thumped in the second before he looked up to see Cori standing next to his picnic table.

"Hey," he said, surprised and thrilled to see her. Especially considering it had been raining for the last few hours. He took his glasses off. The better to see her. "What are you doing here?"

She looked amazing. She always looked amazing, but today she was dressed in a white skirt with a red hoodie and red rain boots. She had streaks of mud on her legs above the boots, as if she'd cut across the playground instead of sticking to the sidewalk. Then Evan realized that of course she'd done that. He wouldn't be surprised if she'd stopped to swing for a few minutes or gone down the slide a couple of times. Her hair was wet, she had no makeup on, and she was smiling at him. All of which made him want her.

No, he already wanted her every second. But her appearance today—mud and all—made him want to put her up on his picnic table and feel those red rubber boots digging into his ass.

Plus she was carrying pie.

"I stopped by your office but Claire told me you were at your main office," she said. "And then pointed me over here."

He laughed. Claire was his receptionist and paralegal. "I like to work here whenever I can."

"Even when it's raining?"

"I hardly notice in here." He was sitting at his usual picnic table under the huge wooden enclosure where he met with ninety percent of his clients. There was something about a picnic table that made people relax, and he liked to think that being in the park was a reminder that there were bigger and better things than whatever legal issue someone was dealing with.

"I don't suppose it's a coincidence that this is the Ethan *Stone* Memorial Pavilion?" Cori asked.

Evan shook his head. "Ethan was my dad. My grandparents built this as well as putting in the big rose garden and the basketball courts after he died."

"Wow. That's a pretty cool memorial."

He smiled. "It is. It's perfect. My dad was well-known as a guy who loved to be outdoors and just have a good time."

"Like you."

He shrugged. "It's more that I'm like him."

She was quiet for a few seconds and Evan just let her study him. Finally, she said, "On purpose, right?"

"What do you mean?"

"You take after him on purpose. You *try* to be like him. That's why you do all the stuff around the community and love to go out and party."

Evan shouldn't have been surprised that she'd figured that out. He and Cori had a lot in common. But where she was doing the opposite of what her father had wanted from her, at least the father she'd known growing up, Evan was trying to fill his father's shoes. And he didn't need a high-priced New York shrink to point that out. He nodded. "My dad was beloved. He was the guy everyone always wanted around. People still talk about how much fun he was. He died when I was twelve and I still remember how packed the church was for his funeral. Standing room only."

Cori pressed her lips together. They were quiet for several seconds. Then she asked, "How did he die?"

"Plane crash."

Her eyebrows shot up. "Really?"

"It was a small plane. He was flying it. Alone."

"Wow, was that what he did for a living?"

Evan shook his head. "The plane was for fun. Though most of his work was fun too. He did a little bit of everything. He was a handyman and helped a few farmers. He trucked for a while. He dabbled in a couple of different businesses. He liked a flexible schedule and working for himself."

"Wow, I can relate to that. It feels like I've done a million different things. Not very stable though." She shook her head. "Sorry, I didn't mean that disrespectfully."

Evan gave a short laugh. "No offense taken. You're right. It was important to him that he enjoy what he was doing. All the time. Whether he was working or relaxing. He didn't want to be tied down to something." Evan frowned as a thought occurred to him. "He liked to be able to move on when it wasn't fun anymore."

Cori took a deep breath. "Yeah, I definitely get that. I'd also move on when things seemed to not be fun for everyone else anymore."

"What do you mean?"

"I was the girl who brought in cookies and arranged Friday happy hours and potlucks. I cracked jokes. I remembered birthdays. When the boss was crabby, I figured out ways to lighten things up. But I was never the girl anyone came to with big issues or important projects. And after a while, the people who do the real work get tired of the one who doesn't take anything seriously."

That caused a different type of squeeze in his chest. How

many times had he heard from his grandfather that he should be more serious and responsible, to not turn out like his father, who could never commit to anything long-term? Even Rudy had told him that he was capable of more than he was doing.

"People don't really get tired of cookies and happy hours, do they?"

She shrugged. "Well, anyone can do cookies and happy hours. It's the attitude and work ethic, or lack of, that people get tired of."

She thought they'd gotten tired of *her*. As someone who didn't think he'd ever get enough of her, everything in him rebelled against that idea. And Evan would have put good money down on the fact that everyone who had ever worked with Cori, remembered her with a smile. Like they did his father. "I bet you were the one they came and got when a customer was pissed off, though."

She tipped her head. "How did you know that?"

"Because you make people feel good, Cori."

She wet her lips, looking very much like she wanted to say something but was carefully considering it. Finally, she thrust out her hand. "I brought you pie."

He really wanted to delve into it more. The whole she-was-amazing thing. But he'd been the one telling her to take it easy on some of her ideas. He still didn't know what a photo booth had to do with a pie shop. Yet, he loved the idea. He'd carefully steered her toward the office and books rather than entertain that idea and that made him feel like crap. And restless. And like he was making a mistake.

"What did I do to deserve pie?" he finally asked.

"Well, I take bacon very seriously. And I realized I'd never introduced you to bacon and Nutella. So..." She sighed. "You were on my mind the other night when you were over having movie night with Ava. And this is what turned out."

He took the pie from her, staring at it. He'd been on her mind.

Thank God. Because he thought about her constantly. "You made me bacon and Nutella *pie*?"

"Hank and the guys said it was really good."

"I'm sure it is." Holy crap. He was already on the verge of begging this woman to let him worship at her feet. And now this? He was a goner.

"I invited them all over," she said. "The other night. To the shop. I..."

She paused and Evan looked up. "You invited Hank and the guys over to the shop?" he asked. "They weren't there at their usual time?"

"It was during the movie night," she said. "I was there...and thinking, or wondering, I guess...about my dad. And I found some pictures of me and my sisters in his drawer and I...suddenly had the urge to talk to someone. About him." She swallowed. "The guys came over and told me stories about him, told me the stories he'd told them. It was...great."

Evan felt a fist squeezing his heart, and he had to try twice to finally get a smile out. She hadn't talked to him because he'd been busy watching a movie with her sister. He was glad that she'd talked to the guys though. They'd known Rudy even better than Evan had. Still, he really wanted to be the one who was there for her. "I'm glad. I'm proud of you," he added, truly meaning it.

She seemed startled. "Proud of me?"

He nodded. "Based on your past with him, it was a risk. You didn't know how those stories would turn out."

She gave him a soft smile. "But I did. Because of you."

The fist around his heart squeezed harder. "Because of the stories I told you about him?"

"Because you loved him."

Evan clenched his teeth and fought the urge to grab her and hug her. Because he'd never let her go once he started. "That means a lot to me."

"Me too."

Not knowing what else to do, besides the hugging, of course, he shuffled some papers into a folder and tucked them inside his bag.

"Where's your briefcase?" she asked, eyeing the bag.

He shook his head. Damn that briefcase. "That case isn't really me."

She grinned. "No kidding."

He narrowed his eyes. She was clearly teasing him. "I was trying to make a good first impression."

"You did," she told him with a nod. "But it was the tennis shoes that did it."

He chuckled. "You want to stay for a little while?"

"Sure. If I'm not interrupting?"

"No, not at all. I just finished my last meeting of the day."

"Some big legal case?" She boosted herself up on the table, her feet resting on the bench next to him. Because Cori didn't even sit at picnic tables like everyone else.

God, he was crazy about her.

"Um, no," he said, focusing on her question instead of the bare legs that were slick from the rain and very much within stroking distance. "I was actually the client in that meeting."

"Oh? Everything okay?"

She looked concerned. He nodded. He hadn't told anyone else about what he'd been looking into, but suddenly he wanted to tell her. "I had this idea and I just wanted to see what it would take."

She tipped her head. "What's the idea?"

"I was talking with a company that builds miniature golf courses. I've been thinking about putting one in. Here in the park."

"Oh, that's so cool!" She grinned. "I love mini-golf."

Of course she did.

"Where are you going to put it?" she asked, scanning the area as if she could see the perfect spot from here.

But she could. The perfect spot was a few yards behind the pavilion.

"I haven't really decided."

"When are you going to do it? Can you get it in before this summer? How long does something like that take to build?"

He shook his head with a smile. He couldn't help it. Her excitement was contagious. "Yeah, they said they could start next month."

"That's really fun! Everyone will be excited."

"But I'm not doing it."

She frowned. "What? Why?"

He sighed. "Because I'm now in charge of a foundation that has a ten million dollar trust."

"Yeah. Exactly. He gave you the money for the town, right?"

"Yeah. Exactly."

Her frown deepened. "What are you talking about?"

"Rudy gave me a shit ton of money to take care of this town. I don't think he meant for me to build a mini-golf course."

"But that was the first thing you thought of?"

"I'd thought of it a while ago—that it would be something fun and that my dad would have loved—but I hadn't looked into the details. I knew it would be too expensive."

"And now you did look into it."

"Yeah."

"And you can definitely afford it now."

"Yeah."

"What's the problem?"

"Don't you think a ten million dollar trust should be used for something more...serious?"

"Serious? Like a library or something?"

"Yeah."

"Does Bliss need a library?"

"No. We have one. But I just...it's ten million dollars."

She laughed. "Well, what did Dad want you to do with the

money?" she asked. "What did you talk about? What did he think the town needed?"

Evan shook his head. "He didn't tell me anything specifically. He told me it was up to me."

Cori shrugged. "Well, then you should build the mini-golf course."

"I think he wanted me to do something more than that," Evan told her.

"Why do you think that?"

"Because he told me I could do more than what I'd been doing."

"Ah." She didn't say anything more for a moment.

Then she shifted, dropping down to straddle the bench beside him. The action made the skirt pull up on her thighs and made him wonder what kind of panties she was wearing today. But he made himself focus on her face.

"Evan, are you sure you're thinking about Rudy here, and not your grandfather?"

Evan felt like she'd just punched him in the chest. "Wh—" He cleared his throat. "What do you mean?"

"I mean that you've been following in your father's footsteps all these years. And you've felt a little guilty about it because your grandfather wants you doing...more...something *different*. Every time you do something fun for this town, you feel like you're honoring your dad on one hand, and disappointing your grandfather on the other." She reached out and covered his hand with hers. "I think you need to figure out who *you* want to be. Not become your father, not rebel against your grandfather, but decide who *you* are. And then be that guy with your whole heart."

His whole heart was thudding almost painfully against his sternum at the moment as he stared at the party girl who had been keeping people firmly on the other side of the wall around *her* heart. The guys at the coffee shop had probably given her some of this insight. No doubt they'd told her about his grandfather. Maybe even his dad. But some of this—maybe a lot of this—was coming from *her*. Because they really were a lot alike. "Like you're working on deciding who *you* want to be?" he asked, his voice gruff.

She didn't seem surprised that he'd figured that out. Or said it. She gave him a nod. "Yeah. Like that."

He turned his hand over and laced his fingers with hers.

"Rudy knew you really well, right?" she asked softly.

He nodded. "Yeah."

"Then I think you need to consider the fact that when he said you could do more, he didn't mean you should do something *different*. It's very possible he meant you should do *more* of what you do."

"What I do?" He gave a short laugh. "I don't really do anything, Cori. I have fun."

"And he knew that. He knew who you were. He knew that you loved this town. He knew that you made people happy. And he loved you, Evan." She squeezed his hand. "He would have wanted you to keep being who you are."

Evan stared at her, his heart pounding suddenly.

"When you and Rudy hung out, what did you do?" she asked.

"Ate pie," Evan said hoarsely. "Went to ball games. Fished. Sat here."

"So you weren't serving soup in a homeless shelter or creating a workable plan for universal health care," Cori said.

He lifted an eyebrow. "He helped us serve breakfast for the veterans on Veterans Day."

She smiled. "My point is, Rudy knew you, he knew the things you loved, he loved those same things with you. He was all about giving people a place to get together and have fun and enjoy each other and the town. It sounds to me like he would have definitely played mini-golf with you if it had been here."

Evan shook his head slightly. "You realize that you're saying nice things about Rudy and you're assuming that he was a different guy than the one you knew."

"I know," she said. "He really did change." She looked a little sad, but she smiled. "I'm glad he was happy here. Evan, there's no way he would have wanted you to be anything other than the guy he got to know and love. And I hate that you don't think you take things seriously. You take this town and your friendships seriously, you've taken Rudy's trust seriously, you take your role as the guy who makes everything more fun seriously."

He leaned in. "Ditto," he said. He swallowed. "You and I are very much alike."

She nodded, her lips pressed together.

"So you don't think I should be using the money on scholarships and helping add on to the medical clinic and reroofing the nursing home?" he asked. Damn, he really wanted to build that mini-golf course suddenly.

She laughed. "Of course you should do all of those things too. But geez, you have ten million dollars. You could do all of those things ten times each." She flipped her hair over her shoulder. "But make sure you invest some of it. You'd be surprised how fast you can spend a couple million dollars."

"Especially when you're giving it away a couple of million dollars at a time, right?"

Her eyes widened. "What do you mean?"

But he could tell she knew what he meant. "You think Rudy didn't know that you'd blown almost your entire trust fund on donations to charities?" he asked.

"He knew?"

"And he loved it, Cori."

Her smile got wobbly.

"Mud pies."

She blinked at him. "What?"

"You should have a place where the kids can make mud pies. Something fun and goofy and pie related."

"At the shop? Ava will have a coronary."

"At the Parking and Pie party," he said.

Her voice got softer. "What are you talking about?"

He couldn't resist any longer. He leaned over, put his hand on her neck and pulled her to stand. Then he brought her up against his body, his hand in her hair. "I can't do this anymore," he told her, staring down into her eyes.

"Do what?" she whispered.

"Hold you back. Squelch your ideas. Tell you to put things on hold and that they're not your domain." He kissed her hot and hard, then pulled back. "You are amazing, Cori. And your dad knew that about you. He really did. I think he realized that he wanted you to keep being you, doing what you do, too. And okay, you aren't supposed to make the pies or wait on the customers, but you should definitely throw that party, and put a photo booth in, and have themes like sweetie pies and kiddie pies—"

"And bacon pies?"

"You have more than just Nutella and bacon?"

She nodded. "Bourbon apple and bacon. And—"

He cut her off with another kiss. "Fuck *yes*, you should do bacon pies," he told her when he pulled back. "And anything else you can dream up."

"But that's not my area. I can't screw up the trust."

"Your area is the business. The money. Anything that helps increase that should be your domain."

Her eyes widened. "A loophole, Counselor?"

He grinned. "Something like that."

"And that's okay?"

"It's more than okay. You have to do it."

"Which thing?"

"All of it."

She paused. Then lifted a hand to his face. "You should never say *all of it* to me," she said quietly. "*All* is a lot with me. I'm best in small doses."

That was the second time she'd said that about herself. "Well, I think you've finally found someone who can take it all. Who wants it all. All at once."

"You sure?" Her voice was almost a whisper now.

"I love that you can't even make plain popcorn," he told her, unable to hold any of these feelings back any longer. "That you can't *not* add garnishes to everything. You immediately added caramel to Hank's coffee. You immediately added color to the shop. You immediately added charity to your park party idea. You always, instantly, make things better." He paused and took a breath. "You've made *me* better."

Her eyes were shimmery and she lifted her other hand, bracketing his face. "You were amazing way before I got here."

He shook his head. "All the things I've done, the fun, the parties, the meetings at the pond, paperwork in the park, were all *efforts* to be a guy people wanted to have around. It was a conscious thing. Something I've been working at. And not feeling particularly successful at, to be honest. But you...you don't even have to try. And you do it in little ways. You add bacon to pie. You add sprinkles to coffee. You let the guys who spent too much time in that shop, give input on the curtains—yes," he said when she opened her mouth, "—I heard about you bringing them fabric swaths to look at. You've asked around town about whose furniture and appliances are in the shop and you've put their names on the stuff. And yes," he said again with a smile at her surprised look. "I heard about that too. You've made your sisters have dinner with you every night and every night they find something on their pillow when they go to bed—a quote, a flower, a chocolate, a bath bomb. Noah told me about that," he said, before she could ask. "You've made people smile all over this town, Cori, and it's just by being you."

She licked her lips, tears in her eyes. "I do try at some of that," she said quietly. "The stuff on their pillows...I do that so they want me around even when I'm talking about photo booths in the pie shop and planning parties in the park and driving them crazy."

He moved his hand to her cheek, his thumb stroking over her cheek. "I love and hate that you don't realize how much people want you around." He took a deep breath. "I want that in my life —that make-every-single-little-thing-even-better—and it makes me look at the little things I can do. I don't need to throw big elaborate parties or help organize street dances or put in a mini-golf course. I can make someone's day with something a lot simpler than that."

"You make my day every time you smile at me."

He felt his own smile drop. He put his forehead against hers and gave a little groan. He needed someone he could make happy just by being himself. She was right, Rudy had known him. And loved him. And all they'd really done was sit and talk. Cori was a lot like her father. "I need you, Cori."

Cori took a deep breath at that and then pulled back. She gave him a big smile. "I'd better go."

She started to turn, but he tightened his hold. "What are you talking about?"

She took another breath and smiled, though her eyes still glistened with tears. "I always leave at the high point."

Uh-huh. He pulled her back to him and put his lips against hers. "I get it. You get out while people are still feeling good, before there's a chance for it to go bad. But you don't have to do that here."

"Things are good right now."

"Yeah, they really are. But," he added, "this is not the high point of this afternoon."

"No?"

"No. That's going to happen about thirty minutes after I get you into my bedroom and out of your clothes."

She hesitated then, her eyes going wider. Finally, she said, "*Thirty* minutes after?"

"I have a lot of things to do before...the high point."

She blew out a breath and seemed to make a decision. "Make it twenty minutes and I'm in."

He grabbed his bag, stuffing the rest of his paperwork inside, and then took Cori's hand as she scooped up the pie. They started across the park.

———

E van called Claire as they hurried across the wet grass. It was still misting slightly, and Cori could only imagine how curly her hair was getting.

"Hey, reschedule my afternoon. I'm heading home early."

Cori didn't hear the other end of the conversation, but he disconnected as they stopped at the corner to let a car pass.

"She'll think you're taking Ava home," she said.

He paused, one foot off the curb, and turned to her. "She thought you were Ava when you stopped at the office?"

She nodded.

"And you didn't correct her?"

"Of course not. Ava's supposed to be making the pies," she reminded him. "And it would be weird for your girlfriend's sister to be seeking you out in the middle of the day." She ignored the pang in her chest. Anyone who saw them together would be able to tell she was crazy about this man, but none of them would know it was *her*. It didn't matter. She knew how she felt. Evan knew how she felt. At least mostly. The whole world didn't have to know.

But she kind of wanted them to.

Evan just looked at her for several seconds. Then he said, "Go to the wedding with me this weekend."

She hadn't been expecting that. She'd been expecting *it doesn't matter what they think* or *just a few more months*. Not an invitation.

"What wedding?"

"A friend's from law school. He's getting married in Great Bend. No one from here will be there."

She thought about that. "I can be with you but be Cori?"

He lifted a hand to her face. "God, yes. Please."

She gave him a bright smile. "Okay. Yes."

He grabbed her hand again and they started across the street at a much faster pace this time. Cori was breathless by the time he tugged her up the front steps to his porch. She barely had time to take in the details of the yard or the wraparound porch or the huge picture window before he had the door open, her through it, and his bag tossed to the side.

"Clothes off," he said as he ran a hand through his wet hair and toed off his shoes.

Cori set the piece of pie on the little table inside the door and turned a full circle, studying his house. It smelled like him. She took a huge deep breath as she made note of the living room to the right, with the big, stone fireplace, the dining room to the left and the door that had to lead to the kitchen. The staircase was almost directly in front of them and she assumed that led to the bedrooms. What was down the hallway just to the right of the stairs?

"Cori."

Her name was low and firm and she turned to face him. He had his shirt unbuttoned and there was heat and amusement in his expression. And she decided she didn't care about that hallway. Or anything else.

"Clothes off," he repeated.

She balanced on one foot as she pulled off one of her boots, then the other, watching him watch her. She pitched them toward the door. Or she thought she did. She couldn't look to see where they'd landed because Evan was walking toward her, definitely more heat than humor in his eyes now, and she couldn't look away.

He stopped in front of her and reached for the zipper on her hoodie, drawing it down quickly and pushing the sweatshirt off her shoulders. It hit the floor at her feet leaving her in only her purple tank and her white denim skirt. His eyes lowered to her breasts and he breathed, "No bra. Thank God."

Cori grinned at that. "I was—"

But she didn't finish the thought as Evan whisked her shirt up and over her head.

"Fucking gorgeous," he muttered, shrugging out of his own shirt as his gaze took her in.

And suddenly, she got nervous. She *never* got nervous about sex. Sex was something she was good at. And enjoyed. Sex and fun. She never doubted herself in those two categories. But since she'd come to Bliss, the fun had gotten complicated. She had to loop other people in, consider their opinions, plan ahead. The photo booth was over the top, her sisters weren't into the kid pies, there were doubts about the park party. Cori had never had to think it all through before and she'd never had to run things past someone else. Either they were into what she was doing or they weren't. But she couldn't just go on without her sisters. And she couldn't leave. And she sure as hell hoped Evan wasn't going to leave right now. Of course it was his house, but...

"Do you have any whipped cream?" she asked, making her voice playful as she stepped forward to run her hand over his chest. His hot, hard, naked chest. She drew in a breath as lust rippled through her.

But Evan flattened his hand over hers, stopping the motion. "No, I don't." There was something in his eyes and voice that tightened her nerves even further.

She focused on his chin rather than his eyes. And thought about how his slight beard would feel rubbing over her breasts and stomach and inner thighs. Yeah, that was better. Concentrate on the sex. "How about chocolate sauce?" She forced playfulness into her voice.

"Cori."

When she didn't look up right away, he tipped her chin up with a finger. "We don't need whipped cream and chocolate sauce."

She gave him a smile that was only half-forced. "Whipped cream makes everything better."

"It makes it different. Like sprinkles in coffee."

Cori wet her lips and nodded. "Right."

"Well, I don't want this changed. I want this straight-up, you and me, all of the delicious stuff *under* the whipped cream."

"The garnishes are what make one dish different from another," she said quietly, also recalling that conversation with him in her kitchen. She wanted to be different for him. She wanted to stand out. And she only knew one way to do that—the same way she always tried to stand out—go over the top.

Evan ran his hand along her jaw to the back of her head. He pulled her close and leaned in, his voice husky. "You are the perfect combination of ingredients from the bottom to the top, Corrine Michelle Carmichael. I don't need one extra thing."

No one had ever said something like that to her. She doubted any of the other men she'd ever been with had ever *thought* something like that. She'd met one boyfriend camping. Another skiing. Another at a charity fundraiser. A couple at bars. But nearly everything they knew about her was about the things she *did*. The activities and the causes and the fun. Because they didn't talk. They partied. But Evan knew so much more than that. And she'd been wearing rain boots and mud and he still wanted her.

Yeah, this was a different dish, no matter what condiments came to the bedroom with them.

She rose on tiptoe and kissed him, sliding her hand into his hair. That was, evidently, enough encouragement, because he turned her and started walking her backward, toward the stairs. His tongue was insistent against hers, his hand gripping her hair gently, his other hand at her hip, steering her. She glanced at the piece of pie on the table by the door. Maybe they should grab that and bring it along. Just in case...

He nudged her to take the first step up the staircase, and she took the first two backward before he stopped her. She was just high enough to put her breasts at mouth level for him and he leaned back to look.

"God, I love your nipples," he said, almost reverently. Then he took one in his mouth, swirling his tongue around the tip, then sucking.

Heat and need blossomed in her core and she moaned.

He pulled back, reluctantly, his eyes on her breasts again as he said, "Okay, keep going. Second door on the left."

Okay, they'd leave the pie. She walked backward up the steps, aware of every bounce her breasts made, the ache between her legs also climbing as she went.

Once they were in his room, Evan pointed at the bed. "Naked. Spread out. Now."

A shiver of desire went through her and she could have sworn her nipples tightened even further. She did love that commanding voice of his.

She watched as Evan kicked off his jeans and dropped his boxers. She blew out a breath at the sight of him fully naked. He was gorgeous. Wide, defined shoulders, thick biceps, sculpted abs, tight ass, big, long fingers and feet. And a thick, hard cock that made her inner muscles tighten and her belly heat.

"Too many skirts on," Evan said huskily, taking his cock in hand and giving it a stroke.

Cori felt a little dizzy and wondered if her blood was all re-routing south the way men said theirs did. She swallowed and unbuttoned her skirt, letting it fall.

"Panties too, Miss Carmichael," Evan said, taking a step toward her, a wicked, sexy smile curling one side of his mouth.

Miss Carmichael. *Yes sir.* She pushed her panties to the floor and kicked them away.

"Bed. Spread out. Wide."

She did as she was told. She would have felt, strangely, a lot less exposed if she had some flavored body powder on or something. Not that it would have covered anything, but it would have been distracting, at least. The way Evan was looking at her, she didn't think she'd have a freckle or a wrinkle unstudied. And she couldn't help but think that this might be the first time she'd ever really been *naked* with a man.

There was no liquor, no toys, no dirty talk, no lingerie. They weren't in a shower or on a table or in the back seat of a limo. There was nothing adding to the moment—or distracting from it being just the two of them in a bedroom on a plain old bed. And it made her feel more exposed than she'd ever been.

Evan climbed onto the bed beside her, just looking, his gaze roaming over her from head to toe. "Dammit, Cori, you are the most beautiful thing I've ever seen."

Her feelings of vulnerability increased. More so than being handcuffed to a bedframe, more so than the experiment with nipple clamps, more so than the time she and Brad—or was it Brian?—had done it on a pool table in a back room of a bar. No one had been around, but there had been the chance of getting caught.

Now with Evan, just the two of them, no garnish, no timeline, no leaving town tomorrow...and she didn't just *feel* vulnerable. She was. Because he knew her. He knew things about her past that none of her other boyfriends ever had. He knew the ways she'd disappointed her father and family. He knew the things she wasn't good at, the way she kept people at a distance, her insecurities.

And he liked her anyway.

He liked her, in part, because of the crazy ideas and things that she typically used to keep people at arm's length.

And she was vulnerable because she was in love with him.

If she did this with him, her heart would be involved in a way that it had never been before.

And she was going to die if she *didn't* do this with him.

"Touch me," she finally said, her voice a little hoarse.

He lay down next to her, stretching out on his side. He lifted a hand and ran it over her hair. "Oh, I intend to. With my hands and my tongue and my lips. Every fucking inch."

She swallowed. "Good."

"But it's going to take me a while. You just get comfortable." He gave her a smile that shot straight through her, heating her blood and making her toes tingle.

She thought about reminding him of the twenty-minute time limit, but then he kissed her. And she forgot about time altogether.

12

He did exactly as he'd promised. He started with her face. His fingers tracing over each spot before his lips did. He kissed her eyebrows, her cheekbones, lingered on her lips and returned there often. He even kissed her earlobes. Then he moved down her neck, over her collar bones, and down the valley between her breasts. His fingers primed her nipples, rolling and plucking until she was writhing, then he lowered his mouth and licked and sucked until she was on the verge of an orgasm just from that.

His fingers continued down her body as his mouth was occupied higher. His fingers trailed over her stomach, making the muscles jump and tighten, then lower, stroking her thighs, and then finally her slick folds. Cori whimpered as he ran the pad of his middle finger over her clit. She arched up, trying to get closer to his touch.

"That's it. Come and get it, darlin'," he said gruffly against one nipple, giving it a flick of his tongue as he circled her clit.

She opened her legs farther and pressed against his hand as Evan continued kissing and licking his way down her body. He licked each rib on both sides as he continued to tease her clit.

Cori gripped the comforter as he dragged his body down hers, the heat and friction of his hot skin on hers winding her tighter and tighter.

When he settled between her knees, his shoulders making her stretch even wider, he moved his hand out of the way of his tongue. But as his mouth settled over her clit, his fingers slid into her.

Cori gasped as sensations sparkled along her nerve endings. The sweet, deep thrusts of his fingers with the achingly perfect suction of his mouth started her climbing toward the crest of an orgasm.

"Evan!"

"Best thing I've ever had in my mouth," he told her as he suddenly moved, turning her to her stomach. But his hand stayed between her legs, his fingers filling her.

"Oh, God," she moaned as he began moving up her back, giving each vertebra a hot kiss.

"Every fucking inch," he reminded her in a gravelly voice that made goose bumps trip down her spine.

When he got to her neck, he moved her hair to the side and placed his lips against her skin. His fingers miraculously still moved in long, slow thrusts right where she needed him, keeping her close to the brink of an orgasm, needy and wanting so much more, yet somehow feeling satisfied, like she'd never been touched like this and it was completely right. He kissed the back of her neck, then dragged his mouth up and down the side of her neck, his beard scraping deliciously. His body pressed into hers from behind, his cock against her ass, and she rocked back into him. The hot length of him combined with the deep groan that rumbled through her from his chest, and his fingers dancing skillfully over her clit, started the hot, glorious climb toward climax again. Cori pushed up onto her hands and knees, dropping her head forward.

"Holy shit, Cori," he groaned.

She was completely at his mercy and wanton at this point, but she didn't care that he'd gotten her here without a single bit of garnish. Just lips and hands and fingers and an incredible amount of...adoring. That's how she felt. Adored. And that was way more powerful than any friction-heated-body-gel she'd ever encountered.

"Please, Evan, please," she gasped.

"What? Tell me, Cori. I want to hear it."

"I need you. Inside," she managed. "Come with me."

He muttered something under his breath—it sounded a little like *rain boots* and *sprinkles*—and the next thing she knew, he'd flipped her onto her back again.

"Like this," he told her. "Good old missionary." He moved between her legs, which she willingly spread. He looked down at her, drawing a deep breath in through his nose. Then he braced a hand beside her head and reached for the drawer in his bedside table. He had a condom on in seconds and then he moved over her. "Who needs vibrators and flavored massage lotion?" he asked, running one hand up her inner thigh.

She laughed breathlessly. "That's what all this has been about? Not all that sweet nonsense about there being more under the whipped cream. You just wanted to prove that you're good enough to not need that stuff?"

"Well," he said, sliding his hand higher and brushing over her clit. "I *am* good enough to take you all the way without all of that stuff."

She moaned quickly as he drew a lazy circle over her clit, his eyes locked on hers.

"But then again," he said. "I knew that from the front seat of my truck the other night."

It was hard to even be fake irritated with a guy who was slowly but surely winding you up toward an orgasm, but she tried to frown. "Sure, let's bring up *that* embarrassing moment right now."

His finger stopped and he dipped his head, putting them almost nose to nose. "Don't you ever fucking be embarrassed about being the sexiest, sweetest, most amazing woman I've ever met. You coming for me in my lap, just like that...Cori, that was the hottest moment of my life. Until now." He slowly slid one long finger into her and Cori felt pleasure streak through her.

She caught her breath and had to clear her throat before she said, "It would have been even more amazing if you hadn't tossed me out of the truck two seconds later."

He curled his finger and she gasped.

"Yeah, well, I was freaked out by how much I wanted to keep you in my lap, with me buried deep, for about fifty years or so."

She wasn't sure if it was the words or the way he pumped his finger deep at the same time, but her head was spinning and she felt her orgasm building hot and fast. And all she could really concentrate on was that she needed him. All of him. Now.

"How about we go with that buried deep thing first?" she asked, pressing up against his hand and rotating her hips.

He groaned and gripped her hips, stopping the motion. Then, with his eyes on hers, he positioned himself and eased forward.

Slow and easy was nice. Being adored was wonderful. She could happily spend hours in this man's arms. But right now, she needed...more. Cori wrapped her legs around his waist, put her heels into his butt, and pulled him close.

He sunk deep and they moaned together. He filled her perfectly, stretched her deliciously. Cori felt her whole body melting and molding around his.

Evan paused, for just a moment, dragging in air. Then he said, "Okay, darlin', here we go."

Hands on either side of her hips, he pulled back and plunged forward, thrusting hard and deep. He withdrew and thrust again, hitting a spot that made every nerve ending shout *yes!* Cori gripped his sides, lifting against him, meeting his strokes, and it was mere minutes before she was spiraling toward the climax she'd been chasing since he'd taken her hand in the park.

"Evan!"

"Best thing I've ever heard," he ground out as he continued to move.

"Evan, please." She sucked in a breath. "Yes, more. Please."

He was such a nice guy. He picked up the pace and a minute later, the orgasm swept over her. Her whole went body hot and tingly and tight, followed by waves of softness and satisfaction and an overwhelming sense of...rightness.

Okay, that was weird. But accurate.

"Cori!" He shouted as he came, clutching her tightly, holding her close as his orgasm swept through him.

He held her like that, breathing raggedly against her neck for several long moments.

Then he rolled to his side, taking her with him. He settled a hand on her ass, took a big satisfied breath, and said, "Now that's what I call *sprinkles* and a cherry on top."

She laughed and snuggled in close. "I had no idea that sex could be like that without whipped cream."

He gave her butt a pinch. "Don't make me take that whipped cream gun away."

"You can try."

He rolled on top of her, tickling along her side. But she was saved a moment later by his phone ringing from the pocket of his jeans. Evan sighed. "Hang on. That's Parker's ring tone." He crawled to the edge of the bed and reached for his jeans. He pulled his phone out and answered, "Hey, I'm taking the after—" He was clearly cut off as his eyes got wide. "Oh, shit."

Cori sat up and was already reaching for her panties on instinct.

"How did he know?" Evan asked Parker. He paused listening. "Great." He didn't sound happy. "Yeah, we'll be right there."

Cori scrambled off the bed as he hung up.

"We have to go." Evan grabbed his boxers.

"What's going on?"

"Your sister is pretending to be you."

Oh. Crap. "Which one?"

"Ava."

"Why?"

"Because my grandfather is at the shop. And Ava is supposedly here with me."

She paused halfway through pulling her skirt up. "How does he know that?"

"Because he stopped by the office and Claire told him we were together. So he stopped by the shop and there were people there who saw us together at the park. And then leaving the park."

"Well...crap."

They got dressed and five minutes later walked through the door of Blissfully Baked together.

"Hey, everyone," Cori greeted, as if there was nothing at all out of place or worth feeling guilty about.

She met Ava's gaze from where her sister was positioned behind the display case that now held six pies, each of which was missing at least one piece. But Cori didn't have a chance to really enjoy that fact. Ava had her hands in the pockets of her apron and a smudge of flour on her face, and it was clear that she was trying to act natural even though she was obviously tense from head to toe. Parker was there too, leaning against the counter behind the cases, his arms folded, not looking happy. Cori gave him a frown. What was his problem?

The only other person in the shop at the moment was a tall man in a suit and tie. He had nearly white hair and light blue eyes. Eyes that his grandson had clearly inherited.

"Welcome back," Ava said. "I was just telling Evan's grandfather that you might not be back since you'd decided to take the afternoon off."

"Evan," the man greeted.

"Hi, Grandpa." Evan steered Cori to the table with a hand on her lower back. He reached a hand out to shake his grandfather's. "I didn't know you were coming to town."

"Just a quick trip to pick up some books your grandmother wanted from the house."

"Grandpa, this is Ava. Ava, my grandfather Judge John McCormick. He's a District Judge for the 20th District. He and my grandmother moved to Great Bend about five years ago but they keep their house here and visit periodically."

"It's very nice to meet you Judge McCormick," Cori said, extending her hand and giving him an Ava smile. A judge, district or otherwise, wouldn't intimidate Ava. But Cori thought the guy was a little imposing even seated on a blue cushion with yellow ruffles.

"You too. I came by specifically for that pleasure," he said, shaking her hand and not even bothering to tell her to call him John rather than Judge. "Not only because you're... dating...my only grandson, but because I'm very curious about the women I read about in Rudy's trust." He lifted his cup for a sip of coffee, watching her over the brim.

She didn't appreciate the way he'd emphasized 'dating' as if they were doing something else entirely—even though they totally were—but she was too distracted by the rest of what he'd said. "You know about the trust?"

"Rudy and Evan had me look it over to ensure they hadn't missed any details," John said with a nod. "It's really a fascinating and unique document."

Well, she'd agree with unique.

"If we'd known you were stopping by, we would have been sure to be here," Evan told him. He pulled a chair out for Cori, then took the seat next to her.

"Would you?" his grandfather asked, setting his cup back on the table. "It sounds like you were busy."

Cori was startled to feel herself blushing.

"Roger was here when Judge McCormick first came in," Ava said. "He told us that he saw you in the park together and then headed to Evan's."

Cori wasn't sure if anyone else would be able to tell, but Ava was pissed. Ava didn't like being caught off guard. She didn't like having meetings she was unprepared for. And she didn't like when the person she was meeting with knew more than she did.

And this was Cori's fault. If she'd been here, then Ava wouldn't have to be faking everything. She would at least be facing all of this as herself.

Cori gave her sister a tight smile. "I needed his opinion on a new pie." She worked hard not to grimace at what sounded very much like a euphemism for sex and hoped that everyone else in the shop was much more mature, and less dirty minded, than she was.

But Parker coughed and she heard the soft choking noise Evan made. Well, terrific.

"Okay, we're going back to the kitchen," Ava said. "We'll let you get to know John." Ava grabbed Parker by the sleeve and pulled him with her into the kitchen.

Cori blew out a breath. Maybe this would be easier with two fewer people trying to keep the lie going. Less chance of someone screwing the story up. She gave John a smile, but just then Evan's phone rang.

He glanced at the screen. "It's...a client."

Cori lifted an eyebrow. Bull. That was Parker's ring tone. Cori gave him a quick frown. He didn't want his grandfather to know that Parker was calling from the kitchen? Yeah, because that was suspicious as hell. Parker was calling to either tell him something he didn't want John to know. Or to chew him out.

No one was happy with Cori and Evan's mid-afternoon break. Except Cori. And Evan. She hoped. She was feeling a little guilty, she had to admit. Not just because John had showed up and Ava had been forced to lie, but because suddenly facing someone else who knew about the trust, she felt jittery. She wasn't sure a district judge would agree that the loopholes they'd all found were no problem.

And she hated the idea that Evan might feel the same way—guilty and jittery. Not the way a woman wanted the man she was falling in love with to feel after sex. Okay, or any man after sex, really.

"I'll be right back." Evan kissed the top of her head and headed outside to the sidewalk.

Leaving her alone with John.

Awesome.

"Rudy would have been thrilled that you and Evan are together," John said, as the little bell over the door tinkled.

That definitely got Cori's attention. "Oh?"

John nodded and picked up his cup again. "Rudy trusted Evan with a lot of responsibility. The foundation, the trust for the town, his own will and trust. When I called him about it, he assured me that you would keep him in line."

Rudy had thought Ava would keep Evan in line? Rudy had known that Ava and Evan would date? "Evan asked...me...out because Rudy wanted him to?" she asked, almost messing it up already by referring to Ava.

John gave a soft chuckle. "No. Rudy didn't ask him to date you." John sipped from his cup, then said, "Rudy knew Evan very well."

Cori could believe that. It seemed Rudy had been incredibly insightful even about her, and he'd spent a lot more time with Evan.

"He would have never flat-out asked him to date you," John went on. "But he planted the seeds. The ways you could be good for him. The ways he could be good for you. He knew that Evan loves being important to people. He loves to make people happy.

All your dad had to do was plant the seeds that you needed more happiness."

Cori's heart clenched at that. He was right. Rudy had been right. That was Evan.

"You and Rudy were friends?" she asked. It seemed John knew her father well.

"No, I wouldn't say that. I was suspicious of him. Strange guy suddenly moves to town and becomes fast friends with my grandson. But he respected that. Then I found out his secret. Or his twelve billion secrets."

"You knew who he was."

"I did. I was, apparently, the only one who thought it was strange that as soon as he showed up, suddenly some company became interested in restoring our buildings and building up Main Street and offering the business owners no-interest loans."

"And you looked into him," Cori said.

"I was, of course, stunned to find out who he really was. But when I went to him about it, I respected the fact that he wanted a new start, a new life."

"You kept his secret." Something about that made her like John a little more.

"I did. And I asked him to help keep an eye on Evan. My grandson has never listened to me very well. But he loved your father."

Cori leaned in, fascinated. "What did you want from Evan?"

"I wanted him to be less like his father," John said. "I wanted him to find a purpose. More than just having a good time."

That was crap. Cori was on the verge of telling him so. Evan had a purpose. He took care of this town and the people he loved. There was definite value in making people happy. Instead she said, "But you approved of Rudy's plan for Evan to date me. To make sure I work less and have more fun."

"Because *you* will make him more balanced too," John said. "You will finally give him a reason to be more responsible."

Oh boy. John thought Evan's feelings for her would make him a better man. No, that his feelings for *Ava* would make him a better man. At least in his grandfather's eyes. John would be incredibly annoyed to find out that not only was she not really Ava, but that Evan wasn't spending that much time with Ava.

Cori felt a niggle of guilt at the back of her mind. Would Evan be better off if he *was* spending more time with Ava?

But no, that wasn't fair. He was a great guy just the way he was. He didn't need any positive influences from anyone.

And Lord knew he wasn't going to get it from her.

She shook that off.

"You know that it was very important to your father that you find happiness, Ava," John said.

His use of her sister's name jolted Cori. She swallowed hard. "So I hear," she said. And it made her heart ache a little. She loved that Rudy wanted Ava to be happy. But it hurt that he hadn't been able to tell her that himself.

"He felt guilty," John went on. "He knew that you worked hard because you thought it made him happy."

"It did," Cori said. That was no secret.

"It did," John agreed with a nod. "For a long time. But he finally realized that he was looking at your successes as proof that he'd done something right as a father. And that that wasn't true. So he decided to be a good father now."

Cori swallowed hard as her throat suddenly tightened. "By bringing me here."

"Yes."

And setting Ava up with Evan. Even if he'd done it indirectly.

That niggle in the back of her mind grew stronger. Yeah, that was definitely guilt. But Evan *had* been making sure Ava had some fun. Yes, Cori had interrupted their dinner, but that had been *helpful* at the time. Supposedly, anyway. Her intentions had been good. And they'd had movie night. Cori had stayed out of the way of that one. That had been fun for Ava. Probably. Game night had been fun. Cori had been there for that and had stayed away from Evan. He'd followed her into the kitchen but...she hadn't even kissed him. And she'd seen Ava laughing that night.

"I've definitely been working less," Cori said to John. But she almost winced. Ava was still working a lot. Too much. She was doing pie shop work and still making conference calls with New York. And who knew who else? She'd supposedly taken movie night off. Cori knew Evan had been gone by eleven because that was when Cori had risked going home. But Ava could have gone to her office to work after he left. Cori hadn't even checked. Because she didn't want to actually hear that Ava had had a good time.

Cori realized that Ava may actually be working longer hours, making up for the time she was taking off here and there with Evan. She was going through the motions with Evan because she had to, but it wasn't actually changing anything for her.

And Evan was just going through the motions with Ava too.

Cori glanced out the window to where Evan was on the sidewalk, still on the phone.

Evan said she was brighter and bolder than he was, but he was still the party guy, fun and spontaneous. He wanted to build a mini-golf course and take clients fishing. He was unconventional. So why was he taking Ava to dinner and doing movie nights at home? Those were...typical dates. Somehow she knew he wouldn't have taken Cori to a steak house. They would have made homemade egg rolls and eaten them picnic style in the back of his truck. And poured the sauces on each other's stomachs for dipping. If they did a movie night, it would have been a marathon and there would have a least been a theme, and cuddling under a blanket, and rewriting the bad dialogue, and acting out how the romantic moments *should* have turned out.

He wasn't really giving Ava the full Evan experience. Because of Cori. Because she was in the way, distracting him with her St. Bernards.

"I'm glad you're going out more," John said. "And it's very tell-tale that Evan hasn't bought the town a Ferris wheel or something." He chuckled and took a final swallow of coffee.

He was drinking it black. That was a definite mark against him. Not to mention how guilty he was making Cori feel.

She frowned. "What do you mean?"

"Evan has ten million dollars all to himself. It's completely under his control and it's for the town. I'm shocked he hasn't bought something absurd like a Merry-Go-Round or a bouncy castle."

Or a mini-golf course. Cori rubbed a finger on the center of her forehead. "He can easily afford some fun things too," she said.

"Oh, no," John said quickly, his smile disappearing. "He'd already got you playing hooky in the middle of a work day and having your sister cover for you when she's not supposed to be baking. Don't fall under his spell."

Well...shit. She couldn't tell him that wasn't true. Or that the hooky thing had been her influence.

"I know my grandson can be very charming, but *you* are supposed to be immune to that."

She was definitely not immune. But yeah, Ava did seem to be. "Did my father tell you that too? That I don't respond to charm?" That was kind of sad. Surely there was someone that had, that could, charm Ava.

"He told me you respond to success and drive," John said. "Which is why forcing you to date someone different was a good plan. You never would have done that on your own."

Cori really hated John's assumption that Evan fit because he was the opposite of successful and driven. But she couldn't defend him too passionately or she wouldn't be Ava.

"I guess there were a lot of good parts to Rudy's plan." Coming to Bliss had been a good thing. Working with her sisters to get the pie shop going had been a good thing. Meeting Hank and the guys had been a good thing. And she couldn't say that

her time with Evan hadn't been *good*. It had been too good, in fact.
It did seem that Rudy had known what he was doing. Which
meant Evan really would be good for Ava...if Cori wasn't in
the way.

"Buying the town a Ferris wheel would somehow indicate
that I'm failing at making Evan more responsible?"

She'd definitely put her vote in *for* the mini-golf course.
Would Ava have done that? No. Cori knew the answer. Ava would
have talked investing.

"Evan wants to be worthy of the responsibility Rudy gave
him," John said. "Evan is well-liked and people trust him with
basic legal matters. But he's not...someone anyone but your
father would have given ten million dollars to."

"But my father wanted me to date him," Cori said, that fact
fully sinking in for the first time. Rudy had wanted Ava and Evan
together. "Seems he must have trusted him if he wanted him with
his daughter."

John laughed. "Well, for one, Rudy didn't worry about you
handling yourself with men. He wanted you to be a little *softer*, if
anything. But he also knew that Evan would never agree to date
you if it was premeditated. Evan doesn't really plan well or
commit easily. And he doesn't like having a lot of expectations
placed on him. But Rudy also knew that once Evan knew what
you needed and that he could meet those needs, he'd step up."

Cori frowned. "Rudy gambled on the fact that Evan is a good
guy who loves to help the people around him."

"He did."

"And he won," Cori said. Evan had done exactly what Rudy
had expected.

"I have a feeling that your father didn't get to where he got to
in business by never gambling."

"No," Cori agreed. "Or by being wrong about people."

John nodded. "Exactly. I thought he was crazy to put Evan in
charge of everything he did. But so far, looks like Rudy was right.

And I know that makes Evan happy—to know that he's making Rudy happy."

Cori sucked in a quick breath, then covered it with a cough. *Dammit.*

Evan probably *wasn't* feeling all that proud and satisfied. After all, he was messing around with her behind everyone's backs, half-assing his dates with Ava, and taking bids on a miniature golf course.

Hell, maybe he wasn't even taking bids. Maybe he was just going to go with the first company that showed him the brightest lights and best music. Because that's what she would do.

Yeah, he could definitely be doing a better job here. And feeling proud of stepping up to help Ava *actually* find balance between work and play—something Ava really did need. If Cori would just get out of the way.

The bell tinkled again and Evan stepped back into the shop.

"Anyway, thank you. I'm not wrong often," John said. "But I'm happy to be wrong about Evan this time."

She didn't really care about John's expectations for Evan. He seemed like a bit of a pompous ass. But she did care about Evan's expectations for Evan.

And once the post-coital buzz wore off and he really thought about how he was failing Ava, he'd be disappointed.

John stood as Evan joined them at the table. "I need to get going."

Evan gave Cori a concerned look. "Already?"

"Just making a quick stop and wanted to say hi, but yes, I need to get back to the city," John said. "Your grandmother has a to-do list for me." He withdrew his wallet and tossed a fifty on the table.

Cori couldn't help but be impressed. If they could sell all their pie and coffee for fifty bucks a piece, their financial situation would improve quickly.

"It was very nice to meet you, Ava," John said. "I look forward to seeing you again."

She gave him a smile. John and Evan shook hands and then John was gone.

Evan gave her a look as he dropped into the chair next to her. "Everything okay?"

"Do you mean does your grandfather believe that I'm Ava and that I've been the good influence on you that he and Rudy wanted me to be? Then yes. You haven't done anything like putting a mini-golf course in, yet. That means I must be doing my job."

Evan sighed. "My grandfather isn't really a fun guy."

She didn't want to know the answer to her next question. But she already kind of did. "Did you know that Rudy wanted you and Ava together?" she asked.

Evan just studied her for a moment. Eventually he nodded. "Yes."

"And you're trying to tell me that doesn't matter?" Cori felt her chest tightening. "You wanted to do what Rudy wanted in every other way, surely you wanted to be the one that helped Ava?"

"I..." He cleared his throat. "I thought about it. But I figured I could help her by being the one to find her the right guy."

"You were afraid of not being the right guy?"

He gave her a small smile. "I never have been the right guy."

Cori felt her heart squeeze. Well, that wasn't true. At all. She hated that he didn't see all the good things he did. "But you've never been with someone like Ava."

"That's true."

Cori wet her lips. "You weren't afraid of messing up with the ten million dollars? Or the will?"

"Of course I was." Evan sighed. "But your dad didn't give me a choice about those."

"So when given the choice, you decided you weren't the right guy."

"Until I slept with Jill," he agreed. "Then I realized maybe helping Ava was my chance to have a good relationship for the right reasons."

Ouch. He hadn't said it, and he maybe hadn't even thought it, but that seemed to insinuate that any other relationship than the one with Ava was not as good. Or right.

"I can't believe you couldn't wait *four months*."

Cori and Evan both turned as Ava came through the kitchen's swinging door. Parker was right behind her.

13

C ori and Evan both rose.

"You couldn't have resisted for a few more weeks?" Ava asked. She focused on Evan. "I thought we talked about how everyone thought us *not* sleeping together was a sign that this was more serious. That everyone was buying that this was something different for you."

"You talked to Ava about *not* sleeping together?" Cori asked Evan.

"I told her how everyone in town had noticed a change to my...typical pattern." His expression was a combination of regret and sheepishness.

Yeah, but *she* and Evan fell right back into their typical patterns when *they* were together. In spite of all the very good reasons to stay apart, they hadn't. No, she hadn't been able to just freaking wait. She never put off having fun and feeling good.

"It was supposed to make it easier to break up later," Ava said. "For now, it looks like we're more serious than he usually is, but in the end, it will be our excuse, that we just never totally felt that way about each other."

"Except now we screwed it up," Cori said. She turned to Evan.

"We're screwing all of it up. We're both doing what we've always done."

He started to respond, then he just took a deep breath and shook his head. "Yeah. I guess we are."

She moved closer to him, not touching him, but meeting his gaze directly. "I feel like being here, in Bliss, in the shop, with my sisters, has been really good for me. And that I've...gotten better. I'm proud of what we're doing. But I want to be proud of everything."

"And you're not proud of being with me," Evan said flatly.

"Because we shouldn't be doing it. And you know it," she said. "You want to be the right guy for Ava. But I got in the way of that."

"I kissed you first."

"When you thought I was Ava. And I sure didn't rush to tell you the truth."

"I haven't fought one second of this, Cori." His voice was low and firm, and he had an intensity in his stare that reminded her of the times he'd defended Rudy.

"You didn't ask for my involvement though. You came to the shop to check in and instead of just telling your mom and everyone that Ava left, I jumped in and pretended to be her. You came over to ask Ava out and I kissed you. You took her to dinner and I interrupted. And you did toss me out of your car the other night."

He made a little growling noise. "We're still on that?"

"I'm just saying, all of the interruptions have been me."

"I haven't *regretted* one second," he said, his gaze boring into hers.

"But—" She took a deep breath. "I'm keeping you from doing what you wanted to do, from doing what Rudy wanted you to do."

"Cori—"

"I want you, Evan," she said before he could say something to change her mind about doing the right thing. "And I've never resisted going after something I've wanted. So this is a way to prove that I'm better now too. I'm going to let us both do what we *should* do. I'm going to let you go. And you're going to help Ava."

"It's only for a few more months," Ava said quickly, suddenly seeming over her annoyance.

But Cori shook her head. "Evan can't go from one sister to the other."

"Then we'll tell them the truth. I started dating Ava but got to know you and fell for you."

"You mean you'll tell everyone that you made a promise to Ava but then couldn't keep your pants zipped?" Cori asked, crossing her arms.

"If that's what people think, fine. That doesn't bother me. We all know the truth," Evan said. "I don't care what everyone else thinks."

"But you do," Cori said. "You care what this town thinks of you, how they feel about you. That's what you care about most. You want to be beloved and wanted here, Evan. And you won't have that if you create this much of a scandal."

"I'm in love with you, Cori."

His words sucked the air out of her lungs. It was the most beautiful thing she'd ever heard. And the most painful. "Well, of course you are," she said. She gave him a half smile. "Because you aren't supposed to be. And you're a contrary personality. Like me."

Evan's jaw ticked and he took a step closer. "If that's your way of telling me you're in love with me too, that kind of sucked."

She fought the urge to wrap her arms around him and refuse to let go. "I'm going to go." She turned for the door.

"Where? You can't *leave*, Cori," Ava said, her tone panicked.

Yeah, that part was definitely inconvenient. She looked back at her sister. "I'm not leaving. I'm...fixing this." Typically, her way of fixing things did include getting out of Dodge. But they were still hanging on by their fingernails and if she left now, she'd mess it all up for her sisters. "It's a big learning curve for me, but I'm trying."

"Where are you going to go?" Ava asked.

"Home," Cori said simply.

"But—"

And she knew Ava wasn't sure where Cori considered home. Well, Cori at least knew that now.

"I'll be at the house, working on the books." And out of everyone's way. "Dinner's at six. And just so you know, we're having three desserts tonight. There will be lots of chocolate. And there's a very good chance I'm using the blowtorch."

Her hand was on the door when she heard, "I love the view from behind, but I'm not letting you walk away from me for long, Cori."

She sucked in a deep breath and gathered her bravado. Then she shot Evan a big Cori grin over her shoulder. "I can absolutely say that you *are* a ton of fun, Evan Stone. Be sure you show my sister that side. There's no reason to hold back."

Then she took the hardest step of her life...out of the pie shop that was full of all of the good things in her life.

———

"We're doing this, Ava."

Ava gave Evan an arched eyebrow. "I'm sorry, did you mean to phrase that as a question?"

"No."

She leaned one elbow onto the table and rested her chin on her hand. "You know, you are hot when you get all bossy, but since you're in love with my sister, that doesn't really do anything useful for me. So how about you tone it down a little?"

Evan blew out a breath.

The past two weeks without talking to or even seeing Cori had been the hardest of his life. Probably not as hard as seeing her and not being able to kiss her, touch her, laugh with her, but still excruciating. He knew he shouldn't appreciate that she was avoiding him, but at the same time, it made it easier to plan this party. He was, however, losing his patience.

"Ava," Evan said, evenly. "This is a good idea. And we're already knee-deep in planning. I need you to be on board here. And maybe even a little excited."

"It is a good idea," she agreed. Then she tossed her pen onto the top of her notebook and sat back in his kitchen chair. "But you and I both know that something's missing."

Evan sighed. He looked down at his own notebook. "Have you told *her* that something's missing?" Because Cori wasn't talking to him.

He and Ava had been working on putting together the Parking and Pie event for the past two weeks. The party was scheduled for a week from today.

As soon as Cori had walked out of the pie shop with his heart, Evan had decided that they were going to do this. They were going to show her that she did not have to stay out of the way, that they not only wanted her around, but they needed her. And putting this together with Ava had showed them both that was even truer than they'd thought. It was supposed to be a kind of tribute to Cori and her amazing, over-the-top-yet-totally-perfect ideas. Instead, it was clear that no one could quite pull it off like she could.

And that made him love her even more.

"She doesn't want to talk about it," Ava said. "She's going to take tickets for us—the money part—but she said we have to do the rest."

Evan shook his head. "Basically, she's gorgeous, sexy, brilliant, and stubborn as hell?"

"Probably a good thing for you to know before you get in any deeper, huh?" Ava asked with a smile.

"I'm in *really* deep now, Ava," he told her honestly.

"Good." She picked her pen up again. "Let's throw a not-bad party that will make her roll her eyes and jump in to save us."

"This isn't going to be the spelling bee all over again?" he asked. "She won't realize what we're trying to do and just walk out?"

Ava shrugged. "I hope not."

"That's not very comforting."

Ava sighed. "Well it won't be a total disaster. So there's that. Everyone knows we're working on it together. They all think it's great. I'm getting everything organized and you're making it fun. They figure this is the perfect type project for us to come together on. Everyone's celebrating us being a couple and all of the wonderful things we're going to be able to do together." She said it dryly.

Evan groaned and ran a hand over his face. "It is great and we are a good team."

Ava laughed. "We are. Just like Dad thought we would be."

Evan looked at Ava. She was beautiful and smart and sophisticated and successful. And he had no desire to kiss her. They were a great team. But they weren't meant to be.

"How is Cori?" he finally asked.

"I've gained five pounds and my kitchen is now bright yellow."

"The kitchen at the house or the shop?"

"Yes."

Evan laughed in spite of himself. "She's bored."

"*Very* bored," Ava said. "Oh, and I do have a Piehole Game in the middle of my dining room."

"Piehole?" Evan repeated.

"You know the saying "shut your piehole?"

"Okay," he said slowly. "Yes."

"And you know of a game called Cornhole?" Ava asked.

"I do." Not that he could imagine Ava Carmichael playing the lawn game where people tossed bean bags through holes in a big wooden board.

"This is a combination. Cori made a game called Piehole. She made bean bags that look like little pies and the holes in the board are all mouths."

Evan honestly wasn't sure what to say to that. But as he thought about it, he felt his grin stretching. "She couldn't resist."

Ava shook her head, also grinning. "Nope. But adding some games is a good idea, right?"

"It is." Evan's mind starting spinning. "We could start everything around four p.m. They could play games for a while before we start the movie at five? I have a couple of ideas for other activities. But I'm sure Cori will have more."

"She won't tell us."

"Maybe she'll tell Noah. He's sweet. A good listener," Evan said.

"She might have written them down."

They both looked up as Brynn came into the room.

"You think so?" Ava asked.

"Well, she's writing something in that notebook while she pretends to work with us every night," Brynn said, taking a chair at the table. She and Noah were both helping with the party too, of course. But the town knew that Ava and Evan were the driving forces.

"Wait what?" Evan asked. "Pretends to work?"

"We have new house rules," Brynn told him. "Cori insists that we all have dinner together every night and then any work we do has to be together at the dining room table. We're not excused until eight."

He liked that. He knew that Rudy had been concerned about his girls and their relationships with one another. At least that was going well.

No, it was *all* going well. The pie shop was up and running. Business was slow, but the party in the park would help. Exactly as Cori had envisioned. And as for their romantic relationships. He looked at the two sisters at his table. He really did want to help them all with the conditions of Rudy's trust. He always had. Because of Rudy. But now it was because of the girls themselves. They'd become his friends.

He wasn't worried about Brynn. She was slow getting into the dating scene maybe, but she'd only been here for a little over two months, and it seemed that Noah was going to be plenty protective when it came to which guys got to take Brynn out. If she didn't go on that first date—especially if Noah was going to keep insisting that his time with Brynn didn't count—then Evan would nudge them in the next couple of months. But there was plenty of time for her to get her six dates in. As for Ava...he wasn't going to be able to keep this up for three and a half more months. That wasn't long. He got that. But he couldn't be away from Cori for that long. He was just going to have to find the right guy—or at least the right-ish guy—for Ava. But he could do that. Probably.

And Cori...well, she wasn't having multiple casual sexual relationships, that was for damned sure. There was going to be nothing *multiple* about her relationships with men in Bliss. Or anywhere else in the world. And there was absolutely nothing casual about what was going on with *him* and Cori.

"Thanks, have a great time." Cori stuffed the money into the money bag and kept her smile in place while the family of five drove their SUV past the table and into the park. Then she turned to survey the scene again.

Ugh. It was...nice. Very nice. The sun was shining and the temperature was just about perfect. Because of course it was. Ava Carmichael wouldn't throw a party in less than ideal temperatures.

Noah was directing people into parking spots facing a huge

movie screen. Almost like a drive-in theater. Cori had no idea how they'd gotten the screen or projector and she hadn't asked. Since they hadn't paid for it out of the pie shop account, it was none of her business. And honestly, the Dream Team of Ava and Evan had so many connections between them that they could probably pull anything off.

And yes, everything was very...nice. They had local high school kids acting as car hops, taking orders and delivering pie and drinks. They had music playing too. It sounded like one of those compilation CDs where kids covered popular songs from the radio. They did have the Piehole game set up along with a couple of other lawn games. And behind the Ethan Stone Memorial Pavilion was a large mud pit where kids were making mud pies. There was even a clean-up station with hoses and towels that bore the logos from Parker's diner, Noah's auto shop, and Evan's law practice.

The other games had nothing to do with pie, but that was a minor detail. It was bugging the crap out of her, but it really was a small thing. The towels were very cool and everyone seemed to be happy to be here. Most of them were sitting in their cars or hanging out in the backs of their trucks, just kind of...waiting. But they were here and eating pie and that was the main point.

There were, however, shrieks of laughter coming from the direction of the mud pit and Cori couldn't help but smile. She was certain Evan had pushed for the mud and Ava had countered with the washing station and had somehow talked the guys into sponsoring the towels. They really were a good team. Exactly as it should be. Evan was part of a carefully laid out plan and Ava was throwing a party. This was the perfect thing for them both.

And Cori wanted to be anywhere else.

"Hi, are you Ava?"

Cori looked at the little boy beside her table. She smiled. "No, I'm Cori. Ava's over there in the yellow shirt." She was even wearing blue jeans.

"Okay. I have to tell her the mac and cheese pie is awesome!"

"Definitely," Cori said with a nod. "She'll love hearing that."

The boy ran off and Cori watched him give Ava the compliment. Her smile was bright and sincere and Cori felt herself smile too. Then Ava looked over at her and gave her a big grin. Ava had made the pies, but it was Cori's recipe. They were a good team too. Cori gave her a thumbs-up. Okay, maybe being here wasn't *all* bad.

"This is pretty good."

Cori turned to find Hank and Walter at her table. "Well, hey guys." Seeing them suddenly made her aware of how much she'd missed seeing them every morning. She'd been sticking close to the house. She couldn't risk being at the shop in case Evan stopped in. Or walked by the window. Or when someone mentioned his name.

"How's it going? It looks nice," Walter said.

Yep. Nice. It sure did. "Okay. We have more pie left than we'd like to. Do you think people are still coming?"

Hank glanced at his watch. "Boy, I don't know, honey. I'd think most everyone would be here by now."

Damn. That's what she'd been afraid of.

"Cori."

Tingles skittered down her spine as Evan's voice came from behind her. *Crap.* She'd avoided him for most of the day. She'd seen him, of course, but they hadn't spoken. She took a deep breath and turned. "Hey."

"Can I show you something?"

No. Hell, no even. She wanted to just sit here, sell tickets, then go home and take a bath. And hope that now that this party was over, Evan and Ava wouldn't need to be spending every evening together.

"I have to take tickets."

He glanced at her table. "Anyone can do that. I need *you* for a minute."

I need you. How was she supposed to respond to that? But before she could come up with anything, Hank piped up. "I can watch the table, Cori."

And the truth was, yeah, anyone could take tickets. Crap, again.

"Fine." She stood. Smoothed her skirt, straightened her T-shirt, and stepped around the table.

Evan reached for her hand, but she shook her head. "Come on. We can't." And if he touched her, even her hand, she'd shatter.

He blew out a breath. "Fine. For now. Over here." He started across the grass toward the mud pit.

They didn't talk and her chest ached. She had so many things —words, emotions—bottled up, it felt like they were constricting her heart, causing each beat to hurt a little. Evan stopped at the edge of the mud. He smiled at the kids who were elbow-deep.

"I saw this," she said. "It's great. I love the towels."

"Yeah?" He finally looked at her again and she saw the same pain in his eyes that she was feeling. He missed her like she missed him. That was...the suckiest thing she'd ever faced. Technically in about three months, he could break up with Ava. But could he really just start dating Ava's sister? He wasn't that guy. He might have dated extensively, even bed hopped a bit, but it was never...scandalous.

"You and Ava did a great job," she finally said.

He gave a nod. "I guess so. But—" He turned to face her fully. "What else would you have done with the party?"

"I don't know what you mean."

"Yes you do. Come on," he said. "What would you have done with it?"

Her heart squeezed. "This whole thing was my idea. Pie and a movie in the park."

"That was your basic idea," he said. He paused then said, "But what about the garnish?"

Oh, boy. She shook her head.

"I thought we'd already covered this." He took a small step forward.

"It doesn't matter."

"Things that are completely fine, good even, are better with your touch."

He'd used the same words before. She shook her head again. "You and Ava—"

"Are fine. But nothing...special."

Cori wet her lips, but again shook her head. "Evan—"

"We need your touch. *I* need your touch." He moved closer again. "In lots of ways. In everything."

She swallowed hard. "It doesn't matter."

"But that's the thing. It does. It really matters."

He took another step, close enough to kiss her. So she stepped back and said quickly, "Pie trivia. And a town vote on what our next new flavor should be."

She had to stop him from...whatever he was doing. Getting closer. Talking. Tempting. Making her miss him even while he was standing right there in front of her.

He did stop. And gave her a half grin that made her heart trip. "Pie trivia? Are there lots of interesting facts about pie?"

Well, she didn't know about *a lot*. But... "Nineteen percent of Americans say apple is their favorite and only nine percent say cherry." Yeah, she'd looked some stuff up working at the dining room table with her sisters.

"I guess there are." Evan gave her another grin.

"But this is all really good as is," she said. "Really."

He clearly wanted to say more, but finally he nodded. "Fine." He took a breath. "Did you see the sign?"

"The sign?" She followed his finger. He was pointing at a wooden sign beside the mud pit.

Future site of the Rudy Carmichael Memorial Miniature Golf Course.

She read it three times, then looked back at Evan, her heart thundering. "Really?"

He nodded. "We needed a mud pit and I needed a ground breaking, so we combined them."

Cori felt tears threatening. "You're going ahead with it?"

"Yeah. Because I realized something." He stepped closer again and she didn't stop him this time. "Rudy was wrong."

Her heart thumped. "He was?"

"The only thing that came of him sending that St. Bernard puppy away was him not having a St. Bernard puppy. He didn't tame or even change your spirit. He just made it so he didn't get to see as much of it. And he missed out."

He moved closer as Cori sniffed. Dammit. She couldn't kiss him here in public in front of the whole town. But he was making it really impossible to resist.

"And I realized if he was so wrong about you, then he could have been wrong about me too," Evan continued. "I don't know if he meant I should do more of what I already do or if I should be doing something else, but it it was something else, then he was wrong. I make people happy. And it took having someone make me incredibly, impossibly happy to realize how truly fucking important that is."

She caught her breath and actually pressed her fingers to her lips.

"Cori, I thought I was happy. I thought I understood fun and goodness. But until you, I didn't realize that things could be even better. And he was completely wrong about Ava being right for me. She's great, but the thing is, I love *your* St. Bernards. I don't mind the mess. I can absolutely handle chaos, and I love surprises. All of which makes me right for *you*. I love you. I want every crazy, over-the-top idea and plan you have. In fact, I need it. This party is fine. But why would I want fine when I can have amazing?"

Cori felt one tear roll over her cheek. This man...he did more than tolerate her craziness. He embraced it. He encouraged it.

Evan started to lift his hand to her face, but she ducked out of the way. "Hold that thought, okay?" She wanted desperately to go into his arms and let him hold her. But once she was there again, she didn't plan on leaving for the next several hours. Or days. Or ever. And there was something she needed to do first.

"What?" He took a step after her. "Where are you going?"

"I have to go...round up some puppies." She shot him a grin, but didn't wait for his response. She turned on her heel and ran for the ticket table, her mind spinning. "Hank!" she puffed a minute later. "Who's the Mayor of Bliss?"

Hank laughed. "Really?"

"Yes, really. I need to talk to him or her. Right away."

"Well, honey, that's me."

"You're the mayor?" How did she not know that? Hank had turned into one of her best friends in Bliss. And she didn't even know he was the mayor. "I feel like this is something we should have talked about."

He winked at her. "I have so many stories. We might need to have afternoon coffee too."

"I'm in. But right now, I need a favor. I'll explain on the way."

Five minutes later, she burst into the pie shop, ran to the back and turned into Parker's kitchen. "I need a can opener."

"You don't have one?" Parker asked.

"I do. But I need another. And another set of hands to use it."

Parker sighed. "Like mine?"

She grinned. "Yep. We need to open every can of pie filling Ava has stashed in our storeroom."

"She has *cans* of pie filling?" Parker asked with a scowl.

Shit. "We'll deal with that later," Cori said quickly. "We need to hurry."

"Tell me why."

"Because I'm in love with your best friend and will make him very happy."

Parker sighed. "You're going to screw up the trust, aren't you?"

"Nope. Just going to use a little loophole. Or two."

E van was nearly out of his mind. Cori had run off over thirty minutes ago and wasn't answering calls or texts.

"What the *hell*?" he asked Ava for the seventh time.

Ava frowned at him. "I'll shove you into that mud pit, Evan. Don't think I won't."

Evan had no doubt. "She just ran off. She—"

Suddenly Parker pulled into the park in his truck. He drove right past the ticket table where Evan was pacing. Evan frowned. Parker didn't do parties. He didn't even let them call football parties, parties. He preferred "gathering" or even better, no label at all. He didn't understand why they couldn't just get together and watch a game without calling it something. As he pointed out every time. Which just made it even more fun to call their get togethers shindigs and bashes. And Parker definitely didn't do parties with kids' movies being shown. But before he could ask his friend what was going on, he saw Cori in the passenger seat. And nothing else mattered.

She jumped out as Parker stopped the truck and ran to the back of the truck. Evan stalked forward, intent on getting his hands on Cori before anything else happened. But she dropped the tailgate—and Evan got distracted. "What the hell is this?"

"This is a kiddie pool filled with pie filling. It's all different kinds. We didn't have enough of any one kind. But that's okay."

Cori climbed into the back of the truck and shot him a grin as she bent over to push the pool to the edge of the tailgate.

Parker moved to grab it and Evan found himself taking the other side as they lowered it to the ground.

"Why?" was all Ava said.

"This is what the winning tug-of-war team will pull the losing team into," Cori said.

"We're having a tug-of-war?" Ava asked.

"We are. The starting high school basketball team against some of the starting football players." Cori jumped out of the truck and wiped her hands on her skirt.

"Where do you want these?" Hank came up to Cori carrying two pie plates.

"Oh, in the pavilion," Cori said.

"What's this?" Evan asked, his heart suddenly racing. He didn't even care really. The look on Cori's face made him want to pull her into that kiddie pool for some pie filling wrestling.

"Those are whipped cream pies," Cori said, almost triumphantly.

"Why?" Ava said again.

Cori kept her eyes on Evan as she said, "There's not much that I do that doesn't involve whipped cream."

Her grin was mischievous and insured that Evan would be getting a can of pie filling on his way home. "What's going on?"

"For two dollars you can throw a pie at a prominent Bliss citizen," Cori said. "If you hit Parker in the face, you get a free breakfast. If you hit Noah, you get a free oil change. For Principal Tompkins, you get a Bliss Bandits sweatshirt. And if you hit Mayor Hank in the face, you get to have coffee with him every day for a week."

"This is—" But Ava apparently didn't know what this was. Or at least what to call it.

"I thought we were maybe missing some demographics. We've got the kids and parents, but now the basketball and football team will get their friends up here and a bunch of Hank's friends want to see him covered in whipped cream."

"Not in the dirty way," Hank said. "Except maybe for Maggie Collins." He winked as Cori snorted.

And Evan had never wanted someone as much as he wanted her.

He grabbed her hand and pulled her close. "Amazing," he said in her ear.

"Well, if I'd had time I would have painted the pool to look like a pie crust," she said with a shrug.

"Of course you would have."

"And we didn't have time to—"

Evan cut her off by wrapping his arm around her, dipping her back, and kissing her. In front of everyone.

She gripped the front of his shirt and opened her mouth under his, but when he lifted his head, she just said, "Evan."

"I love you Corrine Michelle Carmichael," he announced loudly. He righted her and turned to face the people who were watching.

"Then you do realize that the woman you're kissing isn't your girlfriend?" Holly Morris came to stand right in front of them.

"Evan!"

Evan turned, taking Cori with him. To face his mother. "Hi, Mom."

"What are you doing?" Diane looked from Evan to Cori and back. "That's not Ava."

Evan grinned at Cori. "No. It's definitely not."

"But—"

"This is scandalous, even for you," Holly cut Diane off. She crossed her arms. "I don't believe you've ever cheated on someone with her *sister* before. But—" She looked Cori up and down. "— anyone who is as free with her *sprinkles* as this one, probably gets a lot of guys into trouble."

Oh, no. He was not going to let her insult Cori like that. He was not going to let this bitch ruin this day for Cori. "Listen, the only thing you need—"

"Holly."

The quiet but firm voice stopped him from speaking and Holly from scowling at him. They both turned to face Diane.

"What?" Holly asked her old friend.

"Shut up."

Evan felt his eyes widen and Cori start with surprise. Holly looked like Diane had just slapped her.

"Excuse me?" Holly asked.

"Evan has always been one of the happiest people I know," Diane said, calmly. She looked Evan directly in the eye. "But this...how he is since meeting Cori...is so much more than he's ever been before."

Evan heard a tiny gasp from Cori and felt her arm tighten around his waist. But he couldn't look away from his mother.

"So," Diane continued, looking at Holly, "if you have anything to say to him other than 'I'm very happy for you, Evan', then you need to just shut up."

Evan felt shock rumble through him. But right on its heels was an incredible feeling of relief. And then contentment. His mother was sticking up for him. It was late. It was just this one moment. But it still mattered. He didn't care what Holly thought, but Diane did, and she was standing up for him to her friend.

More, she saw his happiness, what Cori had done to him. And *that* mattered.

Evan looked at Holly. "You're not the only one who is going to wonder what happened," he told her. "And I'm sure you're all going to talk about it." He glanced at Hank and Walter, knowing they would definitely help spread the story. "But it's very simple —I was dating Ava." He had been. His intentions had been good. And he and Ava had definitely spent time together. "But that meant I saw a lot of Cori too. And she's..." He glanced at her, his chest filling with warmth and desire and love. "...amazing," he finished, though it didn't seem like a strong enough word. "I fell for her completely. Yes, it might seem 'scandalous' to go from one sister to the other, but Ava and I were nothing more than friends and Cori and I are so much more than a weekend fling."

"And it would take an idiot not to see what was happening between Evan and Cori," Ava said, coming to stand next to her sister. "They belong together and I'm thrilled."

Cori leaned over and hugged Ava, and Evan gave her a grin and a wink over the top of Cori's head.

Holly narrowed her eyes, but said nothing. Diane stepped forward and Evan leaned down so she could kiss his cheek. Then she kissed Cori's, sniffed, and said with a wobbly smile, "I hope we can all get together soon."

"I'd love to make you a cup of coffee tomorrow," Cori told her. "And maybe we could talk for a little while."

"I've never had sprinkles on my coffee," Diane said. She glanced at Evan. "But that sounds like something your dad would have loved."

Evan felt his throat tighten and he could only nod.

"Well, I might even have to pull out my blowtorch for this," Cori said.

Diane's eyes widened. "What?"

"Really?" Evan asked her.

Cori grinned at him, then at Diane. "Toasted marshmallows aren't only for pie. I make a fantastic s'mores latte."

And Evan wanted to throw her over his shoulder and carry her across the park, in front of everyone, and straight up the road to his house.

"Well, that sounds wonderful," Diane told her.

"It's a date then."

"And that better be the only date you're going on."

They turned to find John McCormick standing behind them. Evan sighed. "Grandfather."

"Evan." He looked at Cori. "Corrine, I presume."

She gave him a single nod. "You can call me Cori."

John looked at Ava. "And you're my grandson's latest ex?"

Ava gave him a cool look. "Your grandson's very good friend."

"Ah." John looked back at Evan. "I see you've screwed this up too."

Evan ran his hand up and down Cori's back and shook his head. "Actually, I think I've gotten this more right than anything I've ever done."

Again, he felt Cori's arm tighten around him and he heard her sniff. This time he did look down at her, much preferring her smile to his grandfather's expression of displeasure.

"That was pretty great," she told him softly.

"But there is the one, not so small detail of the trust," John said before Evan could respond.

He looked back to his grandfather. "What do you mean?"

"You've broken one of the main stipulations," John said. "Cori wasn't supposed to date anyone, for six months."

"We haven't broken anything," Evan said calmly.

"Then how do you explain how you are together?"

Evan shrugged. "Rudy didn't want Cori to date. Since he didn't define what 'dating' entailed, I assume he meant he didn't want Cori to have relationships with men like she's had in the past."

"And you are somehow different?" John asked.

"Cori?" Evan asked.

"Oh, there's no question things with Evan and me are different," she told John. "I typically hang out at dance clubs or party on yachts or do crazy stuff like rock climbing or scuba diving with the guys I date."

"You party on *yachts*?" Evan asked.

"Shh," she told him, giving him a little pinch. "I'm making a point." She addressed John again. "And if I'd taken my shirt off in any other guy's car, I definitely would have gotten lucky."

John's eyes widened and now it was Evan that pinched *her*. Right on her ass.

But Cori went on. "And if I was dating Evan, it would already be over. We're past the two-month mark here. Guys never make it that long. And I've baked for him. I've never baked for any other guy."

Evan liked that. A lot.

"And I've never told any other guy about my childhood. Or anything else important," Cori said, her tone softening a little. "I've never paid enough attention to anyone else to know that he prefers half and half to milk in his coffee. And I've definitely never met anyone else's mother...or grandfather."

Evan grinned, the warmth in his chest—and the need to throw her over his shoulder—growing stronger.

"What I'm doing with Evan is definitely not dating. It's making a commitment." Cori looked up at him. "And I can assure you, that's absolutely something different."

Evan kissed her quick and hard on the mouth, then focused on his grandfather again. "And I can promise we haven't done any of the things I typically do when I date someone either. Cori and I haven't been to a single movie, barbecue, or street dance. And I promise we won't be doing any of that for at least another three months or so."

John stood, studying them both, for several long seconds. Then he gave a nod. "A loophole."

"A loophole," Evan confirmed.

"Fine," John agreed. "But, Evan," he added, looking at Cori again. "You need to take this girl miniature golfing as soon as you can."

Evan couldn't believe it. His grandfather had not only agreed with him about the stipulations in Rudy's trust, but he was giving his blessing to the miniature golf course. Evan swallowed hard and extended his hand. "I'll do that."

John took his hand and gave it a long squeeze. Then he said to his daughter, "Can I buy you a pie, Diane?"

She smiled brightly. "I'd love that."

They moved toward the pie stand and Cori turned to face

Evan, her eyes wide and her face lit up. "Wow. That was awesome. This day is perfect, Evan."

"Actually—"

"Look out!"

Noah's shouted warning came just as a large ball of fluff came tearing toward them. Barking.

"*Now* it's perfect," he said with a grin.

Cori froze in his arms. "Is that—"

The puppy was coming straight at them but as Evan leaned to grab him, he veered off, heading for the mud pit. "Stop him!" Evan shouted with a laugh.

Cori gave him a huge, stunned smile. "You got me an actual St. Bernard?" she asked, wonder in her voice.

Evan started to pull her close again, but Noah shouted, "Evan!" as the puppy plunged into the mud.

"It's only fair after all of the amazing figurative St. Bernard's you've given me," Evan said.

"I hope you know what you've done." But her face was full of joy.

"I told you," he said, squeezing her hand. "I can handle chaos and messes."

He looked over as Noah lunged for the dog—and missed. The puppy ran happily through the mud until Cori put her fingers to her lips and gave a sharp whistle. The dog, and all of the humans in the vicinity, paused. She knelt on the grass and the puppy yelped once, then made a beeline for her. The dog jumped up on her, covering her clothes with muddy paw prints and her face with wet, sloppy kisses.

"That might be the hottest you've ever looked," he told her taking in the muddy paw prints on her shirt, the streaks of dirt on her legs and the huge, happy grin on her face.

"What's his name?" she asked as the dog wiggled free and suddenly headed toward Ava.

Ava shrieked and stepped behind Parker just before he scooped up the wriggling ball of fur.

"I think Rudy."

Cori looked up at him. She stretched to standing. "Really? A messy troublemaker? Does that fit?"

Evan brushed her hair back and looked into her eyes. "A big ball of happiness that makes everyone around him smile."

Her eyes suddenly got misty. "I like that idea of him."

"It was him. I promise."

She sniffed and then wrapped her arms around his neck, getting mud all over him too. "I love you, Evan Stone."

He settled his hands on her butt and squeezed. "I love you too. Which is why I got you a puppy. He'll make it harder to leave in nine months."

"Well, no worries," she said, smiling though her voice was thick. "I only leave after we hit the high point, remember? And I have a feeling there's always going to be more of those to come with you."

Relief, love, gratitude—and yes, lust—washed though him. "Well, I might have learned a little bit from Ava about plans and schedules and deadlines, but—" He dipped his head and put his lips against hers, "—high points are my specialty."

Then he kissed her as her St. Bernard, Rudy, went barreling toward the table full of whipped cream pies.

EPILOGUE

Y*ou don't know anything about this huge box of gourmet chocolate-dipped strawberries that are sitting on my desk, do you?*

Evan grinned at the box of strawberries that had not only been dipped in chocolate but that were decorated to look like they were "wearing" wedding dresses and tuxedo jackets using white and dark chocolate. He set his phone aside and returned to his paperwork. Jill could be feeding penguins or...whatever penguin veterinarians did in zoos...and it could be hours before he heard back. But he knew the gift was from her. And it was hilarious.

But it was only ten minutes before she replied.

They didn't have any decorated like eggplants.

Evan snorted. Jill would definitely send him strawberries decorated like eggplants if she could. She loved that particular emoji because she found it so funny that people thought that eggplants were more phallic than cucumbers or bananas.

The dots were still jumping, indicating she was typing, so he waited to reply.

From what mom says, little brides and grooms are appropriate though.

Figured your mom would tell you to send ones that look like piles of crap.

LOL! No, she says you and Cori are really great together, actually. Jill included a heart emoji and then a GIF of someone gagging.

Yeah, Jill wasn't much of a romantic. Evan grinned. *We are really great together. And yes, it really is sickening.* He send a GIF of the kissing-in-the-rain-scene from *The Notebook.*

SOOOO happy I'm in Omaha where I don't have to see that.

I know. But you have to come home to visit and meet Cori. Seriously. She's awesome.

Liz told me the whole story of how she stood up to my mom, Sprinkles. I want to BE Cori.

Evan laughed at that, in spite of the fact that he probably had a new nickname. That Parker and Noah would definitely pick up on immediately.

There's a s'mores pie in it for you if you NEVER call me that in public.

I've heard of this mystical s'mores pie too. Admit it...that's when you fell in love.

It had probably been the mention of Nutella the very first day. But the s'mores pie hadn't hurt.

Wait 'til you see what she can do to peanut butter and jelly.

His office door opened just as he hit *send.*

It was Cori. And his heart actually missed a beat. That would make Jill gag too, he was sure. Which made him grin. He loved being sickeningly in love. "Hey." He stood and rounded the desk.

"Hey."

Her smile made him think about re-enacting *The Notebook* kiss. They didn't really need rain for it...

"You wouldn't happen to know why I got a gift bag today that has a bottle Calamine lotion and box of Benadryl in it, would you?" she asked.

Evan stopped with one hand extended to pull her close. He glanced at his phone and started laughing. "Oh my God."

"So you *do*?"

He grabbed the waistband of Cori's jeans and pulled her to him. "I do, as a matter of fact."

She wrapped her arms around his waist, tipping her head back to look up at him. "You do? Who's it from?"

"Jill."

"Jill?" She frowned slightly, thinking. "You mean *Jill*? Holly's daughter?"

"Yeah." He pointed at the strawberries on his desk. "She sent me something too. Kind of a I'm-so-happy-you're-actually-in-love gift."

Cori peered at the box. "Are those strawberries?"

He nodded.

"I don't get it."

And suddenly he realized that the gift was funny and Jill's way of congratulating him but...it also meant he was going to have to explain what strawberries and Calamine had to do with anything.

That brat.

"Give me a second," he said. He pulled Cori around the desk with him and settled her on his lap as he took his seat again. He grabbed his phone. He ignored the GIF Jill had sent of a guy wagging his eyebrows in response to Evan's comment about Cori being good with PB and J. *You are in HUGE trouble,* he typed and sent.

So she got my gift then?

I hope a penguin poops on your shoe.

LOL! Every damned day, Ev.

Good.

Cori was reading the texts. "Okay, so you and Jill had straw-berries together at some point in the past, I'm guessing."

"Um...right." Dammit. He didn't really want to go into detail here.

"And the Calamine?"

Dammit. "That was...after. Jill's allergic." He winced as he said it.

"And you didn't just eat these strawberries?" Cori guessed. She was a smart cookie.

"Jill's a brat. Her sending this stuff is seriously a congratulations on our relationship," he said quickly. "She's happy for us. And thinks she's hilarious."

Cori wrapped an arm around his neck and reached for a strawberry. She bit into it and gave a little moan. "They're really good."

He felt his body harden just watching her mouth close around the berry. He squeezed her hip. "You're not allergic, right?"

She licked chocolate off her bottom lip, slowly. Then shook her head. "Nope."

He shifted on the chair, his eyes on her mouth, where she was now licking chocolate off the strawberry. "Good. That's *very* good."

Cori kept her eyes on his as she bit into it again. Her lips were wet with the sweet juice, her tongue flicking out as she made that soft moaning sound again. He pulled her down for a kiss, sliding his tongue over her lip, tasting the strawberry and chocolate, then stroking over her tongue with his and giving a little groan of his own.

She lifted her head after a moment and tossed the stem back into the box. Then she pushed off of his lap. But instead of sitting on the edge of his desk, taking her shirt off, and painting her nipples with chocolate and strawberry, she stepped around his desk and started for the door.

"Hey, where are you going?"

"Back to the pie shop," she said. She looked back at him. "Why? What did you think I was going to do?"

"Lay back on my desk and let me eat you like *you're* a giant chocolate covered strawberry."

She stopped at his door and gave him a smile. "That would be fun."

"Get back over here."

"Oh, Evan," she sighed. "That's not going to happen."

He frowned. "What's not?"

"The whole sex with strawberries thing."

"I'll bring them home-—"

"Ever."

He blew out a breath. "Why the hell not?" But he knew.

"Because you did that with Jill."

"But, I—" He glanced at the berries, then the phone, then back to Cori. He sighed. "Dammit."

Cori shrugged. "Yeah. It's too bad. I really like strawberries."

"But we've done other things that we've previously done with other people. If I could take it back, I would."

She held up a hand. "Don't say that. That whole thing with Jill was one of the reasons you pretended to date Ava, which was why we got to spend time together."

"So we *should* have strawberry sex. In celebration and commemoration."

Her eyes widened. "Wait, you think I won't do it because I'm jealous of you and Jill doing it?"

Well, *now* he didn't. "I don't...know."

"I *can't* do it," she said. "Because the whole time I'll be thinking about all the places she had to put Calamine lotion. Huge mood killer."

He opened his mouth, probably to make another argument, but now *he* was thinking about the places she'd had to put Calamine lotion. And, though he felt bad about it, it definitely made him shudder. And suddenly feel the need to scratch what had to be a sympathy itch.

"Fine," he said. "But you'd better bring a can of cherry pie filling over tonight."

Cori gave him a grin. "That I can do."

She blew him a kiss and left.

He immediately grabbed his phone. *You're cock blocking me with Calamine lotion.*

Jill sent a GIF of a woman shrugging with a caption that said "Oops". She didn't look apologetic.

You knew that's how she'd react?

Hey, I owed you that. Hives, Evan. HIVES.

You really are a brat.

She just sent a grinning emoji. Then she said, *You have plenty of other tricks. I'm not worried about your cock staying blocked for long.*

He wasn't either. But the fact that Jill was able to give him a hard time even from hundreds of miles away did increase his respect for her.

At least show me the penguin poop on your shoe, he said. *That would make me feel better.*

A moment later, a photo came through of her shoe, clearly on a sheet of ice, and something that definitely could have been penguin poop on the toe. Or mud. Or chocolate ice cream that she'd had at lunch. But he decided to believe that she was mucking around in bird crap.

Did you know that some penguins have pink poop? From the krill they eat.

Evan sent his own gagging GIF. *Nope, didn't know that.*

Know who does know that?

The next message was another photo. Of the back of a guy, crouching in front of a penguin. The photo was mostly focused on the guy's ass.

You're a horrible photographer, he told her, even though he was certain she'd focused the camera exactly as she'd meant to.

That's Tim.

Is Tim a vet? How many vets did this zoo need, anyway?

Tim is the Executive Director for the zoo foundation. He usually wears a suit and tie and works in an office.

What's he doing in the penguin enclosure?

Don't know. But he's been here almost every day since I got here.

She sent a smiley face with its tongue hanging out.

Evan grinned. *You do realize he doesn't care about penguins having pink poop, right?*

No? That's not even slightly interesting to a regular person?

Nope.

Guess I better work on my conversation topics.

I think you're going to be fine. He sent her GIF of Donald Duck with his heart pounding out of his chest. Literally.

You think?

Penguin crap=true love. Or, at least, he wants in your pants.

Good deal. I want in HIS pants.

Evan laughed and sent her an eggplant, a banana, and a cucumber.

She sent him a thumbs up.

Talk to you later. I have a bunch of strawberries to get rid of.

Later, Sprinkles.

Evan sighed. He was really going to have to shut that down.

Then he headed to the grocery store to put together another gift bag for Cori.

At least nothing could mess with her love of Nutella.

HIGH HEELS AND HAYSTACKS

Don't miss Ava and Parker's story, High Heels and Haystacks!

———

Only three things stand between Ava Carmichael and her twelve billion dollar inheritance:

1.   A year of living in Bliss, Kansas.
2.   A relationship that lasts six consecutive months.
3.   A pie.

Ava has run a multi-billion-dollar company, negotiated with shark investors, and hobnobbed with business royalty, but she's about to be defeated by her inability to turn sugar, flour, and apple pie filling into something edible.

Conveniently, the owner of the diner next door, Parker Blake, is magic in the kitchen. And he technically works for her. So she can make him teach her to bake. And, hey, if everyone assumes they're heating up more than the oven during their time in the kitchen...well, that's called multitasking.

Parker Blake likes his women the way he likes his coffee: not in his diner. But gorgeous, strong-willed, type-A Ava clearly isn't going to stop messing up his kitchen—or his simple, stress-free small town life—until the conditions of her daddy's will are met. So, sure, he'll teach his "boss" to bake.

But once the kitchen door closes, it's pretty clear who's really in charge.

———

Enjoy this excerpt from High Heels and Haystacks!

T he next day, the diner was packed. Every single chair, booth, and stool was filled. There were even a couple of guys standing off to one side, leaning against the wall, eating their burgers.

And every one of the people in those seats turned to look at Ava as she stepped through the front door.

Parker almost dropped the plate he was holding.

Holy hell.

He supposed that she thought she was dressed for fruit picking. Her hair, normally stick straight and sleek, was now pulled back into a pony tail. That alone was strangely sexy. Seeing her in a new way. A less polished way, he supposed. She also had sunglasses propped on top of her head. The bright red rims matched the t-shirt she wore. He'd also never seen her in a t-shirt. She'd worn a hoodie for the game night she and her sisters had hosted at their house about a month ago. That, too, had been surprisingly sexy. Seeing her let go a little. But this... well, this t-shirt was her sister, Cori's. It had to be. It was bright red, nice and fitted to her curves, and read *In my defense, I was left unsupervised.*

That didn't fit Ava at all. But the shirt...it fit a little too well.

And then there were the jeans. He had never seen her in blue jeans. He'd wanted to. In his mind, that was going to be a sign that she was trying to fit in to small town life and that she was going to figure out how to dress for function and comfort rather than the I'll-take-over-your-company-make-a-million-dollars-by-lunch-and-look-hot-as-hell-while-doing-it look she usually had going.

But the jeans hugging Ava's hips, ass, and long legs were making *his* jeans fit a lot *less* comfortably, and the only functions he could come up with her were inappropriate, probably sexist, and involved smudging the lipstick that matched her sunglasses and t-shirt perfectly.

And her heels.

His eyes finally made it past the slim-fitting denim to her feet. And these shoes, if nothing else, reminded him of exactly who Ava Carmichael was. The three-inch red heels weren't practical for fruit picking in the least. They weren't practical for much of anything around Bliss, as a matter of fact.

But he didn't want her to take them off.

Damn, he'd never been a shoe guy before. He was fairly certain he'd never noticed what his dates wore on their feet. But with Ava Carmichael, her heels were as much a part of her as the long blonde hair and the I'm-out-of-your-league attitude.

The silence in the diner stretched, all eyes on her, until she smiled and focused on him.

"It's twelve fifty-five."

That's all she said, looking straight at Parker, but several people turned back to their plates and started eating faster.

"Boss is here," Mark Johnson commented to Parker.

"She the boss of you everywhere?" Don Arnold asked under the diner noise so that only Parker, Mark, and Brian Watson heard.

"I'd let her tell me what to do," Brian agreed.

"Shut the fuck up," Parker told them. But it didn't have a lot of force behind it. He'd expected to get crap about Ava being his boss at the pie shop. And lots of waggled eyebrows and innuendo about the time they spent together.

He didn't care that everyone was enjoying the idea of Ava as his boss. Even outside of the diner. He didn't get too worried about what people thought of him in general. The people here knew him. He'd been the same guy for the past fifteen years and he had no plans to change.

So there was no way anyone here actually thought that he was going to get all worked up about Ava. No way they really thought that he was going to suddenly change all of his habits or shirk his responsibilities even for a chance to peel those blue jeans off of her. So what if he was closing for a couple of hours this afternoon. That was *supposed* to be how this worked every day. Working six a.m. to six p.m. every single day in a little town where everything else was open eight to five left little time for chores at his farm, changing the oil in his truck, errands like picking up a new phone charger, or even stopping at the post office.

And frankly, no one needed a burger at three in the afternoon. He supposed some might say that was just his opinion, but truthfully, it was right. He didn't like the whole breakfast-for-dinner idea either, where people had pancakes and eggs for dinner. Don't even get him started on brunch. Breakfast, lunch, and dinner were three distinct meals that each had their own special tastes and style. In his diner, breakfast ended at nine o'clock, lunch ended at one, and dinner ended at six and that was perfectly reasonable. And had been the schedule for twelve years now. Ever since Parker had taken over.

However, he *did* care that their teasing words about how Ava bossed him around did nothing to get *his* mind away from the idea of her telling him exactly what she liked—how hard, how fast, and how long.

"I'm suddenly in the mood for fruit pie," Mark added.

Parker gave him a stern look. "Knock it off."

It was only because he didn't need his mind wandering to the idea of Ava with pie filling spread all over her...

Fuck.

Parker worked on not reacting. And not moving out from behind the counter that was blocking the erection that was suddenly pressing insistently against his fly.

But he was torn between laughing and rolling his eyes as she crossed the diner, the red purse swinging from her arm, her heels clicking on his tile like some kind of fucking countdown clock ticking away. He simply reached behind the counter and started handing out to go boxes. Which people filled immediately.

This damned town. He'd been trying to get people out of the diner at one p.m. every day for the past twelve years. But the door rarely closed behind the last customer until at least a quarter after. And all Ava had to do was strut in here in her kick-ass red heels and mention the time.

Of course, no one was shoveling their fries in because they were scared of her. It was because they all wanted Parker to get lucky. It should probably be disturbing to think that the entire town was this interested in him getting laid. But he was used to these people being in his business—his actual business and his personal business—and this was exactly where he wanted their minds to be right now.

He didn't respond to Ava as she leaned a hip against the counter next to the cash register, watching as people reached for their wallets. As if she was overseeing her subjects.

Amazingly, the door bumped shut behind the last customer at 1:03 p.m.

Ava hadn't even blinked as people told her to have a good time and that they were happy she was getting Parker out of the diner for a while and to enjoy the fruit picking. If she'd noticed the way they said "fruit picking", she didn't show it. She'd smiled, nodded, and said goodbye sweetly to everyone who had spoken to her.

After they were gone, she crossed back to the door, turned the lock and flipped the CLOSED sign around as if it was her diner, her door and her sign.

ABOUT THE AUTHOR

Erin Nicholas is the New York Times and USA Today bestselling author of over thirty sexy contemporary romances. Her stories have been described as toe-curling, enchanting, steamy and fun. She loves to write about reluctant heroes, imperfect heroines and happily ever afters. She lives in the Midwest with her husband who only wants to read the sex scenes in her books, her kids who will never read the sex scenes in her books, and family and friends who say they're shocked by the sex scenes in her books (yeah, right!).

Never miss any news from Erin!
Sign up for her newsletter today!
Find ALL of her books right here!
www.erinnicholas.com

And find Erin at
www.ErinNicholas.com,
on Twitter and on Facebook

Join her SUPER FAN page on Facebook for insider peeks, exclusive giveaways, chats and more!

———

MORE FROM ERIN

M ore sexy, contemporary romance...

Now Available at all book retailers

Sapphire Falls

Welcome to Sapphire Falls
Getting Out of Hand
Getting Worked Up
Getting Dirty

Naughty and Nice in Sapphire Falls
Getting In the Spirit, Christmas novella
Getting In the Mood, Valentine's Day novella
Getting to the Church On Time, wedding novella

Ferris Wheels & Fireflies in Sapphire Falls
Getting It All

Getting Lucky
Getting Over It
Getting to Her (companion novella)
Getting His Way

Ever After in Sapphire Falls
After All
After You
After Tonight (coming spring 2018)

Lots more from Sapphire Falls at
www.SapphireFalls.net

The Bradfords
Just Right (book 1)
Just Like That (book 2)
Just My Type (book 3)
Just for Fun (book 4)
Just a Kiss (book 5)
Just What I Need: The Epilogue (novella, book 6)

Counting On Love
Just Count on Me (prequel)
She's the One
It Takes Two
Best of Three
Going for Four
Up by Five

The Billionaire Bargains
No Matter What
What Matters Most
All That Matters

Boys of Fall
Out of Bounds
Illegal Motion
Full Coverage

Taking Chances
Twisted Up
Tangled Up
Turned Up

Opposites Attract
Completely Yours
Forever Mine
Totally His

Made in the USA
Middletown, DE
26 January 2018